Praise for Retribution Falls

'O⸱ ⸱ery level, *Retribution* ⸱ ⸱ ⸱n

'*Re⸱ ⸱tion Falls* is the k⸱ ⸱ I did⸱ ⸱ ⸱we were allow⸱ ⸱t-ing ⸱ ⸱s making their haphazard way in a wondrous retro⸱ ⸱ ⸱orld. A fast exhilarating read'

Peter F. Hamilton

'*Ret⸱ ⸱on Falls* picks you up, whisks you swiftly and enter⸱ ⸱ingly along, and sets you down with a big smile on your ⸱e'

Joe Abercrombie

'The⸱ ⸱ce is furious, the action is full-screen, the style is shar⸱ ⸱d polished, the air is full of whizzing bullets and stra⸱ ⸱d cries. What's not to like?'

Tom Holt, *SFX*

'By ⸱ time the story ends, only the grimmest of readers won' ⸱e smiling (and/or punching the air). Sequel soon, pleas⸱ ⸱he *Ketty Jay*'s crew deserve to fly again' *Total Sci Fi*

'*Ret⸱ ⸱tion Falls* is a rip-roaring full blown space-pirate adv⸱ ⸱⸱re . . . It's also one of the best pieces of fun I've read⸱ ⸱a long while'

SFF World

'*Re⸱ ⸱tion Falls* is a superb, ripping yarn. Great characters, tig⸱ ⸱lot, relentless pace, and a fascinating world full of pro⸱ ⸱e for future instalments. Prepare to be entertained'

Speculative Horizons

'W⸱ ⸱s not to love in this book – fast action, great char-act⸱ ⸱great setting and superb one-liners? Highly, highly rec⸱ ⸱nended'

Fantasy Book Critic

RETRIBUTION FALLS

A Tale of the *Ketty Jay*

Chris Wooding

Indigo

The right of Chris Wooding to be identified as the author of
this work has been asserted by him in accordance with the
Copyright, Designs and Patents Act 1988.

First published in Great Britain in 2009 by
Gollancz

This edition published in Great Britain in 2012 by
Indigo
An imprint of the Orion Publishing Group
Orion House, 5 Upper St Martin's Lane,
London WC2H 9EA

An Hachette UK Company

1 3 5 7 9 10 8 6 4 2

A CIP catalogue record for this book
is available from the British Library

ISBN 978 1 78062 056 5

Typeset at The Spartan Press Ltd,
Lymington, Hants

Printed in Great Britain by Clays Ltd, St Ives plc

The Orion Publishing Group's policy is to use papers that
are natural, renewable and recyclable products and
made from wood grown in sustainable forests. The logging
and manufacturing processes are expected to conform to
the environmental regulations of the country of origin.

www.chriswooding.com
www.orionbooks.co.uk

One

Lawsen Macarde – A Question Of Probabilities –
Frey's Cutlass – New Horizons

The smuggler held the bullet between thumb and forefinger, studying it in the weak light of the store room. He smiled sourly.

'Just imagine,' he said. 'Imagine what this feels like, going through your head.'

Grayther Crake didn't want to imagine anything of the sort. He was trying not to throw up, having already disgraced himself once that morning. He glanced at the man next to him, hoping for some sign that he had a plan, some way to get them out of this. But Darian Frey's face was hard, and showed nothing.

Both of them had their wrists tied together, backs against the damp and peeling wall. Three armed thugs ensured they stayed there.

The smuggler's name was Lawsen Macarde. He was squat and grizzled, hair and skin greasy with a sheen of sweat and grime, features squashed across a face that was broad and deeply lined. Crake watched him slide the bullet into the empty drum of his revolver. He spun it, snapped it shut, then turned towards his audience.

'Do you think it hurts?' he mused. 'Even for a moment? Or is it all over – *bang!* – in a flash?'

'If you're that curious, try it out on yourself,' Frey suggested.

Macarde hit him in the gut, putting all of his considerable weight behind the punch. Frey doubled over with a grunt and almost went to his knees. He straightened with some effort until he was standing again.

'Good point,' he wheezed. 'Well made.'

Macarde pressed the muzzle of the revolver against Crake's forehead, and stared at Frey.

'Count of three. You want to see your man's brains all over the wall?'

Frey didn't reply. Crake's face was grey beneath his close-cropped blond beard. He stank of alcohol and sweat. His eyes flicked to the captain nervously.

'One.'

Frey showed no signs of reacting.

'I'm just a passenger!' Crake said. 'I'm not even part of his crew!' His accent betrayed an aristocratic upbringing which wasn't evident from his appearance. His hair was scruffy, his boots vomit-spattered, his greatcoat half-unbuttoned and hanging open. To top it off, he was near soiling himself with fear.

'You have the ignition code for the *Ketty Jay*?' Macarde asked him. 'You know how to fire her up and get her flying?'

Crake swallowed and shook his head.

'Then shut up. Two.'

'Nobody flies the *Ketty Jay* but me, Macarde. I told you that,' Frey said. His eyes flickered restlessly around the store room. Cloud-muffled sunlight drifted in through horizontal slits high up on one stone wall, illuminating rough-sewn hemp sacks, coils of rope, wicked-looking hooks that hung on chains from the ceiling. Chill shadows cut deep into the seamed faces of Macarde and his men, and the air smelled of damp and decay.

'Three,' said Macarde, and pulled the trigger.

Click.

Crake flinched and whimpered as the hammer fell on an empty chamber. After a moment, it sank in: he was still alive. He let out a shuddering breath as Macarde took the gun away, then cast a hateful glare at Frey.

Frey's expression was blank. He was a different person to the man Crake knew the night before. That man had laughed as loud as Malvery and made fun of Pinn with the rest of them. He'd told stories that had them in stitches and drank until he passed out.

That man, Crake had known for almost three months. That man, Crake might have called a friend.

Macarde studied the pistol theatrically. 'Five chambers. One down. Think you'll be lucky again?' He put the muzzle back to Crake's forehead.

'Oh, please, no,' Crake begged. 'Please, please, no. Frey, tell him. Stop playing around and just tell him.'

'One,' said Macarde.

Crake stared at the stranger to his right, his eyes pleading. No doubt about it, it was the same man. There were the same wolfishly handsome features, the same unkempt black hair, the same lean frame beneath his long coat. But the spark in his eyes had gone. There was no sign of the ready, wicked smile that usually lurked in the corner of his mouth.

He wasn't going to give in.

'Two.'

'*Please*,' he whispered. But Frey just looked away.

'Three.'

Macarde paused on the trigger, waiting for a last-moment intervention. It didn't come.

Click.

Crake's heart leaped hard enough to hurt. He let out a gasp. His mouth was sticky, his whole body was trembling and he desperately wanted to be sick.

You bastard, he thought. *You rot-hearted bastard.*

'Didn't think you had it in you, Frey,' Macarde said, with a hint of admiration in his voice. He thrust the revolver back into a holster somewhere amidst the motley of battered jackets that he wore. 'You'd let him die rather than give up the *Ketty Jay*? That's cold.'

Frey shrugged. 'He's just a passenger.' Crake swore at him under his breath.

Macarde paced around the store room while a rat-faced thug covered the prisoners with the point of a cutlass. The other two thugs stood in the shadows: an enormous shaven-headed bruiser and a droop-eyed man wearing a tatty knitted cap. One guarded the only exit, the other lounged against a barrel, idly examining a lever-action shotgun. There were a dozen more like them downstairs.

Crake clawed at his mind for some way to escape. In spite of the shock and the pounding in his head, he forced himself to be rational. He'd always prided himself on his discipline and self-control, which only made the humiliation of the last few moments harder to bear. He'd pictured himself displaying a little more dignity in the face of his own extinction.

Their hands were tied, and they'd been disarmed. Their pistols had been taken after they were found at the inn, snoring drunk at the table. Macarde had taken Frey's beautiful cutlass – *my* cutlass, Crake thought bitterly – for his own. Now it hung tantalisingly from his belt. Crake noticed Frey watching it closely.

What of Malvery and Pinn? They'd evidently wandered off elsewhere in the night to continue their carousing, leaving their companions to sleep. It was just bad luck that Macarde had found them, tonight of all nights. Just a few more hours and they'd have been out of port and away. Instead they'd been dragged upstairs – pausing only for Crake to be sick on his own feet – and bundled into this dank store room where an anonymous and squalid death awaited them if Frey didn't give up the ignition codes for his aircraft.

I could be dead, Crake thought. *That son of a bitch didn't do a thing to stop it.*

'Listen,' said Macarde to Frey. 'Let's be businessmen about this. We go back, you and I. Worked together several times, haven't we? And even though I came to expect a certain *sloppiness* from you over the years – late delivery, cargo that wasn't quite what you promised, that sort of thing – you never flat-out screwed me. Not till now.'

'What do you want me to say, Macarde? It wasn't meant to end up this way.'

'I don't want to kill you, Frey,' said Macarde in a tone that suggested the opposite. 'I don't even want to kill that milksop little pansy over there. I just want what's mine. You owe me an aircraft. I'll take the *Ketty Jay*.'

4

'The *Ketty Jay*'s worth five of yours.'

'Well, consider the difference as the price of me *not* cutting off your balls and stuffing them in your ears.'

'That's fair,' conceded Frey.

'That aerium you sold me was bad stuff. Admit it.'

'What did you expect for that price?'

'You told me it came straight from the refinery. What you sold me was so degraded it wouldn't have lifted a biscuit, let alone twenty tons of aircraft.'

'Sales patter. You know how it is.'

'It must have been through the engines of every freebooter from here to the coast!' Macarde growled. 'I'd have got better quality stuff siphoning it off the wrecks in a junkyard!'

Crake gave Frey a fleeting look of guilt. 'Actually,' grinned Frey, 'it'd have been about the same.'

Macarde was a stocky man, and overweight, but his punch came blindingly fast, snapping Frey's head back so it cracked against the wall. Frey groaned and put his hands to his face. His fingertips came away bloody from a split lip.

'Little less attitude will make this all go a lot smoother,' Macarde advised.

'Right,' said Frey. 'Now *you* listen. If there's some way I can make this up to you, some job I can do, something I can steal, whatever you want . . . well, that's one thing. But you will never get my craft, you hear? You can stuff whatever you like in my ears. The *Ketty Jay* is mine.'

'I don't think you're in much of a position to negotiate,' Macarde said.

'Really? 'Cause the way I see it, the *Ketty Jay* is useless without the ignition code, and the only one who knows it is me. That puts me in a pretty strong position as long as I don't tell you.'

Macarde made a terse gesture towards Droop-Eye. 'Cut off his thumbs.'

Droop-Eye left his shotgun atop the barrel he'd been leaning on and drew a dagger.

'Whoa, wait!' said Frey quickly. 'I'm talking compensation. I'm talking giving you *more* than the value of your craft. You cut off my thumbs and I can't fly. Believe me, you do that and I take the code to my grave.'

'I had five men on that craft,' said Macarde, as Droop-Eye came over. 'They were pulling up out of a canyon. I saw it. The pilot tried to get the lift and suddenly it just wasn't there. Bad aerium, see? Couldn't clear the lip of the canyon. Tore the belly off and the rest of it went up in flames. Five men dead. You going to compensate me for them, too?'

'Listen, there's got to be something you want.' He motioned suddenly at Crake. 'Here, I know! He's got a gold tooth. Solid gold. Show them, Crake.'

Crake stared at the captain in disbelief.

'I don't want a gold tooth, Frey,' said Macarde patiently. 'Give me your thumbs.'

'It's a start!' Frey cried. He glared hard and meaningfully at Crake. 'Crake, why don't you *show them your gold tooth*?'

'Here, let us have a look,' Rat said, leaning closer to Crake. 'Show us a smile, you little nancy.'

Crake took a deep, steadying breath, and gave Rat his most dazzling grin. It was a picture-pose he'd perfected in response to a mortifying ferrotype taken by the family photographer. After that, he vowed he'd never be embarrassed by a picture again.

'Hey! That's not half bad,' Rat commented, peering at his reflection in the shiny tooth. And Crake grinned, harder than he'd ever grinned in his life.

Droop-Eye pulled Frey away from the wall over to a set of cob-webbed shelves. He swept away a few empty jars with his arm, and then forced Frey's bound hands down onto the shelf. Frey had balled his fists and was refusing to extend his thumbs. Droop-Eye hammered him in the kidney, but he still held fast.

'What I'm *saying*, Macarde, is that we can *both* come out ahead,' he argued through gritted teeth. 'We'll work off the debt, me and my crew.'

'You'll be halfway to New Vardia the second I take my eyes off you,' Macarde replied.

'What about collateral? What if I leave you one of the fighters? Pinn has a Skylance, that thing's faster than greased owl shit. You ought to see it go!'

Droop-Eye drove a knee into his thigh, making him grunt, but he still wouldn't extend his thumbs. The thug by the door smirked at his companion's attempts to make Frey co-operate.

'Here, listen!' Rat shouted. Everyone stopped and turned to look at him, surprised by the volume of his voice. A strange expression crossed his face, as if he was puzzled to find himself the centre of attention. Then it disappeared beneath a dawning revelation.

'Why don't we let them go?' he suggested.

Macarde gave him a reptilian glare. 'What?' he said slowly.

'No, wait, hear me out,' said Rat, with the attitude of one caught up in an idea so brilliant that it would require careful explanation to his benighted audience. 'I mean, killing 'em won't do no good to us. They don't look like they've got a shillie to their name anyways. If we let 'em go, they could, you know, spread the good word and stuff: "That Lawsen Macarde is a reasonable man. The kind of man you can do business with."'

Macarde had been steadily reddening as Rat's speech went on, and now his unshaven jowls were trembling with fury. Droop-Eye and Bruiser exchanged wary glances. Neither of them knew what had possessed their companion to pipe up with his opinion, but they both knew the inevitable outcome. Macarde's hand twitched towards the hilt of Frey's cutlass.

'You should listen to the man,' said Crake. 'He talks a lot of sense.'

Macarde's murderous gaze switched to Crake. Absurdly, Crake was still smiling. He flashed his toothy grin at Macarde now, looking for all the world like some oily salesman instead of a man facing his imminent demise.

But then Macarde noticed something. The anger drained from his face and he craned in to look a little closer.

'That's a nice tooth,' he murmured.

Yes, keep looking, you ugly bag of piss, Crake thought. *You just keep looking*.

Crake directed every ounce of his willpower at the smuggler. Rat's idea wasn't so bad, when you thought about it. A show of generosity now could only increase Macarde's standing in the eyes of his customers. They'd come flocking to him with their deals, offering the best cuts for the privilege of working with him. He could own this town!

But Macarde was smarter than Rat. The tooth only worked on the weak-minded. He was resisting; Crake could see it on his face. Even bewitched as he was by the tooth, he sensed that something was amiss.

A chill spread through Crake's body, something icier and more insidious than simple fear. The tooth was draining him. Hungover and weak as he was, he couldn't keep up the fight for long, and he'd already used his best efforts on Rat.

Give it up, he silently begged Macarde. *Just give it up.*

Then the smuggler blinked, and his gaze cleared. He stared at Crake, shocked. Crake's grin faded slowly.

'He's a daemonist!' Macarde cried, then pulled the pistol from his holster, put it to Crake's head and pulled the trigger.

Click.

Macarde was as surprised as Crake was. He'd forgotten that he'd loaded his pistol with only a single bullet. There was an instant's pause, then everything happened at once.

Frey's cutlass flew out of Macarde's belt, leaping ten feet across the room, past Droop-Eye and into the captain's waiting hands. Droop-Eye's final moments were spent staring in incomprehension as Frey drove the cutlass double-handed into his belly.

Macarde's bewilderment at having his cutlass stolen by invisible hands gave Crake the time he needed to gather himself. He drove a knee hard into the fat man's groin. Macarde's eyes bulged and he staggered back a step, making a faint squealing noise like a distressed piglet.

His hands still bound, Crake wrestled the revolver from Macarde's beefy fingers just as Rat shook off the effects of the tooth and drew his cutlass back for a thrust. Crake swung the gun about and squeezed the trigger. This time the hammer found the bullet. It discharged point-blank in Rat's face, blowing a geyser of red mist from the back of his skull with a deafening bang. He tottered a few steps on his heels and collapsed onto a heap of rope.

Macarde was stumbling towards the door, unwittingly blocking Bruiser's line of fire. As the last thug fought to get an angle, Frey dropped his cutlass, darted across the room and scooped up the lever-action shotgun that Droop-Eye had left on the barrel. Bruiser shoved his boss behind him to get a clear shot at Crake, and succeeded only in providing one for Frey, who unloaded the shotgun into his chest with a roar.

In seconds, it was over. Macarde had gone. They could hear him running along the landing outside, heading downstairs, shouting for his men. Frey shoved the shotgun into his belt and picked up his cutlass.

'Hold out your hands,' he said to Crake. Crake did so. The cutlass flickered, and his bonds were cut. He tossed the cutlass to Crake and held out his own hands.

'Now do me.'

Crake weighed the weapon in his hands. To his ears, it still sang faintly with the harmonic resonance he'd used to bind the daemon into the blade. He considered what it would feel like to shove it into the captain's guts.

'We don't have time, Crake,' Frey said. 'Hate me later.'

Crake was no swordsman, but he barely had to move his wrist and the cutlass did the rest. It chopped neatly through the gap between Frey's hands, dividing the cord in two. He threw the cutlass back to Frey, walked over to Rat's corpse and pulled the pistol from his holster.

Frey chambered a new round into the shotgun. 'Ready?'

Crake made a sweeping gesture of sarcastic gallantry towards the door. *Be my guest.*

Beyond was a balcony that overlooked a dim bar-room, musty with smoke and spilled wine. It was empty at this hour of the morning, its tables still scattered with the debris of the previous night's revelries. Tall shutters held off the pale daylight. Macarde was yelling somewhere below, raising the alarm.

Two men were racing up the stairs as Frey and Crake emerged. Macarde's men, wielding pistols, intent on murder. They saw Frey and Crake an instant before the foremost thug slipped on Crake's vomit-slick, which no one had thought to clear up. He crashed heavily onto the stairs and his companion tripped over him. Frey blasted them twice with his shotgun, shattering the wooden balusters in the process. They didn't get up again.

Frey and Crake ran for a door at the far end of the balcony as four more men appeared on the bar-room floor. They flung the door open and darted through, accompanied by a storm of gunfire.

Beyond was a corridor. The walls were painted in dull, institution-green paint, flaking with age. Several doors in chipped frames led off the corridor: rooms for guests, all of whom had wisely stayed put.

Frey led the way along the corridor, which ended in a set of tall, shuttered windows. Without breaking stride, he unloaded the remainder of the shotgun's shells into them. Glass smashed and the shutters blew from their hinges. Frey jumped through the gap that was left, and Crake, possessed of an unstoppable, fear-driven momentum, followed him.

The drop was a short one, ending in a steeply sloping, cobbled lane between tall, ramshackle houses. Overhead, a weak sun pushed through hazy layers of cloud.

Crake hit the ground awkwardly and went to his knees. Frey pulled him up. That familiar, wicked smile had appeared on his face again. A reminder of the man Crake had thought he knew.

'I feel a sudden urge to be moving on,' Frey said, as he dusted Crake down. 'Open skies, new horizons, all of that.'

Crake looked up at the window they'd jumped from. The sounds of pursuit were growing louder. 'I have the same feeling,' he said, and they took to their heels.

Two

'There she is,' said Malvery, with a grand sweep of his arm. 'The *Ketty Jay.*'

Jez ran a critical eye over the craft resting on the stone landing pad before them. A modified Ironclad, originally manufactured in the Wickfield workshops, unless she missed her guess. The *Ketty Jay* was an ugly, bulky thing, hunched like a vulture, with a blunt nose and two fat thrusters mounted high up on her flanks. There was a stubby tail assembly, the hump of a gun emplacement and wings that swept down and back. She looked like she couldn't decide if she was a light cargo hauler or a heavy fighter, and so she wouldn't be much good as either. One wing had been recently repaired, there was cloud-rime on the landing struts and she needed scrubbing down.

Jez wasn't impressed. Malvery read her reaction at a glance and grinned: a huge grin, springing into place beneath his thick white walrus-moustache.

'Ain't the loveliest thing you'll ever see, but the bitch does fly. Anyway, it's what's in the guts that counts, and I speak from experience. I'm a doctor, you know!'

He gave an uproarious laugh, holding his sides and throwing his head back. Jez couldn't help a smile. His guffaw was infectious.

There was something immediately likeable about Malvery. It was hard to withstand the force of his good humour, and despite his large size he seemed unthreatening. A great, solid belly pushed out from his coat, barely covered by a faded pullover that was stained with the evidence of a large and messy appetite. His hair had receded to a white circlet around his ears, leaving him bald on top, and he wore small round glasses with green lenses.

'What happened to your last navigator?' she asked.

'Found out he'd been selling off spare engine parts on the side. He navigated himself out the cargo door with the Cap'n's toe up his arse.' Malvery roared again, then, noticing Jez's expression, he added, 'Don't worry, we were still on the ground. Not that the thieving little bastard didn't deserve dropping in a volcano.' He scratched his cheek. 'Tell you the truth, we've had bad luck with navigators. Been through seven in the past year. They're always ripping us off or disappearing in the night or getting themselves killed or *some* damn thing.'

Jez whistled. 'You're making this job sound awfully tempting.'

Malvery clapped her on the back. 'Ah, it ain't so bad. We're a decent lot. Not like the cut-throat scum you might take on with otherwise. Pull your weight and keep up, you'll be fine. You take a share of whatever we make, after maintenance or whatnot, and the Cap'n pays fair.' He studied the *Ketty Jay* fondly, balled fists resting on his hips. 'That's about as much as you can ask for in this day and age, eh?'

'Pretty much,' said Jez. 'So what are you lot into?'

Malvery's look was unreadable behind his glasses.

'I mean, cargo hauling, smuggling, passenger craft, what? Ever work for the Coalition?'

'Not bloody likely!' Malvery said. 'The Cap'n would sooner gulp a pint of rat piss.' He reddened suddenly. 'Pardon the language.'

Jez waved it away. 'Just tell me what I'm signing up for.'

Malvery harumphed. 'We ain't what you'd call a very *professional* lot, put it that way,' he said. 'Cap'n sometimes doesn't know his arse from his elbow, to tell you the truth. Mostly we do black market stuff, smuggling here and there. Passenger transport: people who want to get somewhere they shouldn't be going, and don't want anyone finding out. And we've been known to try a bit of light piracy now and again when the opportunity comes along. I mean, the haulage companies sort of *expect* to lose one or two cargoes a month, they budget for it, so there's no harm done.' He made a vague gesture in the air. 'We sort of do anything, really, if the price is right.'

Jez deliberated for a moment. Their operation was clearly a shambles, but that suited her well enough. They didn't seem like types who would ask many questions, and she was lucky to find work at all in Scarwater, let alone something in her field of expertise. To keep moving was the important thing. Staying still too long was dangerous.

She held out her hand. 'Alright. Let's see how it goes.'

'Fine decision! You won't regret it. Much.' Malvery enfolded her hand in thick, meaty fingers and shook it enthusiastically. Jez couldn't help wondering how he managed to button his coat with fingers like that, let alone perform complex surgery.

'You really a doctor?' she asked.

'Certified and bona fide!' he declared, and she smelled rum on his breath.

They heard a thump from within the belly of the craft. Malvery wandered round to the *Ketty Jay*'s stern, and Jez followed. The cargo ramp was down. Inside, someone was rolling a heavy steel canister along the floor in the gloom. The angle prevented Jez from seeing anything more than a pair of long legs clad in thick trousers and boots.

'Might as well introduce you,' said Malvery. 'Hey there! Silo! Say hello to the new navvie.'

The figure in the cargo hold stopped and squatted on his haunches, peering out at them. He was tall and narrow-hipped, but his upper body was hefty with muscle, a thin cotton shirt pulled tight across his shoulders and chest. Sharp eyes peered out from a narrow face with a beaked nose, and his head was shaven. His skin was a dark yellow-brown, the colour of umber.

He regarded Jez silently, then got to his feet and resumed his labour.

'That's Silo. Engineer. Man of few words, you could say, but he keeps us all in the sky. Don't mind his manner, he's like that with everyone.'

'He's a Murthian,' Jez observed.

'That's right. You *have* been around.'

'Never seen one outside of Samarla. I thought they were all slaves.'

'So did I,' said Malvery.

'So he belongs to the Cap'n?'

Malvery chuckled. 'No, no. Silo, he ain't no slave. They're friends of a sort, I suppose, though you wouldn't know it sometimes. *His* story . . . well, that's between him and the Cap'n. They ain't said, and we ain't asked.' He steered Jez away. 'Come on, let's go meet our flyboys. The Cap'n and Crake ain't about right now. I expect they'll be back once their hangovers clear up.'

'Crake?'

'He's a daemonist.'

'You have a *daemonist* on board?'

Malvery shrugged. 'That a problem?'

'Not for me,' Jez replied. 'It's just . . . well, you know how people are about daemonists.'

Malvery made a rasping noise. 'You'll find we ain't a very judgemental lot. None of us are in much of a position to throw stones.'

Jez thought about that, and then smiled.

'You're not in with those Awakener fellers, are you?' Malvery asked suspiciously. 'If so, you can toddle off right now.'

Jez imitated Malvery's rasp. 'Not likely.'

Malvery beamed and slapped her on the back hard enough to dislodge some vertebrae. 'Good to hear.'

They walked out of the *Ketty Jay*'s shadow and across the landing pad. The Scarwater docks were half-empty, scattered with small to medium-sized craft. Delivery vessels and scavengers, mostly. The activity was concentrated at the far end, where a bulbous cargo barque was easing itself down. Crews were hustling to meet the newcomer. A stiff breeze carried the metallic tang of aerium gas across the docks as the barque vented its ballast tanks and lowered itself gingerly onto its landing struts.

The docks had been built on a wide ledge of land that projected out over the still, black lake which filled the bottom of the barren mountain valley. It was a wild and desolate place, but then Jez had seen many like it. Remote little ports, hidden away from the world, inaccessible by any means but the air. There were thousands of towns like Scarwater, existing beneath the notice of the Navy. Through them moved honest traders and smugglers alike.

It had started as a rest stop or a postal station, no doubt. A dot on the map, sheltered from the treacherous local winds, with a ready source of water nearby. Slowly it grew, spreading and scabbing as word filtered out. Opportunists arrived, spotting a niche. Those travellers would need a bar to quench their thirst, someone thought. Those drunkards would need a doctor to see to their injuries when they fell off a wall. And they'd need someone to cook them a good breakfast when they woke up. Most major professions in the cities were harshly regulated by the Guilds, but out here a man could be a carpenter, or a baker, or a craftbuilder, and be beholden to nobody but himself.

But where there was money to be made, there were criminals. A place like Scarwater didn't take long to rot out from the inside. Jez had only been here a week, since leaving her last commission, but she'd seen enough to know how it would end up. Soon, the honest people would start to go elsewhere, driven out by the gangs, and those who were left would consume each other and move on. They'd leave a ghost town behind, like all the other ghost towns, haunted by abandoned dreams and lost possibilities.

To her left, Scarwater crawled up the stony hillside from the lake. Narrow lanes and winding stairways curved between simple rectangular buildings set in clusters wherever the land would take them. Aerial pipe networks cut across the streets in strict lines, steaming gently in the chill morning air, forming a scaffold for the jumble beneath them. Huge black mugger-birds gathered on them in squads, watchful for prey.

This isn't the place for me, she thought. But then, where was?

Ahead of them on the landing strip were two small fighter craft: a Caybery Firecrow and a converted F-class Skylance. Malvery led her to the Skylance, the closer of the two. Leaning against its flank, smoking a roll-up cigarette and looking decidedly the worse for wear, was a man Jez guessed was the pilot.

'Pinn!' Malvery bellowed. The pilot winced. 'Someone you should meet.'

Pinn crushed out the cigarette as they approached and extended a hand for Jez to shake. He was short, stout and swarthy, with a shapeless thatch of black hair and chubby cheeks that overwhelmed his eyes when he managed a nauseous smile of greeting. He couldn't have been more than twenty, young for a pilot.

'Artis Pinn, meet Jezibeth Kyte,' said Malvery. 'She's coming on as navigator.'

'Jez,' she corrected. 'Never liked Jezibeth.'

Pinn looked her up and down. 'Be nice to have a woman on board,' he said, his voice deep and toneless.

'Pinn isn't firing on all cylinders this morning, are you, boy?' Malvery said, slapping him roughly on the shoulder. Pinn went a shade greyer and held up his hand to ward off any more blows.

'I'm an inch from losing my breakfast here,' he murmured. 'Lay off.' Malvery guffawed and Pinn cringed, pummelled by the doctor's enormous mirth.

'You modified this yourself?' Jez asked, running a hand over the Skylance's flank. The F-class was a racer, a single-seater built for speed and manoeuvrability. It had long, smoothly curved gull-wings. The cockpit was set far back along the fuselage, to make space for the enormous turbine in its nose that fed to a thruster at the tail end. This one had been bulked out with armour plate and fitted with underslung machine guns.

'Yeah.' Pinn roused a little. 'You know aircraft?'

'Grew up around them. My dad was a craftbuilder. I used to fly everything I could get my hands on.' She nodded towards the *Ketty Jay*. 'I bet I could even fly *that* piece of crap.'

Malvery snorted. 'Good luck getting the Cap'n to let you.'

'What was your favourite?' Pinn asked her.

'He built me an A-18 for my sixteenth birthday. I loved that little bird.'

'So what happened? You crash it?'

'She gave up the ghost five years back. I put her down in some little port up near Yortland and she just never took off again. I didn't have two shillies to bash together for repairs, so I took on with a crew as a navvie. Thought I could do long-haul navigation easy enough; I mean, I'd been doing it for myself all that time on the short-haul. That first trip I got us lost; we wandered into Navy airspace and a couple of Windblades nearly blew us out of the sky. Had to learn pretty quick after that.'

'I like her,' Pinn said to Malvery.

'Well, good,' he replied. 'Come on, let's say hi to Harkins.' They nodded their farewells.

'He ain't a bad lad,' said Malvery as they walked over to the Firecrow. 'Dumb as a rock, but he's talented, no doubt about that. Flies like a maniac.'

Firecrows had once been the mainstay of the Navy, until they were succeeded by newer models. They were built for dogfighting, with two large prothane thrusters and machine guns incorporated into the wings. A round bubble of windglass was set into the blunt snout to give the pilot a better field of vision from the cockpit, which was set right up front, in contrast to the Skylance.

Harkins was in the Firecrow, running rapidly through diagnostics. He was gangly, unshaven and hangdog, wearing a leather pilot's cap pushed far back. His dull brown hair was thin and receding from his high forehead. Flight goggles hung loosely around his neck. He moved in rapid jerks, like a mouse, tapping gauges and flicking switches with an expression of fierce concentration. As they approached, he burrowed down to examine something in the footwell.

'Harkins!' Malvery yelled at the top of his considerably loud voice. Harkins jumped and smashed his head noisily on the flight stick.

'What? What?' Harkins cried, popping up again with a panicked look in his eyes.

'I want to introduce you to the new navvie,' Malvery said, beaming. 'Jez, this is Harkins.'

'Oh,' he said, taking off his hat and rubbing his crown. He

looked down at Jez, then launched into a quick, nervous babble, his sentences running into each other in their haste to escape his mouth. 'Hi. I was doing, you know, checking things and that. Have to keep her in good condition, don't I? I mean, what's a pilot without a plane, right? I guess you're the same with maps. What's a navigator without a map? Still a navigator, I suppose, it's just that you wouldn't have a map, but you know what I mean, don't you?' He pointed at himself. 'Harkins. Pilot.'

Jez was a little stunned. 'Pleased to meet you,' was all she could say.

'Is that the Cap'n?' Harkins said suddenly, looking away across the docks. He pulled the flight goggles up and over his eyes. 'It's Crake and the Cap'n,' he confirmed. His expression became alarmed again. 'They're, um, they're running. Yep, running down the hill. Towards the docks. Very fast.'

Malvery looked skyward in despair. 'Pinn!' he called over his shoulder. 'Something's up!'

Pinn sloped into view around his Skylance and groaned. 'Can't it wait?'

'No, it bloody can't. Tool up. Cap'n needs help.' He looked at Jez. 'Can you shoot?'

Jez nodded.

'Grab yourself a gun. Welcome to the crew.'

Three

A Hasty Departure – Gunplay –
One Is Wounded – A Terrifying Encounter

They were passing out weapons, gathered behind a stack of crates that had been piled up astern of the *Ketty Jay*, when Crake and the captain reached them.

'Trouble?' Malvery asked.

'Must be that time of the week,' Frey replied, then yelled for Silo.

'Cap'n,' came the baritone reply from the Murthian, who was squatting at the top of the cargo ramp.

'You get the delivery?'

'Yuh. Came an hour ago.'

'How long till you can get her up?'

'Aerium's cycling through. Five minutes.'

'Fast as you can.'

'Yes, Cap'n.' He disappeared into the hold.

Frey turned to the others. 'Harkins. Pinn. Get yourselves airborne. We'll meet you above the clouds.'

'Is there gonna be a rumble?' Pinn asked hopefully, rousing briefly from his hangover. Harkins was already halfway to his aircraft by the time he finished the sentence.

'Get out of here!' Frey barked at him. Pinn mumbled something sour under his breath, stuffed his pistol into his belt and headed for the Skylance, oozing resentment at being cheated of a fight.

'Macarde's on his way,' said Frey, as Malvery passed him a box of bullets. 'Bringing a gang with him.'

'We're low on ammo,' Malvery murmured. 'Make 'em count.'

'Don't waste too many on Crake, then,' Frey said, loading the lever-action shotgun he'd taken from Droop-Eye. 'He couldn't hit the side of a frigate if he was standing next to it.'

'Right-o, Cap'n,' said Malvery, giving Crake a generous handful anyway. Crake didn't rise to the jibe. He looked about ready to keel over from the run.

Frey nodded at Jez. 'Who's this?'

'Jez. New navvie,' Malvery said with the tone of someone who'd got tired of introducing the same person over and over.

Frey gave her a cursory appraisal. She was small and slight, which was good, because it meant she wouldn't take up too much space and would hopefully have an equally small appetite. Her hair was tied in a simple ponytail which, along with her unflatteringly practical clothes, suggested a certain efficiency. Her features were petite and appealing but she was rather plain, boyish and very pale. That was also good. An overly attractive woman was fatal on a craft full of men. They were distracting and tended to substitute charm and flirtatiousness for doing any actual work. Besides, Frey would feel obliged to sleep with her, and that never worked out well.

He nodded at Malvery. She'd do.

'So who's Macarde, then?' Jez asked, chambering bullets as she spoke. When they looked at her, she shrugged and said, 'I just like to know who I'm shooting.'

'The story, in a nutshell,' said Malvery. 'We sold the local crime lord twelve canisters of degraded aerium at cut price rates so we could raise the money to buy three canisters of the real stuff, since we barely had enough to get off the ground ourselves.'

'Problem is, our contact let us down,' said Frey, settling into position behind the crates and sighting along his shotgun. 'His delivery came late, which meant he couldn't get us the merchandise on time, which meant we were stuck in port just long enough for one of Macarde's bumble-butt pilots to fly into a wall.'

'Hence the need for a swift departure,' said Malvery. 'Flawless plans like this are our stock-in-trade. Still want to sign on?'

Jez primed her rifle with a satisfying crunch of metal. 'I was tired of this town anyway.'

The four of them took up position behind the crates, looking out at the approach road to the docks. The promontory was accessed by way of a wide, cobbled thoroughfare that ran between a group of tumbledown warehouses. The dockers who worked there were moving aside as if pushed by a bow wave, driven to cover by the sight of Lawsen Macarde and twenty gun-wielding thugs storming down the street.

'That'll be us outnumbered and outgunned, then,' Malvery murmured. He looked back to where the Skylance and the Firecrow were rising from the ground, aerium engines throbbing as their electromagnets turned refined aerium into ultralight gas to fill their ballast tanks. Separate, prothane-fuelled engines, which powered the thrusters, were warming up with an ascending whine.

'Where's Bess, anyway?' Frey asked Crake.

'Do I look like I've got her in my pocket?' he replied irritably.

'Could do with some help right now.'

'She'll be cranky if I have to wake her up.'

'Cranky is how I want her.'

Crake pulled out a small brass whistle that hung on a chain around his neck, and blew it. It made no sound at all. Frey was about to offer a smart comment concerning Crake's lack of lung power when a bullet smashed into a crate near his head, splintering through the wood. He swore and ducked reflexively.

Crake replaced the whistle, then leaned out of cover and unleashed a wild salvo of pistol fire. His targets yelled and pointed fearfully, then scattered for cover, throwing themselves behind sacks and barrels that were waiting to be loaded into the warehouses.

'Ha!' Crake cried in triumph. 'It seems *they* don't doubt my accuracy with a pistol.'

An instant later his hair was blown forward as Pinn's Skylance tore through the air mere feet above him, machine guns raking the street. Barrels were smashed to matchwood and several men jerked and howled as they were punched with bullets. The Skylance shrieked up the street and then twisted to vertical, arrowing into the clouds and away.

'Yeah,' said Frey, deadpan. 'You're pretty scary with that thing.'

The dockers had all fled inside by now, leaving the way clear for the combatants. Macarde's men were at the edge of the landing pad, fifty feet away. Between them was a small, two-man flyer and too much cover for Frey's liking. The smugglers had been shocked by Pinn's assault, but they were regrouping swiftly.

Frey and Jez began laying down fire, making them scuttle. One smuggler went down, shot in the leg. Another unwisely took shelter behind a large but empty packing crate. Malvery hefted a double-barrelled shotgun, aimed, and blew a ragged hole through the crate and the man behind it.

'Silo! How we doing?' Frey called, but the mechanic couldn't hear him over the return fire from the smugglers.

'Darian Frey!' Macarde called, from his hiding place behind a stack of aircraft tyres. 'You're a dead man!'

'Threats,' Frey murmured. 'Honestly, what's the point?'

'They're trying to flank us!' said Jez. She fired at one of the smugglers, who was scampering from behind a pile of broken hydraulic parts. The bullet cut through the sleeve of his shirt, missing him by a hair. He froze mid-scamper and fled back into hiding.

'Cheap kind of tactic, if you ask me,' Crake commented, having recovered sufficient breath for a spot of nervous bravado. He knocked the shells from the drum of his revolver and slotted five new ones in. 'The kind of sloppy, unoriginal thinking you come to expect from these mid-level smuggler types.'

Jez peered round the side of the crates, looking for the man she'd shot at. Instead she saw another, making his way from cover to cover, attempting to get an angle on them. He disappeared before she could draw a bead on him.

'Can I get a bit less wit and a bit more keeping your bloody eyes open for these sons of bitches coming round the side?' she snapped.

'She's no shrinking violet, I'll give her that,' Frey commented to Malvery.

'The girl's gonna fit right in,' the doctor agreed.

More of Macarde's gang had moved up and taken shelter behind the two-man flyer. Crake was peppering it with bullets.

'Ammo!' Malvery reminded him.

Frey ducked away as a salvo of gunfire blasted chips from the stone floor and splintered the wood of the crates. Malvery answered with his shotgun, loudly enough to discourage any more, then dropped back to reload.

Jez stuck her head out again, concerned that she'd lost sight of the men who were trying to flank them. Despite her warning, her companions were still preoccupied with taking pot-shots at the smugglers approaching from the front.

A flash of movement: there was another one! A third man, edging into position to shoot from the side, where their barricade of crates would be useless.

'Three of them over here!' she cried.

'We're a little busy at the moment,' Frey replied patiently.

'You'll be busy picking a bullet out of your ear if you don't—' she began, but then she got shot.

It was a white blaze of pain, knocking the wind from her and blasting her senses. Like being hit by a piston. The impact threw her backwards, into Crake, who half-caught her as she fell.

'She's hit!' he cried.

'Already?' Frey replied. 'Damn, they usually last longer than *that*. Malvery, take a look.'

The doctor blasted off two shots to keep the smugglers' heads down, then knelt next to Jez. Her already unhealthy pallor had whitened a shade further. Dark red blood was soaking through her jacket from her shoulder. 'Ah, girl, come on,' he murmured. 'Don't be dying or anything.'

'I'm alright, Doc,' she said, through gritted teeth. 'I'm alright.'

'Just you stay still.'

'Haven't got *time* to stay still,' she replied, struggling to her feet, clutching her shoulder. 'I *told* you they were coming round the side! Where's the one who . . . ?' She trailed off as she caught sight of something behind them, coming down the cargo ramp, and her face went slack. 'What is *that*?'

Malvery turned and looked. 'That? That's Bess.'

Eight feet tall and five broad, a half-ton armoured monstrosity loomed out of the darkness into the light of the morning. There was nothing about her to identify her as female. Her torso and limbs were slabbed with moulded plates of tarnished metal, with ragged chain mail weave beneath. She stood in a hunch, the humped ridge of her back rising higher than her enormous shoulders. Her face was a circular grille, a criss-cross of thick bars like the gate of a drain. All that could be seen behind it were two sharp glimmers: the creature's eyes.

Jez caught her breath. A golem. She'd only heard of such things.

A low growl sounded from within the creature, hollow and resonant. Then she came down the ramp, her massive boots pounding the floor as she accelerated. Cries of alarm and dismay rose from the smugglers. She jumped off the side of the ramp and landed with a rattling boom that made the ground tremble. One gloved hand scooped up a barrel that would have herniated the average human, and flung it at a smuggler who was hiding behind a pile of crates. It smashed through the crates and crushed the man behind, burying him under an avalanche of broken wood.

'Well, she's cranky, alright,' said Frey. 'Good old Bess.'

The golem tore into the smugglers who had been sneaking round the flanks, a roaring tower of fury. Bullets glanced from her armour, leaving only scratches and small dents. One of the smugglers, panicking, made a break from cover. She seized him by the throat with a loud crack and then flung his limp corpse at his companions.

Another man tried to race past her while her back was turned, but she was quicker than her bulk suggested. She lunged after him, grabbing his arm with massive fingers. Bone splintered in the force of her grip. Her victim's brief shrieks were cut short as she tore the arm from its socket and clubbed him across the face with it, hard enough to knock him dead.

The remainder of Macarde's men suddenly lost their taste for the fight. They turned tail and ran.

'What are you doing?' Macarde screamed at them, from his

hiding place near the rear of the conflict. 'Get your filthy yellow arses back there and shoot that thing!'

Bess swung around and fixed her attention on him, a deep rattling sound coming from her chest. He swallowed hard.

'Don't ever come back here, Frey, you hear me?' he called, backing off a few steps as he did so. 'You ever come back, you're dead! You hear me? Dead! I'll rip out your eyes, Frey!'

His parting shot was barely audible, since he was bolting away as he delivered it. Soon he had disappeared, chasing his men back into the tangled lanes of Scarwater.

'Well,' said Frey. 'That's that.'

'She up and ready, Cap'n!' Silo hollered from the top of the cargo ramp.

'Exquisite timing, as always,' Frey replied. 'Malvery, how's the new recruit?'

'I'm okay,' Jez said. 'It went right through.'

Malvery looked relieved. 'So you won't need anything taking out, then. Just a little disinfectant, a bandage, and you'll be right.'

Jez gave him an odd look. 'I suppose so.'

'She's a tough little mite, Cap'n,' Malvery declared with a tinge of pride in his voice, as if her courage was some doing of his.

'Next time, try not to get shot,' Frey advised her.

'I wouldn't have *been* shot if you'd bloody listened to me.'

Frey rolled his eyes. 'Doc, take her to the infirmary.'

'I'll be fine,' Jez protested.

'You just had a bullet put through your shoulder!' Frey cried.

'It'll heal.'

'Will you two just get on that damn aircraft?' Frey said. 'Crake! Bring Bess. We're leaving ten minutes ago!'

Frey followed Malvery and Jez up the ramp and into the *Ketty Jay*. Once they were out of sight, Crake stepped gingerly through the wreckage and laid a hand on the golem's arm. She turned towards him with a quiet rustle of chain mail and leather. He reached up and stroked the side of her face-grille, tenderness in his gaze.

'Well done, Bess,' he murmured. 'That's my girl.'

25

Four

There were very few moments in Jandrew Harkins' life when he could be said to be truly relaxed. Even in his sleep he'd jitter and writhe, tormented by dreams of the wars or, occasionally, dreams of suffocation brought on by Slag, the *Ketty Jay*'s cat, who had a malicious habit of using his face as a bed.

But here, nestled in the cramped cockpit of a Firecrow with the furnace-roar of prothane thrusters in his ears, here was peace.

It was a calm day in the light of a sharp autumn sun. They were heading north, following the line of the Hookhollow Mountains. The *Ketty Jay* was above him and half a mile to starboard. Pinn's Skylance droned alongside. There was nothing else in the sky except a Navy frigate lumbering across the horizon to the west, and a freighter out of Aulenfay, surfacing from the sea of cloud that had submerged all but the highest peaks. To the east it was possible to see the steep wall of the Eastern Plateau, tracing the edge of the Hookhollows. Further south, the cloud was murky with volcanic ash, drifting towards the Blackendraft flats.

He looked up, through the windglass of his cockpit canopy. The sky was a perfect, clear, deep blue. Never ending.

Harkins sighed happily. He checked his gauges, flexed his gloved hand on the control stick and rolled his shoulders. Outside this tight metal womb, the world was strange. *People* were strange. Men were frighteningly unpredictable and women more so, full of strange insinuations and cloaked hunger. Loud noises made him jump; crowds made him claustrophobic; smart people made him feel stupid.

26

But the cockpit of a Caybery Firecrow was his sanctuary, and had been for twenty years. No awkwardness or embarrassment could touch him while he was encased in this armour. Nobody laughed at him here. The craft was his mute servant, and he, for once, was master.

He watched the distant Navy frigate for a time, remembering. Once, as a younger man, he'd travelled in craft like that. Waiting for the call to clamber into his Firecrow and burst out into the sky. He remembered with fondness the pilots he'd trained with. He'd never been popular, but he'd been accepted. Part of the team. Those were good days.

But the good days had ended when the Aerium Wars began. Five years fighting the Sammies. Five years when every sortie could be the one you never came back from. Five years of nerve-shredding dogfights, during which he was downed three times. He survived. Many of his friends weren't so fortunate.

Then there was the peace, although the term was relative. Instead of Sammies the Navy were after the pirates and free-booters who had prospered during the war, running a black market economy. Harkins fought the smugglers in his own lands. The enemy wasn't so well equipped but they were more desperate, more savage. Turf wars became grudge matches and things got even uglier.

Then, unbelievably, came the Second Aerium War, a mere four years after the first, and Harkins was back fighting alongside the Thacians against the Sammies and their subjects. After all they'd done the first time, all the lives that were lost, it was the politicians who let them down. Little had been done to defang the Samarlan threat, and the enemy came back with twice the vigour.

It was a short and dirty conflict. People were demoralised and tired on all sides. By the end – an abrupt and unsatisfying truce that left everyone but the Sammies feeling cheated – Harkins was out of it. He'd had too many near misses, lucked out a little too often, seen death's face more than any man should have to. He was a trembling shell. They discharged him two weeks before the end of the war, after fourteen years in the service. The meagre

27

pension they gave him was all the Navy could afford after such a ruinous decade.

Those years were the worst years of all.

Harkins had come to realise that the world changed fast these days, and it wasn't kind to those who weren't adaptable. He had no skills other than those he'd learned as a fighter pilot, and nobody wanted a pilot without a plane. A bleak, grey time followed, working in factories, doing odd jobs, picking up a pittance. Scraping a living.

It wasn't Navy life that he missed, with its discipline and structure. It wasn't the camaraderie – that had soured after enough of his friends had died. It was the loss of the Firecrow that truly ached.

Though he'd flown almost a dozen different Firecrows, with minor variations and improvements as time went on, they were all the same in his mind. The sound of the thrusters, the throb of the aerium engines pumping gas into the ballast tanks, the enclosing, unyielding hardness of the cockpit. The Firecrow had been the setting for all his glories and all his tragedies. It had carried him into the wondrous sky, it had seen him through the most desperate dogfights, and occasionally it had failed him when it had no more to give. Everything truly important that had ever happened in his life, the moments of purest joy and sheer, naked terror, had happened inside a Firecrow.

Then in his darkest hour, there came a light. It was almost enough to make him believe in the Allsoul and the incomprehensible jabber of the Awakeners. Almost, but not quite.

His overseer at the factory knew about Harkins' past as a pilot for the Coalition Navy. It was all Harkins talked about, when he talked at all. So when the overseer met a man in a bar who was selling a Firecrow, he mentioned it to Harkins.

That was how Harkins met Darian Frey, who had won a Caybery Firecrow on an improbably lucky hand of Rake and now had no idea what to do with it. Harkins had barely enough money to keep a roof over his head, but he went to Frey to beg. He'd have sold his soul if it got him back into the cockpit. Frey didn't think his soul was worth much, so he suggested a deal instead.

Harkins would fly the Firecrow on his behalf. The pay would be lousy, the life unpredictable, probably dangerous and usually illegal. Harkins would do exactly as he said, and if he didn't, Frey would take his craft back.

Harkins had agreed before Frey had even finished laying out the terms. The same day, he left port as an outflyer for the *Ketty Jay*. It was the happiest day of his life.

It had been a long journey from that Navy frigate to here, flying over the Hookhollow Mountains under Darian Frey. He'd never again have the kind of steel in his spine he had as a young pilot. He'd never have the obscene courage of Pinn, who laughed at death because he was too dim to comprehend it. But he'd tasted what life was like trapped on the ground, unable to rise above the clouds to the sun. He was never going back to that.

He glanced around apprehensively, as if someone, somewhere might be watching him. Then he settled back into the hard seat of the Firecrow and allowed himself a broad, contented smile.

For Crake, there was no such contentment. Listless, he wandered the tight confines of the *Ketty Jay*. There was a strange void in his belly, as if the wind had been knocked out of him. He drifted about, a spectre of bewildered sadness.

At first he'd confined himself to the near-vacant cargo hold, until the space began to oppress him and his mood started to make Bess uneasy. After that he went to the mess and drank a few mugs of strong coffee while sitting at the small communal table. But the mess felt bleak with no one to share it with.

So he climbed up the ladder from the mess to the passageway that linked the cockpit at the fore of the craft to engineering in the aft. In-between were several rooms that the crew used as quarters, their sliding doors stained with ancient, oily marks. Electric lights cast a dim light on the grimy metal walls.

He thought about going up to the cockpit to have a look at the sky, but he couldn't face Frey right now. He considered going to his quarters, perhaps to read, but that was unappealing too. Finally he remembered that their new recruit had managed to get herself shot, and decided it would be the decent thing to go and enquire after her health. With that in mind, he walked down the passageway to Malvery's infirmary.

The door was open when he got there, and Malvery had his feet up, a mug of rum in his hands. It was a tiny, squalid and unsanitary little chamber. The furniture comprised little more than a cheap dresser bolted to the wall, a washbasin, a pair of wooden chairs and a surgical table. The dresser was probably intended for plates and cutlery, but it had found new employment in the display of all manner of unpleasant-looking surgical instruments. They were all highly polished – the only clean things in the room – and they looked like they'd never been used.

Malvery hauled his feet off the chair where they were resting, and shoved it towards Crake. Then he poured a stiff measure of rum into another mug that sat on the dresser. Crake obligingly sat down and took the proffered mug.

'Where's the new girl?' he asked.

'Up in the cockpit. Navigating.'

'Didn't she just get shot?'

'You wouldn't think so, the way she's acting,' Malvery said. 'Damnedest thing. When she finally let me have a look at her, the bleeding had already stopped. Bullet went right through, like she said.' He beamed. 'All I had to do was swab it up with some antiseptic and slap on a patch. Then she got up and told me she had a job to do.'

'You were right, she *is* tough.'

'She's lucky, is what she is. Can't believe it didn't do more damage.'

Crake took a swig of rum. It was delightfully rough stuff, muscling its way to his brain where it set to work demolishing his finer mental functions.

Malvery adjusted his round, green-tinted glasses and harumphed. 'Out with it, then.'

Crake drained his mug and held it out for a refill. He thought for a moment. There was no way to express the shock, the betrayal, the resentment he felt; not in a way that Malvery would truly understand. So he simply said: 'He was going to let me die.'

He told Malvery what had happened after he and Frey were captured. It was an effort to keep everything factual and objective, but he did his best. Clarity was important. Emotional outbursts went against his nature.

When he'd finished, Malvery poured himself another shot and said, 'Well.'

Crake found his comment somewhat unsatisfying. When it became clear the doctor wasn't going to elaborate, he said, 'He let Macarde spin the barrel, put it to my forehead and pull the trigger. *Twice!*'

'You were lucky. Head wounds like that can be nasty.'

'Oh, spit and blood!' Crake cried. 'Forget it.'

'Now *that's* good advice,' Malvery said, tipping his mug at his companion. He hunkered forward in his chair. 'I like you, Crake. You're a good one. But this ain't your world you're living in any more.'

'You don't know a thing about my world!' Crake protested.

'Don't think so?' He swept out a hand to indicate the room. 'Time was I wouldn't set foot in a place like this. I used to be Guild approved. Worked in Thesk. Earned more in a month than this little operation makes in a year.'

Crake eyed him uncertainly, trying to imagine this enormous, battered old drunkard visiting the elegant dwellings of the aristocracy. He couldn't.

'This ain't no family, Crake,' Malvery went on. 'Every man is firmly and decidedly for himself. You're a smart feller; you knew the risks when you threw your lot in with us. What makes you think he'd give up his craft in exchange for you?'

'Because . . .' Crake began, and then realised he'd nothing to say. *Because it would have been the right thing to do.* He'd spare himself Malvery's laughter.

'Look,' Malvery said, more gently. 'Don't let the Cap'n fool you. He's got a way with people, when he has a mind to try. But it's not here nor there to him if you live or die. Or me, for that matter, or anyone else on board. I wonder if he even bothers about himself. The only thing he cares about is the *Ketty Jay*. Now if you think that's heartless, then you ain't seen the half of what's out there. The Cap'n's a good 'un. Better than most. You just got to know how he is.'

Crake didn't have an answer to that. He didn't want to say something childishly bitter. Already he felt faintly embarrassed at bringing it up.

'Maybe you're right,' he said. 'Maybe I shouldn't be here.'

'Hey now, I didn't say *that*!' Malvery grinned. 'Just saying, you got to realise not everyone thinks like you. Hard lesson, but worth it.'

Crake said nothing and sipped his rum. His sad mood was turning black. Perhaps he *should* just give it up. Get off at the next port, turn his back on all this. It had been six months. Six months of moving from place to place, living under an assumed name, muddying his traces so nobody could find him. At first he'd lived like a rich hobo, haunting shabby hotels all over Vardia, his days and nights spent in terror or drunken grief. It was three months before the money began to run short and he collected himself a little. That was when he found Frey, and the *Ketty Jay*.

Surely the trail had gone cold by now?

'You're not *really* thinking of packing it in, are you?' Malvery prompted, turning serious again.

Crake sighed. 'I don't know if I can stay. Not after that.'

'Bit daft if you leave now. The way I understand it, you paid passage for the whole year with that cutlass.'

Crake shrugged, morose. Malvery shoved him companionably with his boot, almost making him tip off his chair.

'Where you gonna go, eh?' he said. 'You *belong* here.'

'I *belong* here?'

'Of course you do!' Malvery bellowed. 'Look at us! We're not smugglers or pirates. We're not a *crew*! The Cap'n's only the cap'n 'cause he owns the aircraft; I wouldn't trust him to lead a bear to honey. None of us here signed on for adventure or riches, 'cause

32

sure as spit there's little enough of either.' He gave Crake a conspiritorial wink. 'But mark me, ain't one of us that's not running from something, you included. I'll bet my last swig of rum on that.' He swigged the last of his rum, just to be safe, then added, '*That's* why you belong here. 'Cause you're one of us.'

Crake couldn't help a smile at the cheap feeling of camaraderie he got from that. Still, Malvery was right. Where would he go? What would he do? He was treading water because he didn't know which direction to swim in. And until he did, the *Ketty Jay* was as good a place as any to hide from the sharks.

'I just . . .' he said. 'It's just . . . I thought he was my friend.'

'He *is* your friend. Kind of. Just depends on your definition, really. I had lots of friends, back in the day, but most of 'em wouldn't have thrown me a shillie if I was starving.' He opened a drawer in the dresser and pulled out a bottle of clear liquid. 'Rum's done. Have a suck on this.'

'What is it?' Crake asked, holding out his mug. He was already pleasantly fogged and long past the point of being capable of refusing.

'I use it to swab wounds,' Malvery said.

'I suppose this is a medicinal-grade kind of conversation,' Crake said. Malvery blasted him with a hurricane of laughter, loud enough to make him wince.

'That it is, that it is,' he said, raising his glasses to wipe a teary eye.

'So why are *you* here?' Crake asked. 'Guild-approved doctor, big job in the city, earning a fortune. Why the *Ketty Jay*?'

Malvery's mood faltered visibly, a flicker of pain crossing his face. He looked down into his mug.

'Let's just say I'm exactly where I deserve to be,' he said. Then he rallied with a flourish, lifting his mug for a toast.

'To friends!' he declared. 'In whatever form they come, and howsoever we choose to define them.'

'Friends,' said Crake, and they drank.

Five

Flying In The Dark – Pinn And
The Whores – A Proposition Is Made

Night had fallen by the time they arrived at Marklin's Reach. The decrepit port crouched in the sharp folds of the Hookhollows, a speckle of electric lights in the darkness. Rain pounded down from a slow-rolling ceiling of cloud, its underside illuminated by the pale glow of the town. A gnawing wind swept across the mountaintops.

The *Ketty Jay* sank out of the clouds, four powerful lights shining from her belly. Her outflyers hung close to her wings as she descended towards a crowded landing pad. Beam lamps swivelled to track her from below; others picked out an empty spot on the pad.

Frey sat in the pilot seat of the *Ketty Jay*'s cockpit, his eyes moving rapidly between the brass-and-chrome dials and gauges. Jez was standing with one hand resting on his chair back, looking out at the clutter of barques, freighters, fighters and privateer craft occupying the wide square of flat ground on the edge of the town.

'Busy night,' she murmured.

'Yeah,' said Frey, distracted. Landing in foul weather at night was one of his least favourite things.

He watched the aerium levels carefully, venting a little and adding a little, letting the *Ketty Jay* drift earthward while he concentrated on fighting the crosswinds that bullied him from either side. The bulky craft jerked and plunged as she was shoved this way and that. He swore under his breath and let a little more gas from the trim tanks. The *Ketty Jay* was getting over-heavy now, dropping faster than he was comfortable with, but he needed the extra weight to stabilise.

'Hang on to something,' he murmured. 'Gonna be a little rough.'

The *Ketty Jay* had picked up speed now and was coming in far too fast. Frey counted in his head with one eye on the altimeter, then with a flurry of pedals and levers he wrenched the thrusters into full reverse, opened the air brakes and boosted the aerium engines to maximum. The craft groaned as its forward momentum was cancelled and its descent arrested by the flood of ultralight gas into its ballast tanks. It slowed hard above the space that had been marked out for her, next to the huge metal flank of a four-storey freighter. Frey dumped the gas from the tanks and she dropped neatly into the vacant spot, landing with a heavy thump on her skids.

He sank back in the chair and let a slow breath of relief escape him. Jez patted him on the shoulder.

'Anyone would think you were worried for a moment there, Cap'n,' she said.

Water splattered in puddles on the landing pad as the crew assembled at the foot of the *Ketty Jay*'s cargo ramp, wrapped in slickers and stamping their feet.

'Where's Malvery and Crake?' Frey asked.

Silo thumbed at the ramp, where a slurred duet could be faintly heard from the depths of the craft.

'Hey, I know that one!' Pinn said, and began to sing along, off-key, until he was silenced by a glare from Silo.

'What are we doing here, Cap'n?' Jez asked. The others were hugging themselves or stuffing their hands in their pockets, but she seemed unperturbed by the icy wind.

'There's a man I have to see. A whispermonger, name of Xandian Quail. There shouldn't be any trouble, but that's usually when there's the most trouble. Harkins, Pinn, Jez, grab your guns and come with me. Silo, you take care of the docking permits, watch the aircraft and all that.' The tall Murthian nodded solemnly.

'Think I might need to do some diagnostics,' blurted Harkins suddenly. 'Check out the Firecrow, you know? She was all tick-tick-tick on the port side, don't know what it was, best check it out, probably, if you know what I mean. Don't want to fall out of the sky, you know, zoooooom, crash, haha. That wouldn't be much good to anyone, now would it? Me dead, I mean. Who'd fly it then? Well, I suppose there'd be nothing to fly anyway if I crashed it. So all round it'd be best if I just ran my eye over the internals, make sure everything's ship-shape, spickety-span.'

Frey gave him a look. He squirmed. It was transparently obvious that the thought of a gunfight terrified him.

'Diagnostics,' he said, his voice flat. Harkins nodded eagerly. 'Fine, stay.'

The pilot's face split in a huge grin, revealing a set of uneven and lightly browned teeth. 'Thank you, Cap'n!'

Frey surveyed the rest of his crew. 'What are we all standing around for?' he said, clapping his hands together. 'Get to it!'

They hurried through the drenched streets of Marklin's Reach. The thoroughfares had become rivers of mud, running past the raised wooden porches of the shops and houses. Overhead, strings of electric light bulbs fizzed and flickered as they were thrown about by the wind. Ragged children peered from lean-to shacks and alleyways where they sheltered. Water ramped off awnings and gurgled down gutters, the racket all but drowning out the clattering hum of generators. The air was thick with the smell of petrol, cooking food, and the clean, cold scent of new rain.

'Couldn't we go see this guy tomorrow instead?' Pinn complained. 'I'd be dryer underwater!'

Frey ignored him. They were already cutting it fine. Being held up in Scarwater had put them behind schedule. Quail had been clear in the letter: get here before the end of Howl's Batten, or the offer would go dead. Frey had been lazy about picking up his mail, so he hadn't got the message for some time. With one thing and another, it was now the last day of the month of Howl's Batten, and Frey didn't have time to delay any longer.

'Gonna end up with pneumonia, that's what's gonna happen,'

Pinn was grumbling. '*You* try flying when your cockpit's waist-deep in wet snot.'

Xandian Quail lived in a fortified compound set in a tumble-down cluster of alleys. His house hulked in the darkness, square and austere, its tall, narrow windows aglow. The grinding poverty experienced by the town's denizens was shut out with high walls and stout gates.

'I'm Darian Frey!' Frey yelled over the noise of the downpour. The guards on the other side of the gate seemed nonplussed. 'Darian Frey! Quail's expecting me! At least, he bloody well better be!'

One of the guards scampered over to the house, holding the hood of his slicker. A few moments later he was back and indicated to his companion that he should let them in.

They were escorted beneath the stone porch, where another guard – this one wearing a waistcoat and trousers and sporting a pair of pistols – opened the main door of the house. He had a long face and a patchy black beard. Frey recognised him vaguely from previous visits. His name was Codge.

'Guns,' he said, holding out his hand. 'And don't keep any back. You'll make me real upset if you do.'

Frey hesitated. He didn't like the idea of going into a situation like this without firepower. He couldn't think of any reason for Quail to want him dead, but that did little to ease his mind.

It was the mystery that unnerved him. Quail had given no details in his letter. He'd only said that he had a proposition for Frey, for Frey in *particular*, and that it might make him very rich. That in itself was enough to make him suspicious. It also made him curious.

I just have to hear him out, Frey thought to himself. Anyway, they were here now, and he didn't much fancy tramping back to the *Ketty Jay* until he'd warmed up a bit.

He motioned with his head to the others. *Hand 'em over.*

Once he'd collected their weapons, Codge stepped out of the way and let them into the entrance hall, where they stood dripping. Three more armed guards lounged about in the doorways, exuding an attitude of casual threat. A pair of large, lean dogs loped over to investigate them. They were white, short-haired and pink-eyed. Night hunters, that could see in the dark and tracked their prey by following heat traces. They sniffed over the newcomers, but when they reached Jez, they shied away.

'Time for a new perfume, Jez,' Frey quipped.

'I do have a way with animals, don't I?' she said, looking mildly put out.

Quail's house was a marked contrast to the dirty streets that had led to it. The floor and walls were tiled in black granite. Thick rugs had been laid underfoot.

Coiled-brass motifs ran along the walls towards two curving staircases. Between the staircases was a large and complicated timepiece. It was a combination of clock and calendar, fashioned in copper and bronze and gold. Behind the hands were rotating discs with symbols for all ten months of the year and each of the ten days of the week. Frey was slightly relieved to see that the calendar read: Queensday Thirdweek, Howl's Batten – the last day of the month. He'd not been certain he had the date right until now.

'Just you,' said Codge, motioning up the stairs and looking at Frey. Frey shucked off his slicker and handed it to Pinn, who took it absently. The young pilot's attention had been snared by the four beautiful, seductively dressed women who had appeared in one of the doorways to observe the newcomers. They giggled and smiled at Frey as he headed for the stairs. He gave them a gallant bow, then took the hand of the foremost to kiss.

'You can butter up the whores later. The boss is waiting,' Codge called. One of the women pooched out her lip at him, then favoured Frey with a dirty smirk.

'He'll have to come down again, though, won't he?' she said, raising an eyebrow.

'Good evening, ladies,' said Frey. 'I'm sure my friend over there would love to entertain you until I return.'

Pinn licked his palm, smoothed down the little thatch of hair atop his potato-like head, and put on his best nonchalant pose. The whores eyed him, unimpressed.

'We'll wait.'

'Frey!' said Xandian Quail, as the captain entered the study. 'Dramatically late, I see. I didn't think you'd come.'

'Far as I'm concerned, a margin for error is just wasted space,' Frey said, then shook hands with a hearty camaraderie far above what he actually felt for the man. Quail offered a glass of wine and did a magnificent job of not noticing the trail of muddy footprints that Frey had brought in with him.

Frey sat down and admired the room while Quail poured the drinks. The front of Quail's desk was carved in the likeness of a huge Cloud Eagle, stern and impressive. An ornate and valuable brass barometer hung behind it, the arrow pointing firmly towards RAIN. The windows had complicated patterned bars set on the outside, for security and decoration alike. A black iron candelabra hung from the ceiling, bulbs glowing dimly with electric power. The walls were panelled in mahogany and lined with books. Frey read some of the titles, but didn't recognise any. It was hardly a surprise. He rarely read anything more complicated than the sensationalist broadsheets they sold in the cities.

Quail gave Frey a crystal glass of rich red wine, then sat opposite him with a glass of his own. He'd probably been handsome once, but no longer. A fiery crash in a fighter craft had seen to that. Now half his bald head was puckered with scar tissue, and there was a small metal plate visible on one side of his skull. A brassy orb sat in the socket where his left eye should have been, and his left arm was entirely mechanical.

In spite of this, he carried himself like an aristocrat, and dressed like one too. He wore a brocaded black jacket with a stiff collar and his patent leather shoes shone. Wet, sweaty and dishevelled, Frey was unimpressive by comparison.

'I'm glad you made it,' said Quail. 'Another day and I'd have offered my proposition elsewhere. Time is a factor.'

'I just came to hear what you have to say,' said Frey. 'Make your pitch.'

'I have a job for you.'

'I know your rates,' Frey said. 'I don't have that kind of money.'

'I'm not selling the information. This one's for free.'

Frey sipped his wine and studied the other man.

'I thought whispermongers always stayed neutral,' Frey said.

'Those are the rules,' said Quail. He looked down at his mechanical hand and flexed the fingers thoughtfully. 'You don't get involved, you don't take sides, you never reveal your sources or your clients. Just hard information, bought and sold. You trade secrets but you never take advantage of them.'

'And you certainly don't offer *jobs*.'

'With what we know, you think we're never tempted? We're only human, after all.' Quail smiled. 'That's why we're very particular about who we use. It wouldn't be good for our profession if it were known that we occasionally indulge in a little self-interest.'

'I'm listening.'

'There's a barque out of Samarla, heading for Thesk. The *Ace of Skulls*. Minimum escort, no firepower. They want to keep things low-key, like it's just another freight run. They don't want attention. From pirates *or* the Navy.'

The *Ace of Skulls*. As a keen player of the game of Rake, Frey didn't miss its significance. The Ace of Skulls was the most important card in the game. 'What are they carrying?'

'Among other things, a chest of gems. Uncut gems, bound for a Jeweller's Guild consortium in the capital. They cut a deal with a mining company across the border, and they're flying them back in secret to avoid the Coalition taxes. The profit margin would be huge.'

'*If* they got there.'

'If they got there. But they won't. Because you'll bring those gems to me.'

'Why trust me? Why wouldn't I head for the hills with my newfound riches?'

'Because you'd be a fool to try it. I know about you, Frey. You don't have the contacts or the experience to fence them. You've no idea how dangerous that kind of wealth can be. Even if you didn't get your throat slit trying to sell them, you'd be ripped off.'

'So what do you propose as payment?'

'Fifty thousand ducats. Flat fee, non-negotiable, paid upon delivery of the gems to me.'

Frey's throat went dry. Fifty thousand. He couldn't possibly have heard that right.

'You did just say fifty *thousand* ducats, didn't you?'

'It's a better offer than you'll get trying to sell them yourself, and the deal will be straightforward and safe. I'm rather hoping it will help you avoid temptation.'

'How much is the chest worth?'

'Considerably more, once the gems are cut. But that doesn't concern you.'

'Let me get this straight. You said fifty thousand *ducats*?'

'On delivery.'

Frey drained his wine in a gulp.

'More wine?' Quail offered politely.

'Please,' Frey rasped, holding out his glass.

Fifty thousand ducats. It was a colossal amount of money. More than enough riches to live in luxury for the rest of his days, even after he'd cut the others their share. *If* he cut them a share, he corrected himself.

No, don't think about that yet. You just need to decide if this really is too good to be true.

His heart pounded in his chest, and his skin felt cold. The opportunity of a lifetime. He wasn't stupid enough to think it came without a catch. He just couldn't see it yet.

Ever since he became a freebooter he'd stuck to one hazy and ill-defined rule. *Keep it small-time.* Ambition got people killed. They reached too far and got their hands bitten off. He'd seen it happen time and again: bright-eyed young captains, eager to make a name for themselves, chewed up in the schemes of businessmen and pirates. The big-money games were run by the *real* bad men. If you wanted to play in that league, you had to be ready for a whole new level of viciousness.

And then there was the Navy. They didn't concern themselves with the small-time operators, but once you made a reputation they'd take an interest. And if there was one thing worse than the backstabbing scum-sacks that infested criminal high society, it was the Navy.

Frey wasn't rich. What money he made was usually gambled away or spent on drink or women. Sometimes it was a struggle just to keep craft and crew together. But he was beholden to no one, and that was the way he liked it. Nobody pulled his strings. It was what he told himself whenever money was tight and things looked bad.

At least I'm free, he thought. *At least there's that.*

In the murky world of bottom-feeders, Frey could count himself among the larger fishes, simply by dint of smarts. The world was full of morons and victims. Frey was a cut above, and he was comfortable there. He knew his level, and he knew what happened when people overestimated themselves.

But it was one job. Fifty thousand ducats. A life of appalling, obnoxious luxury staring him in the face.

'Why me?' he asked as Quail refilled his glass. 'I must have dealt with you, what, three times?'

'Yes,' said Quail, settling again. 'You sold me a few titbits. Never bought anything.'

'Never could afford it.'

'That's one point in your favour,' he said. 'We're barely acquainted. The scantest of links between us. I couldn't risk offering this opportunity to most of my clients. My relationship with them is too well known.' He leaned forwards across the desk, clasping his hands together, meshing metal fingers with flesh. 'Make no mistake, if this operation goes bad, I don't know you, and you never heard about those gems from me. I will not allow this to be traced back here. I have to protect myself.'

'Don't worry. I'm used to people pretending they don't know me. Why else?'

'Because fifty thousand ducats is an absurd amount of money to you and I believe it will keep you loyal. Because you're too small-time to fence those gems for yourself, and you're beneath the notice of the Navy and other freebooters alike. And because no one would believe you if you told them I was involved. You're frankly not a very credible witness.'

Frey searched his face, as if he could divine the thoughts beneath. Quail stared back at him patiently.

'It's an easy take, Frey. I know her route. She'll be following the high ground, hugging the cloud ceiling, staying out of sight. No one's going to know she's there but you. You can bring her down over the Hookhollows. Then you pick up the gems, and you fly them to me.'

Frey didn't dare hope it was true. Was it possible that he was simply in the right place at the right time? That a man like him could have a chance to make a lifetime's fortune in one swoop? He wracked his memory for ways he might have given Quail offence, some reason why the whispermonger would send him into a trap.

Could Quail be working on someone else's behalf? Maybe. Frey had certainly made enemies in his time.

But what if he's not *setting you up? Can you really take that chance?*

The clammy, nauseous feeling he had at that moment was not unfamiliar to him. He'd felt it many times before, while playing cards. Staring at his opponent over a hand of Rake, a pile of money between them, his instincts screaming at him to fold and walk away. But sometimes the stakes were just too high, the pot too tempting. Sometimes, he ignored his intuition and bet everything. Usually he lost it all and left the table, kicking himself. But sometimes . . .

Sometimes, he won.

'Tell you what. Throw in some female company, a bed for the night and all the wine we can drink, and you got a deal.'

'Certainly,' said Quail. 'Which lady would you like?'

'All of them,' he said. 'And if you have one who's particularly tolerant – or just blind – she might see to Pinn, too. I'm gonna need his head straight for flying, and the poor kid's gonna split his pods if he doesn't empty them soon.'

Six

The Ghostmoth – Frey's Idea Of Division –
The Ace Of Skulls – Harkins Tests His Courage

In the steep heights of the Hookhollows, where the lowlands of Vardia smashed up against the vast Eastern Plateau, silence reigned. Snow and ice froze tight to the black flanks of the mountains, and not a breath of wind blew. A damp mist hazed the deep places, gathering in crevasses and bleak valleys, and a glowering ceiling of cloud pressed down hard from above, obscuring the peaks and blocking out any sight of open sky. Between sat a layer of clear air, a sandwich of navigable space within which an aircraft might pick its way through the stony maze.

It was isolated and dangerous, but this claustrophobic zone was the best way to cross the Hookhollows unobserved.

A distant drone came floating through the quiet. It steadily rose in volume, swelling and thickening. Around the side of a mountain came a lone, four-winged corvette. A heavily armed Besterfield Ghostmoth.

Lurking in the mist layer, barely a shadow, the *Ketty Jay* stayed hidden as it passed.

Frey watched the Ghostmoth from the cockpit, its dark outline passing overhead. Crake watched it with him.

'That's not the one we're after, is it?' he asked, rather hoping it wasn't.

'No,' said Frey. He wouldn't have taken on a Ghostmoth for any money. He was only concerned that its pilot might spot them and decide to take an interest. You could never be sure. There were a lot of pirates out here. *Real* pirates, not fairweather criminals like they were.

Nothing sat right with Frey about this whole plan. Nothing except the colossal payoff, anyway.

He'd never liked piracy, and historically he'd displayed a lack of talent in the field. Of the four times he'd tried it, three had been failures. Only once had he successfully downed and robbed a craft, and even then the loot had been meagre and his navigator got stabbed and killed in the process. Twice they'd been forced to flee in the face of superior firepower. On the most recent attempt they'd actually managed to board the craft only to find it had already delivered its cargo. That was the closest his crew had ever come to mutiny, until he hit on the idea of placating them with a night out at the nearest port. The following morning, the incident was forgotten, along with most of their motor skills and their ability to speak.

In general, Frey didn't like being shot at. Piracy was a risky business, and best left to the professionals. Even Quail's assurances of an easy take did little to quell his fears.

The Ghostmoth slid out of view, and Frey relaxed. He checked on Harkins and Pinn, hovering a little way above them and to starboard, dim in the mist. The *Ketty Jay* drifted silently, but for the occasional hiss of stabilising gas-jets as Frey's hands twitched across the brass-and-chrome dashboard. The cockpit lights had been turned off, leaving the interior gloomy. Jez was sitting at the navigator's station, studying a map. Crake, who had dropped in uninvited, stood behind the pilot's seat, wringing his hands. Frey thought about ordering him back to his quarters but couldn't be bothered with the argument that might ensue.

'Quail said they'd be coming through here?' Crake murmured.

'That's what he said,' Frey replied.

'Makes sense,' Jez told Crake. 'You want to get through the Hookhollows without being spotted, you follow the mountains that rise closest to the cloud ceiling. That way you can't be seen from above and you minimise possible sight-lines from below. Two of the most obvious routes converge on this point.'

Frey turned around in his seat and looked at her. 'I'm beginning

45

to think that, after many months, I've finally found a navigator who actually knows what they're doing,' he said.

'We're few and far between, Cap'n.'

'How's the shoulder?'

'Fine.'

'Good. Don't get shot again. You're useful.'

'I'll do my best,' she said, with a quirky little grin.

Frey settled back to watching. He'd begun to think that Jez was a lucky find. In the few days she'd been on board, she'd shown herself to be far more efficient and reliable than he'd expected. Competence was by no means a prerequisite to joining the crew of the *Ketty Jay*, but Jez was head and shoulders above the other navigators Frey had worked with. He suspected that she was accustomed to better crews than Frey's mob, but their slapdash technique didn't seem to bother her. And she was good at what she did. She'd brought them in from Marklin's Reach with pinpoint accuracy, with only a featureless sea of cloud and a few mountain peaks to plot their position by. Frey had dropped down through the cloud and found himself dead in the middle of the pass they'd selected for their ambush.

She was a smart one. He only hoped she wasn't *too* smart.

Perhaps the others hadn't noticed, but Jez knew something was wrong with this job. He kept catching a glimpse of the question in her eyes. She'd open her mouth as if to say something, then shut it again and look away.

She feels it too, Frey thought. *Instinct.*

Instinct. Perhaps. Or perhaps she sensed that her captain intended to rip them off good and proper.

He tried to feel bad, but he really couldn't manage it. After all, you couldn't be robbed of what you never had. Quail had promised *him* fifty thousand ducats, not *them*. Granted, he'd always maintained a system of fair shares for his crew, dividing the booty according to pre-arranged percentages, but these were exceptional circumstances. By which he meant an exceptional amount of money. Too much to share.

46

It was just this one time, he promised himself. Because after this, he'd never need to work again.

He'd informed the crew that Quail had given them the tip-off in exchange for one thing. There was a chest on board that he wanted. They were to bring it to him. Everything else was theirs for the taking.

Frey had obtained a full description of the chest, and he knew it would be locked tight. Quail had also assured him there were plenty more pickings besides. The crew could loot to their hearts' content, and everyone would be happy. They didn't need to know what was inside the chest. They didn't need to know about the arrangement between Frey and Quail.

But Jez kept giving him that look.

'I hear something,' Crake said suddenly.

Frey listened. He was right: a low throb, accompanied by the higher whines of smaller engines. Hard to make out how many.

'Jez,' Frey murmured. 'Ready on the electroheliograph.'

'Cap'n,' she said, reaching over to the switch.

'This is the one, isn't it?' Crake asked, squinting through the windglass, trying to catch a glimpse.

'This is the one,' Frey said.

The *Ace of Skulls* slid into the pass, cruising majestically between two broken peaks. Long, blunt-faced and curve-bellied, she had stubs for wings and a tail assembly like an enormous fin. Thrusters pushed her along as she glided through the air, buoyed up with huge tanks of aerium gas. Decals on her flanks displayed her name, printed across a fan of cards. She was a heavy, no-nonsense craft, without frills, solid. Nothing about her gave away the value of the cargo within.

Buzzing alongside, dwarfed in size, were four Swordwings. Frey recognised them by their distinctive conical, down-slanting muzzles and aerodynamic shape. They were fast fighter craft. Nothing exceptional in their design, but in the hands of a good pilot they could be deadly.

'It's not exactly *minimum escort*,' Crake murmured.

47

Frey made a distracted noise of agreement. He didn't like the look of those Swordwings. He'd expected two, not four.

'Just give me the word,' Jez said, fingertip hovering over the press-pad of the electroheliograph switch.

Frey stared up at the freighter. It wasn't too late to listen to the voice that told him to back out of this. The voice that told him to lay his cards down when he knew his hand was beat. The voice of caution.

You could just keep going on as you are, he thought. *It's not a bad life, is it? You've got your own craft. You don't answer to anyone. The whole world's there for you. Now what's wrong with that?*

What was wrong with it was that he didn't have fifty thousand ducats. He hadn't really minded before, but suddenly the lack had become intolerable.

'Cap'n?' Jez prompted. 'Time's a factor.'

Frey had picked a spot just below the mist layer and in the shadow of a peak, to give them a good view of the pass above. But if he could see the *Ace of Skulls*, she might see him, and without the element of surprise they'd have no chance.

You know this is too good to be true, Frey. Stuff like this just doesn't happen to guys like you. Ambition gets people killed.

'Cap'n?'

'Do it,' he said.

Pinn wiped his running nose with the back of his hand and stared at the grey bulk of the *Ketty Jay*.

'Come on! What's taking so long?' he cried. The need to get up there and shoot something was like a physical pull. His boots tapped against the complicated array of pedals; his gloved fingers flexed on the flight stick. These were the moments he lived for. This was where the action was. And Pinn, as he never tired of telling everyone, was all about action.

The Second Aerium War fizzled out mere days before he had the chance to sign up. Those miserable Sammies called it off just as he was about to get in there and bloody his guns. It was as if they'd intended to spite him personally. As if they were afraid of what would happen when Pinn got into the thick of things.

Well, if the Sammies were too chickenshit to face him in the air, then he'd just take it out on the rest of the world, every chance he got. Having been cheated once, he reasoned it was only his due. A man deserved the opportunity to prove himself.

He snatched up the small, framed ferrotype of his sweetheart Lisinda, that hung on a chain from his dash. The black and white portrait didn't do her justice. Her long hair was fairer, her innocent, docile eyes more beautiful in his memory.

It had been taken just before he left. He wondered what she was doing now. Perhaps sitting by a window, reading, patiently awaiting his return. Did she sense his thoughts on her? Did she turn her pretty face up to the sky, hoping to see the cloud break and the sun shine through, the glimmer of his wings as he swooped triumphantly in to land? He pictured himself stepping down from the Skylance, Lisinda rushing joyously towards him. He'd sweep her up in his arms and kiss her hard, and tears would run uncontrollably down her face, because her hero had returned after four long years.

His thoughts were interrupted by a series of flashes from a lamp on the *Ketty Jay*'s back. A coded message from the electroheliograph.

Go.

Pinn whooped and rammed the prothane thrusters to maximum. The Skylance boomed into life and leaped forward, pressing him back in his seat. He stamped down on a pedal, wrenched the stick, and the craft came bursting out of the mist, arcing towards the small flotilla high above. They'd all but passed overhead now, so he came at them from below and behind, hiding in their blind spot. A fierce grin spread across his chubby face as the engines screamed and the craft rattled all around him.

'This ain't your lucky day,' he muttered as he lined his enemy up in his sights. He believed true heroes always said something dry and chilling before they killed anybody. Then he pressed down on his guns.

The pilot of the nearest Swordwing had only just heard the sound of Pinn's engine when the bullets ripped through the underbelly of his craft. They pierced the prothane tanks and blasted the Swordwing apart in a dirty cloud of flame. Pinn howled with joy, corkscrewed through the fire and burst out of the far side. He craned in his seat to look back, past his port wing, and saw Harkins coming up, machine guns blazing, shredding the rudder of another Swordwing as he shrieked by.

'Yeah!' he cried. 'Nice shooting, you twitchy old freak!'

He hauled the Skylance into a loop, hard enough to make his vision sparkle at the edges, and headed back towards the flotilla. The two remaining Swordwings had broken formation now, taking evasive action. Harkins' target was coiling its way down to a foggy oblivion, leaving a trail of smoke from its ruined tail. Far below, the *Ketty Jay* had broken cover and was heading towards the slow bulk of the freighter.

Pinn picked another Swordwing and plunged towards it. He dropped into position on its tail, machine guns spitting a broken row of blazing tracer bullets. The pilot banked hard and rolled, darting neatly out of the way. Pinn raised an eyebrow.

'Not bad,' he murmured. 'This is gonna be fun.'

'She's heading for the clouds!' Jez said.

She was right. The *Ace of Skulls* had turned her nose up towards the cloud ceiling and was gliding towards it. Visibility would be almost nil in there.

'I'm on it,' Frey said, then suddenly yelled, 'Doc!'

'What?' came the bellowed reply through the open doorway of the cockpit.

'Start hassling the fighters! I've got the big fish!'

'Right-o!'

There was the thumping of autocannon fire as Malvery, in the gunner's cupola, began unleashing lead at all and sundry. Frey fed a little more into the prothane engines and the *Ketty Jay* responded, surging upwards. She was surprisingly light for such a big craft, but Frey was long used to the way she handled. Nobody knew her like he did.

Harkins and Pinn had the Swordwings occupied, chasing them around the sky, leaving the way clear for him. He hunched forward in his seat, frowning intently at his target. Jez and Crake stood behind him, hanging on as best they could as the *Ketty Jay* rocked and swayed.

The freighter swam higher, thrusters pushing as hard as they were able, but she was a lumbering thing and she couldn't get a steep enough angle without tearing herself apart under her own weight. Frey would only get one chance, but one chance was all he needed. The aerium tanks on a craft like this were an enormous target. Though there was nothing on the outer skin to indicate their location, Frey knew his aircraft. It would be hard to miss.

Just graze the tanks with your guns, he reminded himself. Holed tanks would vent aerium gas, and the steady loss of lift would force the pilot to either land the craft or have her drop out of the sky. A landing might be a bit violent in this kind of terrain, but Frey didn't much care as long as the cargo was intact. The prothane tanks – the dangerous part – were well armoured and buried deep within the craft. It would take a really bad landing to make them go up.

The *Ace of Skulls* swelled in his view, growing larger as he approached. In attempting to escape she'd exposed her belly. He zeroed in on the spot just under her stubby, finlike wings.

Closer . . . closer . . .

He squeezed the trigger on his flight stick. The *Ketty Jay*'s front-mounted machine guns clattered, punching a pattern of holes across the freighter's side.

And the *Ace of Skulls* exploded.

The windglass of the cockpit filled with a terrible bloom of fire, lighting up Frey's astonished face for a split second. Then the impact hit them.

The detonation was ear-shattering. A concussion wave swamped the *Ketty Jay*, making her roll sharply and sending Jez and Crake slamming into the navigator's station. Frey wrestled with the controls, yanking on the flight stick with one hand, hitting switches with the other. The engines groaned and stuttered, but Frey had flown this craft for more than a decade and he knew her inside out. Teeth gritted, he gentled her through the chaos, and in seconds they were level again.

Frey looked out of the cockpit. He felt sick and faint. An oily black cloud of smoke, blistering with red and white flame, roiled in the air. The *Ace of Skulls'* enormous bow was plummeting into the pass far below; her tail assembly crashed against the side of a mountain and broke into pieces. A cloud of lesser debris spun lazily away, thrown out by the colossal force of the explosion.

And in among the debris, charred, limp things fell towards the earth. Some of them were still almost whole.

Bodies. Dozens of bodies.

Harkins stared at the slow cascade of wreckage as it tumbled from the sky. He wasn't sure he'd exactly grasped the full implications of what had just happened, but he knew this was bad. This was very, very bad. And not just because they'd screwed up yet another attempt at sky piracy.

Then, suddenly, the Swordwing he'd been chasing broke left and dived. Harkins' attention switched back to his target.

He's running! Harkins thought. A glance told him that the second Swordwing was doing the same, spearing up towards the clouds. Pinn was hot on its tail, spraying tracer fire. Smoke trailed from one of its wings.

Harkins threw the Firecrow into a dive. Whatever had just happened, Harkins was certain of one thing. They were in trouble.

But only if someone lived to tell about it.

The Swordwing was dropping hard, towards the layer of mist that had hidden the *Ketty Jay*. Harkins rattled off a short burst from his guns, but he was still too far away. He opened the Firecrow's throttle and screamed after the Swordwing as it was swallowed up by the mist.

Oh no, he fretted to himself. *I don't want to go in there, I really don't!*

But it was too late for second thoughts. The mist closed over him, greying his vision. The Swordwing was a dark smudge ahead. It had pulled level, skimming through the upper layers of mist where visibility was just the right side of suicidal. Harkins tried to close the distance, but they were evenly matched on speed.

Sweat began to trickle down the deep folds of his unshaven cheeks. They were going too fast, they were going way too fast. This pilot was a maniac! Was he trying to get himself killed?

Harkins pressed down on his guns, hoping for a lucky hit. The tracer fire blazed away into the gloom.

A mountain loomed out of the mist to starboard, an unending slope of snowy rock fading into view. The Swordwing swung in recklessly close to it, hugging the mountainside. The shockwave of its passage threw up clouds of loose snow, whipping them into Harkins' path. The pilot was trying to blind him further. But the tactic was ineffective: the powdery snow dispersed too fast, and did nothing to slow him. Harkins angled himself on an intercept trajectory and closed in on his target.

The mountainside ended without warning, and the Swordwing made a dangerously sharp turn, almost clipping the corner. Harkins followed out of reflex. The only safe place in this murk was where his target had already been.

An outcrop of black stone came at him like a thrown fist.

His reactions responded in place of conscious thought. He shoved the flight stick forward and the Firecrow dived, skimming under the jutting stone with barely a foot to spare. It thundered over him for a terrifying instant and was gone.

He pulled away from the mountainside, gibbering. That was too close, too close, too close! His legs had begun to tremble. This was insane! Insane! Who did that pilot think he was, anyway? Why was he putting Harkins through such torment?

But there it was: the Swordwing. Still visible through the bubble of windglass on the Firecrow's snout. It was heading down, further into the dull blankness, a ghostly blur.

Harkins followed. Afraid as he was, he was also afraid to face the consequences of giving up. He couldn't take Frey's wrath if he let the Swordwing go. Death in the cockpit was one thing, but confrontation was quite another. Confrontation was a special kind of hell for Harkins, and he'd do just about anything to avoid it.

Dense, threatening shadows came into view on either side of them: mountains, pressing in close. Harkins bit his lip to stop his teeth chattering. The Firecrow's engines cocooned him in warm sound, but he was acutely aware of how fragile this metal shell would be if it hit something at a hundred knots. He'd seen Firecrows shatter like eggs, some of them with his friends inside.

But that never happened to me! he told himself, firming his will, and he pushed harder on the throttle.

The mountains slid closer on either side, pushing together, and he realised they were heading into a defile. Then, suddenly, the Swordwing slowed. Harkins bore down on it. The blur took on form and shape, growing before him. He pressed down his guns just as the Swordwing went into a steep climb, and the tracers fell astern as it shot upwards and disappeared into the haze.

At that moment, Harkins realised what his opponent was doing. Panic clutched at him. He yanked back on the flight stick, hauling on the throttle and stamping the pedal that opened the flaps for emergency braking. The Firecrow's blunt nose came up; the craft squealed in protest. Harkins felt a weight like a giant's hand shoving him down into his seat.

A wall of grim stone filled his vision. Massive, immovable, racing towards him. The end of the defile. He screamed as the Firecrow clawed at the air, scrabbling to climb. Blood pounded in his thighs and feet. His vision dimmed and narrowed as he began to brown out.

You're not gonna faint . . . you're not gonna faint . . .

Then everything tilted, vertical became horizontal, and the wall that had been in front of him was rushing beneath his wings. He let off on the stick, blood thumping back into his head, and the Firecrow shot out of the defile and upwards. There were a few seconds of nothing but grey, then he burst out of the mist and into the clear air.

Stillness.

As if in a trance, he cut back the throttle and gently brought the Firecrow to a hover, letting it float in the air, resting on the buoyancy of its aerium tanks. A dozen kloms away, visible between the peaks, the *Ketty Jay* hung listlessly, waiting for his return. He looked down into the sea of mist, but his quarry was long gone.

His hands were quivering uncontrollably. He held one up before him and stared as it shook.

Seven

*An Argument – Crake Accuses – What The
Cat Thinks Of Jez – Frey Has A Dream*

The eastern edge of the Hookhollows was full of hiding places. Secret valleys, sheltered ledges. There were folds in the crumpled landscape big enough to conceal a small fleet of aircraft. Freebooters treasured these bolt holes, and when they found a good one they guarded its location jealously.

Nightfall found the *Ketty Jay* and her outflyers in one of Frey's favourite spots, a long tunnel-like cave he usually employed when he was running from something bigger than he was. It was wider than it was high, a slot in the plateau wall that ran far back into the mountainside. A tight fit for a craft the size of the *Ketty Jay*, but Frey had brought them in without a scratch. Now the *Ketty Jay* hunkered in the dark, its dim underbelly lights reflected by the shallow stream that ran along the floor of the cave. There was no sound but for a rhythmic dripping and the relentless chuckle of the water.

Inside the *Ketty Jay*, things were not so calm.

'What in the name of the Allsoul's veiny bollocks were you aiming at, you shit-wit?' Pinn demanded of his captain, who punched him in response.

Slag, the *Ketty Jay*'s cat, watched the ensuing scuffle with feline disinterest from his vantage point atop a cabinet. The whole crew had gathered in the mess, crowding into one small room, and the comical jostle to separate Pinn and Frey involved a lot of bashing into things and knocking chairs over. The mess was a cheerless place, comprising a fixed central table, a set of metal cabinets for utensils and a compact stove, where Slag warmed himself when Silo chased him out of the engine room.

Slag was an ancient warrior, a grizzled slab of muscle held together by scar tissue and a hostile disposition. Frey had brought him on board as a kitten the day after he took ownership of the *Ketty Jay*, fourteen years ago. Slag had never known anything beyond the *Ketty Jay*, and never been tempted to find out. His life's purpose was here, as the nemesis of the monstrous rats that bred in the air ducts and pipeways. For more than a decade the battle had been fought, generations of sharp-toothed rodents versus their indestructible antagonist. He'd seen off the best of them – their generals, their leaders – and hunted their mothers until they were near-extinct. But they always came back, and Slag was always waiting for them.

'Will you two stop acting like a pair of idiots?' Jez cried, as Malvery and Silo pulled Pinn from their captain. Pinn, red-faced with anger, assured Malvery he was calm so the doctor would release him, then made the obligatory second lunge at Frey. Malvery was ready for it, and punched him hard in the stomach, knocking the wind out of him.

'What'd you do that for?' Pinn rasped weakly, wide-eyed with the injustice of it all.

'Fun,' replied Malvery, with a broad grin. 'Now calm down before I club your stupid block off. You ain't helping.'

Frey shook Silo off with a baleful glare and dusted himself down. 'Right,' he said. 'Now we've got *that* out of the way, can I say something, nice and slow so everyone gets it? *It – wasn't – my – fault!*'

'You did blow up the freighter, though,' Crake pointed out.

'If you knew *anything* about aircraft you'd know they always put the prothane tanks as deep inside as possible, well armoured. Otherwise people like us might be able to hit them and blow the whole thing to smithereens.'

'The way you did,' Crake persisted, out of malice. He hadn't forgotten Frey's behaviour when Lawsen Macarde had a gun to his head.

'But I didn't!' Frey cried. 'Machine guns couldn't have penetrated deep enough to even *get* to the prothane tanks. Silo, tell them.'

The Murthian folded his arms. 'Could happen, Cap'n. But it's one in a million.'

'See? It *could* happen!' Pinn crowed, having recovered his breath.

'But it's *one in a million*!' Frey said through gritted teeth. 'About the same chance as you shutting up for five minutes so I can think.'

Slag unfurled from his spot on top of the cabinet and dropped down to the countertop with a thump. He thought little, if at all, of the other beings with whom he shared the craft, but he was feeling unaccountably piqued that nobody was paying any attention to him amid this puzzling furore. Harkins, who had been keeping his head down anyway, cringed into the corner as he caught sight of the cat. Slag gave him a stare of utter loathing, then leaped to the table so he could get into the middle of things.

'The question isn't whose fault it is—' Jez began.

'Not mine, that's for sure!' Frey interjected.

Jez gave him a look and continued. 'It's not whose fault it is. The question is whether we're going to get *blamed* for it.'

'Well, thanks to Harkins being a bloody great chicken, we probably will,' Pinn said sullenly.

'That guy was a good pilot!' Harkins protested. 'He was a . . . he was a fantastic pilot! Well, fantastic, or he had a death wish or something. What kind of idiot flies full throttle through mountain passes in the mist? The . . . the crazy kind, that's what kind! And I'm a good pilot, but I'm not some crazy idiot! You said minimum escort, someone said minimum escort! No one said anything about . . . about four Swordwings and one of them being a pilot like that! What's a pilot like that doing flying escort to some grubby old freighter?'

'I'd have caught him,' said Pinn. 'I caught the one *I* was chasing.'

'Well, yours was probably shit,' Harkins muttered.

Jez was pacing around the mess as the pilots argued, head bowed thoughtfully. As she drew close to Slag, he arched his back and hissed at her. Something about this human bothered him. He didn't understand why, only that he felt threatened whenever she was around, and that made him angry. He hated Harkins for being weak, but he was afraid of Jez.

'What's got into him?' Crake wondered.

'Ugly sack of mange,' sneered Pinn. 'It's finally lost its tiny little mind.'

'Hey!' said Frey, defensive. 'No bitching about the cat.' He put out his hand to stroke Slag, and quickly withdrew it as Slag took a swipe at him.

'Why not? Bloody thing's only fit to use as a duster anyway. Wring its neck, stick a broom handle up its—'

'Shut up about the cat!' Jez said, surprising them into quiet. For such a little thing she'd proved herself unusually feisty, and she commanded respect far out of proportion to her physical size. 'We've got more important things to deal with.'

She walked in a slow circle around the mess, stepping between them as she spoke. 'We caught them by surprise. Even if that Swordwing got away – he might have crashed in the mist – then he'd have barely had time to work out what was going on before he ran. Harkins was on his tail almost immediately. He'd have had other things on his mind.'

'You don't think he could identify us?' Frey said.

'I doubt it,' Jez replied. 'There are no decals on the craft that identify us as the *Ketty Jay*, and we're not exactly famous, are we? So, what do they have? Maybe he saw an Wickfield Ironclad accompanied by a Firecrow and a Skylance. You'd have to be pretty dedicated to hunt us down on the basis of that.'

'Quail won't say a word,' said Frey, warming to her optimism. 'Though it's probably best if our paths never cross again. Just to be safe, let's stay out of Marklin's Reach. Silo, put it on our list of no-go ports. Scarwater, too.'

'Aren't that many ports left to go to,' Malvery grumbled.

'Well, now there are two fewer.' He looked around the room.

'Alright, are we done here? Good. Let's keep our heads down, forget this ever happened, and it's business as usual.' He began to leave, but was stopped by a soft voice.

'Am I the only one who remembers there were *people* on that freighter?' Crake said.

Frey turned around to look over his shoulder at the daemonist.

'That thing was hauling passengers,' Crake said. 'Not cargo.'

Frey's eyes were cold. 'It wasn't my fault,' he said, and clambered up the ladder to the exit hatch.

The crew dispersed after that, some still arguing between themselves. Slag remained in the middle of the table in the empty mess, feeling neglected. After a swift and resentful bout of self-grooming with his tongue, he resolved to make Harkins suffer tonight by creeping into his quarters and going to sleep on his face.

Frey stepped into his quarters and slid the heavy iron door shut behind him, cutting off the voices of his crew. With a sigh, he sat on the hard bunk and dragged his hand down his face, mashing his features as if he could smear them away. He sat there for a while, thinking nothing, wallowing in the bleak depression that had settled on him.

Every time, he thought bitterly. *Every damned time.*

Suddenly, he surged to his feet and drew back his hand to strike the wall, but at the last instant he stopped himself. Instead he pressed forehead and fist against it, breathing deeply, hating. A hatred without target or focus, directed at nothing, the blind frustration of a man maligned by fate.

What had he done to deserve this? Where was it written that all his best efforts should come to nothing, that opportunity should flirt with him and leave him ragged, that money should rust to powder in his hands? How had he ended up living a life surrounded by the witless, the desperate, drunkards, thieves and villains? Wasn't he better than that?

That bastard Quail! *He'd* done this. Somehow, he was responsible. Frey had known the job was too good to be true. The only people who ever made fifty thousand ducats out of a deal were people who already had ten times that. Just one more way the world conspired to keep the rich where they were, and keep everyone else down.

The *Ace of Skulls* should *never* have exploded. It was impossible. What happened to those people . . . Frey never meant for that. It was an accident. He couldn't be blamed. He'd only meant to hit the aerium tanks. He *had* hit the aerium tanks. It was just one of those things, like a volcano erupting, or when a craft got caught in a freak hurricane. An act of the Allsoul, if you believed all that Awakener drivel.

Frey sourly reflected there might be something in the idea of an all-controlling entity. Someone was certainly out to get him, intent on thwarting his every endeavour. If there was an Allsoul, then he sure as spit didn't like Frey very much.

He walked over to the steel washbasin and splashed water on his face. In the soap-streaked mirror he studied himself. He smiled experimentally. The lines at the edges of his eyes seemed to have deepened since last time he looked. He'd first noticed them a year ago, and had been shocked by the first signs of decline. He'd unconsciously assumed he'd always stay youthful.

Though he'd never admit it aloud, he knew he was handsome. His face had a certain something about it that pulled women towards him: a hint of slyness, a promise of danger, a darkness in his grin – *something*, anyway. He never was exactly sure what. It had given him an easy confidence in his youth, a self-assured air that only attracted women more strongly still.

About the only piece of luck I ever got, he thought, since he was in the mood to be peevish.

Even men could be drawn into his orbit, sucked in by a vague envy of his success with the opposite sex. Frey had never had a problem making new friends. Charm, he'd discovered, was the art of pretending you meant what you said. Whether complimenting a man, or offering feathered lies to a woman, Frey never seemed less than sincere. But he'd usually forget them the moment they were out of his sight.

Now here he was, thirty, with lines around his eyes when he

smiled. He couldn't trade on his looks for ever, and when they were gone, what was left? What would he do when his body couldn't take the rum any more and the women didn't want him?

He threw himself away from the sink with a snort of disgust.

Self-pity doesn't suit you, Frey. No one likes a whiner.

Still, he had to admit, it had been a pretty bad decade and his thirties had got off to an unpromising start. Waiting for his luck to change had worn his patience thin, and trying to change it himself invariably ended in disaster.

Look on the bright side, he thought. *At least you're free.*

Yes, there was that. No boss to work for, no Coalition Navy breathing down his neck. No woman tying him down. Well, not in the metaphorical sense, anyway. Some of his conquests had been more sexually adventurous than others.

But damn, this time . . . this time he really thought he had a chance. The sheer disappointment had shaken him badly.

It could have been different, though. Maybe if you'd taken a different path, ten years ago. Maybe you'd have been happy. You'd certainly have been rich.

No. No regrets. He wouldn't waste his life on regrets.

The captain's quarters were cramped, although they were still the biggest on the craft. He didn't keep them particularly clean. The metal walls were coated in a faint patina of grime and the floor was filthy with bootprints. His bunk took up most of the space, beneath a string hammock of luggage which threatened to snap and bury him in the night. A desk, drawers and cabinets were affixed to the opposite wall, with catches in the drawers and doors to prevent them opening during flight. In the corner was his mirror and washbasin. Sometimes he used the washbasin as a toilet in the night, rather than climb two levels down to use the head. There were advantages to being male.

He got up and opened a drawer. Inside, atop a mess of papers and notebooks, sat a tiny bottle of clear liquid. He took it, and returned to the bunk.

Might as well, he thought, sadly.

He unscrewed the stopper, which also functioned as a pipette.

He squeezed the bulb and drew in a little liquid, tipped his head back and administered one drop to each eye. Blinking, he lay back on the bed.

Drowsy relief billowed over his senses. The aches in his joints faded away, to be replaced by a warm, cloudy sensation that erased his cares and smoothed his brow. His eyes flickered shut, and he drifted on the cusp of sleep for a long while before succumbing.

He dreamed that night of a young woman, with long blonde hair and a smile so perfect it made his heart glow like burning embers. But when he woke the next morning, he remembered none of it.

Eight

Tavern Banter – Crake Visits An Old Friend –
The Sanctum – An Unpleasant Surprise

Old One-Eye's tavern was a swelter of heat and smoke, pungent with sweat and meat and beer. The gas lamps were muted by the fug that hung in the air. Stoves, lit to keep the chill of dusk away, made the room stifling. The din of conversation was such that people had to shout to be heard, raising the volume ever further. Waitresses passed between the crude wooden tables, expertly avoiding the attentions of rough-eyed men with ready hands.

Buried amid the standing crowd, Frey held court at a table littered with pewter flagons. He was just finishing a tale about his early days working for Dracken Industries as a cargo hauler. The story concerned an employee's senile mother, who had somehow got to the controls of an unattended tractor and driven it into a pile of caged chickens. The punchline was delivered with enough panache to make Pinn spew beer from his nose, which had Malvery laughing so hard he retched. Crake observed the scene with a polite smile. Harkins looked nervously at the people standing nearby, clearly wishing he was anywhere but here. The gangly pilot had been cajoled along on this expedition by Malvery, who thought it would do him good to get out among people. Harkins hated the idea, but had agreed anyway, to avoid the slightest risk of giving offence by refusal.

Jez and Silo were absent. Jez didn't drink alcohol, and kept herself to herself; Silo rarely left the ship.

Crake sipped at his beer as Pinn and Malvery recovered. His companions were all merrily drunk, except Harkins, who radiated discomfort despite having sunk three flagons already. Crake was still working on his first. They'd given up bullying him to keep pace once he'd convinced them he wouldn't be swayed. He had other business tonight, and it didn't involve getting hammered on cheap alcohol.

How easily they forgot, he thought. As if Macarde holding a gun to his head was a trifling matter not worthy of comment. As if the mass murder of dozens of innocent people was something that could be erased with a few nights of heavy drinking.

Was that their secret? Was that how they lived in this world? Like animals, thinking only of what was in front of them. Did they live in the moment, without thought for the past or concern for the future?

Certainly that was true of Pinn. He was too dim to comprehend such intangibles as past or future. Whenever he spoke of them, it was with such a devastating lack of understanding that Crake had to leave the room.

Pinn rambled endlessly about Lisinda, a girl from his village, the sweetheart who waited for him back home. His devotion and loyalty to her were eternal. She was a goddess, a virginal idol, the woman he was to marry. After a brief romance – during which Pinn proudly declared they'd never had sex, as if through some mighty restraint on his part – she'd told him she loved him. Not long afterward, he'd left her a note and gone out into the world to make his fortune. That had been four years ago, and he'd neither seen nor contacted her since. He'd return a rich and successful man, or not at all.

Pinn saw himself as her shining knight, who would one day return and give her all the wonderful things he felt she deserved. The simple truth – which, in Crake's opinion, was obvious to anyone with half a brain – was that the day would never come. What little money Pinn had was quickly squandered on pleasures of the flesh. He gambled, drank and whored as if it was his last day alive, and he flew the same way. Even if he somehow managed to survive long enough to luck his way into a fortune, Crake had no doubt that the bovine, dull-looking girl – whose picture Pinn enthusiastically showed to all and sundry – had long since given up on him and moved on.

In Crake's eyes, Pinn had no honour. He'd lie with whores, then lament his manly weakness in the morning and swear fidelity to Lisinda. The following night he'd get drunk and do it again. How he could believe himself in love on the one hand and cheat on her on the other was baffling. Crake considered him a life-form ranking somewhere below a garden mole and just above a shellfish.

The others, he couldn't so easily dismiss. Harkins was a simple man, but at least he knew it. He didn't suffer the same staggering failure of self-awareness that Pinn did. Malvery had a brain on him when he chose to use it, and he was a good-hearted sort to boot. Jez, while not luminously cultured, was very quick and knew her stuff better than anyone on board, with the possible exception of their mysterious Murthian engineer. Even Frey was smart, though clearly lacking in education.

How, then, could these people live so day-to-day? How could they discard the past and ignore the future with such enviable ease?

Or was it simply that the past was too painful and the future too bleak to contemplate?

He finished his drink and got to his feet. This was a question for another time.

'Excuse me, gentlemen,' he said. 'I have to pay someone a visit.'

His announcement was greeted by a rousing *wa-hey!* from the table.

'A lady friend, eh?' Malvery enquired with a salacious nudge that almost unbalanced him. 'I knew you'd crack! Three months I've known him and he's not so much as looked at a woman!'

Crake managed to maintain a fixed smile. 'You must admit, the quality of lady I've been exposed to hasn't been terribly inspiring.'

'Hear that?' jeered Pinn. 'He thinks he's too good for our sort! Or maybe it's just that women aren't to his taste,' he finished with a smirk.

Crake wasn't sinking to that level. 'I'll be back later,' he said stiffly, and left.

'We'll be here!' Frey called after him.

'You great big ponce!' Pinn added, to raucous howls of laughter from his companions.

Crake pushed his way out of the tavern, cheeks burning. The cold, clear air off the sea soothed him. He stood outside Old One-Eye's, collecting himself. Even after several months on board the *Ketty Jay*, he wasn't used to being mocked quite so crudely. It took him a short while before he felt calm enough to forgive the crew. Not Pinn, though. That was just one more score against him. *Ponce*, indeed. That moron didn't know *how* to love a woman.

He buttoned up his greatcoat, pulled on a pair of gloves and began to walk.

Tarlock Cove at dusk was rather picturesque, he thought. A fraction more civilised than the dives he'd become accustomed to, anyway. With the Hookhollows rising steeply at the back of the town and the wild Poleward Sea before it, there was a dramatic vista at every corner. It was built into the mountainside and straggled around the encircling arms of the bay, connected by steep stairs and winding gravel paths. Houses were narrow, wooden and generally well kept once you got away from either of the two docks. Vessels of both air and sea made port here, as Tarlock Cove was built on fishing. The ships trawled the shoals and sold their catch to the aircraft crews for distribution.

It was, in fact, the reason they'd come here. Having been burned by their last endeavour, Frey decided to play it safe with some nice, legal work that wasn't liable to get them all killed. He'd all but emptied the *Ketty Jay*'s coffers to buy a cargo of smoked bloodfish, which he planned to sell inland for a profit. Apparently, it was 'easy work' and 'nothing could go wrong', both phrases Crake had learned to mistrust of late.

He headed up railed stone stairways and along curving lanes. The houses pressed close to a waist-high barrier wall, which separated pedestrians from the sheer cliffs on the other side. Lamplighters were making their way along the cobbled streets, leaving a dotted line of hazily glowing lamp-posts in their wake. Tarlock Cove was preparing for dusk.

As Crake climbed higher, he could see the lighthouse at the mouth of the bay, and he was pleased when he noticed it brighten and begin to turn. Such things, signs of a well-run and orderly world, gave him a sense of enormous satisfaction at times.

Orderliness was one of the reasons he'd liked Tarlock Cove on his previous visits. It was overseen by the family whose name it bore, and the Tarlocks ensured their little town wasn't left to ruin. Houses were well painted, streets swept clean, and the Ducal Militia made certain that the ragamuffin traders who passed through were kept from bothering the respectable folk higher up the mountainside.

Dominating it all from the highest point of the town was the Tarlock manse. It was unassuming in its grandeur, a wide, stout building with many windows, benevolently overlooking the bay. A classically understated design, Crake thought: the picture of aristocratic modesty. He'd visited with the Tarlocks once, and found them delightful company.

But it wasn't the Tarlocks he planned to see tonight. He went instead down a winding, lamp-lit lane and knocked at the door of a thin, three-storey house sandwiched between other houses of a similar design.

The door was opened by a rotund man in his sixties wearing pince-nez. The top of his head was bald, but stringy grey hair fell around his neck and over the collar of his brown-and-gold jacket.

He took one look at his visitor and the colour drained from his face.

'Good evening, Plome,' Crake said.

'*Good evening*?' Plome spluttered. He looked both ways up the alley, then seized him by the arm and pulled him over the threshold. 'Get off the street, you fool!' He shut the door the moment Crake was inside.

The hallway within was shadowy at this hour: the lamps hadn't yet been lit. Gold-framed portraits and a floor-to-ceiling mirror hung on panelled walls of dark wood. As Crake began to unbutton his greatcoat, he glanced through the doorway into the sitting room. Tea and cakes for two had been laid out on a lacquered side table next to a pair of armchairs.

'You were expecting me?' Crake asked, bemused.

'I was expecting someone entirely different! A judge, if you must know! What are you *doing* here?' Before Crake could answer, Plome had taken him by the elbow and was hurrying him down the hall.

At the end of the hall was a staircase. Plome steered Crake around the side to a small, innocuous door. It was a cupboard under the stairs, to all appearances, but Crake knew by the prickling of his senses that appearances were deceptive here. Plome drew a tuning fork from his coat and rapped it smartly against the door frame. The fork sang a high, clear note, and Plome opened the door.

Inside was a single shelf with a lantern, and a set of wooden steps leading down. Plome held the fork high, still ringing, and ushered Crake past. Crake felt himself brushed by the daemon that had been thralled into the doorway. A minor glamour. Anyone opening the door before subduing the daemon with the correct frequency would have seen nothing but a cluttered cupboard, probably accompanied by a strong mental suggestion that there was nothing interesting inside.

'Watch yourself,' said Plome. 'I'll go first. Third step from the bottom will paralyse you for an hour or so.'

Crake stopped and waited for Plome to shut the door, strike a match and touch it to the lantern. He led the way down the stairs, and Crake followed him. At the bottom Plome struck another match and lit the first of several gas-lamps set in sconces on the walls. A soft glow swelled to fill the room.

'Electricity hasn't caught on here yet, I'm afraid,' he said apologetically, moving from lamp to lamp with the match. 'The Tarlocks banned small generators. Too noisy and smelly, that's the official line. But really it's so they can build their own big generator and charge us all for the supply.'

The sanctum under the house had changed little since Crake's last visit. Plome, like Crake, had always leaned towards science rather than superstition in his approach to daemonism. His sanctum was like a laboratory. A chalkboard was covered with formulae for frequency modulation, next to a complicated alembic and books on the nature of plasm and luminiferous aether. A globular brass cage took pride of place, surrounded by various resonating devices. There were thin metal strips of varying lengths, chimes of all kinds, and hollow wooden tubes. With such devices a daemon could be contained.

Crake went cold at the sight of an echo chamber in one corner. It was a riveted ball of metal, like a bathysphere, with a small circular porthole. He felt the strength drain out of his limbs. A worm of nausea crawled into his gut.

Plome followed his gaze. 'Oh, yes, that. Rather an impulse purchase. I haven't used it yet. Need to wait for the electricity to get here. To provide a constant vibration to produce the echo, you see.'

'I know how it works,' Crake assured him, his voice thin. He felt suddenly out of breath.

'Of course you do. And I expect you know how dangerous and unpredictable the echo technique is, too. Can't risk a battery conking out on me while I've got some bloody great horror sitting inside!' He laughed nervously, before noticing that Crake had lost the colour in his face. 'Are you quite alright?'

Crake tore his eyes away from the echo chamber. 'I'm fine.'

Plome didn't pursue the matter. He produced a handkerchief and mopped his brow. 'The Shacklemores were here looking for you.'

'The Shacklemores?' Crake was alarmed. 'When?'

'Sometime around the end of Swallow's Reap, I think. They said they were visiting all your associates.' He wrung his hands. 'Made me quite uncomfortable, actually. Made me think they knew about . . . well, this.' He made a gesture to encompass the sanctum. 'It'd be very awkward if this got out. You know how people are about us.'

But Crake was too busy thinking about himself. The Shacklemore

Agency was bad news. Bounty hunters to the rich and famous. He'd expected they'd be involved, but the confirmation still came as a blow.

'Sorry, old chap,' Plome said. 'I suppose they found you out, eh?'

'Something like that,' he replied. *Something much, much worse.*

'Barbarians,' he snorted. 'They take one look at a sanctum, then cry "daemonist" and hang you. Doesn't matter who you are or what you've done. Ignorance will triumph over reason every time. That's the sad state of the world.'

Crake raised an eyebrow. He hadn't expected such a comment from this generally conservative man. 'You don't think I should have stayed to face the music? Argued my case?'

'Dear me, no! Running was the only thing you could have done. They just don't understand what we're about, people like us. They're afraid of the unknown. And those blasted Awakeners don't help, shooting their mouths off about Allsoul this and daemonism that, riling up the common folk. Why do you think I'm brown-nosing up to the local judge, eh? So I've got a fighting chance if anyone discovers what I've got hidden under my house!'

Plome had reddened during his tirade, and he had to take a few breaths and mop his brow when he was done. 'Speaking of which, he could be here any minute. What can I help you with?'

'I need supplies,' Crake said. 'I need to get back into the Art, and I don't have any of the equipment.'

'It's practising the Art that got you into this pickle in the first place,' Plome pointed out.

'I'm a daemonist, Plome,' Crake said. 'It's what I am. Without that, I'm just another shiftless rich boy, good for nothing.' He gave a sad, resigned smile. 'Once you've touched the other side, you can't ever go back.' A sudden, unexpected surge of tears surprised him. He fought them down, but Plome saw his eyes moisten and looked away. 'A man should . . . a man should get back on a horse if it throws him.'

'What happened to you?' Plome asked, getting worried now.

'The less you know, the better,' he said. 'For your own good. I don't want you involved.'

'I see,' said Plome, uncertainly. 'Well, you can't go to your usual suppliers. The Shacklemores will have them staked out.' He hurried over to a desk, snatched up a sheet of paper that was lying there, and scribbled down several addresses. 'These are all trustworthy,' he said, handing Crake the paper.

Crake ran his eye over the addresses. All in major cities, dotted around Vardia. Well, if he couldn't persuade Frey to visit one of them, he could always take leave of the *Ketty Jay* and make his own way.

'Thanks. You're a good friend, Plome.'

'Not at all. Our kind have to stick together in these benighted times.'

Crake folded the paper over, and saw that Plome had written it on the back of a handbill. He opened it out, and went grey.

'Where did you get this?'

'They're posted all over. Whoever that is, they want him badly. Him and his crew.'

'You don't say,' Crake murmured weakly.

'You know, the Century Knights just turned up in town looking for him, if you can believe that!' Plome enthused. 'The Archduke's personal elite!' He whistled and pointed at the flyer. 'He must have *really* messed up. I wouldn't want to be in his shoes when the Knights catch up with him!'

Crake stared at the handbill, as if he could simply will it out of existence.

WANTED FOR PIRACY AND MURDER, it said. LARGE REWARD.

Staring back at him was a picture of Frey.

Nine

*A Matter Of Honour – Bree And Grudge – 'One More Town
We're Not Coming Back To' – Departure Is Delayed*

C rake hurried through Tarlock Cove as fast as he dared. The streets were dark now, deepening towards true night, and stars clustered thickly overhead. The beam of the lighthouse swept across the town and out to sea. Crake walked with his collar up and his head down, his blond hair blowing restlessly in the salt wind, trying not to draw attention to himself.

Run, he told himself. *Just run. You weren't a part of it. They don't even know you're on the crew.*

But run where? His assets had been seized, so he had only the money he'd taken when he fled, and there was little enough of that left. His only contact here was Plome, and the last thing Plome needed was to shelter a fugitive. He had his own secrets to keep. No, Crake wouldn't implicate him in this matter. He'd deal with it on his own.

Run!

But he couldn't. Because the only way he was going to stay ahead of the Shacklemore Agency was to keep on the move, and the only way he could do that was aboard the *Ketty Jay*.

And there was more, besides. It was a matter of honour. He didn't care for Frey at all, and Pinn was beneath consideration, but the others didn't deserve to be hung out to dry like that. Especially not Malvery, of whom Crake was becoming quite fond.

But if he was honest with himself, even if he'd hated them all, he'd have gone back. If only to warn them. Because it was the right thing to do, and because it made him better than Frey.

He traced his steps back to Old One-Eye's, and paused at the threshold, listening for signs of a disturbance. He'd been seen drinking with the crew. If they'd already been caught, there was no sense getting himself picked up as well.

There was a good chance Frey hadn't been recognised, though. The ferrotype on the handbills must have been taken a long while ago, ten years or more. It didn't look much like Frey. He had a little less weight and a lot less care on his face. He was clean-shaven and looked happy, smiling into the camera, squinting in the sun. There were mountains and fields in the background. Crake wondered when it was taken, and by whom.

The drinkers were merry and the noise inside the tavern was customarily deafening. All seemed well. Peering through the windows, which were bleared with condensation, he detected nothing amiss.

Get in, grab them, and get out of town.

He took a breath, preparing himself to face the throng inside. That was when he spotted a pair of Knights heading up the street towards him.

He knew them from their ferrotypes. Everyone knew the Knights. Broadsheets carried news of their exploits; cheap paper-backs told fictional tales of their adventures; children dressed up and pretended to be them. Most citizens of Vardia could identify twenty or thirty of the hundred Century Knights. But nobody knew all of them, for they operated as much in secret as in public.

These two were among the most famous, and they attracted stares from passers-by as they approached. The smaller Knight was Samandra Bree, wearing a long, battered coat and loose hide trousers that flared over her boots. Perched on her head was her trademark tricorn hat. Her coat flapped back in the wind as she strode along, offering glimpses of twin lever-action shotguns and a cutlass at her belt. Young, dark-haired and beautiful, Samandra was a darling of the press. By all accounts she did little to encourage their attention, which only made the people love her more and the press chase her harder.

Her companion was Colden Grudge, who wasn't quite so photogenic. He was a man of bruising size with a face like a cliff.

Thick, shaggy brown hair and an unkempt beard gave him a spiteful, simian look. Beneath a hooded cloak, time-dulled plates of armour had been strapped over his massive limbs and chest. He bore the insignia of the Century Knights on his breastplate. Two double-bladed hand-axes hung at his waist, and an autocannon was slung across his back.

Crake's mouth went dry and he almost fled. It took him a few moments to realise that they weren't heading for him at all, but for the tavern he was standing in front of. They were going to Old One-Eye's.

He didn't have time to think. In moments they'd be inside. Before he knew what he was doing, he thrust the handbill at them and blurted: 'Excuse me. You're looking for this man, aren't you?'

The Knights stopped. Grudge glared at him, tiny eyes peering out from beneath a beetling brow. Samandra tipped back her tricorn hat and smiled. Crake found himself thinking that she really was quite strikingly gorgeous in person.

'Why, yes we are, sir,' she said. 'Seen him?'

'I just . . . yes, I just did, yes,' he stammered. 'At least I think it was him.'

'And where was that?' Samandra asked, with a faintly amused expression. She took his nervousness to be the reaction of a man intimidated by a pretty woman, instead of someone strangled by the fear of discovery.

'In a tavern . . . that way!' Crake improvised, pointing up the road.

'*Which* tavern?' Grudge demanded impatiently.

Crake grasped for a name. 'Oh, it's the one with lanterns out front, you know . . . The Howling Wolf or something . . . The Prowling Wolf! That's it! That's where I saw him!'

'You sure about that?' Grudge asked, unconvinced.

'You're not from around here, are you?' Samandra asked, in that charmingly soft voice that made Crake feel like pond scum for lying to her.

'Does it show?' he said, with a grin. He gave them a smile, a glimpse of the golden tooth. Putting just a little power into it, letting the daemon suck a tiny fraction of his vital essence, just enough to allay their suspicions, just enough to say: *believe him*. 'I'm visiting a friend.'

Samandra's eyes had flicked to his tooth for just an instant, drawn by the glimmer. Now they were back on him.

'Be where we can find you,' she said.

Crake looked at her blankly.

'The reward!' she said, pointing at the handbill. 'You do want the reward?'

'Oh, yes!' Crake said, recovering. 'I'll just be in here.' He thumbed towards Old One-Eye's.

Samandra and Grudge exchanged glances, then they hurried off up the road in the direction of The Prowling Wolf. Crake let out a slow, shaky breath and plunged into the tavern.

Frey was having a rare old time. He was exhausted from laughing and perfectly drunk, hovering in that elusive zone of inebriation where everything was in balance and all was right with the world. He never wanted this night to end. He loved Malvery and Pinn and even silent Harkins as brothers in arms. And if things began to wind down, well, the waitress had been giving him looks. She had a homely sort of face, but he liked her red hair and the freckles on her button nose, and he was in the mood for something curvy and soft tonight.

What a life it was! A fine thing to be a captain, a freebooter, a lord of the skies.

Crake's arrival was something of a downer. 'We're getting out of here,' he said, slapping the handbill onto the table and thrusting a finger at the picture of Frey. 'Now!'

Frey, a little slow off the mark, was more surprised by the picture than the danger it represented. He recognised it immediately. How did they get their hands on *that* one? Who gave it to them?

Crake snatched the handbill away and stuffed it in his pocket. 'I just had to head off Samandra Bree and Colden Grudge. They're looking for us. They'll be back in a few minutes. I suggest we not be here when they do.'

'You met Samandra Bree?' Pinn gaped. 'You lucky turd!'

'Spit and blood! Get moving, you idiots!'

The penny had finally dropped. They surged up and pushed their way through the crowd towards the door.

By the time they emerged from the tavern, Frey's mood had see-sawed from elation to cold, hard fear. The Century Knights? The *Century Knights* were on his tail? What had he done to deserve that?

'Back to the *Ketty Jay*?' Malvery suggested, scanning the street.

'Bloody right,' Frey muttered. 'This is one more town we're not coming back to.'

'Why don't we just emigrate and be done with it?'

'Not a bad idea at that,' Frey said over his shoulder, as he hurried away in the direction of the docks.

The town's landing pad was situated halfway along one of the mountainous arms that sheltered the bay. Houses became sparser as they approached, and the streets were whittled down to a single wide path that dipped and curved with the land. It was flanked by storage sheds, the occasional tavern and a customs house. The vast, moist breathing of the sea was loud here. Waves crashed and spumed on the rocks far below.

Frey hugged his coat tight around him as he led his crew along the stony path. The previously welcoming town seemed suddenly threatening and nightmarish. He glanced over his shoulder for signs of pursuit, but nobody came running after them. Perhaps they'd given the Knights the slip.

Wanted for *murder*? Piracy, fine, he'd own up to that (to himself, at least. Damned if he'd admit it to a judge). But murder? He was no murderer! What happened to the *Ace of Skulls* wasn't his fault!

It didn't matter that piracy and murder carried the same penalty of hanging. In real terms, whether he did both or only one was moot: his end would be the same. But it was the principle of the thing. It was all so tragically unfair.

He slowed as they spotted a trio of Ducal Militiamen coming towards them. They were striding along the road from the docks, clad in the brown uniform of the Aulenfay Duchy, all buttoned-up jackets and flat-topped caps. The path afforded nowhere to duck away without looking suspicious.

'Cap'n . . .' Malvery warned.

'I see them,' Frey said. 'Keep walking. It's only me they'll recognise.'

Frey tucked his head down into his collar and shoved his hands into his pockets, playing the frozen traveller hurrying to get somewhere warm. He dropped back into the group, keeping Malvery's bulk between him and the militiamen.

Their boots crunched on the path as they approached. Frey and his crew moved to the side of the path to let them pass. Their eyes swept the group as they neared.

'Bloody chilly when the sun goes down, eh?' Malvery hailed them with his usual booming good humour.

They grunted and walked on. So did Frey and his men.

The landing pad was busy with craft and their crews, loading the day's catch onto the vessels for the overnight flight inland. A freighter was rising slowly into the air, belly-lights bright. Its aerium engines pulsed as electromagnets pulverised refined aerium into ultralight gas, flooding the ballast tanks.

Frey had planned to avoid the rush and leave in the morning, since his cargo wasn't nearly as perishable as fresh fish, but now he was glad of the chaos. It would provide cover for their departure.

They passed the gas-lamps that marked the edge of the pad and wended their way towards the *Ketty Jay*. Crews laboured in the dazzling shine of their aircrafts' lights, long shadows blasted across the tarmac by the dark hulks that loomed above them. Thrusters rumbled as the freighter overhead switched to its prothane engines and began pushing away from the coast. The air was heavy with the smell of fish and the tang of the sea.

'Harkins, Pinn. Get to your craft and get up there,' said Frey. 'Harkins, I know you're drunk but that's *my* Firecrow and if you crash it I'll stuff you into your own arsehole and bowl you into the sea. Clear?'

Harkins belched, saluted, and staggered away. Pinn scurried off towards his Skylance without a word. The mention of the Century Knights had intimidated him enough that he was glad to get out of there.

Silo was standing at the bottom of the *Ketty Jay*'s cargo ramp when Frey, Malvery and Crake arrived. He was idly smoking a roll-up cigarette made from an acrid Murthian blend of herbs. As they approached, he spat into his hand and crushed it out on his palm.

'Where's Jez?' Frey demanded.

'Quarters.'

'Good. We're going.'

'Cap'n.'

Silo joined the others as they headed up the ramp and into the cargo hold. The hold was steeped in gloom as always, stacked high with crates that were lashed untidily together. The reek of fish was overpowering in here.

Frey was making for the lever to raise the cargo ramp when a gravelly voice called out:

'Make another move and everybody dies.'

They froze. Coming up the cargo ramp, revolvers in both hands, was a figure they all knew and had hoped to never see. The most renowned of all the Century Knights. The Archduke's merciless attack dog: Kedmund Drave.

He was a barrel-chested man in his late forties, his clumsily assembled face scarred along the cheek and throat. Silver-grey hair was clipped close to his scalp, and he wore a suit of dull crimson armour, expertly moulded to the contours of his body by the Archduke's master artisans. A thick black cloak displayed the Knights' insignia in red, and the hilt of his two-handed sword could be seen rising behind his shoulder.

'Back away from that lever,' he commanded Frey. One revolver was trained on him; the other covered the rest of the crew. 'Get over with your friends.'

Frey obliged. He'd sobered up fast. The effects of the alcohol had been cancelled by the chill shock of adrenaline. He wracked his brains frantically to think of a way out of this, because he knew one thing for sure: if Kedmund Drave took him in, he'd swing from the gallows.

'Guns!' Drave snapped, as he herded them together. 'Knives. All of it.'

They disarmed, throwing their weapons down in a small heap in front of them. Drake looked them over critically.

'Step back. Against the crates.'

They did as they were told.

'Now. Who's this Jez I heard you mention?'

'She's the navigator,' Frey replied.

Drave glanced at the stairs leading out of the cargo hold. Deciding whether it was worth the risk of going up and getting her.

'Anyone else?'

'No,' said Frey.

Drave took a sudden step towards them and pressed the muzzle of his revolver to Crake's forehead. 'If you're lying, I'll blow his brains out!'

Crake whimpered softly. He'd had just about enough of people putting guns to his head.

'There's not another soul on board!' Frey said. He started with himself, and then pointed to each of the crew in turn. 'Pilot. Engineer. Doctor. Navigator is in her quarters. You've got a full crew here. This one . . .' he waved at Crake, 'he's just along for the ride.'

'The others? The outflyers?'

'Already gone.'

Drave glared at him, then took the revolver off Crake and backed away to a safer distance.

'Both of them?'

'Already gone,' Frey repeated, shrugging. 'They took off when they heard the Knights were on the case. Could be halfway to anywhere by now. We're all alone here.'

Deep in the shadows between the piles of crates, two tiny lights glimmered. There was the heavy thump of a footstep and a rustle of chain mail and leather. Drave spun around to look behind him, and the colour drained from his face.

'Well, unless you count Bess,' Frey added, and the golem burst from the darkness with a metallic roar.

Drave's reactions saved him. The armour of the Century Knights was legendarily light and strong, made using secret techniques in the Archduke's own forges, and it slowed him not at all as he flung himself aside to avoid Bess's crushing punch. He hit the ground in a roll and came up with both revolvers blazing. Bess flinched and recoiled as the bullets ricocheted from her armour and punched through her leather skin, but the assault did nothing more than enrage her. She bellowed and swept another punch at Drave, who jumped backwards to avoid it.

As soon as the Knight was distracted, the crew scattered. Frey dived for the guns, came up with Malvery's shotgun in his hands and squeezed the trigger. As he did so, he realised he'd forgotten to prime it first. He hoped the doctor had been careless enough to keep a round in the chamber.

He had. Drave saw the danger, raised his pistol, and was a split second from firing when Frey hit him full in the chest. The impact blasted him off his feet. He landed hard on the cargo ramp and rolled helplessly down it and off the end.

Silo lunged across the hold and raised the lever to close the cargo ramp. Bess started to run down it, chasing the fallen Knight, but Crake shouted after her. She stopped, somewhat reluctantly, and settled for guarding the closing gap. Drave was already trying to pick himself up off the ground. He was groggy but otherwise unharmed, saved by his chestplate.

Frey had bolted for the stairs that led up to the main passageway before the cargo ramp had even closed. He sprinted into the cockpit, past Jez, who was just opening the door to her quarters.

'Was that *gunfire*?' she asked.

He leaped into his chair and punched in the ignition code, then boosted the aerium engines to full. The *Ketty Jay* gave a dolorous

81

groan as its tanks filled and began to haul the craft skyward. He could hear gunfire outside over the sound of the prothane thrusters: Drave shooting uselessly at the hull. The dark aircraft that shared the landing pad sank from view as they lifted into the night sky.

'Cap'n?' Jez enquired, from the doorway of the cockpit. 'Are we in trouble?'

'Yes, Jez,' he said. 'We're in trouble.'

Then he hit the thrusters and the *Ketty Jay* thundered, tearing away across the docks and racing out to sea.

Ten

Jez Has Visions – Trinica Dracken –
An Ultimatum From Crake – Frey Takes A Stand

It was a still day. Light flakes of snow drifted from a sky laden with grey cloud. The silence was immense.

Jez stood on the edge of the small landing pad, wrapped up in pelts, holding a cup of cocoa between her furred mittens. She'd bought her new arctic attire soon after arriving. Her meagre possessions had been left behind in her room at the lodging-house in Scarwater. Truth be told, despite the temperature, she didn't need to wear anything at all. The cold didn't seem to affect her nowadays. But it was essential to keep up appearances: her safety depended on it. Anyone in their right mind would kill her if they knew what she was.

The landing pad was set on a raised plateau above a great, icy expanse. On the horizon, a range of ghostly mountains lay, blued by distance. A herd of snow-hogs were trekking across the plain.

Yortland. A frozen, hard and cruel place, but the only place on the continent of North Pandraca where the Coalition Navy held no sway, and Coalition laws didn't apply. The only place left for the crew of the *Ketty Jay* to run to.

She took a sip of her cocoa.

I could stay here, she thought. *I could walk out into that wilderness and never be seen again.*

Behind her sat the *Ketty Jay* and her outflyers. Snow had settled on the *Ketty Jay*'s back and wings, several inches deep. Nearby, an elderly Yort was hammering at the struts of his craft, knocking off icicles. He looked strong despite his age, with a thick neck and huge shoulders. He was bundled up in heavy furs, only his bald and tattooed head exposed to the elements. His ears, lips and nose were pierced with rings and bone shards. Otherwise, there was nobody to be seen.

Besides the *Ketty Jay* there were a couple of Yort haulers and some small personal racers, which Jez had already examined and mentally criticised – a habit born from a life as a craftbuilder's daughter. They were blockish, dark and ugly, built for efficiency, without a care for aesthetics. Typical Yort work. In such an excessively masculine society, owning a craft of elegant design was viewed at best as pointless, at worst as potential evidence of homosexuality. Not something to be taken lightly, since sodomy carried the death penalty out here. As a result, Yorts designed everything to suggest that the owner was so enormously virile, a woman would need armour-plated ovaries to survive a night with him.

Jez's eyes unfocused as she stared out across the plain.

Get away from everyone, she thought. *Maybe that's best. Get away from everyone, before it's too late.*

But the loneliness. She couldn't take the loneliness. What was the point in existence, if you were forever alone?

Scattered across the plateau was the settlement of Majduk Eyl. Yorts built mostly underground for insulation, and their dwellings were barely visible. All that could be seen from the pad were the shallow humps of their dome-shaped roofs, the doorways that thrust through the snow, the skylights sheltered by overhanging eaves. Smoke rose from three dozen chimneys, curling steadily up to join the clouds. A small figure, hooded and cloaked, was scattering grit from a sack over the slushy trails that ran between the dwellings.

The crew of the *Ketty Jay* were in one of those buildings. They were just another set of companions, like the ones before, and the ones before that. She kept herself aloof from them. It would make it hurt less when she had to leave.

Sooner or later, they'd notice something was different about her. The little things would begin to add up. The way her bullet wound had healed so fast, the way she never seemed to sleep, the way she never got tired. The way animals reacted to her.

Then she'd have to move on again, find a new crew. Keep going.

Going where? Doing what?

Anywhere. Anything. Just keep going.

She drank her cocoa. She only ate or drank these days because she liked the taste, not out of need. During the month of Swallow's Reap, as an experiment, she'd gone without food or water for a week. Nothing happened except a vague, instinctive suspicion that something was missing in her daily routine. After that, she'd made sure to join the crew at mealtimes, and occasionally comment loudly on her hunger or thirst; but she ate little, because she wasn't wasteful by nature.

The snow-hogs were inching across the ice-plain, shambling heaps of muscle and tusk and shaggy white fur. She could see a pair of predators tracking them, huge doglike things, a type of creature she didn't recognise. They loped along hungrily, hoping for a chance at a straggler.

Here I am again, she reflected, as she scanned the landscape. A few years ago, she'd been a frequent visitor to the wild, icebound northern coast, part of a scientific expedition in search of the relics of a lost civilisation. It hadn't been a conscious decision to stay away from Yortland, but it was only now that she realised she'd never been back since . . . well, since . . .

Her thoughts flickered away from the memory, but it was too late. A dreadful sensation washed over her, beginning at her nape and sweeping through her body. Her skin tightened, then relaxed; her muscles clenched and unclenched. The world flexed, just a fraction, and when it sprang back into shape, everything was different.

A strange twilight had fallen. Though it seemed darker, her vision had sharpened. It was as if she'd been looking at the world through a steamed-up pane of glass, and it had suddenly been removed. Details were thrust at her eyes; edges became stark as razors.

85

The herd of snow-hogs prickled with a faint purplish aura. Though they were several kloms away, she could count their teeth, and see the pupils of their rolling eyes. She sensed the path of the faint wind chasing along the plain; she could picture its route in her mind.

There was so much she was sensing, hearing, smelling. She could hardly breathe under the assault of information. It felt like she was being battered by an irresistible river. At any moment she'd lose her footing and be swept into oblivion.

One of the predators suddenly broke into a run. Its aura was deep crimson, and it left a slowly dispersing trail as it ran. Then suddenly she was with the predator, *in* the predator, its blood pumping hard, heart slamming, tongue-loll and tooth-sharp, all paws and look-see yes yes yes that one is weak, *that* one, and my kin-brother alongside and wary of the sharp sharp tusks of the mother but oh oh *the hunger*—

Jez gulped in a breath, like a drowning woman who had just broken the surface. Reality snapped into place: the world was once again as it had always been. Snow drifted down, undisturbed by her panic. She took a step back, disorientated, wanting to be away from that edge of the plateau. The mug had fallen from her hands and lay on the ground before her. Brown, steaming cocoa ate through the ice.

She began to tremble, helplessly, and not from the cold. She clutched herself and looked about. The Yort was nowhere to be seen. Nobody was there. Nobody had witnessed it.

Witnessed what? she demanded of herself. *What's happening to me?*

A gust of wind blew from the north, and there was a sound on the wind, something she sensed rather than heard. Voices, raised in a cacophony, calling. A terrible, desperate longing swelled in her.

She looked to the north, and it was as if she could see past the mountains, past the sea, her vision carried on bird's wings. She rushed onward, over icebergs and waves until there came fog and mist and a vast wall of churning grey.

She knew this place. It was the swirling cloud-cap they called the Wrack, which cloaked the north pole. The frontier than no one had ever returned from. Not alive, anyway.

There was something behind the cloud. A shape, an aircraft, black and vast, looming towards her. The voices.

Come with us.

She screwed her eyes shut and staggered away with a cry, stumbling towards the *Ketty Jay*. Her mind rung like a struck bell, resounding with the howling, the Wrack, and the terror of what lay beyond.

The bar was empty, but for the crew of the *Ketty Jay* and the bartender. The menfolk of the village were in the mines or out hunting; the women generally stayed out of sight. During the day, Frey and the others had the place to themselves.

Frey stared dejectedly at his picture. This time it was no hand-bill. He'd made the national broadsheets now.

'It's only on page ten!' Malvery bellowed, giving him a thump on the shoulder. 'It doesn't even look like you! Besides, that issue's a week old. Mark me, they'll have forgotten about it by now.'

Frey took little comfort in that. It was true that he looked less and less like his picture, but that was mostly because the Frey in the picture was so happy and carefree. The real Frey was becoming less so by the day. His stubble had grown out to an untidy beard and his hair was getting beyond the control of a comb. His eyes were sunken and there were dark bags beneath them. In the two weeks since they'd fled Tarlock Cove he'd become ever more sullen and withdrawn.

And now this: a broadsheet from Vardia, given to Silo by a trader who bought their cargo of smoked fish at a rock-bottom price. Frey had hidden angrily in his quarters during the transaction, in case he was recognised.

DRACKEN JOINS THE HUNT

On this day the *Vardic Herald* has learned of an Announcement by Trinica Dracken, Feared Captain of the *Delirium*

87

Trigger, to the effect that she will devote all her Will and Effort to the task of bringing to Justice, be it Dead or Alive, the Fugitive Darian Frey and his crew, wanted for Piracy and Murder, and for whom a large Reward is offered for information that might lead to their Capture. The *Herald* could not reach Captain Dracken for comment, but it is this reporter's humble Opinion that with such a Famous and Deadly Lady upon their trail, it cannot be long before these Scoundrels are brought to face Justice for their crimes.

'The bloody *Delirium Trigger*,' Pinn groaned. He'd been almost constantly drunk for a fortnight now, having nothing else to occupy himself with. His eyes were bloodshot and he reeked of alcohol. 'Queen bitch of the skies.' He paused for a moment, then added, 'I'd do her.'

The bar was a small, round room, with a domed roof criss-crossed by stout rafters and a south-facing skylight. A fire-pit burned red in the centre, beneath a large stone chimney. The wooden floor was strewn with pelts, the walls hung with the skulls of horned animals. Tables and seats were made from tree stumps. There was a counter against one wall. Behind it, a surly Yort guarded a barrel of beer and a few shelves stocked with unlabelled liquor in jars.

The bartender was in his mid-fifties, with thick arms and a face weathered like bark. His head was shaved and his long red beard was gathered into a queue by iron rings. He only spoke in grunts, yet somehow he made it clear that Frey and his men were not welcome here. He'd rather have an empty bar. They ignored him and came anyway.

'Why don't you go home, Pinn?' Crake asked. He was looking up at the rafters, where several arctic pigeons cooed softly to each other. He'd noted the lumpy white streaks among the dried-in bloodstains on the floor, and was covering his flagon of dark beer with his hand.

'What?' Pinn asked blearily.

'I mean, what's stopping you? You've got your own craft.

88

You haven't been named or identified. Why not go back to your sweetheart?'

Frey didn't even raise his head at the mutinous tone of the suggestion. Crake was just baiting Pinn. Those who even believed Pinn *had* a sweetheart – Malvery was of the opinion that he might have made her up – knew full well he'd never go back to her. In his mind, she waited to welcome him with open arms on the day he returned home swathed in glory; but he seemed to be the only one who didn't realise that day would never come. Pinn was waiting for glory to happen to him, rather than seeking it out.

Lisinda was the heroic conclusion to his quest, the promise of home comforts after his great adventure. But what if she wasn't there when he returned? What if she was holding another man's child? Even in the dim clouds of Pinn's mind, the possibility must have made itself known, and made him uneasy. He'd never risk the dream by threatening it with reality.

'Not going back till I made my fortune,' Pinn said, a note of resentment in his voice. 'She deserves the best. Gonna go back . . .' He raised his flagon and his voice at the same time, challenging anyone to defy him. 'Gonna go back a rich man!' He slumped again and sucked at his drink. 'Till then, I'm stuck with you losers.'

An idea struck him. He stabbed a thick finger at Crake and said: 'What about you, eh? Mister La-di-da, I-talk-so-cultured? Don't you have a . . . a banquet to attend or something?' He folded his arms and smirked, pleased at this cunning reversal.

'Well unfortunately, in the process of saving all your lives at Old One-Eye's, I let two of the Century Knights get a rather good look at me,' Crake replied. 'But it is something I've been meaning to bring up.' He leaned forward on his elbows. 'They know Jez's name but they haven't seen her. Kedmund Drave saw us all but he doesn't have our names. As a group, we're rather easy to identify. Apart, they'll probably never catch us. They'll only get Frey.'

Harkins looked uneasily around the table. Malvery shifted and cleared his throat. Frey didn't react.

'Now, I don't know about all of you,' Crake continued, 'but I am not spending the rest of my life hiding in an icy wasteland. So what I want to know,' he said, looking directly at Frey, 'is what you intend to do next. *Captain.*'

There was a loud *plop* as something fell from the rafters and into Crake's beer. Without taking his eyes from Frey, he pushed it away from him with his fingertips.

Frey was still staring at the article, but he wasn't really seeing it. His mind was working furiously, struggling to puzzle out this crisis, getting nowhere. He'd spent a fortnight raking over the coals of recent events, searching for some buried truth, but there were simply no answers to be had.

It didn't make any sense. Why him? If this was a set-up, why choose him? An obscure freebooter, his name all but unknown in pirate circles. Yet Quail had asked for him specifically. Quail, to whom he'd done no wrong.

Of course, maybe someone had used Quail to set him up, that was always a possibility. But who had he offended? To whom had he done such a grievous slight? It must be someone powerful, if they could orchestrate something serious enough to involve the Archduke's personal elite. The Century Knights didn't usually concern themselves with affairs unconnected to the Archduke.

Was it an accident? A million-to-one shot that destroyed that craft? No. Frey didn't believe in million-to-one chances. He'd been set up. Someone rigged that freighter to blow, and they put him in position to take the blame.

At least one of the pilots in the escort craft was superb. Whoever arranged all this must have banked on someone living to tell the tale. Even if no one had escaped, they'd have pinned it on him somehow, he had no doubt. But this way they had a witness, presumably unconnected to the real brains behind the operation.

What was on board that freighter?

'Frey?' Crake prompted, snapping him out of his reverie. Frey's head came up. 'I asked what you intend to do now?'

Frey shrugged helplessly. 'I don't know.'

'I see,' said Crake, his voice dripping with scorn. 'Well, let me know when you do. I'd be interested in finding out. If I'm still here.' With that, he got up and left.

There was a long silence. The crew were not used to seeing Frey so beaten. It unsettled them.

'What about New Vardia?' Malvery suggested. 'Fresh start. Unknown lands. Just the sort of thing for a bunch of lads in our position.'

'No!' Harkins cried, and they all looked at him. He went red. 'I mean to say, umm, the *Ketty Jay* might make it – I say *might* – but the fighters, nuh-uh. The Storm Belt's still too bad to the west, and they can't carry enough fuel to go the other route. We'd have to leave the fighters behind and me, no way, I ain't leaving that Firecrow, even if she does belong to the Cap'n. He leaves the Firecrow behind, I stay behind with her. Final.'

Frey was surprised at Harkins' unusual assertiveness on the matter.

'Retribution Falls,' said Pinn. 'That's what my money's on. Nobody'd find us in Retribution Falls.'

'Nobody would find us because it's impossible to find,' explained Frey patiently. 'Any ideas how *we* would find *it*?'

Pinn thought for a moment and came up blank. 'Well, there's got to be a way,' he muttered. 'You hear about all those pirates who've been there. You hear about Orkmund, don't you?'

Frey sighed. Retribution Falls: the legendary hidden pirate town. A place safe from the dangers of the world, where you could fight and drink and screw to your heart's content and the Navy could never touch you. It was said to be founded by the renowned pirate Orkmund, who mysteriously disappeared ten years ago and had never been reliably sighted since. Other famous pirates who were no longer around were often said to have retired to Retribution Falls. It made a more romantic story than a slow death by syphilis or alcoholism, or being murdered in the night by your own crew.

But that was all it was: a story. Orkmund was dead. The other pirates were dead. Retribution Falls was a myth.

Pinn saw that nobody was taking up his idea and began to sulk.

Frey returned to the same obsessive thoughts that had been keeping him up at night.

New Vardia. Maybe he *could* go to New Vardia. Leave the fighters behind.

The idea wasn't appealing. It was a long and dangerous journey to the other side of the world, and once there, there was nowhere to hide. A few small settlements. A frontier lifestyle, lived without luxuries. If his pursuers tracked him to New Vardia, he'd be easily caught.

He ticked off options in his head. Samarla? They wouldn't last two days, and Silo would never go. Thace? They'd be caught and deported if they tried to stay. Thacians were very defensive of their little utopia. Kurg? Populated by monsters.

Of the countries this side of the Great Storm Belt, only Yortland provided a haven, and it was a cold and bitter one, entirely too close to Vardia. They couldn't hide there for ever. Not with the Century Knights and Trinica Dracken on their tail.

His eyes fell to the broadsheet spread out on the table. Bitterness curdled in his guts. The sanctimonious tone of the writer, exulting in Frey's imminent downfall, enraged him. The memory of Crake's snide dismissal made him grit his teeth. The picture of himself smiling out from the page inspired a deep and intolerable hatred. That they should use *that* picture. *That* one!

This was too much. He could take the vagaries of chance that robbed him at cards time and again. He could handle the knowledge that his best efforts at self-improvement were doomed to be thwarted by some indistinct, omnipotent force. He could live with the fact that he was captain of a crew who were only staying with him because they had nowhere else to go.

But to be so thoroughly stitched up, without any idea who was behind it or even what he'd done to deserve it? It was so tremendously, appallingly unfair that it made his blood boil.

'I can't run any more,' he murmured.

'What'd you say?' asked Malvery.

He surged to his feet, knocking his flagon aside with the back of his hand, his voice rising to a shout. 'I said I can't *run* any more!'

He snatched up the broadsheet and flung it away, pointing after it. 'There's nowhere I can go that *she* won't find me! She'll never stop! Now I'm a man well accustomed to being shat on by fate, but everyone has their limits and I've bloody well reached mine!'

The others stared at him as if he was mad. But he wasn't mad. Suddenly, he felt inspired, empowered, alive! Swept up in the excitement of a resolution, Frey thundered on.

'I'm damned if I'm going to run halfway round the planet to get away from these people! I'm damned if I'm going to hang for a crime without even knowing what I've done! And I'm damned if I'm going to rot out the rest of my days in some icebound wasteland!' He pounded his fist down on the table. 'There is one person who might know who's behind all this. That brass-eyed bastard who gave me the tip: Xandian Quail. We all know his kind never reveal their sources, but he made one big mistake. He left me nothing else to lose. So I'm gonna go back. I'm gonna head right back there even if the whole bloody country is looking for me and I'm gonna find out who did this! I'll make them sorry they ever heard the name of Darian Frey!' He thrust his fist in the air. '*Who's with me?*'

Malvery, Pinn and Harkins gaped at him. Silo watched him inscrutably. The bartender cleaned flagons. The only sound in the silence that followed was the squeak of cloth against pewter.

'Oh, piss on you all,' snapped Frey, then stormed off towards the door. 'If you're not on the *Ketty Jay* in half an hour I'll leave you here to freeze.'

Eleven

Crake Mixes With The Common Man – A Bad Case Of Indigestion –
Smoking Out The Enemy – Questions and Answers

O n reflection, Crake had spent rather a lot of time in taverns lately. As a man who had once prized study and discipline it made him feel vaguely decadent. He was used to drawing rooms and social clubs, garden parties and soirées. During his university days he'd frequented fashionably seedy dives, but they were usually full of similarly educated folk eager for a taste of the low life. His drinking binges had always been disguised as evenings of intelligent debate. There was no threat of that with the crew of the *Ketty Jay*.

Nowadays, he simply drank to forget.

He sat at the bar, two mugs of the foul local grog before him. It was late afternoon in Marklin's Reach, and a sharp winter sun cut low across the town. Dazzling beams shone through the dirty windows and into the gloomy, half-empty tavern. Slowly writhing smoke formed hypnotic patterns, unfurling in the light.

Crake checked his pocket watch and scanned the room. His new friend was late. He wondered if he'd overdone things last night by buying all the drinks. Maybe he'd laid on the flattery a bit thick. Tried too hard.

He thought they'd got on well, all things considered. He thought he'd done a good job bridging the vast gulf in intellect. Still, Crake was never sure with these simple types. He suspected they had a certain intuition. They sensed he wasn't one of them.

But Rogin had seemed to take to him. He'd been happy to chat with anyone, as long as they were buying the drinks. At the end of the night, they agreed to meet up for a quick mug of grog the next day, before he went on duty. 'It'll help me ease into my shift, so to speak,' he'd said. Crake had brayed enthusiastically and promised to have a drink waiting.

He scratched at his beard. He'd considered shaving it off, since the Century Knights would be looking for a blond-bearded man. But the others who were chasing him were looking for somebody clean-shaven, which was why he'd grown it in the first place. He feared the Shacklemore Agency just as much as the Century Knights, and so, all things being even, he decided the beard suited him and kept it. He thought it made him look pleasingly rugged.

He checked his pocket watch again. Where *was* that oaf? After all the effort he'd spent following the man home, tracking him to his local haunt and plying him with booze, Crake would be sorely annoyed if he got stood up now.

He was in a sombre mood. Memories of the past and doubts about the future flocked up to meet him. Was he doing the right thing, staying with the *Ketty Jay*? Wouldn't he be better off cutting them loose, making his own way? After all, he didn't exactly owe Frey a huge debt of loyalty after their run-in with Macarde.

But Frey had promised him they'd get to a big city as soon as it was safe. There, Crake could get the supplies he needed to practise his daemonism. He'd allowed himself to be placated by that. He could wait a little longer.

The need to practise the Art was nagging at him. After the accident, he'd imagined he'd never be tempted by it again. But he'd abandoned his studies out of fear, and that was a cowardly thing. Since university, his every spare moment had been secretly devoted to daemonism. It was the only thing that set him apart from the herd of over-educated, moneyed idiots that had surrounded him all his life. He thought himself better than that. He disdained them. He'd been brave enough to look into the unknown, to reach towards the arcane. He could do things that powerful men would marvel at. Shortly before they hanged him.

But no matter the dangers, he couldn't give it up. To return to the grey unknowing, the humdrum day-to-day, was unimaginable.

He'd tasted grief and despair and the highest terror, he'd made the most terrible mistakes and he bore a shame that no man should have to bear; but he'd stared into the fires of forbidden knowledge, and though he might look away for a moment, his gaze would always be drawn back.

You can start small. Start with the easy procedures. See how you go.

Besides, with only enough money to buy the most basic supplies – let alone pay for transport – he wasn't in a good position to leave. At least on the *Ketty Jay* he was surrounded by people who asked no questions, people untrained in the aristocratic arts of vicious wit and backstabbing. He rather liked that about them, actually.

A disturbing notion occurred to him. Spit and blood, was it possible he was getting *comfortable* in their company? He took a swig from his mug to wash away the bad taste that left in his mouth, then choked as he realised the grog tasted even worse.

'Went down the wrong pipe, eh?' said a voice behind him, and he was pummelled on the back hard enough to break a rib.

Crake smiled weakly and wiped his tearing eyes as the man sat down next to him. Grubby and balding, with a lumpy nose and cheeks red with gin blossoms, Rogin wasn't easy on the eye. Nor on the nose, for that matter. He had the sour and faintly cabbagey smell of a man accustomed to stewing in his own farts.

Crake made a heroic attempt to summon some manly gusto and slapped Rogin on the shoulder in greeting. 'Good to see you, my friend,' he said, with his best picture-pose grin. The low shafts of sunlight glinted on his gold tooth. 'I got you a drink.'

Rogin picked up the mug provided for him – a mug Crake had laced with Malvery's special concoction – and lifted it up so they could clink them together.

'To your health!' said Rogin, and downed his grog in one swallow.

'Oh, no,' murmured Crake, with a self-satisfied smirk. 'To yours.'

The warmth drained from the air as the sun dipped beneath the horizon. Frost gathered on the churned mud of the thoroughfares, and the people of Marklin's Reach retreated into their homes. A thin blue mist of fumes hung near the ground, seeping from portable generators that hummed and clattered in the alleys behind the wooden shanties. Chains of electric bulbs brightened and dimmed as the power fluctuated.

Frey huddled in the mouth of an alleyway, concealed by a patch of shadow conveniently created when Pinn smashed the bulbs overhead. Silo and Jez stood with them. Crake and Harkins had been left back at the *Ketty Jay*, since both of them were a liability in a firefight. Harkins would be reduced to a dribbling wreck in seconds, and Crake was more likely to hit a friend than an enemy.

Xandian Quail's house stood across the street, secure behind its high walls and its wrought-iron gate. Frey had been watching the two guards behind the gate for an hour now as they stamped back and forth, bundled up in jackets and hoods. He was cold and impatient, and was wondering whether Crake had put enough of Malvery's concoction into Rogin's drink.

Malvery himself loitered a little way away, near the wall but out of sight of the guards. A black doctor's bag lay at his feet. His hands were thrust into his coat pockets and he looked as miserable as Frey felt. As Frey watched he leaned down, opened the bag and took a warming hit of medicinal alcohol from the bottle within.

Then, finally, a groan from behind the wall. Malvery stiffened, listening. After a moment Rogin swore and groaned again, louder still. His companion's voice was too muffled to hear the words, but Frey detected alarm in his tone.

Malvery looked for him expectantly. Frey stepped out of the shadows and waved the doctor into action.

Go.

Malvery scooped up the doctor's bag and set off. Rogin's groans had become low cries of pain now, foul oaths forced through gritted teeth. Malvery passed in front of the gate, halted theatrically as if he'd only just heard the sounds of Rogin's distress, and then peered through the bars.

Rogin was curled in a ball on the other side, clutching his

stomach. His companion, a tall, wiry man with ginger hair and a broken nose, looked up as Malvery hailed him.

'Get lost, old feller!' the guard snapped.

'Is your friend alright?' Malvery enquired.

'Does he *look* alright?'

'It's my guts!' Rogin gasped. 'My bloody guts! Hurts like a bastard.' He grimaced as another spasm of agony racked him.

'Let me help him. I'm a doctor,' Malvery said. The ginger-haired guard looked up suspiciously. Malvery brandished his doctor's bag. 'See?'

The guard glanced back at the doorway of the house, wondering if he should tell someone inside.

'For shit's sake! Let him in!' Rogin cried, his voice getting near to hysteria. 'I'm dying, damn it!'

The guard fumbled out a set of keys and opened the gate, then stepped back to allow Malvery through.

'Thank you,' said Malvery as he passed. Then, since the guard had one hand on the gate and the other on the key, he drew out a pistol and pressed it to the unfortunate man's temple. 'Why don't you leave it open, eh?' he suggested.

Frey, Silo, Pinn and Jez sallied out from the shadows and across the deserted thoroughfare, then slipped through the open gate. Silo went to the fallen man and quickly disarmed him while Jez did the same to Malvery's guard. Rogin made a strangled sound of mingled fury and pain, but Silo crouched down next to him and tapped the barrel of a revolver against his skull.

'Sssh,' he said, finger on his lips.

Jez closed the gate and Frey kept his gun on the ginger-haired guard while Silo and Malvery trussed Rogin up. They gagged him with a length of rag and one of Pinn's balled-up socks, which Malvery had chosen for additional anaesthetic effect. Then they carried him off to the nearby guardhouse.

'Don't worry, mate,' said Malvery as they went. 'The prognosis is good. The pain'll pass in a few hours, although I'd suggest you send your loved ones out of town before you take your next dump.'

Frey scanned the house quickly. The curtains were drawn across the windows and no one seemed to have paid any attention to Rogin's cries. If they'd heard him at all, they probably assumed it was someone on the street outside.

He didn't dare to hope that all might be going well. That would only put the jinx on him.

'Right, you,' he said to the remaining guard, as Malvery returned. 'I've got a job for you. Do it well, and you don't get hurt. Understand?'

The guard nodded. He was angry and humiliated, but he was mostly terrified. Probably his first time being held at gunpoint. Good. Frey didn't want to shoot him if he didn't have to.

Jez tossed Malvery his shotgun as he and Silo returned from the guardhouse. Malvery always felt better with a bit of proper firepower. He didn't trust pistols; he thought them fiddly.

They assembled on either side of the heavy oak doors, beneath the stone porch. Frey dragged the guard up by his arm and stepped back, pistol trained on him.

'Get them to open the door,' he said. 'Don't try anything, if you want to keep your brains in your head.'

The guard nodded. He took a nervous breath and rapped on the door.

Frey's hand was trembling, just a little. His throat had gone dry. He wondered if the guard knew how scared he was himself.

I don't want to die.

'Yeah?' came a voice from inside.

'It's Jevin. Open the door,' said the guard.

The door opened a little way. It was Codge, he of the long face and the patchy black beard.

'What's up?'

Frey shoved the guard aside and aimed his revolver point-blank at the white expanse of Codge's forehead. Codge stared at him in surprise for an instant. Then he went for his gun.

Frey's reaction was as instinctive as Codge's had been. He pulled the trigger. Codge's head snapped back; tiny beads of blood spattered Frey's face. Codge tipped backwards and crumpled to the ground.

Frey wasted a moment on shock. He hadn't wanted to fire. What was that idiot doing, going for his gun like that?

Malvery shouldered the door hard and it opened a little way before jamming against the dead weight of Codge's body. Frey wriggled through the gap and into the hallway. There was a panicked moment as he found himself alone and exposed, face to face with a guard who had been too bewildered to react until now. The man's hand moved for the pistol in his holster, but Frey's weapon was out and ready, and he was faster. His arm snapped out straight, finger poised over the trigger.

Don't.

To Frey's relief, this one had more sense than Codge. He slowly raised his hands. Malvery shoved the door open the rest of the way, barging Codge's corpse aside. There was a swell of women's voices from one of the doorways leading off the hallway, crying variations of 'Stop!' But a guard came stumbling out anyway, naked from waist to ankle, his engorged penis waggling ridiculously. One hand was struggling to pull up the pair of trousers that tangled his legs, while he attempted to aim a pistol with the other. Malvery sighted and blew him away before he'd taken two steps.

Frey pulled the guard who had surrendered over to him, pressing the pistol to his back, using him as a shield. He disarmed his prisoner and tossed the gun aside as Malvery moved out of the way of the door and Jez and Pinn came in after him.

'Silo?' Frey asked.

'Covering the guard outside,' Jez replied. 'Jevin, or whatever his name is.'

Frey was thankful that someone had the presence of mind to do that. He'd half-expected them all to come rushing in when he did.

He wrapped his arm around his prisoner's throat from behind. 'Where's the other one?' he hissed. There had been four guards inside, last time he'd visited. Without waiting for an answer, he called: 'We got your friend here! Step out and you won't get hurt! I've got no business with you!'

There was silence, but for the ticking of the clock that over-looked the hall. Then a voice drifted out from another doorway:

'Bren? That you?'

'It's me, Charry,' Frey's prisoner replied. 'They got a gun to my head. There's four of 'em.'

Another long silence. 'Alright,' said Charry. 'I'm coming out. Don't nobody shoot. Nobody's gonna shoot, are they?'

'Nobody's gonna shoot,' said Frey, with a pointed glare at Pinn.

A rifle skidded out from one of the doorways, followed by a pistol and a knife. A young, swarthy-looking man emerged, his hands held high. Jez took him over to stand with the other prisoner. Silo came in from outside.

'Where's the guard you were covering?' Frey asked, appalled.

'Tied him up. Put him in the guardhouse with the other,' said Silo.

'Right, right,' Frey said, relieved. He allowed himself to relax a little. 'Should've thought of that myself.'

Pinn and Malvery exchanged a glance. Malvery looked skyward in despair.

'Your boss is upstairs?' Frey asked the prisoners. They nodded. 'No more guards?' They shook their heads. 'The whores?'

'In there,' said Charry, indicating the room the half-naked man had come from. 'Obviously.'

Frey looked at Silo. 'You're in charge. Anyone moves, shoot them. Malvery, you and me are going to have a word with Quail.' As an afterthought, he added: 'Bring your bag. I don't want him dying before he talks.'

'Right-o,' said Malvery, heading outside to collect the doctor's bag that he'd left on the porch.

Frey walked up to the whores' doorway and stood to one side. The dead man with his trousers round his ankles had a comically astonished expression on his face.

We can all but hope to die with such dignity and elegance, he thought.

'Ladies?' he called. There was no reply. He stuck his head

around the doorway, and drew it back rapidly as a shotgun blast blew part of the door frame to splinters.

'Ladies!' he said again, slightly annoyed this time. His ears were ringing. 'We're not going to hurt you!'

'No, you're bloody not!' came the reply. 'I know your sort! We give what we give 'cause we're paid to! Nobody takes it by force!'

'Nobody's taking anything,' said Frey. 'You might remember me. Darian Frey? We were introduced just a few weeks ago.'

'Oh,' came the reply, rather less harsh than before. 'Yes, I remember you. Stick your head out, let us have a look.'

'I'd rather not,' he replied. 'Listen, ladies, our business is with Quail. We'll be done with it and go. Nobody's going to bother you. Now will you let us past?'

There was a short debate in low voices. 'Alright.'

'You won't shoot?'

'Long as nobody tries to come in. Specially that one who looks like a potato. He's enough to turn a woman to the other side.'

Silo grinned at Pinn, who kicked an imaginary stone and swore under his breath.

'Especially not him,' Frey agreed.

'Well. Okay then.'

Malvery returned with his bag. He took another swig of swabbing alcohol and stuffed it back inside. Pinn bleated for a taste, but Malvery ignored him.

They hurried past the doorway. Frey caught a glimpse of the whores, hidden behind a dresser with a double-barrelled shotgun poking over the top. They held a pair of white, pink-eyed dogs on leashes, for extra protection. One of the whores waved and made a kiss-face as he passed, but he was out of sight too quickly to respond.

He headed up the stairs, Malvery close behind. The coiled-brass motif from the hallway continued on the upper level, but here the walls and floor were panelled in black wood and lit by electric bulbs in moulded sconces. The place had a dark, grand feel to it. Frey was feeling pretty dark and grand himself right now.

As they approached Quail's study they heard something crash inside. The sound of a desk tipping over. Presumably he was making a barricade. Frey remembered the bars on the windows from his last visit. They couldn't be opened from the inside. Quail wasn't going anywhere.

They took position either side of the door. Frey kicked it open and stepped back as a pistol fired twice. The door rebounded and came to rest slightly ajar. There were two coin-sized holes in the wood panelling of the corridor at chest-height.

'Anyone comes through that door, they'll be sorry!' Quail cried. His attempt to sound fierce was woeful. 'I've got a couple of guns and enough ammo for the whole night. The militia will be here sooner or later! Someone will have heard the racket you made downstairs!'

Frey thought for a moment. He waved at Malvery. 'Give me the bottle.'

'What?' Malvery said, feigning ignorance.

'The bottle of alcohol in your bag. Give it here.'

Malvery opened his bag reluctantly. 'This bottle?' he asked querulously, rather hoping Frey would reconsider.

'I'll buy you another one!' Frey snapped, and Malvery finally handed it over. He snatched it off the doctor and pulled out the stopper. 'Now a rag.'

'Oh,' Malvery murmured, divining Frey's plan. He passed Frey a bit of cloth with the expression of one about to witness the cruel extinction of some lovable, harmless animal.

Frey stuffed the rag into the neck of the bottle and upended it a few times. He pulled out a match – one of several that had lived in the creases of his coat pocket for many years – and struck it off the door jamb. He touched it to the rag and flame licked into life.

'Fire in the hole,' he grinned, then booted open the door and lobbed the bottle in. He ducked back in time to avoid the gunfire that followed.

The throw had been pitched into the corner of the room – he didn't want to incinerate Quail quite yet – but the whispermonger started howling as if he were on fire himself, instead of just the bookshelves.

Frey and Malvery retreated a little way down the corridor to another doorway, where they took shelter and aimed. Black smoke began to seep out of Quail's study. They could hear him clattering around inside, cursing. Glass smashed, bars rattled. The smoke became a thick, churning layer that spread out along the ceiling of the corridor. Quail began to cough and hack.

'You think this is gonna take much longer?' Malvery asked, and an instant later Quail burst from the room, his good eye watering, waving a pistol in one hand.

'*Drop it!*' Frey yelled, in a voice so loud and commanding that he surprised himself. Quail froze, looking around, and spotted Frey and Malvery with their guns trained on him. 'Drop it, or I'll drop you.'

Quail dropped his gun and raised his hands, coughing. His smart jacket was smoke-stained and his collar had wilted. His sleeve was ripped, revealing the polished brass length of his mechanical forearm.

Frey and Malvery emerged from hiding. Frey grabbed the whispermonger by the lapels and dragged him down the corridor, away from the smoke and flames of the study. He slammed Quail bodily up against the wall. Quail glared at him, teeth gritted, defiance on his face. Frey saw himself reflected in Quail's mechanical eye.

'Right then,' said Frey, then stepped back and shot him in the shin.

Quail screamed and collapsed, writhing on the ground, clutching at his leg. 'What the shit did you do that for, you rotting whoreson?' he yelled.

Frey knelt down on one knee next to him. 'Look, Quail. I don't have time for the preliminaries, and to be honest, I'm pretty unhappy with you right now. So let's pretend you've already put up a spirited resistance to my questioning and just tell me: who set me up? Because if I have to ask again, it's your kneecap. And after that I'm going for something you *can't* replace with a mechanical substitute.'

'Gallian Thade!' he blurted. 'It was Gallian Thade who gave me the job, that's all I know! It came through a middleman but I knew something was funny so I traced it back to him. He's a rich landowner, a nobleman who lives out in—'

'I know who Gallian Thade is,' Frey said. 'Go on.'

'They said it should be you, specifically *you* that I offered the job to. But they said . . . aaah, my leg!'

'*What* did they say?' Frey demanded, and punched him in his wounded shin. Quail shrieked and writhed, breathless with pain.

'I'm telling you, I'm telling you!' he protested. 'They said if you couldn't be found, I could offer it to someone else, last-minute. The important thing . . . the important thing was that the *Ace of Skulls* was passing through the Hookhollows on that date, they *knew* that, and they wanted someone to attack it. Preferably you, but if not, any lowlife would do.'

'You're not in much of a position to make insults, Quail.'

'Their words! Their words!' he said frantically, holding up a hand to ward off further punishment. 'Someone who wouldn't be missed, that's what they said. You'll forgive me if I'm not thinking too clearly since you just shot me in my damn leg!'

'Pain does cloud one's judgement,' Malvery observed sagely, crouched alongside Frey.

'You've no idea what was on that aircraft?' Frey pressed the whispermonger. He coughed into his fist. Time was getting short. The corridor was filling with hot smoke, and the only breathable air was low down. The militia wouldn't be far away.

'He told me jewels! He said he'd buy them from me if you came back. If not, he'd pay me a fee anyway. It was a cover story, I knew that, but I didn't . . . didn't find out what was underneath.'

'You don't want to speculate? Any idea why the Century Knights are all over me? Why there's such a big reward offered that Trinica Dracken is involved?'

'Dracken!' His eyes widened. 'Wait, I do know this! Trinica Dracken . . . she's put the word out in the underground. Anyone sees you, they tell her. Not the Century Knights. She's offering an even bigger reward. But it's for information only . . . she wants to catch you herself.'

'Well, of course she does—'

'No, you don't understand. Dracken doesn't have that kind of money. Someone's funding her. I don't know who. But whoever it is, they want her to get you before the Century Knights do. This isn't just about a reward, Frey. This is something more. Someone doesn't want the Knights to find you.'

Frey's jaw tightened. Deeper and deeper. Worse and worse.

'We'd better go, Cap'n,' said Malvery, coughing. 'Smoke's getting bad.'

'Alright,' Frey muttered. 'Come on.'

'What about me?' Quail said, as they got up. 'You can't just—'

'I can,' said Frey. 'You still have one good leg.' With that, they left, the whispermonger hurling oaths after them.

'Should we truss up the rest of his men?' Malvery asked, as they hurried down the stairs at the end of the hall. Pinn, Jez and Silo still had the surviving guards at gunpoint at the far end.

'No time. Besides, I think they'll have their hands full saving the house.' Frey raised his voice to address everyone in the hall. 'Ladies, gentlemen, we're out of here! Your boss is upstairs, and only mildly wounded. Go help him if you have the inclination. You'll also notice that the house is on fire. Make of that what you like.'

Militia whistles were sounding in the distance as the crew of the *Ketty Jay* slipped through the front gate, their breath steaming the air. Bright yellow flames were pluming from the eaves of the house behind them.

'This time we're *really* not coming back,' said Frey, as they headed for the dock.

'One question,' said Malvery as he huffed alongside. 'Gallian Thade, this noble feller, you know him?'

'No,' said Frey. 'But I knew his daughter very well. Intimately, you could say.'

Malvery rolled his eyes.

Twelve

*The Awakeners – Frey Apologises –
A Game Of Rake*

Olden Square sat in the heart of Aulenfay's trade district, a wide paved plaza surrounded by tall apartment buildings with pink stone facias. On a clear winter day such as this, the square was filled with stalls and people, everyone buying or selling. Hawkers offered food or theatre tickets or clockwork gewgaws; street performers imitated statues and juggled blades. Visitors and locals wandered between the attractions, the ladies in their furs and hats, men in their leather gloves and greatcoats. Children tugged at their parents' arms, begging to investigate this or that, drawn by the smell of candied apples or cinnamon buns.

The centrepiece was a wide fountain. The water tumbled down through many tiers from a high column, on which stood a fierce warrior. He was wielding a broken sword, fighting off three brass bears that clawed at him from below. On the rooftops, pennants of brown and green snapped and curled in the breeze, bearing the Duke's coat of arms.

Frey and Crake sat on the step of a small dais. Behind them four stone wolves guarded an ornate, black iron lamp-post, one of several dotted around the square to illuminate it at night. Frey was holding a white paper bag in one hand and chewing on a sugar-plum. He offered the bag to Crake, who took a sweet absently. Both of them were watching a booth in the corner of the square, from which three Awakeners were plying their trade.

The booth was hung with banners showing a symbol made up of six spheres in an uneven formation, connected by a complicated pattern of straight lines. The three Awakeners were dressed identically, in white single-breasted cassocks with high collars and red piping that denoted their status. They were Speakers, the rank and file of the organisation.

One of them was kneeling in front of a circular chart laid out on the ground. An eager-eyed man knelt opposite, watching closely. The Speaker was holding a handful of tall sticks upright in the centre of the chart. He let go and they fell in a clutter. The Speaker began to study them intently.

'Seriously, though,' said Frey. 'What's all that about?'

'It's rhabdomancy,' said Crake. 'The way the sticks fall is significant. The one behind him is a cleromancer: it's a similar technique. See? He drips a little animal blood in the bowl, then casts the bones in there.'

'And you can tell things from that?'

'Supposedly.'

'Like what?'

'The future. The past. You can ask questions. You can find out if the Allsoul favours your new business enterprise, or see which day would be most auspicious for your daughter's wedding. That kind of thing.'

'They can tell all that from some sticks?'

'So they say. The method isn't really that important. Each Awakener specialises in a different way of communicating with the Allsoul. See the other one? She's a numerologist. She uses birthdates, ages, significant numbers in people's lives and so on.'

Frey looked over at the third Awakener, a young woman, chubby and sour-faced. She was standing in front of a chalkboard and explaining a complicated set of mathematics to a bewildered audience of three, who looked like they could barely count on their fingers.

'I don't get it,' Frey confessed.

'You're not supposed to get it,' said Crake. 'That's the point. Mystical wisdom isn't much good if everyone possesses it. The Awakeners claim to be the only ones who know the secret of communicating with the Allsoul, and they don't intend to share. If you want something from the Allsoul, you go through them.'

Frey scratched the back of his neck and looked askance at Crake, squinting against the sun. 'You believe any of that?'

Crake gave him a withering look. 'I'm a daemonist, Frey. Those people in there, they'd like to see me hanged. And do you know why? Because what I do is *real*. It *works*. It's a *science*. But a century of this superstitious twaddle has made daemonists the most vilified people on the planet. Most people would rather associate with a Samarlan than a daemonist.'

'*I'd* associate with a Samarlan,' said Frey. 'War or no war, they've got some damned fine women.'

'I doubt Silo would think so.'

'Well, he's got a chip on his shoulder, what with his people being brutally enslaved for centuries and all that.'

Crake conceded the point.

'So what about this Allsoul thing?' asked Frey, passing over another sugarplum. 'Enlighten me.'

Crake popped the sugarplum in his mouth. 'Why the interest?'

'Research.'

'Research?'

'Gallian Thade, the man who put Quail up to framing us. He's the next one we need to talk to if we want to get some answers. I want to find out what he's framing us for.' He stretched, stiff from sitting on the step. 'Now, getting to Gallian, that's gonna be no easy task. But I can get to his daughter.'

Crake joined the dots. 'And his daughter is an Awakener?'

'Yeah. She's at a hermitage in the Highlands. They keep their acolytes cut off from the outside world while they study. I need to get in there and get to her. She might know something.'

'And you think she'll help you?'

'Maybe,' said Frey. 'Best idea I've got, anyway.'

'Shouldn't you be asking someone who believes this rubbish?'

Frey shifted on the step and settled himself again. 'You're educated,' he said, with slightly forced offhandedness. 'You know how to put things.'

'That's dangerously close to a compliment, Frey,' Crake observed.

'Yeah, well. Don't let it go to your head. And it's *Captain* Frey to you.'

Crake performed a half-arsed salute and slapped his knees. 'Well, then. What *do* you know?'

'I know *some* things. I've heard of the Prophet-King and how they put all his crazy pronouncements in a book after he went mad, except *they* think he was touched by some divine being or something. And how they all say they can solve your problems, just a small donation required. But I never was that bothered. None of it seemed to make much sense. Like some street scam that got out of control, you know? Like the thing with the three cups and the ball and no matter what you do, you never win. Except with this, half the country plays it and they never get that it's rigged.' He snorted. 'Nobody knows *my* future.'

'Fair enough.' Crake cleared his throat and thought for a moment. When he spoke it was as a teacher, crisp and to the point. 'The basic premise of their belief posits the existence of a single entity called the Allsoul. It's not a god in the sense of the old religions they wiped out, more like a sentient, organic machine. Its processes can be seen in the movement of wind and water, the behaviour of animals, the eruption of volcanoes and the formation of clouds. In short, they believe our planet is alive, and intelligent. In fact, vastly more intelligent than we can comprehend.'

'Okaaay . . .' Frey said uncertainly.

'The Awakeners think that the Allsoul can be understood by interpreting signs. Through the flights of birds, the pattern of fallen sticks, the swirl of blood in milk, the mind of the planet may be known. They also use rituals and minor sacrifices to communicate with the Allsoul, to beg its favour. Disease can be cured, disaster averted, success in business assured.'

'So let me get this straight,' Frey said, holding up his hand. 'They ask a question, they . . . release some birds, say. And the way the birds fly, what direction they go, that's the planet talking to them. The Allsoul?'

'When you strip out all the mumbo-jumbo, yes, that's exactly it.'

'And you say it doesn't work?'

'Ah!' said Crake scornfully, holding up a finger. 'That's the clever part. They've got it covered. Margin for human error, you see. Their understanding of the Allsoul is imperfect. Human minds aren't yet capable of comprehending it. You can ask, but the Allsoul might refuse. You can predict, but the predictions are so vague they'll come true more often than not. The Allsoul's schemes are so massive that the death of your son or the destruction of your village can be explained away as part of a grand plan that you're just too small to see.' He gave a bitter chuckle. 'They've got all the angles figured out.'

'You really hate them, don't you?' Frey said, surprised at the tone in his companion's voice. 'I mean, you *really* hate them.'

Crake clammed up, aware that he'd let himself get out of control. He gave Frey a quick, tense smile. 'It's only fair,' he said. 'They hated me first.'

They strolled up the hill from Olden Square, along a tree-lined avenue that led towards the wealthier districts of Goldenside and Kingsway. Passenger craft flew overhead and motorised carriages puttered by. There were fine dresses in the windows of the shops, displays of elaborate toys and sweetmeats. As they climbed higher they began to catch glimpses of Lake Elmen through the forested slopes to the west, vast as an inland ocean. All around, stretching into the distance as far as the eye could see, were the dark green pines and dramatic cliffs of the Forest of Aulen.

'Pretty part of the world,' Frey commented. 'You'd think the Aerium Wars never happened.'

'Aulenfay missed the worst of it the first time round, and got none of it on the second,' said Crake. 'You should see Draki and Rabban. Six years on and they're still half rubble.'

'Yeah, I've seen 'em,' he replied distantly. He was watching a young family who were approaching on their side of the avenue: a handsome husband, a neat wife with a beautiful smile, two little girls singing a rhyme as they skipped along in their frilly dresses.

After a moment the woman noticed his interest. Frey looked away quickly, but Crake bid them a pleasant 'Good day,' as they passed.

'Good day,' the couple replied, and a moment later the girls chimed 'Good day!' politely. Frey had to hurry on. The sight of their happiness, the sound of those little voices, was like a kick in the chest.

'What's the matter?' Crake enquired, noticing Frey's sudden change in demeanour.

'Nothing,' he muttered. 'Nothing, I just suddenly . . . I was worried they'd recognise me. Shouldn't have made eye contact.'

'Oh, I wouldn't worry. I told you, I picked up a broadsheet in Marklin's Reach yesterday. There was no mention of you. And Aulenfay isn't the kind of place where they stick "Wanted" posters everywhere. I think you've been forgotten by the general public.' He patted Frey on the shoulder. 'Besides, considering the age of the photograph and your newly raddled and insalubrious appearance, I don't think anyone would recognise you unless they had a particular interest.'

'Raddled and insalubrious?' Frey repeated. He was beginning to suspect Crake of showing off, in an attempt to belittle him.

'It means formidable and rugged,' Crake assured him. 'The beard, you see.'

'Oh.'

They came to a crossroads and Crake stopped on the corner. 'Well, I must be leaving you. I have to go and pick up my equipment, and the kind of people who sell daemonist paraphernalia are the kind of people who don't like non-daemonists knowing who they are.'

'Right,' said Frey. 'Have it delivered to the dock warehouse. We'll pick it up from there. No names, though.'

'Of course.' The daemonist turned to go.

'Crake.'

'Yes?'

Frey looked up the street, rather awkwardly. 'That thing with Macarde . . . him holding a gun to your head and so forth . . .'

Crake waited.

'I'm sorry it went that way,' Frey said at last.

Crake regarded him for a moment, his face unreadable. Then he nodded slightly and headed away without another word.

Frey made his way to the South Quarter, a less affluent part of the city, where he visited a tailor and a shop that specialised in theatrical make-up. After that, he went looking for a game of Rake.

The South Quarter was about as seedy as Aulenfay got, which meant it was still quite picturesque in a charmingly ramshackle kind of way. The winding lanes and cobbled alleyways were all but free of filth and litter. Statues and small, well-kept fountains still surprised visitors at every turn. There were no rag-tag children or crusty beggars. Aulenfay had a strict policy against that kind of thing.

The Ducal Militia were in evidence, patrolling in their stiff brown uniforms. Frey kept out of their way.

Despite the risks of coming to a big city, Frey had allowed himself to be persuaded by Crake. He did have some preparation to do before he went looking for Amalicia Thade in her secluded hermitage, but that wasn't the whole reason. The crew needed a break. The disastrous attack on the freighter, the escape from the Century Knights, that frustrating time spent bored and freezing in Yortland – all these things had worn them down, and they were sick and tired of each other's company. A little time off would do them all good, and Aulenfay was a fine place for it.

Whether they'd all come back or not was another matter, but Frey wasn't worried about that. If they left, they left. He'd understand. They'd each make their own choice.

It took a little searching to locate the Rake den. He hadn't been this way for a few years. But it was still there, in the cellar bar of an old tavern: a little room with three circular tables and a vaulted ceiling of old grey brick. Smoke drifted in the air and the shadows were thick, thrown by oil lanterns. Rake players didn't like their games too brightly lit. Most of them only had a passing acquaintance with daylight.

Only one of the tables was in use when Frey was shown in. Three men sat there, studying their cards, dull piles of coins before them. There was a thin, po-faced man who looked like an undertaker, an elderly, toothless drunk, and a whiskery, rotund fellow with a red face and a battered stovepipe hat. Frey sat down and they introduced themselves as Foxmuth, Scrone and Gremble, which amused Frey, who thought they sounded like a firm of lawyers. Frey gave a false name. He ordered a drink, emptied out his purse on the table, and set to the game.

It wasn't long before he realised his opponents were terrible card players. At first he suspected some kind of trap: perhaps they were feigning incompetence to sucker him. But as the game went on he became ever more convinced they were the real deal.

They went in big with their money, chasing runs that never came up. They jittered with excitement when they made a low three-of-a-kind and then bet it as if it was unbeatable. They allowed themselves to be bluffed away whenever they saw Frey pick up a dangerous card, frightened that he was holding something that could crush them.

From the moment he sat down, he was winning.

Several hours passed, and several drinks. Scrone was too plastered to keep his attention on the game, and his money was whittled away on silly bets. Eventually, he made a suicidal bluff against Foxmuth who was holding Crosses Full and lost it all. After that, he fell asleep and began to snore.

Foxmuth was knocked out shortly afterwards, following a chancy call against Gremble's Ace-Duke paired. Foxmuth's last card failed to produce the hand he needed, and Gremble scooped up all his money.

Frey was only mildly disheartened. All his careful work in maintaining his lead had been undermined by the bad play of the other two. They'd given all their money to Gremble, making the two remaining players roughly even. He settled down to the task of demolishing his final opponent.

'Just my luck,' Foxmuth moaned. 'The wife's going to rip me a new arse when I come home. I wouldn't have even been here if they'd had the parade today.'

Frey was only half-listening. He dealt the cards, three each, then picked up his. A thin chill of excitement ran through him. Three Priests.

'Why didn't they have the parade?' Frey asked, making idle chatter to cover his anticipation.

'Earl Hengar was supposed to be coming to see the Duke. Big parade and all. But with what's happened . . . well, I suppose they thought it was in bad taste or something. Cancelled last-minute.'

'I should think so. Bloody disgrace,' muttered Gremble. He rapped the table to indicate that he didn't wish to bet.

'Bet,' said Frey. 'Two bits.' He pushed the coins in. It was a high opening bid, but he knew Gremble's style of play by now. Instead of being frightened off, Gremble would assume it was a bluff and match it. Which was exactly what he did.

Frey dealt four more cards to the middle, two for each player in the game. Two face up, two face down. The face-up cards were the Lady of Wings and the Priest of Skulls.

His heart jumped. If he could get that Priest, he'd have an almost unbeatable hand. But Gremble, to the left of the dealer, got to pick his card first from the four in the middle.

'What's a disgrace?' he asked, trying to keep the conversation up. He wanted Gremble distracted.

'About Hengar and that Sammie bitch.'

Frey gave him a blank look.

'You don't know? You been living in a cave or something?'

'Close,' said Frey.

'It's not been in the broadsheets,' said Foxmuth. 'They don't dare print it. But everyone knows. It's been all over this past week.'

'I've been away,' he said. 'Yortland.'

'Chilly up there,' Gremble commented, taking the Lady of Wings as he did so. Frey thrilled at the sight.

'Yeah,' Frey agreed. The Priest was his. He made a show of

deliberating whether to take one of the two face-down mystery cards or not. 'So what's the story with Hengar?'

Hengar, Earl of Thesk and the only child of the Archduke. Heir to the Nine Duchies of Vardia. It sounded like something Frey should be paying attention to, but he was concentrating on depriving this poor sap of all his coins. He picked up the Priest. Four Priests in his hand. If he played this right, the game would be his.

'So there were all these rumours, right?' Foxmuth said eagerly. 'About Hengar and this Sammie princess or something.'

'She wasn't a princess, she was some other thing,' Gremble interrupted, frowning as he looked at his hand.

'Yeah, well, anyway,' Foxmuth continued. 'Hengar was having secret meetings with her.'

'Political meetings?'

'The other kind,' Gremble muttered. 'They was lovers. The heir to the Nine Duchies and a bloody Sammie! The family wanted it stopped, but he wouldn't listen, so they was covering it all up. But this past week, well . . . All I can say is someone must've shot their mouth off.'

'What's so wrong with him seeing a Sammie?' Frey asked.

'Did you miss the wars or something?' Gremble cried.

'I wasn't on the front line,' said Frey. 'First one, I was working as a cargo hauler. Never saw action. Second one, I was working for the Navy, supply drops and so on.' He shut up before he said any more. He didn't want to revisit those times. Rabby's final scream as the cargo ramp closed still haunted him at night. He could never forget the awful, endless, slicing agony of a Dakkadian bayonet plunging into his belly. Just the thought made him sick with fury at the people who had sent him there to die. The Coalition Navy.

Gremble humphed, making it clear what he thought of Frey's contribution. 'I was infantry, both wars. I saw stuff you can't imagine. And there are a lot of people out there like me. Curdles my guts to think of our Earl Hengar snuggling up to some pampered Sammie slut.'

'So how did the news get out?'

'Search me,' growled Gremble. 'But the Archduke ain't happy about it, I bet. There's already all them rumours about the Archduchess, how she's secretly a daemonist and that. You know they say the Archduke has a regiment of golems helping guard his palace in Thesk? And that he's planning to make more regiments to fight on our front lines?'

'Didn't know that,' said Frey.

'It's what they say. They say the Archduchess is behind it. They say that's why they're doing all that stuff to undermine the Awakeners. Awakeners and daemonists hate each other.'

'Yeah, I gathered,' said Frey, thinking back to his earlier conversation with Crake.

'And now there's Hengar behaving like this . . .' Gremble tutted. 'You know, I always used to like him. He's a big Rake player, you know that?' He folded his arms and sucked his teeth. 'But now? I don't know what that family's coming to.'

'Speaking of Rake, are you gonna bet?'

'Five bits!' Gremble snapped.

'Raise five more,' Frey replied.

'I bet all of it!' said Gremble immediately, piling the rest of his money into the centre of the table. Then he sat back and looked at his cards with the air of someone wondering what he'd just done.

Frey considered for only a moment. 'Okay,' he said. Gremble went pale. He hadn't expected that.

Frey laid down his cards with a smile. 'Four Priests,' he said. Gremble groaned. His own four cards were the Ace, Ten, Three of Wings and the Lady of Wings he'd just picked up. He was going for Wings Full, but even if he made it, he couldn't beat Four Priests.

Unless Frey drew the Ace of Skulls.

The Ace of Skulls was the wild card. Usually it was worse than worthless, but in the right circumstances it could turn a game around. In most cases, if a player held it, it nullified all their cards and they lost the hand automatically. But if it could be made part of a high-scoring hand, Three Aces or a Run or Suits Full or higher, it made that hand unbeatable.

If Frey drew the Ace of Skulls, his Four Priests would be cancelled and he'd lose everything.

There were two cards left on the table, face down. Gremble reached out and turned one over. The Duke of Wings. He'd made his Wings Full, but it didn't matter now. He sat back with a disgusted snort.

Frey reached out for his card, but there was a commotion behind him, and he turned around as a tavern-boy came clattering down the stairs.

'Did you hear?' he said urgently. Scrone jerked in his chair, startled halfway out of sleep, and then slipped back into unconsciousness.

'Hear what, boy?' demanded Foxmuth, rising.

'There's criers out in the streets. They're saying why the parade got cancelled. It's because of Hengar!'

'There, what did I tell you?' said Gremble, with a note of triumph in his voice. 'They're ashamed of what he's done, and so they should be!'

'No, it's not that!' said the boy. He was genuinely distressed. 'Earl Hengar's dead!'

'But that's . . . He's bloody *dead*?' Foxmuth sputtered.

'He was on a freighter over the Hookhollows. There was some kind of accident, something went wrong with the engine, and . . .' The boy looked bewildered and shocked. 'It went down with all hands.'

'When?' asked Frey. The muscles of his neck had tightened. His skin had gone cold. But he hadn't taken his eyes from that face-down card on the table.

'Excuse me, sir?'

'*When* did it happen?'

'I don't know, sir. They didn't say.'

'What kind of damn fool question is that?' Gremble raged. 'When? When? What does it matter *when*? He's dead! Buggering piss-bollocks! It's a tragedy! A fine young man like that, taken from us in the prime of his life!'

'A good man,' Foxmuth agreed gravely.

But the *when* did matter. *When* meant everything to Frey. *When* was the final hope he had that maybe, against all the odds, he could avoid the terrible, crushing weight that he felt plummeting towards him. If it happened yesterday, or the day before . . . if it could somehow be that recent . . .

But he knew when it had happened. It had happened three weeks ago. They just hadn't been able to keep it quiet any longer.

The Century Knights. The job from Quail. All those people, travelling incognito on a cargo freighter. The name of the freighter. It all added up. After all, wouldn't Hengar travel in secret, returning from an illicit visit to Samarla? And wasn't he a keen Rake player?

Gallian Thade had arranged the death of the Archduke's only son. And he'd set Frey up to take the fall.

He reached over and flipped the final card.

The Ace of Skulls grinned at him.

Thirteen

Frey Is Beleaguered –
A Mysterious Aircraft – Imperators

F rey stumbled through the mountain pass, his coat clutched tight to his body, freezing rain lashing his face. The wind keened and skirled and pushed against him while he kept up the string of mumbled oaths and curses that had sustained him for several kloms now. On a good day, the Andusian Highlands at dawn could be described as dramatic – stunning, even – with its wild green slopes and deep lakes nestling between peaks of grim black rock. Today was not a good day.

Frey dearly wished for the sanctuary and comfort of his quarters. He remembered the grimy walls and cramped bunk with fondness, the luggage rack that ever threatened to snap and drop an avalanche of cases and trunks on his head. Such luxurious accommodation seemed a distant dream now, after hours of being pummelled by nature. He was woefully underdressed to face the elements. His face felt like it had been flayed raw and his teeth chattered constantly.

He lamented his bad luck at being caught out in the storm. So what if he'd set out completely unprepared? How could he have known the weather would turn bad? He couldn't see the future.

It seemed like days had passed since he left the *Ketty Jay* hidden in a dell. He couldn't risk landing too close to his target for fear of being seen, so he put her down on the other side of a narrow mountain ridge. The journey through the pass should have taken five hours or so. Six at the most.

When he set off the skies had been clear and the stars twinkling as the last light drained from the sky. There had been no hint of the storm to come. Malvery had waved him on his way with a cheery *ta-ra* and then taken a swig of rum to toast the success of his journey. Crake had been playing with the new toys he'd picked up in Aulenfay. Bess was having fun uprooting trees and tossing them around. Pinn had stolen the theatrical make-up pen that Frey had bought in the South Quarter and painted the Cipher on his forehead – the six connected spheres, icon of the Awakener faith. He was prancing around in the ill-fitting Awakener robes that had been tailored for Frey, pulling faces and acting the clown.

Frey had been unusually full of good cheer as he walked. All of them had come back from Aulenfay. Frey took that as a vote of confidence, even if the truth was they had no better alternatives. But even with the news of Hengar's death looming over him, he felt positive. Bullying Quail had energised him. Having a name to put to the shadowy conspiracy against him gave him a direction and a purpose. He'd got so used to running away that he'd forgotten how it felt to fight back, and he was surprised to learn that he liked it.

Besides, he thought sunnily, things were about as bad as they could possibly get. After a certain point, it didn't really matter if they hung him for piracy, mass murder, or for assassinating Earl Hengar, heir to the Archduchy. He'd be just as dead, any way you cut it. That meant he could do pretty much whatever he liked from here on in.

His buoyant mood survived while the first ominous clouds came sliding in from the west, blacking out the moon. He remained persistently jolly as the first spots of rain touched his face. Then the howling wind began, which took the edge off his jauntiness a little. The rain became torrential, he got lost and then realised he had no map. By this time he'd begun to freeze and was desperately searching for shelter, but there was none to be found and, anyway, he didn't have the supplies to wait out a really bad storm. He decided to keep going. Surely he was almost there by now?

He wasn't.

Dawn found him exhausted and in bad shape. His face was as

dark as the clouds overhead. He stumped along doggedly, head down, forging through the tempest. His good mood had evaporated. It wasn't positivity but spite that drove him onward now. He refused to stop moving until he'd reached his destination. Every time he crested a rise and saw there was another one ahead, it made him angrier still. The pass had to end eventually. It was him against the mountain, and his pride wouldn't let him be beaten by a glorified lump of rock, no matter how big it thought it was.

Finally the wind dropped and the rain dwindled to a speckling. Frey's heart lifted a little. Could it be that the worst was over? He didn't dare admit the possibility to himself, for fear of inviting a new tempest. Fate had a way of tormenting him like that. The Allsoul punished optimists.

He struggled up another sodden green slope and looked down into the valley beyond. There, at last, he saw the Awakener hermitage where Amalicia Thade was cloistered.

The hermitage sat on the bank of a river, a sprawling square building constructed around a large central quad. It was surrounded by lawns which opened on to fields of bracken and other hardy highland plants. With its stout, vine-laden walls, deeply sunken windows and frowning stone lintels, it looked to Frey like a university or a school. There was a quiet gravity to the place, a weightiness that Frey usually associated with educational institutions. Academia had always impressed him, since he'd only a passing acquaintance with it. All that secret knowledge, waiting to be learned, if only he could ever be bothered.

A little way from the hermitage, linked to it by a gravel path, was a small landing pad. There were no roads into the valley. Like so many places in Vardia, it was only accessible from the air. In a country so massive and with such hostile geography, roads and rail never made much sense once airships were invented. A small cargo craft took up one corner of the pad. It was their only link with the outside world, most likely, although there would certainly be other visitors from time to time.

Frey could see the tiny figures of Awakener Sentinels patrolling the grounds, carrying rifles. They issued from a guardhouse, which had been built outside the hermitage. He'd intended to arrive under cover of deepest night, but getting lost in the storm had put him severely behind schedule. There was no way he could approach the hermitage during the day without being seen.

The last of the rain disappeared, and he saw hints of a break in the clouds. Shafts of sun were beaming down on the mountains in the distance, warm searchlights slowly tracking towards him. There was nothing for it but to find a nook and rest until nightfall. Now that the storm had given up and he'd reached his destination, he was tired enough to die where he stood. A short search revealed a sheltered little dell, where he piled dry bracken around himself and fell asleep in the hollow formed by the roots of a dead tree.

He woke to the sound of engines.

It was night, clear and cold. He extricated himself from the tangle of bracken and stood up. His skin was fouled with old sweat, his clothes were stiff and he desperately needed to piss. His body ached as if he'd been expertly beaten up by a squad of vicious midgets. He stood, groaned and stretched, then spat to clear the rancid taste in his mouth. That done, he went to investigate what that noise was all about.

He looked down into the valley while he relieved himself against the side of a tree. The moon had painted the world in shades of blue and grey. The windows of the hermitage glowed with an inviting light, a suggestion of heat and comfort and shelter. Frey was looking forward to breaking in, if only to get a roof over his head for a while.

The craft he'd heard was a small black barque, bristling with weapons. A squat, mean-looking thing, possibly a Tabington Wolverine or something from that line. It was easing itself down onto the landing pad, lamps on full, a blare of light in the darkness.

A visitor, thought Frey, buttoning himself up. *Best get down there while they're occupied.*

He made his way down into the valley, staying low in the bracken when he could, scampering across open ground when he had to. He got to the river, where there was better cover from the bushes that grew on the bank, and followed it up towards the hermitage. There was a lot of activity surrounding the newly arrived vessel. The Sentinels had all but abandoned their patrol duties to guard it. They stationed themselves along the path between the house and the landing pad.

You should leave it alone, he told himself. *Take advantage of the distraction. Get inside the building. Do what you came here to do.*

A minute later he was creeping through the bracken, edging his way closer to the landing pad to get a better look. He just wanted to know what all the fuss was about.

The craft rested on the tarmac, bathed in its own harsh light. Though the cargo ramp was down, it still had its thrusters running and the aerium engines fired up. Evidently it wasn't staying for long.

When he'd got as close as he dared, Frey squatted down to watch. The wind rustled the bracken around him. The craft had a name painted on its underside: the *Moment of Silence*. He'd never heard of it.

The Sentinels had organised themselves as though they expected an attack, guarding the route between the craft and the door of the building, which stood open. They were dressed in grey, high-collared cassocks of the same cut that all the Awakeners wore. They carried rifles and wore twinned daggers at their waists. The Cipher was emblazoned in black on their breasts: a complex design of small, linked circles.

Sentinels, Crake had explained, were not true Awakeners. They lacked the skill or the intelligence to be ordained into the mysteries of the order. That was why they only wore the Cipher on their breast, not tattooed on their foreheads. They devoted themselves to the cause in other ways, as protectors of the faith. They were not known to be especially well trained or deadly, but they were disciplined. Frey resolved to treat them with the same respect he gave anyone carrying a weapon capable of putting a hole in him.

Everyone was on the alert. Something important was happening.

There was movement by the house, and several Sentinels

emerged. They were carrying a large, iron-bound chest between them, straining under its weight. The chest was a work of art, lacquered in dark red and closed with a clasp fashioned in the shape of a wolf's head. Frey was suddenly very keen to find out what was inside.

The Sentinels had hauled it up the path and had almost reached the craft when two figures came down the cargo ramp to meet them. Frey felt a chill jolt at the sight of them. Being so close to the craft didn't seem like such a good idea any more.

They were dressed head to toe in close-fitting suits of black leather. Not an inch of their skin was showing. They wore gloves and boots, and cloaks with their hoods pulled up. Their faces were hidden behind smooth black masks, through which only the eyes could be seen.

Imperators. The Awakeners' most dreaded operatives. Men who could suck the thoughts right out of your head, if the stories were to be believed. Men whose stare could send you mad.

Frey hunkered down further into the bracken.

The Sentinels put the chest down in front of the Imperators, then one of them knelt and opened it. Frey was too far away to see what was within.

One of the Imperators nodded, satisfied, and the chest was closed. The Sentinels lifted it and carried it up the *Moment of Silence*'s cargo ramp. They emerged seconds later, having left their burden inside. A few words were exchanged, and then one of the Imperators boarded the craft. The other turned to follow, but suddenly hesitated, his head tilted as if listening. Then he turned, and fixed his gaze on the spot where Frey hid in the bracken.

An awful sensation washed over him: foul, seething, corrupt. Frey's heart thumped hard in terror. He ducked down, out of sight, burying himself among the stalks and leaves. The loamy smell of wet soil and the faintly acrid tang of bracken filled his nostrils. He willed himself to be a stone, a rabbit, some small and insignificant thing. Anything that would be beneath the Imperator's notice. Some distant part of him was aware that such overwhelming fear wasn't natural, that there was some power at work here; but reason and logic had fled.

Then, all at once, the feeling was gone. The fear left him. He stayed huddled, not daring to move, breathing hard, soaked in relief. It had passed, it had passed. He murmured desperate thanks, addressed to no one. Never again, he swore. Never again would he go through that. Those few seconds had been among the most horrible of his life.

He heard the whine of the hydraulics as the cargo ramp slid shut. Electromagnets throbbed as the aerium engines got to work. The *Moment of Silence* was taking off.

Frey gathered his courage and raised his head, peering out above the bracken. The Imperators were gone. All eyes were on the craft. Frey took advantage of the moment, and scampered away towards the hermitage.

By damn, what did that thing do to me?

He could only remember one event vaguely comparable to the ordeal he'd just suffered. He'd been young, perhaps seventeen, and he and some friends went out to some fields where some very 'special' mushrooms grew. The night had started off with hilarity and ended with Frey seized by a crushing paranoia, afraid that his heart was going to burst, and being mobbed by hallucinatory bats. That senseless, primal fear had turned a confident young man into a quivering wreck. Now he'd been brushed by it again.

His breathing had returned to normal by the time he got to the hermitage, and he had himself under control again. Shaken, but unharmed. He approached the building from behind, where there were no guards to be seen, and pressed himself against the cool stone of the wall. Security was lax here. He had that to be thankful for. The guards didn't expect any trouble. They were only here for protection against pirates and other marauders, who might find the idea of a hermitage full of nubile, sex-starved young women somewhat alluring.

Frey cheered at the thought. He'd forgotten about the nubile, sex-starved part. It made his mistake back in Aulenfay twinge a little less, although his cheeks still burned at the memory.

He'd studied the Awakeners in Olden Square and picked Crake's brains about their faith for a purpose. His idea was to disguise himself as a Speaker, to blend in seamlessly, and thereby move about the hermitage unopposed. Congratulating himself on his unusually thorough preparations, he'd surprised Crake by appearing in full Speaker dress: the high-collared white cassock with red piping, the sandals, the Cipher painted on his forehead in a passable impression of a tattoo.

'What do you think?' he asked proudly.

Crake burst out laughing, before explaining to the rather miffed captain that Awakener hermitages were always single sex institutions. Acolytes were allowed no contact with the opposite gender. In Amalicia's hermitage, all the tutors and students would be female. The male guards would be forbidden to go inside except under special circumstances, and even then the female acolytes would be kept to their rooms. Lust interfered with the meditation necessary to communicate with the Allsoul.

'So you're telling me that there's a building full of women who haven't even *seen* a man in years?' Frey had demanded to know.

'What I'm telling you is that your cunning disguise is going to be pretty useless in there, since there shouldn't be a male Speaker within twenty kloms of that hermitage,' said Crake. 'However, it's interesting that you jumped to the other conclusion first. I never pegged you as a glass-half-full kind of person.'

'Well, a man must make the best of things,' Frey replied, already envisioning a pleasant death by sexual exhaustion, after being brutally abused by dozens of rampant adolescent beauties.

So Frey had discarded the uniform. Pinn found it later and had been wearing it ever since, for a joke, pretending to be an Awakener. It was funny for the first few hours, but Pinn, encouraged, had carried the joke far past its natural end and now it was just annoying. Frey wouldn't be surprised if Malvery had beaten him up and burned the robe by the time he got back. He rather hoped so.

He found two small doors, recessed in alcoves, but the Awakeners who ran the hermitage were sensible enough to keep them locked. He considered breaking a window, but they were set high up in the wall and were very narrow. He wouldn't want to get stuck in one. Finally he found the entrance to a storm cellar which looked as if it led under the house. Hurricanes were frequent in these parts. A padlock secured a thick chain, locking the doors to the cellar. Both were stout and new. It looked like it would take a lot of sawing and hammering to get through that. An intruder would certainly be caught before they gained access.

Frey drew his cutlass and touched its tip to the lock.

'Think you can?' he asked it. He didn't really believe it could understand him, but as ever, it seemed to know his intention. He felt it begin to vibrate in his hands. A thin, quiet whine came from the metal. Soon it was joined by another note, setting up a weird, off-key harmonic that set Frey's teeth on edge. The lock began to jitter and shake.

Suddenly, by its own accord, the cutlass swept up and down, smashing into the lock. The shackle broke away from the padlock and the chain slithered free. The blade itself was unmarked by the impact. Frey hadn't even felt the jolt up his sword arm.

He regarded the daemon-thralled cutlass that Crake had given him as the price of his passage. Best deal he ever made, he reckoned, as he sheathed it again.

He climbed into the storm cellar before anyone came to investigate the noise. Steps led down to a lit room, from which he could hear the growl and rattle of machinery. He slipped inside, shut the cellar door behind him, and crept onward into the hermitage.

Fourteen

A Ghastly Encounter – Intruder In The
Hermitage – A Heartfelt Letter – Reunion

F rey stepped warily into the dim electric glow of smoke-
grimed bulbs. The room at the bottom of the stairs was
the powerhouse of the hermitage, dominated by a huge old
generator that whined and screeched and shook. It took Frey a
while to persuade himself that the ancient machine wasn't in
imminent danger of detonation, but in the end logic triumphed
over instinct. Since it had obviously been running for fifty years or
more, the idea that it would explode just as he was passing would
be such incredible bad luck that even Frey couldn't believe it
would happen.

Pipes ran from the generator to several water boilers and storage
batteries, linking them to the central mass like the legs of some
bloated mechanical spider. The air pounded with the unsteady
rhythm of the generator and everything stank of prothane fumes.
Frey's head began to swim unpleasantly.

He crept forward, his cutlass held ready. He always preferred
blades in close quarters. The powerhouse was shadowy and full of
dark corners and aisles from which someone could emerge and
surprise him. He hadn't discounted the possibility that he might
run into a mechanic down here, or maybe even a guard, although
they'd need lungs like engines to breathe these fumes for long.

The generator banged noisily and he shied away, threatening it
with the tip of his cutlass. When nothing calamitous happened, he
relaxed again, feeling a little stupid.

Just get out of here, he told himself. Abandoning caution, he hurried through the room with his arm over his face, breathing through the sleeve of his coat.

If there was anyone else down there, he neither saw nor heard them. A few stone steps led up to a heavy door, which was unlocked. He peered in, and found himself in an untidy antechamber full of tools. Dirty gloves and rubber masks with gas filters hung on pegs. Frey shut the door behind him, muffling the sound of the generator. There was another door leading to a room beyond, and now he could hear loud snoring from the other side.

Snoring was good. Unless it was a particularly cunning decoy – Frey briefly imagined a sharp-eyed assassin waiting behind the door, dagger raised, snoring loudly – then it suggested the enemy was unaware, unarmed and at a massive disadvantage, which was the only way Frey would fight anyone if he could help it.

He lifted the door on its hinges to minimise the squeak, pushed it open, and immediately recoiled. The room beyond reeked overwhelmingly of cheesy feet and stale flatulence, strong enough that Frey had to fight down the urge to gag. He glanced briefly at one of the gas masks hanging on the wall, then took a deep breath and slipped inside.

The place was a wreck. Every surface was covered in discarded plates of food, half-drunk bottles of milk that had long gone bad, and pornographic ferrotypes from certain seedy publications (Frey saw several women he recognised). In the corner, on a pallet bed surrounded by discarded chicken bones and bottles of grog, lay a mound of hairy white flesh entangled in a filthy blanket. It took Frey a few moments to work out where the head was. He only found it when a gaping wet hole appeared in the crumb-strewn black thatch of a face, and there emerged a terrible snore like the death-rattle of a congested warthog.

Frey kept his sword pointed at the quivering mass of the caretaker's naked belly, and edged through the room towards the door at the far end. Finding it locked, he cast around the room and located a key under a scattering of toenail clippings. He extracted it gingerly, slipped it in the lock and went through. The caretaker, deep in his drunken slumber, never stirred.

It took him some time to find his way to the dormitories. A quick search established that the basement level of the building was a maze of gloomy corridors and pipes, sealed off from the hermitage proper, presumably to stop the caretaker getting in and giving the acolytes a nasty shock. There must have been another entrance for the caretaker, since the storm doors had been locked on the outside, but Frey never found it. What he did find was a chimney flue, which he climbed with considerable difficulty and much discomfort.

When he emerged, sooty and dishevelled, from the fireplace, he found himself in a small hall. Doors led off to other rooms, and a wide staircase went up to the floor above. The place had a clean, quiet, country feel: the cool, pensive atmosphere of an old house at night. Bulbs shone from simple iron sconces; decoration was understated and minimal. There were no idols of worship or shrines, such as the old gods might have demanded. The only evidence of this building's purpose was a shadowy, gold-framed portrait of King Andreal of Glane, father of the Awakeners and the last ever King. He'd been painted in his most regal pose. It betrayed none of the madness that later took him, and set him to burbling prophecies which ended up having far more influence over the country than he ever did while he ruled it.

There was little here to distract the mind from its devotions. Instead, there were only panelled doors, strong beams, smooth banisters, and the frowning sensation of trespass that settled heavier on Frey with every passing moment.

There are no guards. Only women inside, he reminded himself. *Since when have you been scared of women?*

Then he remembered Trinica Dracken, and he felt a little nauseous. Of all the people in the world he never wanted to see again, she was top of the list.

Forget her for now, he thought. *You've a job to do.*

He dusted himself down as best he could, though he was still covered in sooty smears when he finished. Having made himself as presentable as possible, he looked through the nearest doorway.

A short corridor led to an empty wooden room, with only a small brazier in the centre. Mats were laid out in a circle around it. A skylight let in the glow of the moon.

A meditation chamber, Frey guessed, backtracking. The Awakeners were very keen on meditation, Crake had told him. Sitting around doing nothing took many years of practice, he'd added with a sneer.

Other doorways let out on to other corridors, which took him to a small study, a filing room full of cabinets and paper, and a classroom with desks in rows of three. Any windows he saw were set high up on the wall, too high to look through without using a stepladder. Obviously interest in the outside world was discouraged.

He soon came upon a room with a stone table, red-stained blood-gutters running down it. Frey's alarming visions of human sacrifice faded when he remembered that many Awakeners used the reading of entrails to understand the Allsoul. As he was wondering how it all might work, he heard the distant whisper of footsteps and female voices in conversation. Someone was up, even at this hour. It was difficult to tell if they were heading his way or not, but he returned to the hall to be safe, and then went up the stairs.

The problem of actually *finding* Amalicia once he was inside the hermitage hadn't greatly troubled Frey during the planning of his daring infiltration. He'd been sidetracked by delicious visions of what an army of cloistered girls might do when a man turned up in their midst. In the face of that, the details seemed rather unimportant. But now he realised that he hadn't the faintest idea where his target was, and his only option was to keep nosing around until something presented itself.

There was another small concern that had been nagging him. It had been two years, more or less, since Amalicia's father sent her to the hermitage. Granted, the point of a hermitage was to keep acolytes in isolation for twice that, but still, two years was a long time. He wasn't even certain she was here at all. Maybe her father had forgiven her and let her out?

No. He didn't think so. He knew Gallian Thade's reputation, and forgiveness wasn't something he approved of.

Besides, Amalicia herself had said as much, in the last letter she'd sent him.

Moilday Firstweek, Thresh, 145/32

Dearest one,

Through the investigations of those still loyal to me and sympathetic to our cause, I have discovered the location of the hermitage to which my father intends to condemn me. He is sending me to the Highlands. I enclose the co-ordinates, which I am sure your navigator can decode, as they are mysterious to me.

Please forgive the cruel and shameful words I wrote in my last letter. I see now that you were wise to flee when you could, for my father's mood has not improved. He still swears terrible vengeance, and likely will desire your death until the day his own comes. My heart should break if harm were to come to you. My anger was not towards you, but towards the injustice that made me my father's daughter and you a man born without noble blood. But our love makes mockery of such things, and I know it will make you brave.

Find me, Darian, and rescue me. You have your craft, and we have the world before us. You will be a great man of the skies, and I shall be at your side, the way we always dreamed.

This letter will depart by my most trusted handmaiden, and I hope it will reach you and find you well. There will be no further opportunity to communicate.

With love everlasting,
Amalicia

Well, I got here eventually, Frey thought.

At the top of the stairs was another corridor, and more doors on either side. Each one was a private study cell, with a small lectern on the floor, a mat for kneeling, and a window slit, high up. There were more classrooms, and a door to a library, which was locked. He was just about to try the next door when suddenly a voice came to him, startlingly close.

'It's Euphelia, that's who it is. She's the one bringing the others down.'

He bolted into a classroom and crouched inside the doorway just as two women came gliding round the corner on slippered feet.

'She's taking her studies very seriously,' argued the other. 'She's terribly earnest.'

'She's just not very bright, then,' replied the first. 'Her understanding of the Cryptonomicon is woeful.'

Two figures swept past in the corridor. Frey caught a glimpse of them. They were middle-aged, with greying hair cut in masculine, efficient styles, and they wore the white cassocks of Speakers.

'She has a talent for casting the bones, though,' the second woman persisted.

'That she does, that she does. The signals are very clear. But I wonder if she'll ever learn to interpret them.'

'Perhaps if we focused her more towards cleromancy and lightened her other studies?'

'Make her a special case? Goodness, no. If we start with her, we have to do it with everyone, and then where will we be?'

The voices faded as they turned the corner, and Frey relaxed. It seemed the hermitage was still patrolled, even in the dead of night. Out to catch acolytes sneaking into the pantry, or some such thing. Well, he'd have to be careful. He didn't think his conscience could handle punching out a woman.

He found the girls' dormitory shortly afterwards, and slid inside.

For a time he stood just inside the door, in the dark. Moonlight fell from a pair of skylights onto two rows of bunk beds. Perhaps fifty girls were sleeping here, their huddled outlines limned in cold light. The room was soft with sighing breath, broken by the occasional delicate snore. There was a scent in the air, not perfume but something indefinable and female, present in a dangerous concentration. Frey began to feel strangely frisky.

He was something of an expert in the art of creeping through women's rooms without disturbing them. By waiting, he was being careful. The slight disturbance caused by his entry may have brought some of the girls close to the surface of sleep, and any small noise might wake them. He was giving them time to slip back into the depths before proceeding.

That, and he wanted to exult in the moment. It really was quite special, being here.

He moved silently between the beds, looking at the moonlit faces of each girl in turn. Disappointingly, they were not quite as luscious in person as he'd imagined they might be. Some were just too young – he had standards – and others were too plain or too fat or had eyes too close together. Their hair was cut in boring styles, and none were in any way prettified. One or two slept beneath their pillows or obscured their faces with their arms, but they didn't have Amalicia's black hair, and their hands – always a giveaway – were too old.

He'd almost reached the end of the room when he saw her. She was sleeping on one of the bottom bunks, her head pillowed by her folded hands, mouth slightly open, face relaxed. Even without the elegant hairstyles and the expertly applied make-up he remembered her wearing, she was beautiful. Her long black hair had fallen across her face in strands; the curve of the lips, the tilt of the nose, the line of her jaw were just as they were in his memory. Frey felt a throb of regret at the sight of her, and smothered it quickly.

He knelt down, reached out and touched her shoulder. When she didn't respond, he shook her gently. She stirred and her eyes opened a little. They widened as she saw him; she took a breath to say his name. He quickly put his finger to his lips.

For a few moments, they just looked at each other. Her gaze flickered over his face, absorbing every detail. Then she pushed her blanket aside and slid out of bed. She was wearing a plain cotton nightdress that clung to her hips and the slope of her breasts. Frey felt a sudden urge to take her in his arms as he'd often done before, but before he could act on it she grabbed his hand and led him towards a door at the far end of the dormitory.

Outside was another corridor, as dark and spartan as the rest.

She checked the coast was clear and then pulled him down it. She took him through a door which led to a narrow set of stairs. At the top was an attic room, with a large skylight looking up at the full moon. It had a small writing desk in a corner, with several books piled atop it. A private study chamber, perhaps. Frey closed the door behind them.

'Amalicia . . .' he began, but then she roundhouse-kicked him in the face.

Fifteen

Amalicia's Revenge – Frey's Talent For Lying –
Plans Are Made – Invitations, Lewd and Otherwise

It wasn't so much the force of the kick but the surprise that sent Frey stumbling back. He tripped and fell to the ground, holding his face, shock in his eyes.

'What'd you do *that* f—'

'Two years!' she hissed, and her bare foot flashed out again and cracked him around the side of the head, knocking him dizzy. 'Two years I've waited for you to come!'

'Wait, I—' he began, but she booted him in the solar plexus and the breath was driven out of him.

'Did you know they teach us the fighting arts in this place? It's all about being in harmony with one's body, you see. Only when we're in harmony with ourselves can we find harmony with the Allsoul. Utter rubbish, of course, but it does have its benefits.' She punctuated the last word with another vicious kick in the ribs.

Frey gaped like a fish, trying to suck air into his lungs. Amalicia squatted down in front of him, pitiless.

'What happened to your promises, Darian? What happened to "Nothing can separate us"? What happened to "I'll never leave you"? What happened to "You're the only one"?'

Frey had a vague recollection of saying those things, and others like them. Women did tend to take what he said literally. They never seemed to understand that because they expected – no, *demanded* – romantic promises and expressions of affection, they forced a man to lie to them. The alternative was frosty silences, arguments, and, in the worst case, the woman would leave to find a man who *would* lie to her. So if he'd said some things he hadn't exactly meant, it was hardly his fault. She only had herself to blame.

'Your father . . .' he wheezed. 'Your father . . . would've had . . . me killed.'

'Well, we'll never know that for sure, will we? You turned tail and ran the moment you realised he'd found out about us!'

'Tactical withdrawal,' Frey gasped, raising himself up on one hand. 'I told you . . . I'd be back.'

She stood up and drove her heel hard into his thigh. His leg went dead.

'Will you stop bloody hitting me?' he cried.

'Two years!' Her voice had become a strangled squeak of rage. 'It took me two years to find you!'

'Oh, what rot!'

'It's the truth! You think your father advertised your whereabouts? You think it was easy finding you? He sent me away so once you'd gone you'd be hidden from me. I've spent two years trying to get my hands on Awakener records, mixing with the wrong kind of people, trying to stay one step ahead of your father and the . . . the *assassins* he set on my trail. You know he's hired the Shacklemores? The Shacklemores have been after me ever since the day I left, and every day I've been trying to make my way back to you.'

It was an outrageous lie, but Frey had a talent for lying. When he lied even *he* believed it. Just for that moment, just for the duration of his protest, he was convinced that he really *had* done right by her. The details were unimportant.

Besides, he knew for sure that Gallian Thade really did still want him dead. Thade had framed him. In such a light, it was rather heroic that he'd come back at all.

But Amalicia wasn't so easily swayed. 'Spit and blood, Darian, don't give me that! I sent you a letter telling you where I was! I sat here in this horrible place waiting for— '

'I never got any letter!'

'Yes, you did! The letter I sent you with the co-ordinates of this place.'

'I never got any co-ordinates! In your last letter you called me a coward and a liar, among other things. In fact, the last letter I got from you left me in very little doubt that you never wanted to see me again.'

Amalicia's hand went to her mouth. Suddenly, all the anger had gone out of her and she looked horrified.

'You didn't get it? The letter I sent after that one?'

Frey looked blank.

Amalicia turned away, an anxious hand flying to her forehead, pacing around the room. 'Oh, by the Allsoul! That silly cow of a handmaiden. She must have written the wrong address, or not paid the right postage, or—'

'Maybe it got lost in the post?' Frey suggested generously. 'Or someone at one of my pick-up points mislaid it. I had to stay on the move, you know.'

'You really didn't receive my letter?' Amalicia asked. Her voice had taken on a note of sympathy, and Frey knew he'd won. 'The one where I took back all those foul things I said?'

Frey struggled to his feet with difficulty. His jaw was swelling, and he could barely stand on his dead leg. Amalicia rushed over to help him.

'I really didn't,' he said.

'And you still came? You still searched for me all these years, even when you thought I hated you?'

'Well,' he said, then paused for a moment to roll his jaw before he delivered his final blow. 'I made a promise.'

Her eyes shimmered with tears in the moonlight. Wide, dark, trusting eyes. He'd always liked those eyes. They'd always seemed so innocent.

She flung herself at him, and hugged him close. He winced as his injuries twinged, then slid his arms around her slender back and buried his face in her hair. She smelled clean. Cleaner than he'd smelled for a long time, that was for certain. He found himself wondering how things might have been with her, if not for her father, if not for the unfortunate circumstances that drove them apart.

No. No regrets. If he opened that door he'd never be able to close it.

She pulled herself away a little, so she could look up at his face. She was desperately sorry now, ashamed for having tragically misjudged him. Grateful that he'd come for her in spite of everything.

'You're the only man I've ever been with, Darian,' she breathed. 'I haven't seen another since my father sent me to this awful place.'

Darian leaned closer, sensing the moment was right, but she drew back with a sharp intake of breath. 'Have you?' she asked. 'Have you been with anyone?'

He looked at her steadily, letting her feel how earnest he was. 'No,' he lied, firmly and with authority.

Amalicia sighed, and then kissed him hard, clutching at him with unpractised, youthful fury. She tore at his clothes, frantic. He struggled free of his sooty greatcoat as she fumbled at the laces of his shirt before finally tugging it off and throwing it away. He pulled her nightshirt up and over her head, and then swept her up and kissed her, gratified to realise that at least part of his fantasy about sex-starved young women in a hermitage was about to come true.

Afterwards, they lay together naked on Frey's coat, his skin prickling deliciously in the chilly night. He ran a finger along the line of her body while she stared at him adoringly. There was a dazed look in her eye, as if she was unable to quite believe that he was here with her again.

'I saw some Imperators on the way here,' he said.

She gasped. 'You didn't!'

'Right outside. A bunch of Sentinels carried a chest out to them, and they put it on their craft and took off. One of them looked right at me.'

'How frightening.'

'They were guarding that chest very closely.'

'Are you asking me if I have any idea what might have been inside?'

'In a roundabout way, yes.'

'I don't know, Darian. Some stuffy old scrolls, no doubt. Perhaps it was an original copy of the Cryptonomicon. They're terribly careful with those things.'

'Remind me what that is again?'

'The book of teachings. They wrote down all the insane little mutterings of King Andreal the Demented, and put them in that book.'

'Oh,' said Frey, losing interest immediately.

'We have to leave together,' she said. 'Tonight.'

'We can't.'

'It's the only way, Darian! The only way we can be together!'

'I want that, more than anything in the world. But there's something I haven't told you. Your father . . .'

'What did he do?' she snapped, jumping immediately to Frey's defence.

'You might not want to hear this.'

'Tell me!'

'Your father . . . well, he's . . . Something terrible happened. An aircraft blew up, and people died. Nobody knows who did it, but your father has pinned it on me. Me and my crew. If you were caught with me, they'd hang you. It's too dangerous. You're safer here.'

Amalicia looked at him suspiciously.

'I'm a lot of things, but I'm no cold-blooded killer!' he protested. 'The Archduke's son was on that craft, Amalicia. Your father arranged it, but half of Vardia is after *me*.'

'Hengar is dead?' she gaped.

'Yes! And your father is in on it.'

Amalicia shook her head angrily, eyes narrowing. 'That bastard. I hate that bastard!'

'You believe me, then?'

'Of course I believe you! Spit and blood, I know what he's capable of. Look at me! His only daughter, condemned to this

141

place because I went against his wishes just once! He doesn't have a heart. Money is all he cares about . . . money and that rotten Allsoul.' She glanced around guiltily, as if afraid she'd gone too far. Then, emboldened by Frey's presence, she went on. 'It's all stupid! I don't believe any of it! They say it's all about faith, but it's not, because I can do it and I don't even care about the Allsoul! It's brought me nothing but misery. Any idiot can study the texts and learn to read the signs. Anyone with half an education can tell the Mistresses what they want to hear. But there's nothing there, Darian! I don't feel anything! I'm just stuck here in this prison, and after two more years they'll put that awful tattoo on my forehead, and after that I'll be an Awakener for ever!' She cupped his bruised jaw with her hands and gazed desperately into his eyes. 'I can't let that happen. I'll die first. You have to get me out of here.'

'I will,' he said. 'I will. But first I have to get to your father.'

'Oh, Darian, no! He'll have you hanged for sure!'

'Gallian Thade is the only lead I've got. If I can find out why he killed Hengar . . . well, maybe I can do something about it.' Then, seeing Amalicia's expectant expression, he added, 'And then I'll come back for you, and we'll escape together as we planned.'

'But if you pin it on my father . . .' Amalicia said, with dawning realisation. 'Why, *he'll* be the one that hangs.'

Frey stumbled mentally. He'd forgotten about that. In clearing his name, Gallian would have to hang. He was asking a daughter to help send her own father to the gallows.

A cruel smile spread across Amalicia's face, the terrifying smile of a child about to stamp on an insect. Malice for the sake of malice. She saw her revenge, and it pleased her. Frey was surprised; he hadn't imagined her capable of such thoughts. Her time in the hermitage had made her bitter, it seemed.

'If he hangs,' she said slowly, 'that makes *me* head of the family. And no one can keep me here when I'm mistress of the Thades.'

'I hadn't even considered that,' Frey said, truthfully. 'I was so wrapped up in the idea of rescuing you . . . well, it had never occurred to me that, if your father died . . .'

'Oh, Darian, it's brilliant!' she said, eyes shining. She threw one leg over his thigh and pressed herself to him eagerly. Frey's mind began to wander from his machinations and back to baser thoughts. 'Kill him! Let the bastard hang! And then I'll be free, and we can be together, and we won't have to run from anyone! We'll marry, and damn what anyone says!'

Frey's ardour dampened at the mention of marriage. *But why?* he asked himself. *Why not this one? She's richer than shit and foxy to boot! Not to mention she's almost a decade younger than you and she thinks the sun rises and sets in your trousers. Since you can't make fifty thousand ducats any other way, why not marry them?*

But however good the reasons, Frey couldn't deny the life-sucking sense of oblivion that overtook him whenever he heard the M-word.

'I daren't even hope for that yet,' he said. 'Things are so dangerous right now . . . simply to survive would be . . . maybe, just maybe, I can win out of this. And then you'll be free, and we can be together.'

Can, he mentally added. *Not will*.

'What can I do?' she asked, missing the fact that Frey had deftly evaded any promise of marriage. She'd heard what she wanted to hear. Frey noted that the women in his life had a tendency to do that.

'Can you think of any reason why your father would want Hengar dead? How would it profit him?'

She lay on her back and looked up at the ceiling. Frey admired her, half-listening as she spoke. 'Well, he's very close to the Awakeners, you know that. But the Awakeners don't have any-thing against Hengar. It's the Archduchess they hate, and the Archduke by association.'

'Why?'

'Because Eloithe is a big critic of the Awakeners. She doesn't believe in the Allsoul. She says they're just a business empire that trades in superstition. And she's obviously inspired the Archduke, since he's started making all kinds of moves to diminish their power. But none of that's anything to do with Hengar.' She thought for a moment, then said, 'You know what I think? I don't think my father's behind this at all.'

'Amalicia, there's no doubt. I spoke to a—'

'No, no, I mean . . . We're landowners, Darian. We make our money from tenants. There's no reason to murder the son of the Archduke.' She sat up suddenly, her face taut with certainty. 'I know him, Darian, he wouldn't come up with something like this. Someone else is behind it.'

'You think there's someone else?'

'I'd bet on it.'

'Well . . . who?'

'That I don't know. I've been away a long time, in case you'd forgotten. It's hard to keep up with my father's business dealings when I've been locked in this prison for two years.'

Her tone grew harsher as she spoke, and Frey – fearing another beating – placated her hurriedly. 'It's okay, it's okay. I'll look into it. I just have to find a way to get close to him.'

'Well, there's the Winter Ball coming up,' she suggested.

'The Winter Ball?'

'You know! The ball! The one my father has every year at our estate on the Feldspar Islands.'

'Oh, the ball!' Frey said, though he'd no idea what she was talking about. Presumably they'd discussed it, although he was reasonably sure he'd never been to one.

'My father always does business there. All the important people come to it. If someone put him up to this whole business of murder, I'm sure you'd find them there. And you'd be well hidden among all the people. It's quite the event of the season, you know!'

'Can you get me in?'

She jumped up and went to the writing desk, drew out a pen and paper and began to scribble. Frey lay on his side, idly studying the curve of her back, the bumps of her spine.

'There are still people in the family who don't agree with what father did. This is a letter of introduction. You can take it to my second cousin – he'll do the rest.'

'I need two invitations.'

Her shoulders tensed and she stopped writing.

'Neither are for me,' he assured her. 'I won't be going. Don't fancy meeting your father again. And you know I'm not very well trained in etiquette. But I do have a friend who is. I'll need his help.'

'And the other?'

'Well, you have to take a lady to these things, don't you? Turning up without a date looks a bit odd.'

'And I suppose you happen to know one?'

'She's my navigator, Amalicia,' said Frey. He leaned over and kissed her between the shoulder blades. 'Just my navigator. And it won't be me that's taking her.'

'Alright,' she said. 'Two invitations.' She resumed writing, then signed with a flourish and laid the letter on top of his piled-up clothes.

Frey began getting to his feet. 'Thank you,' he said. 'I'll get you out of here. I promise.'

'Where do you think you're going?'

Frey looked towards the door of the attic. 'Well, I'm technically not supposed to be here, so I should really be gone before everyone wakes up.'

Amalicia pulled him back down again. 'It's not even close to dawn,' she said. 'I've had nobody to lie with for two years, Darian. We still have some catching up to do.'

Sixteen

*A Triumphant Return – Frey Takes
On New Crew – Silo's Warning*

It was midday by the time Frey made it back to the grassy valley where the *Ketty Jay* waited. There was a cold breeze, but the sun warmed the skin pleasantly, and most of the crew were outside. Harkins was tinkering with the Firecrow; Jez was reading a book she'd picked up in Aulenfay; Malvery was lying on his back, basking. Silo was nowhere to be seen. Frey presumed he was inside, engaged in one of his endless attempts to modify and improve the *Ketty Jay*'s engine.

Frey strolled into their midst, whistling merrily. Pinn – who was lying propped up against the wheel strut of his Skylance – lifted the wet towel off his forehead and gave an agonised groan. He was still wearing his Awakener garb, although the Cipher he'd painted on his head was now just a red smear.

'I see you managed to keep yourself entertained while I was gone,' Frey said. 'Heavy night?'

Pinn groaned again and put the towel back on his forehead.

'Mission accomplished, Cap'n?' Jez called, looking up from her book. 'What happened to your face?'

Frey touched fingertips to his bruised jaw, probing the skin delicately. 'Little misunderstanding, that's all,' he said. Jez ran her eye over his shabby, soot-covered clothes and let the issue drop.

Bess was sitting on the grass, her short, stumpy legs sticking out in front of her, like some vast and grotesque mechanical infant. Crake was cleaning her with a bucket and a rag. She was making a soft, eerie cooing noise, like wind through distant trees. Crake said it meant she was happy, rather like the purring of a cat, but it unsettled Frey to hear the voice of the daemon that inhabited that massive armoured shell.

'You look chipper today,' Crake observed.

Malvery sat up, took off his round, green-lensed glasses and peered at Frey. 'Yes, he has a definite glow about him, despite the battle damage. I'd say he had a very happy reunion with someone. That's my professional opinion.'

'A gentleman never tells,' said Frey, with a broad grin that was as good as a confession.

'I'm very pleased for you,' said Crake, disapprovingly.

'How did your new toys work out?' Frey enquired.

Crake brightened. 'I think I can do quite a lot with them. A daemonist needs a sanctum, really, but some processes are more portable than others. I won't be fooling around with anything too dangerous, that's for sure, but I can still do beginner's stuff.'

'What's beginner's stuff? Stuff like my cutlass?'

Crake choked in amazement and almost flung down his rag. 'Your cutlass,' he said indignantly, 'is a work of bloody art that took me years of study to accomplish and almost –'

He stopped as he caught the look of wicked amusement on Frey's face. 'Oh,' he said. 'I see. You caught me. Very droll.'

Frey walked over and slapped him on the shoulder. 'No, seriously, I'm interested. What can you do?'

'Well, for example . . .' He drew out two small silver earcuffs from his pocket. 'Take one of these and put it on your ear.'

Frey fixed it to his ear. Crake did the same with the other. They looked like any other innocuous ornament. Bess stirred restlessly, her huge bulk rustling and clanking as she moved. Crake patted her humped back.

'Don't worry, Bess. We're not finished yet. I'll clean the rest in a moment,' he assured her. The golem, mollified, settled down to wait.

'Now what?' asked Frey.

'Go over there,' said Crake, pointing. 'And ask me a question. Just talk normally, don't raise your voice.'

Frey shrugged and did as he was told. He walked fifty yards and then stopped. Facing away from Crake, he said quietly, 'So what exactly are you doing on the *Ketty Jay*?'

'I gave you my cutlass on the condition that you'd never ask me that,' Crake replied, close enough to his ear so that Frey jumped and looked around. It was as if the daemonist was standing right next to him.

'That's incredible!' Frey exclaimed. 'Is that really you? I can hear your voice right in my ear!'

'The range could be better,' said Crake modestly. 'But it's quite a simple trick to thrall two daemons at the same resonance. They're the most rudimentary type; stupid things, really. Little sparks of awareness, not even as smart as an animal. But they can be very useful if put to a task.'

'I'll say!'

'I was thinking, if I can whip up some better versions, that you could use them to communicate with your pilots or something. Better than that electroheliograph thing you have.'

'That's a damn good idea, Crake,' he said. 'Damn good idea.'

'Anyway, better take it off. These things will tire you out if you wear them too long. Daemons have a way of sucking the energy out of you.'

'My cutlass doesn't,' Frey replied.

He heard the slight hesitation. *My* cutlass, Crake was undoubtedly thinking.

'One of many reasons it's such a work of art,' he said.

Frey unclipped the earcuff and returned to Crake, who had resumed scrubbing the golem. 'I'm impressed,' he said, handing it back. 'You want to go to a party?'

'Excuse me?'

'A ball, actually. Formal ball, held by Gallian Thade.'

'The Winter Ball at Scorchwood Heights?'

'Ummm . . . yes?' Frey replied uncertainly.

'You have invitations?'

Frey brandished the letter from Amalicia. 'I will have soon. I was thinking you might go, and take Jez with you.'

Crake looked at him, searching for a sign of mockery.

'I mean it,' he said. 'I could really use your help, Crake. Thade will be there, and if he's working with someone else, it's our best chance of finding out what he's up to.'

Crake was still watching him narrowly, indecision in his eyes.

'Look,' said Frey. 'I know I have no right to ask. You're a passenger. That's what you signed on for. You don't owe me anything.' He shrugged. 'But, I mean, you and Bess . . .'

Bess shifted at the sound of her name, a quizzical coo coming from deep within her. Crake patted her back.

Frey coughed into his fist, looked away into the distance, and scratched his thigh. He was never very good with honesty. 'You and Bess, the both of you saved our lives back in Marklin's Reach. I've kind of got to thinking that, well . . .' He shrugged again. Crake just kept on looking at him. The daemonist wasn't making it easy. 'What I'm saying – badly – is that I've started to think of you more as part of the crew, instead of just dead weight. I'm saying, well . . . look, I don't know what business you're really on, or why you took up with me in the first place, but it's getting to be pretty bloody handy having the two of you around. Especially if you're gonna start making more little trinkets like those ear things.'

'That's very kind of you, Frey,' said Crake. 'Are you offering me a job?'

Frey hadn't really thought about that. He just knew that he needed Crake to help him out. 'Would you take one if I offered it?' he heard himself saying. 'Part of the crew? Just till . . . well, until we get this whole mess sorted out. Then you could decide.'

'Do I get my cutlass back?'

'No!' Frey said quickly. 'But I'll cut you in on a share of what we make.'

'We don't seem to *make* a great deal of anything.'

Frey made a face, conceding the point.

'What would I have to do in return?' Crake asked. He returned to scrubbing Bess's massive back. A deep, echoing groan of pleasure came from the golem's depths.

'Just . . . well, stick around. Help us out.'

'I thought I was doing that already.'

'You are! I mean . . .' Frey was getting frustrated. He was a supremely eloquent liar, but he struggled when he had to talk about things that he actually felt. It made him vulnerable, and that made him angry at himself. 'I mean, you and Bess could just up and walk, right? It's like you said back in Yortland: they'd never come looking for you. It's me they're after. And I'm sure you've other business you want to be getting on with, something to do with all that daemonism stuff you picked up.'

'So what you're saying is that you'd like us to stay around?' Crake prompted.

'Yes.'

'And that you . . . well, that you *need* us.'

Frey didn't like the triumphant tone creeping into Crake's voice. 'Yes,' he said warily.

'And what are you going to do next time someone puts a gun to my head and spins the barrel?'

Frey gritted his teeth. 'Give them the ignition codes to the *Ketty Jay*,' he said, glaring malevolently at the grass between his feet. 'Probably.'

Crake grinned and gave Bess a quick buff on the hump. 'You hear that, Bess? We're pirates now!' Bess sang happily, a ghostly, off-key nursery rhyme.

'So you'll go to the ball?' Frey asked.

'Alright,' he said. 'Yes, I'll go.'

Frey felt a flood of relief. He hadn't realised how much he'd been counting on Crake's co-operation until this moment. He was about to say something grateful-sounding when he was interrupted by a cry from further up the valley.

'Cap'n!'

It was Silo. The tall Murthian wasn't in the engine room after all, but running down the valley towards them with a haste that could only spell trouble. He was carrying a spyglass in his hand.

'Cap'n! Aircraft!' Silo cried, pointing. The others – with the exception of Pinn – scrambled to their feet or ran to look.

'I see it,' said Jez.

'Damn, you've got good eyes!' said Malvery. 'I don't see a thing!'

'Nor me!' added Crake.

Jez looked around guiltily. 'I mean, I can't make it out or anything, not really. Just saw a flash of light, that's all.'

Silo reached them and passed the spyglass to Frey. Frey put it to his eye.

'She coming . . . from the south . . .' he panted. 'Think she . . . heading for the . . . hermitage . . .'

'Then she'll pass over us?'

'Yuh-huh. See us for sure.'

Frey cast about with the spyglass, struggling to locate the incoming threat. It swung into view and steadied. Frey's mouth went dry.

She was a big craft. Long and wide across the deck, black and scarred, yet for all her ugliness she was sleek. A frigate, built more like an ocean vessel than an aircraft: a terrible armoured hulk bristling with weaponry. Her wings were little more than four stumpy protuberances: she was too massive to manoeuvre quickly. But what she lacked in speed, she more than made up for in firepower. This was a combat craft, a machine made for war with a crew of dozens.

Frey took the spyglass away from his eye.

'It's the *Delirium Trigger*,' he said.

Seventeen

Dracken Catches Up – Equalisers –
Jez Makes A Plan – Pinn's Defence – Lightning

The reaction among the crew was immediate. Frey had never seen them scramble into action so fast. He vainly wished he had half the authority that the *Delirium Trigger* apparently did.

'Everyone! Get to stations! We're airborne!' Frey yelled, even though Silo, Jez and Malvery were already bolting up the cargo ramp. Harkins had scampered into the cockpit of the Firecrow like a frightened spider, and Pinn was grumbling nauseously to himself as he set about getting himself into the Skylance.

'Crake! Get Bess inside and shut the ramp!' he ordered, as he raced aboard the *Ketty Jay*. He made his way to the cockpit with speed born of panic, flying up the steps from the cargo hold two at a time. He squeezed past Malvery, who was climbing into the autocannon cupola on the *Ketty Jay*'s back, and found Jez already at her post. He threw himself into his chair, punched in the ignition code, and opened up everything he could for an emergency lift.

How did she find me?

Harkins was in the air by the time the *Ketty Jay* began to rise, and Pinn took off a few moments later, still clad in his half-buttoned Awakener cassock and with a red smear across his forehead. There was a look of frantic bewilderment on his face, like someone rudely awakened from sleep to find their bed is on fire.

The *Ketty Jay* was facing the *Delirium Trigger* as she rose. The frigate was coming in fast. Now it was easily visible to the naked eye, and growing larger by the second. She couldn't fail to have spotted the craft lifting into the sky, directly in her path. The question was, would she recognise the *Ketty Jay* at this distance?

As if in answer, four black dots detached from her, and began to race ahead. Outflyers. Fighter craft.

'She's on to us!' Frey cried. He swung the craft around one hundred and eighty degrees, and hit the thrusters. The *Ketty Jay* bellowed as she accelerated to the limit of her abilities.

'Orders, Cap'n?' Jez asked.

'Get us out of here!'

'Can we outrun her?'

'The *Trigger*, yes. The outflyers are Norbury Equalisers. We can't outrun them.'

'Okay, I'm on it,' said Jez, digging through her charts with a loud rustling of paper.

'Heads up, everyone!' Malvery called from the cupola. 'Incoming!'

Frey wrenched the control stick and the *Ketty Jay* banked hard. A rapid salvo of distant booms rolled through the air, followed a moment later by a sound like the end of the world. The sky exploded all around them, a deafening, pounding chaos of shock and flame. The *Ketty Jay* was shaken and thrown, flung about like a toy. Pipes shrieked and burst in the depths of the craft, spewing steam. Cracks split the glass of the dashboard dials. A low howl of metal sounded from somewhere in the guts of the craft.

And then suddenly the chaos was over, and somehow they were still flying, the majestic green canvas of the Highlands blurring beneath them.

'Ow,' said Frey weakly.

'You alright, Cap'n?' asked Jez, brushing her hair out of her eyes and gathering up her scattered charts.

'Bit my damn tongue,' Frey replied. His ears were whistling and everything sounded dim.

'They're firing again!' cried Malvery, who had a view of the *Delirium Trigger* from the blister on the *Ketty Jay*'s back.

'What kind of range do those guns *have*?' Frey murmured in

dismay, and sent the *Ketty Jay* into a hard dive. But there was no cataclysm this time. The explosions fell some way behind them, and the concussion was barely more than a sullen shove.

'Not enough, apparently,' said Jez.

'Malvery! Where are those fighters?' called Frey through the door of the cockpit.

'Catching us up!' the doctor replied.

'Don't fire till they're close enough to hit! We've not got much ammo for that cannon!'

'Right-o!'

He turned to his navigator. 'I need a plan, Jez.'

She was plotting frantically with a pair of compasses. 'This craft has Blackmore P-12s, right?'

'Uh?'

'The thrusters. P-12s.'

'Yeah.'

'Okay.' She looked up from her chart. 'I have an idea.'

Pinn's mouth tasted like decomposing mushrooms and his peripheral vision was a swarming haze. He felt like there wasn't a drop of moisture in his body and yet his bladder throbbed insistently. He was utterly detached from the world. Reality was somewhere else. He was cocooned in his own private suffering.

And yet, some faint part of him was alarmed to find that he was in the cockpit of his Skylance, racing over the Highlands, pursued by four fighter craft intent on shooting him down. That part was urging him to sharpen up pretty quickly and pay attention. Eventually, he began to listen to it.

With some difficulty, he craned around and looked over his shoulder. The enemy craft were close enough to make out now. He recognised the distinctive shape of Norbury Equalisers: their bulbous, rounded cockpits right up front; their straight, thick wings, cut off at the ends; their narrow, slightly arched bodies. Norburys were a pain in the arse. Speedy and highly manoeuvrable. They were like flies: annoyingly hard to swat. And when you got frustrated, you made mistakes, and that was when they took you out.

He could outrun them, for sure. He could outrun just about anything in his modified Skylance. But an outflyer's job wasn't to save his own neck. He had to protect the *Ketty Jay*. Besides, running was for pussies.

The *Ketty Jay* was to starboard. He saw her change tack, swinging towards the west, and he banked to match. The horizon became uneven as the edge of the Eastern Plateau came into view, a hundred kloms ahead of them. Beyond it, invisible, the land fell away in the steep, sheer cliffs and jagged, crushed peaks of the Hookhollows.

Pinn frowned. Where did they think they were going? They might be able to make it to the mountains, where there would be ravines and defiles to use as cover, but there was still no way the *Ketty Jay* could outmanoeuvre an Equaliser.

He glanced to port. The *Delirium Trigger* was safely out of the race, but the Equalisers were banking to intercept the *Ketty Jay* on her new course, and they were closing the gap even faster than before.

Minutes ticked by. The slow, excruciating minutes of the long-distance chase. Pinn's world shrank back to the pulsing of his hangover, the low roar of the thrusters, the shudder and tremble of the Skylance. But every time he looked around, the Equalisers were closer. One thing was clear: whatever the *Ketty Jay* was heading for, she wouldn't make it before the Equalisers reached her.

Then, in the far distance, he saw an indistinct fuzz in the air. Gradually the fuzz darkened, until there could be no question as to what it was. Just beyond the lip of the Eastern Plateau was a line of threatening clouds. The clear blue of the sky ended abruptly in a piled black bank of gathering thunderheads.

The *Ketty Jay* was running for the storm.

'How'd you know *that* was there, you clever bitch?' he murmured, out of grudging respect for Jez. He naturally assumed it wasn't the captain's doing.

He checked where the Equalisers were. Behind him now, but closer still, flying in tight formation. Organised. Disciplined. Soon they'd be within firing range.

He shook his head and spat into the footwell. 'I've had enough of this,' he snarled. He was bored with the chase and angry at his nagging headache. The fact that the enemy were flying in such neat formation inexplicably annoyed him. If someone didn't do something soon, those Equalisers would start taking shots at them, and Pinn was damned if he was going to present his tail to four sets of machine guns.

'Alright,' he said. 'Let's play.'

He broke away from the *Ketty Jay* in a high, curving loop. At its apex, he rolled the craft to bring him right-side up again. The pursuing fighters were below and ahead of him now. They'd seen the threat but were slow to react, unsure if he was fleeing or fighting. Nobody expected a single craft to take on four: it was suicidal.

But death was a concept that Pinn wasn't really smart enough to understand. He didn't have the imagination to envisage eternity. Oblivion was unfathomable. How could he be scared of something when he only had the vaguest notion of it? So he dived down towards the pursuing fighters with a whoop of joy, and opened up with his machine guns.

The Equalisers scattered as he plunged among them like a cat among birds. They banked and rolled and dived, darting out of his line of fire as he cut through the formation and out the other side. Lesser craft would have been tagged, but the Equalisers were just quick enough to evade him.

Pinn pulled the Skylance into a climb, rolling and banking as he did, making himself a difficult target. G-forces wrenched at him. His hangover throbbed in protest at the abuse, but the adrenaline was kicking in now, clearing away the cobwebs. He fought to keep track of the Equalisers as they wheeled through the sky. Three of them were reorganising, continuing their pursuit of the *Ketty Jay*. One had peeled off and was angling for a shot at Pinn.

One? *One?* Pinn was insulted. Ignoring the fighter that was trying to engage him, he flew towards the main formation. They'd streaked ahead, dismissing him. They thought they'd got too much of a head start while he was turning around. They thought he had no chance of catching them.

They were wrong.

Pinn hit the thrusters and left his pursuer aiming at empty sky. The Skylance howled gleefully as it accelerated, eating up the distance between Pinn and his targets. He came in from directly behind, growing in their blind spot. He was forced to fly straight to avoid notice, but he was acutely aware that by doing so he was allowing the fourth Equaliser to line up on his tail. He held steady for a dangerous moment, then loosed off a fusillade at the nearest plane.

Whether it was luck, instinct, or skill, the pilot spotted him an instant before he fired. The Equaliser banked hard and the bullets chipped across its flank and underwing, instead of hitting the tail assembly. Pinn cursed and rolled away just as the Equaliser on his tail sent a volley of tracer fire his way. The Skylance danced between the bullets and dived out of the line of fire.

Pinn jinked left and right, keeping his movements unpredictable. He twisted his neck round, trying to get a fix on his opponents. The most important factor in aerial combat was knowing where your enemies were. He kept up a frantic evasion pattern until he spotted two of the Equalisers dwindling in the distance, continuing their pursuit of the *Ketty Jay*. The plane he'd damaged was still in the air and still a threat, though it was trailing a thin line of smoke that made it easy to find. Burned by his sneak attack, that pilot had decided to deal with Pinn.

He felt better once he'd located the fourth Equaliser. He had two of them on his tail now. They respected him enough that they couldn't turn their backs on him. Now all he had to do was keep them busy awhile.

He launched into a new sequence of evasions, leading them away from the *Ketty Jay* as he corkscrewed and twisted and rolled. The Equalisers homed in on him from different angles, doing their best to trap him, but he could see their tactics and refused to play along. The one he'd damaged was limping slightly, a little slow and clumsy, and its pilot couldn't lock in with his companion. Their manoeuvres were pretty but came to nothing. Sporadic machine-gun fire chattered behind him, but it was more hopeful than effective.

I should just turn around and take these bastards out, thought Pinn. But then he caught sight of the *Delirium Trigger*, much larger than he remembered when he last looked. Their aerobatics had allowed the bigger craft to catch them up, and Pinn didn't fancy dealing with her guns on top of everything else.

The *Ketty Jay* was barely visible in the distance. He'd taken two of the Equalisers out of the chase, and he'd delayed the other two and bought the *Ketty Jay* time to reach the storm. He'd done his part.

He reached over and grabbed a lever underneath the dash. The Skylance had been built as a racer long before he'd modified it for combat, and it still had a racer's secret weapon installed. He levelled up and aimed for the horizon.

'Bye bye, shit-garglers!' he yelled, then rammed the Skylance to full throttle and engaged the afterburners. The Skylance rocketed forward, slamming him back in his seat with enough force to press his chubby cheeks flat against his face. His pursuers could only watch, hopelessly outpaced, as the Skylance dwindled into the distance, carrying its whooping pilot with it.

'Two still with us!' called Malvery from his cupola. 'Pinn's drawn off the others.'

Frey grinned. 'I'd kiss that kid if he wasn't so hideous and stupid.' He looked about. 'Where's Harkins?'

Jez pointed up through the windglass to the Firecrow hanging high on their starboard side.

'Tell him to engage,' he said, then shifted in his seat and hunched forward over the controls. 'Keep 'em off my tail.'

Jez reached over to the electroheliograph and tapped a rapid code. The lamp on the *Ketty Jay*'s back flashed the sequence. Harkins gave a wing-waggle and broke away.

The winds were rising as the storm clouds rolled ever closer. Frey's admiration for Jez had grown a great deal in the moment he saw those thunderheads appear on the horizon. She'd been right on the money. Again. It was an unfamiliar feeling, having someone reliable on his crew. He was rather liking it.

'Wind is from the northwest today, and it's sunny,' she'd said. 'Warm air rising off the mountains up the side of the plateau, cooled by the airstream coming down from the arctic. This time of the day, this kind of weather, you're gonna get a storm there.'

The kind of storm a small fighter craft couldn't handle. But a bigger one, driven by the notoriously robust Blackmore P-12 thrusters – that kind of craft could make it through.

Crake stuck his head round the door. 'Anything I can do?'

'Where've you been?'

'Bess was upset. All the explosions, you see.'

'We'll try and keep it down,' Frey replied dryly. 'Get me a damage report from Silo.'

Crake ran off down the corridor to comply. Frey returned his attention to the storm. The *Ketty Jay* rocked and shivered as the winds began to play around her. Machine-gun fire sounded from behind them.

'There goes Harkins,' Frey said. 'Malvery! What's going on back there?'

'They dodged round him! Still coming!'

'Well make sure you—' he began, but was drowned out by the heavy thudding of the autocannon as Malvery opened up on their pursuers.

Frey cursed under his breath and swung the *Ketty Jay* to starboard. He heard the chatter of machine guns, and a spray of tracer fire passed under them and soared away towards the clouds.

'Will you hold still?' Malvery bellowed. 'I ain't gonna hit anything if you keep jigging around like that!'

'I'm jigging around so they don't hit *us!*' Frey shouted back, then banked again, dived, and yawed to port. The *Ketty Jay* was a sizeable target, but she could move faster than her bulk suggested.

Her pursuers were still at the limit of their range, but they were catching fast.

'You know the worst thing about flying an aircraft like this?' he asked Jez. 'You can't see behind you. I'm just *guessing* where those sons of bitches are while they take pot-shots at my arse. I wish, just once, someone would have the guts to take us on from the front so I could shoot 'em.'

'Sounds like it wouldn't be a very wise tactic, Cap'n,' she replied. 'But we can hope.'

The storm was filling the sky now. They were flying in low, and the thunderheads had swallowed the sun. The cockpit darkened, and the air got choppier still. The *Ketty Jay* began to rattle around, buffeted this way and that.

'Let's see 'em aim straight in *this*,' he murmured. 'Signal Harkins. Tell him to get out of here. He knows the rendezvous.'

Jez complied, tapping the electroheliograph.

A few moments later, Malvery yelled: 'Hey! Harkins is turning tail! That yellow toad was supposed to be—'

'My orders!' Frey yelled back. 'He can't follow us into the storm. It's up to you now.'

'You're giving orders now?' Malvery sounded surprised. 'Blimey.' Then the autocannon began thumping again in clipped bursts.

Crake appeared at the door. 'Silo says the engines have taken a hit and they're overheating, but it's nothing too serious. Other than that there's only minor structural—'

There was a shattering din as a salvo of bullets punched into the *Ketty Jay*'s hull from behind. She yawed crazily, hit a pressure pocket in the storm and plunged fifteen metres, fast enough to lift Crake off the ground and slam him to the floor again. The engines groaned and squealed, reached a distressing crescendo, then slowly returned to their usual tone.

Crake pulled himself up from the floor, wiping blood from a split lip. 'I'll get a damage report from Silo, shall I?' he enquired.

'Don't bother,' said Frey. 'Just hang on to something.'

Crake clutched at the metal jamb of the cockpit door as the

Ketty Jay began to shake violently. Frey dumped some of the aerium gas from the tanks to add weight and stability to the craft, letting the thrusters take the strain instead. Getting the balance right was crucial. A craft like the *Ketty Jay*, unlike its outflyers, wasn't aerodynamic enough to fly without the aid of its lighter-than-air ballast. It couldn't produce enough lift to maintain its bulk.

The thunderheads rushed towards them, inky billows flashing with angry lightning. Wind and pressure differentials began to shove them this way and that. The world outside darkened rapidly as they hit the outer edge of the clouds. A blast of blinding light, terrifyingly close at hand, made Crake cower. Jez glanced over at him and gave him a sympathetic smile. He firmed his resolve and stood straighter.

'Doc! Are they still with us?' Frey howled over the rising wail of the wind. There was no reply. 'Doc!'

'What?' Malvery cried back irritably.

'Are they still with us?'

A long pause.

'*Doc!*' Frey screamed.

'*I'm bloody looking!*' Malvery roared back. '*It's dark out there!*' Then, a moment later, he boomed a triumphant laugh. 'They're turning tail, Cap'n! Running off home!'

Jez beamed in relief.

The *Ketty Jay* was pushed from beneath by a pressure swell and veered steeply, dislodging Crake's grip on the jamb and sending him careering into a wall. It was black as night outside. Frey flicked on the headlights, but that only lit up the impenetrable murk that had closed in on them.

'I can't help noticing we're still in the storm,' said Crake.

Jez supplied the answer, since Frey was concentrating on flying. 'We need to put some distance between them and us. Otherwise they might just pick up the chase again when we emerge.'

'And what happens if some of that lightning hits us?' he asked, not really wanting to know the answer.

'We'll probably explode,' Frey said. Crake went grey. Jez

opened her mouth to say something but at that moment the craft was shaken again. Frey could hear things clattering about in the mess, and something cracked and burst noisily out in the corridor. Water began to spray everywhere.

'Is this tub even going to hold together?' Crake demanded.

'She'll hold,' Frey murmured. 'And if you call her a tub again, I'll kick you out right now, and you and your metal friend can fly home.'

'What, and miss my chance to attend Gallian Thade's Winter Ball? Just try and—'

There was a stunning flash of light and everything went black. All lights, inside and out, were suddenly extinguished. There was a brief sensation of unreality, as if time itself had been stunned. The air snapped and crawled with wild energy. For long seconds, no one spoke. An uncanny peace blanketed the chaos. The engines droned steadily, pushing them through the storm. The darkness was utter.

Then the lights flickered on again, and the *Ketty Jay* began to rattle once more.

'What was that?' Crake whispered.

'Lightning,' said Jez.

'You said we'd explode!' Crake accused the captain.

Frey only grinned. 'Time to get out of here,' he said. He hauled back on the control stick and the *Ketty Jay* began to climb.

The ascent through the clouds was rough, but the turbulence was nothing the *Ketty Jay* couldn't handle. She'd seen worse than this in her time. Though she was jostled and battered and harassed every klom of the way, Frey fought with her against the storm, and the two of them knew each other well. Frey didn't realise it, but a fierce smile was plastered across his face as he flew. *This* was what being a freebooter was all about. *This* was how it felt to be a lord of the skies. Outwitting your enemies, snatching victory from defeat. Braving the storm.

Then the clouds ended, and the *Ketty Jay* soared free. The dark carpet of thunderheads was spread out below them as far as they could see, obscuring everything beneath. Above them was only an endless crystalline blue and the dazzle of the sun.

'Malvery?' Frey called.

'All clear, Cap'n!' came the reply.

Frey looked over his shoulder at Jez and Crake, who were glowing with excitement and relief.

'Good job, everyone,' he said. Then he slumped back in his seat with a sigh. 'Good job.'

Eighteen

Civilisation – A Musical Interlude – Fredger
Cordwain – Vexford Swoops In – Morcutt The Boor

The night was warm, and the air shrilled with the song of insects. Lush plants hissed and rustled in the tropical breeze. Electric lamps, hidden in the foliage, lit up an ancient stone path that wound up the hill, towards the lights and the distant music. Northern Vardia might have been frozen solid, but here in the Feldspar Islands winter never came.

Crake and Jez disembarked arm in arm from the luxurious passenger craft that had shuttled them from the mainland. Crake paused to adjust the cuffs of his rented jacket, then smiled at his companion to indicate his readiness. Jez tried not to look ill at ease in her clinging black dress as they made their way down from the aircraft. They were greeted at the bottom of the stairs by a manservant, who politely asked for their invitations. Crake handed them over and introduced himself as Damen Morcutt, of the Marduk Morcutts, whom he'd recently made up.

'And this is Miss Bethinda Flay,' he said, raising Jez's hand so the manservant might bob and kiss it. The manservant looked at Crake expectantly for elaboration, but Crake gave him a conspiratorial wink and said, 'She's rather new to this game. Be gentle with her, eh?'

'I quite understand, sir,' said the manservant. 'Madam, you are most welcome here.'

Jez curtsied uncertainly, and then the two of them went walking up the path towards the stately manor at the top of the hill.

'Small steps,' murmured Crake out of the corner of his mouth. 'Don't stride. Remember you're a lady.'

'I thought we agreed that I was a craftbuilder's daughter,' she replied.

'You're supposed to be a craftbuilder's daughter trying to be a lady.'

'I *am* a craftbuilder's daughter trying to be a lady!'

'That's why the disguise is flawless.'

Crake had spent the last week coaching Jez in the basics of etiquette. She was a fast learner, but a crash course in manners would never convince anyone that she was part of the aristocracy. In the end, Crake had decided that the best lies were those closest to the truth. She'd pose as a craftbuilder's daughter – a life she knew very well. He'd play the indolent son of a wealthy family who had fallen in love with a low-born woman and was determined to make her his bride.

'That way, they'll think your mistakes are naïve rather than rude,' he told her. 'Besides, they'll feel sorry for you. They've seen it all before a dozen times, this breathless romance between a young aristocrat and a commoner. They know full well that as soon as it gets serious, Mother will step in and you'll be dumped. Nobody's going to waste a good marriage opportunity on a craftbuilder's daughter.'

'What a charming lot you are,' Jez observed.

'It's an ugly business,' Crake agreed.

It *was* an ugly business, but it was a business Crake had known all his life, and as he made his way along the winding path through the restless trees towards Scorchwood Heights, he felt an aching sorrow take him. The feel of fine clothes on his skin, the sound of delicate music, the cultured hubbub of conversation that drifted to them on the warm breeze – these were the familiar things of his old life, and they welcomed him back like a lover.

Seven months ago, he'd taken all of this for granted and found it shallow and tiresome. Having an allowance great enough to keep him in moderate luxury had permitted him to be disdainful about the society that provided it.

But now he'd tasted life on the run: hunted, deprived of comfort and society. He'd been trapped on a craft with people who mocked his accent and maligned his sexuality. He'd stared death in the face and been witness to a shameful act of mass-murder.

The world he'd known was for ever lost to him now. It hurt to be reminded of that.

'Do I look okay?' Jez fretted, smoothing her dress and patting at her elaborately styled hair.

'Don't do that! You look very pretty.'

Jez made a derisive rasp.

'That ruins the illusion somewhat,' said Crake, scowling. 'Now listen to what I tell you, Miss Bethinda Flay. Beauty is all about confidence. You actually clean up rather well when you change out of your overalls and put on a little make-up. All you need to do is believe it, and you'll be the equal of anyone here.' He stroked his beard thoughtfully. 'Besides, the competition will be weak. Most of the women in this party have been inbred to the point of complete genetic collapse, and the others are more than half horse.'

Jez snorted in surprise and then burst out laughing. After a moment, she caught herself and restrained her laughter to a more feminine chuckle.

'How kind of you to say so, sir,' she managed in an exaggerat- edly posh accent. She wobbled on the verge of cracking up, then swallowed and continued. 'May I compliment you on the sharpness of your wit tonight.'

'And may I say how radiant you look in the lamplight,' he said, kissing her hand.

'You may. Oh, you may!' swooned Jez, then she hugged herself to his arm and followed him jauntily up the path to the manor. She was beginning to have fun.

Scorchwood Heights was set amid a grove of palm trees, its broad porticoed face looking out over a wide lawn and garden. It was a place of wide spaces, white walls, smooth pillars and marble floors. The shutters were thrown open and the sound of mournful string instruments and Thacian pipes wafted out into the night.

The lawn was crowded with knots of society's finest. The men dressed stiffly, many in Navy uniform. Others wore uniform of another type: the single-breasted jackets and straight trousers that were the fashion of the moment. They laughed and argued, loudly discussing politics and business. Some of them even knew something about the subject. The women showed off in daring hats and flowing dresses, fanning themselves and leaning close to criticise the clothes of passers-by.

Crake felt Jez's good humour falter at the sight of so many people, and he gave her a reassuring smile. 'Now, Miss Flay. Don't let them intimidate you.'

'You sure you couldn't have just come on your own?'

'That's just not how it's done,' he said. 'Deep breath. Here we go.'

Flagged paths meandered round pools and fountains towards the porch. Crake led them through the garden, stopping to take two glasses of wine from a passing waiter. He offered one to Jez.

'I don't drink,' she said.

'That doesn't matter. Just hold it. Gives you something to do with your right hand.'

It was a little cooler inside the manor. The high-ceilinged rooms with their white plastered walls sucked some of the heat out of the night, and the open windows let the breeze through. Servants fanned the air. The aristocrats had gathered in here, too, bunching into corners or lurking near the canapés, moving in swirls and eddies from group to group.

'Remember, we're looking for Gallian Thade,' Crake murmured. 'I'll point him out when I see him.'

'And then what?'

'And then we'll see what we can find out.'

A handsome young man with carefully parted blond hair approached them with a friendly smile. 'Hello there. I don't think we've met,' he said, offering a hand. He introduced himself as Barger Uddle, of the renowned family of sprocket manufacturers. 'You know! Uddle Sprockets! Half the craft in the sky run on our sprockets.'

'Damen Morcutt, of the Marduk Morcutts,' said Crake,

shaking his hand vigorously. 'And this charming creature is Miss Bethinda Flay.'

'My father used to use your sprockets all the time,' she said. 'He was a craftbuilder. Swore by them.'

'Oh, how delightful!' Barger exclaimed. 'Come, come, I must introduce you to the others. Can't have you standing around like wet fish.'

Crake let this puzzling metaphor pass, and soon they were absorbed into a crowd of a dozen young men and women, all excitedly discussing the prospect of making ever more money in the future.

'It's only a matter of time before the Coalition lifts the embargo on aerium exports to Samarla, and then the money will come rolling in. It's all about who's ready to take advantage.'

'Do you think so? I think we'll find that the Sammies don't even need it any more. Why do you think the last war ended so suddenly?'

'Nobody knows why they called the truce. The Allsoul alone knows what goes on inside that country of theirs.'

'Pffft! It was aerium, pure and simple. They fought two wars because they didn't have any in their own country and they couldn't stand buying it from us. Now they've found some. Bet you anything.'

'We shouldn't even be trading with those savages. We should have gone in there and flattened them when we had the chance. Mark my words, this is only a lull. They're building a fleet big enough to squash us like insects. There'll be a third Aerium War, and we won't win this one. New Vardia, that's where I'm going. New Vardia and Jagos.'

'The frontier. That's where the money is, alright. Get right in on the ground floor. But I think I'd miss the society. I'd just shrivel out there.'

'Oh, you've no sense of adventure!'

After a while, Crake and Jez excused themselves and made their way into an enormous drawing room. Here was the source of the music they'd been hearing ever since they arrived. A quintet of

Thacian women played delicate folk songs from their homeland. They were slender, olive-skinned, black-haired, and even the least attractive among them could still be called pretty. They wore coloured silks and held exotic, exquisitely made instruments of wood and brass.

'Listen,' said Crake, laying a hand on Jez's shoulder.

'Listen to what?'

'Just listen,' he said, and closed his eyes.

In the field of the arts – as in science, philosophy, culture and just about everything else – Thacians were the leaders in the known world. Vardic aristocracy aspired to the heights of Thacian achievement, but usually all they could manage were clumsy imitations. To hear real Thacian players was a treat, which came at a hefty price – but then Gallian Thade wasn't a man known to be short of money. Crake allowed himself to be swept away in the tinkling arpeggios, the haunting moan of the pipes, the counterpoint rhythms.

This was what he missed. The casual elegance of music and literature. To be surrounded by wonderful paintings and sculpture, perfect gardens and complicated wines. The upper classes insulated themselves against the world outside, padding themselves with beauty. Without that protection, things became ugly and raw.

He wished, more than anything, that he could go back. Back to how it was before everything went bad. Before . . .

'Excuse me.'

He opened his eyes, irritated at the interruption. The man standing before him was taller than he was, broad-shouldered and bull-necked. He was fat, but not flabby, bald-headed, and sported a long, thin moustache and expensively cut clothes.

'Sorry to spoil your enjoyment of the music, sir,' he said. 'I just had to introduce myself. Fredger Cordwain is my name.'

'Damen Morcutt. And this is Miss Bethinda Flay.' Jez curtsied on cue, and Cordwain kissed her hand.

'Charmed. I must ask you, sir, have we met? Your face seems very familiar to me, very familiar indeed, but I can't place it.'

Crake felt a small chill. *Did* he know this person? He'd been quite confident that nobody who knew his face would be here tonight. His crime had been kept out of the press – nobody wanted a scandal – and the Winter Ball was simply too exclusive for the circles Crake had moved in. Invitations were almost impossible to secure.

'I'm terribly sorry,' he said. 'I can't quite recall.'

'Perhaps we met on business? At a party? May I ask what it is you do?'

'You may well ask, but I'm not sure I could answer!' Crake brayed, falling into his role. 'I'm sort of in between occupations at the moment. Father wants me to go into law, but my mother is obsessed with the idea that I should be a politician. Neither of them appeals much to me. I just want to be with my sweetheart.' He smiled at Jez, who smiled back dreamily, bedazzled by her rich boyfriend. 'May I ask what it is that *you* do?'

'I work for the Shacklemore Agency.'

It took all of Crake's control to keep his expression steady. The news was like a punch in the gut. Suddenly, he was certain that Cordwain was watching for a reaction from him, and he was determined to give none.

'And what does the Shacklemore Agency do?' asked Jez innocently, though she must have already known. Crake silently thanked her for the distraction.

Cordwain favoured her with a patronising smile. 'Well, Miss, we look after the interests of our clients. We work for some very important people. My job is to deal with those people, keep things running smooth.'

'Hired guns and bounty hunters, that's what they are,' sniffed Crake. He was quick on his feet in social situations, and he'd already decided on the best tactic for getting away as fast as possible. 'I must say, I find it very distasteful.'

'Damen! Don't be rude!' Jez said, appalled.

'It's alright, Miss,' said Cordwain, with an unmistakable hostility in his gaze. 'There's some that don't understand the value of the work we do. The law-abiding man has nothing to fear from us.'

'I say, sir, do you dare to imply something?' Crake bristled, raising his voice. People nearby turned and looked. Cordwain noticed the attention their conversation had drawn.

'Not a thing, sir,' he said coldly. 'I apologise for disturbing you.' He bowed quickly to Jez and walked away. The people around them resumed their conversations, glancing over occasionally in the hope of further drama.

Crake felt panicked. Had there been a warning in the man's tone? Had he been recognised? But then, what was the point in confronting him? Was it just monstrous bad luck that he'd run into a Shacklemore here?

The warm sensation of being surrounded by familiar things had faded now. He felt paranoid and uneasy. He wanted to get out of here as soon as possible.

Jez was studying him closely. She was an observant sort, and he had no doubt that she knew something was up. But she kept her questions to herself.

'Let's go find Gallian Thade, hmm?'

Crake found him shortly afterwards, on the other side of the room. He was a tall, severe man with a hawk nose and a deeply lined, narrow face. For all his years, his pointed beard and black hair had not a trace of grey. His eyes were sharp and moved rapidly about as he spoke, like an animal restlessly scanning for danger.

'That's him,' said Crake, admiring their host's stiff, brocaded jacket.

Thade was in conversation with several men, all of them stern and serious-looking. Some of them were smoking cigars and drinking brandy.

'Who's that with him?' murmured Jez, looking at the man next to Thade.

Crake studied Thade's companion with interest. 'That's Duke Grephen of Lapin.'

Crake knew him from the broadsheets. As ruler of one of the

Nine Duchies that formed Vardia, he was one of the most influential people in the land. Only the Archduke held more political power than the Dukes.

Grephen was a dour-looking man with a squarish build and a sallow face. His eyes were deeply sunken and ringed with dark circles, making him look faintly ill. His short blond hair was limp and damp with sweat. Though he was thirty-five, and he wore a fine uniform with the Lapin coat of arms on its breast, he looked like a pudgy boy playing at being a soldier.

Despite his less than formidable appearance, the others treated Grephen with the greatest respect. He didn't speak often, and never smiled, but when he had something to offer, his companions listened intently.

'Bet you never thought you'd see *him* when you came here tonight,' said a voice to their right. They looked over to see a gaunt man with white hair and bushy eyebrows, flushed from alcohol and the heat. He was wearing a Navy uniform, his buttons and boots polished to a high shine.

'Why, no, I hadn't imagined I would,' said Jez.

'Air Marshal Barnery Vexford,' he said, taking her hand to kiss it.

'Bethinda Flay. And this is my sweetheart, Damen Morcutt.'

'Of the Marduk Morcutts,' Crake added cheerily, as he shook Vexford's hand. Vexford wasn't quick enough to keep the fleeting, predatory glitter from his eyes. Crake had already surmised what was on his mind. He was after Jez, and that made Crake his competition.

'You know, ferrotypes don't do him justice,' Jez twittered. 'He's so very grand in real life.'

'Oh, he is,' agreed Vexford. 'A very serious man, very thoughtful. And so devout. A credit to his family.'

'Do you know the Duke very well?' Jez asked.

Vexford glowed. 'I have had the privilege of meeting the Duke on many occasions. The Archduke is also a personal friend of mine.'

'Perhaps you could introduce us to Duke Grephen?' Crake

suggested, pouncing. Vexford hesitated. 'We'd be honoured to meet him, and offer our thanks to the host. I know Bethinda would be very grateful.'

'Oh! It would be a dream come true!' she gushed. She was getting to be quite the little actress.

Vexford's reservations were obvious. You didn't introduce just *anyone* to the Duke. But he'd talked himself into a corner, and he'd seem foolish if he backed out now. 'How can I refuse such a beautiful lady?' he said, with a hateful smile at Crake. Then he laid his hand on Jez's back, claiming her as his prize, and led her over towards the Duke's group without another look at her 'sweetheart'. Crake was left to follow, rather amused by the Air Marshal's attempt to snub him.

Vexford's timing was perfect. The conversation had lulled and his arrival in the group caused everyone to take notice of the newcomers.

'Your Grace,' he said, 'may I introduce Miss Bethinda Flay.' After a pause long enough to be insulting, he added, 'And also Damen Morcutt, of the Marduk Morcutts,' as if he'd just remembered Crake was there.

On seeing the blank looks of his companions, someone in the group exclaimed knowingly, 'The Marduk Morcutts, ah, yes!' The others murmured in agreement, enough to imply that the Marduk Morcutts were indeed a fine family, even if none of them knew who the Marduk Morcutts actually were.

Jez curtsied; Crake bowed. 'It's a great honour, your Grace,' he said. 'For both of us.'

The Duke said nothing. He merely acknowledged them silently with nods, then gave Vexford a look as if to say: *why have you brought these two here?* The conversation had fallen silent around them. Vexford shifted uncomfortably and sipped his sherry.

'And you must be Gallian Thade!' Crake suddenly exclaimed. He took up Thade's hand and pressed it warmly between his palms, then gave the older man a companionable pat on the hip. 'Wonderful party, sir, just wonderful.'

Vexford almost choked on his drink. The others looked

shocked. Such familiarity with a man who was clearly his social superior was unpardonable. The worst kind of behaviour. Nobody expected such oafishness in a place like this.

Thade kept his composure. 'I'm so glad you're enjoying it,' he said frostily. 'You should try the canapés. I'm sure you would find them delicious.'

'I will!' said Crake enthusiastically. 'I'll do it right now. Come on, Bethinda, let's leave these gentlemen to their business.'

He took her by the arm and marched her away towards the canapés, leaving Vexford to face the silent scorn of his peers.

'What was that about?' asked Jez. 'I thought you wanted to find out what Thade was up to.'

'You remember this?' he said, taking a tiny silver earcuff out of his pocket.

'Of course I do. You showed the Cap'n how they worked. He didn't stop talking about them for two days. I think you impressed him.' She watched him affix it to his ear. 'Looks a bit tacky for this kind of party,' she offered.

'Can't be helped.'

'Where's the other one?'

Crake flashed her a gold-toothed grin. 'In Thade's pocket. Where I put it, when I patted him on the hip.'

Jez was agape. 'And you can hear him now?'

'Loud and clear,' he said. 'Now let's get some canapés, settle down, and see what our host has to say.'

Nineteen

An hour later, and Crake had begun to remember why he'd been so bored with the aristocracy. He seemed to be encountering the same people over and over again. The faces were different, but the bland niceties and insipid observations remained the same. He was yet to meet anyone more interesting than the clothes they wore.

The guests fell neatly into the pigeonholes he made for them. There was the Pampered Adventurer, who wanted to use Father's money to explore distant lands and eventually set up a business in New Vardia. They had no real concept of hardship. Then there was the Future Bankrupt, who talked enthusiastically of investing in dangerous projects and bizarre science, dreaming of vast profits that would never materialise. They were often attached to the Vapid Beauty, whose shattering dullness was only tolerable because they were so pleasant to look at. Occasionally he spotted a Fledgling Harpy, spoiled daughter of a rich family. Unattractive, yet intelligent enough to realise that their fiancée was only with them for their money. In revenge for thwarting their fantasies of romance, they intended to make the remainder of his life a misery.

These, and others, he recognised from long experience. A procession of stereotypes and clichés, he thought scornfully. Each one desperately believing themselves to be unique. They parrot their stupid opinions, plucked straight from the broadsheets, and hope that nobody disagrees. How had he ever communicated with these people? How could he ever go back among them, knowing what he knew?

They'd moved into the magnificent ballroom, with its swirled marble pillars and copper chandeliers. The floor was busy with couples, some of them lovers but most not. They exchanged partners as they moved, men and women passed around in a political interplay, gossiping and spying on one another. Crake stood to one side with Jez, talking with a pair of brothers who had recently bought an aerium mine and clearly had no idea how to exploit it.

Gallian Thade and Duke Grephen stood on the other side of the room. Crake listened. It was hard to concentrate on two conversations at once, but luckily he needed less than half his attention to keep up with either. Jez was fielding the Aerium Brothers, and Thade and his companions were saying nothing of any interest. Their talk consisted of possible business ventures, witticisms and pleasantries. He was beginning to wonder if Frey had been wise to believe Thade might give something away.

'We should go elsewhere,' he heard Thade murmur, through the silver earcuff. 'There are things we must discuss.'

Crake's eyes flickered to the host, who was talking to the Duke. Grephen nodded, and they excused themselves and began to move away across the ballroom. This was promising.

'Miss Flay!'

It was Vexford, the rangy old soak who had taken a fancy to Jez. He gave Crake a poisonous glare as they made their greetings. He'd not forgotten his recent embarrassment at Crake's hands. It hadn't embarrassed him enough to keep him from trying to steal his adversary's sweetheart, apparently.

'Air Marshal Vexford!' Jez declared, with false and excessive enthusiasm. 'How good to see you again!'

Vexford puffed up with pleasure. 'I was wondering if I might have the honour of this dance?'

Jez glanced uncertainly at Crake, but Crake wasn't listening. He was concentrating on the sounds in his ear. Grephen and Thade were exchanging greetings with people as they passed through the ballroom towards a doorway at one end. The greetings were getting fainter and fainter as they moved out of range.

'Damen?' Jez enquired. He noticed her again. 'Air Marshal Vexford wishes to dance with me.' Her eyes were urgent: *Save me!*

Crake smiled broadly at the Air Marshal. 'That would be fine, sir. Just fine,' he said. 'Excuse me, I must attend to something.' He slipped away with rude haste, to spare himself Jez's gaze of horrified betrayal.

He made his way towards the doorway Grephen and Thade were heading for, glancing around nervously as he went. He was searching for a sign of Fredger Cordwain, the man who worked for the Shacklemores. Crake hadn't spotted him since their conversation earlier, and it worried him deeply.

When he was a child, he'd been afraid of spiders. They seemed to like his bedroom, and no matter how the maids chased them out they always came back. But frightened as he was, he found their presence easier to bear if he could see them, hiding in a corner or motionless on the ceiling. It was when he looked away, when the spider disappeared, that the fear came. A spider safely on the far side of the room was one thing; a spider that might already be crawling over the pillow towards his face was quite another. Crake wanted Cordwain where he could see him.

The sound of Thade's voice strengthened in his ear as he drew closer to them. They passed through the grand doorway at the end of the ballroom and away. Crake followed at a distance.

Beyond was a corridor, leading through the manor to other areas: smoking rooms, galleries, halls. Guests were scattered about in groups, admiring sculptures or laughing among themselves. Crake was sweating, and not only because of the heat. He felt like a criminal. The casual glances of the doormen and servants seemed suddenly suspicious and knowing. He sipped his wine and tried to look purposeful.

'Where are we going?' Grephen said quietly to Thade, looking around. 'Somewhere more private than this, I hope.'

'My study is off-limits to guests,' Thade replied. He halted at a heavy wooden door with vines carved into its surface, and unlocked it with a key. Crake stopped a little way up the corridor, pretending to admire a painting of some grotesque aunt of the

Thade dynasty. Thade and Grephen stepped inside and closed the door behind them.

He waited for them to speak again. They didn't. Wait: was that a murmur in his ear? Perhaps, but it was too faint to make out. The study evidently went back some distance into the manor, and they were right at the limit of his range.

Spit and blood! I knew I should have made these things more powerful, he thought, fingering his earcuff in agitation.

He looked both ways up the corridor, but nobody was paying attention to him. He walked across to the door that led to the study. If anyone asked, he could just say he got lost.

He tried the door. It didn't open. He tried again, more forcefully. Locked.

'I don't think you can go in there,' said a portly, middle-aged man who had spotted his plight.

'Oh,' said Crake. 'I must be mistaken.' He lowered his voice, and moved close to murmur: 'I thought this was the lavatory. It's quite desperate, you see.'

'Other end of the corridor,' said the man, giving him a pat on the shoulder.

'Much obliged,' he said, and hurried away.

His mind was racing. If Thade had anything worth hearing, he was saying it right now, and Crake was too far away to listen. This whole excursion would be wasted if he couldn't get back in range, and quickly.

Just then he passed the foot of a staircase. It was relatively narrow and simple, with white stone steps and elegant, polished banisters. A manservant stood on the first step, barring entry to guests.

And suddenly Crake had an idea.

'Excuse me,' he said. 'Would you mind terribly if I had a nose around up there?'

'Guests are not allowed, sir,' said the manservant.

Crake grinned hugely. His best grin, his picture-grin. His gold tooth glinted in the light of the electric bulb. The manservant's eyes glittered like a magpie's.

'I'd be most grateful if you could make an exception,' he said.

The corridors upstairs were cool and hushed and empty. The gabble of conversation and music from the ballroom were muted by the thick floors. Crake could hear a pair of maids somewhere nearby, talking in low voices, giggling as they prepared the bedrooms.

He chose a direction that he judged would take him towards Thade's study chambers. Despite the awful thrill of trespass, his limbs were beginning to feel heavy. Using the earcuff, and now his tooth, had sapped his energy. Years of practice had trained him to endure the debilitating effect of employing daemons, but the sustained, low-level usage had worn him down.

A man's voice joined the women's. A butler. Chiding. *Get on with your work.* The three of them were up ahead, just around a bend in the corridor. They might step into view at any moment, and Crake would be seen. He could feel his pulse throbbing against his collar. His palms were clammy and wet with the terror of being caught doing something wrong. He marvelled at how people like Frey could flout authority with such ease.

Then, a murmur. The faintest of sounds. The daemon thralled to his earcuff was humming in resonance with its twin. He was picking up the conversation again.

Stealthily, holding his breath, he moved down the corridor. The butler was issuing instructions as to how the master wanted his guests' rooms arranged. His voice grew in volume. Frustratingly, Thade's didn't. Crake was skirting around the limit of his earcuff's range. Somewhere on the floor below him, Thade and Grephen were discussing the secret matters he'd come here to learn about. He had to get closer.

Crake crept up to the corner, pressing himself against it. He peered round. The butler was in the doorway of a nearby bedroom, a little way inside. His back was to the corridor, and he was talking to the maids within.

Crake took a shallow breath and held it. He had to do this now, before his nerve failed him. Soft-footed, he padded past the doorway. No voice was raised to halt him. The butler kept talking.

Unable to believe his luck, Crake kept going, and the conversation in his ear grew audible.

'. . . concern that . . . still haven't caught . . .'

He opened a plain-looking door and ducked inside, eager to get out of the corridor. Within was a small, green-tiled room, with a shuttered window, a scalloped white sink, and a flush toilet at the end.

Well, he thought. *I found the lavatory after all.*

'It's imperative that Dracken finds him before the Archduke's Knights do,' said Grephen in his ear. 'It should have been done properly the first time.'

Crake felt a guilty shiver, the chill of an eavesdropper who hears something scandalous. They were talking about Frey.

'Nobody expected him to get away,' said Thade. 'I had four good pilots flying escort.'

'So why didn't they do their jobs?'

The lavatory had a lock on the inside, with a large iron key. Crake eased the door closed and quietly turned it, then sat down on the toilet lid. Grephen and Thade were almost directly below him now. He could hear them perfectly.

'The survivor said they launched a surprise attack.'

'Well, of course they did! We told them the route the *Ace of Skulls* would be flying! So why weren't our pilots warned?'

'The pilots were independents, hired through middlemen, that couldn't be connected to you. We needed them to be reliable, untainted witnesses. We could hardly warn them an attack was coming without giving away the fact that we set up the ambush.'

Amalicia Thade was right, thought Crake. *Her father wasn't in this alone. This goes all the way up to the Duke.*

'The *Ketty Jay* had two outflyers – fighter craft,' Thade went on patiently. 'We didn't even know Frey travelled with outflyers. He's such an insignificant wretch, it's a miracle he keeps his own craft in the sky, let alone three.'

'You didn't *know*?'

'Your Grace, do you have any idea how hard it is to keep track of one maggot amid the swarming cess of the underworld? A man like that puts down no roots and leaves little trace when he's gone. The sheer size of our great country makes it—'

'You underestimated him, then.'

Crake heard a resentful pause. 'I miscalculated,' Thade said at last.

'The problem was that you didn't *calculate* anything,' Grephen said. 'You allowed your personal hatred of this man to blind you. You saw a chance for revenge because he disgraced your daughter. I should never have listened to you.'

'The Allsoul itself thought that Darian Frey was an excellent choice for our scheme.'

'The auguries were unclear,' said Grephen, coldly. 'Even the Grand Oracle said so. Do not presume to know the mind of the Allsoul.'

'I am saying that I trust in the Allsoul's wisdom,' Thade replied. 'This is merely a hiccup. We will still emerge triumphant.'

Crake couldn't help a sneer and a tut. *Superstition and idiocy*, he thought. *Strange how your Allsoul can't stop me using my daemons to listen to every word you say.*

'The survivor told us that the *Ketty Jay*'s outflyers were fast craft with excellent pilots,' Thade explained. 'The surprise attack threw them into chaos and took out half of our men. We were lucky that one witness escaped to report to the Archduke.'

Nobody spoke for a time. Crake imagined a sullen silence on Grephen's part.

'This is not a disaster,' said Thade, soothingly. 'Hengar is out of the way, and our hands remain clean. Don't you see how things have fallen in our favour? That fool's dalliance with the Samarlan ambassador's daughter gave us the perfect opportunity to remove him and make it look like a pirate attack. If he'd not been travelling in secret, if your spies hadn't discovered his affair, our job would have been that much more difficult.'

Grephen grunted in reluctant agreement, allowing himself to be mollified.

'Not only that,' Thade went on, 'but leaking information about the affair to the public has turned them against Hengar and the

Archduchy in general. Hengar was the one they loved, remember? He stood aside when his parents began their ridiculous campaign to deprive the people of the message of the Allsoul. His death could have strengthened the family, made them sympathetic in the eyes of the common man, but instead they have never been so unpopular.'

'That's true, that's true.'

Thade was warming to his own positivity now. 'Don't you see how kindly the Allsoul looks on our enterprise? We have cleared the line of succession: the Archduke has no other children to inherit his title. The people will welcome you when you seize control of the Coalition. You will be *Arch*duke Grephen, and a new dynasty will begin!'

Crake's mind reeled. *This* was what it was all about? Spit and blood, they were planning a coup! They were planning to over-throw the Archduke!

It was all but inconceivable. Nobody alive remembered what it was like to live without a member of the Arken dynasty ruling the land. The rulers of the duchy of Thesk had been the leaders of the Coalition for almost a century and a half. They'd been the ones who forcefully brought the squabbling Coalition to heel after they deposed the King and threw down the monarchy. The first Archduke of Vardia had been of the family of Arken, as had every one since. The Arkens had been the ultimate power in the land for generations, overseeing the Third Age of Aviation and the Aerium Wars, the discovery of New Vardia and Jagos on the far side of the world, the formation of the Century Knights. They'd abolished serfdom and brought economic prosperity and industry to a land strangled by the stagnant traditions of millennia of royal rule.

Crake felt history teetering. Riveted, he listened on.

'It . . . *concerns* me that Darian Frey is still on the run,' said the Duke. 'He has already been to the whispermonger you employed.'

'Don't worry about Quail. Dracken has made sure he won't speak to anyone ever again.'

'But Frey is already on the trail. He was spotted near your daughter's hermitage.'

'Amalicia has been questioned by the Mistresses, at my request. She swears that he never visited her. Dracken probably caught up to him before he had a chance to—'

'What if she's lying?'

'You know I can't go in there or bring her out. She must stay in isolation. We have to trust her, and the Mistresses.'

'My point is, he must know about you. That means he may learn about *me*.'

'Peace, your Grace. Who'll believe him? With Quail dead, there's nothing to link us but the word of a mass-murderer.'

'It's not a chance I want to take. If he digs deep enough, he might find something. I don't want the Century Knights getting hold of him and giving him the chance to spout his theories to the Archduke.'

Crake was sitting atop the toilet, elbows on his knees, one hand on his forehead with his fingers clenched anxiously through his hair. Finally he understood the true seriousness of their situation. Unwittingly, they'd become entangled in a power-play for the greatest prize in the land. The only problem was they'd been inconvenient enough not to die when they were supposed to. Now they were hunted, both by those who thought they were responsible, and those who wanted them silenced. Small fry dodging the mouths of the biggest fish in the sea.

Thade's voice was soothing again. 'Dracken will have him soon. She guessed that he'd go to Quail, and she surmised he'd go after your daughter rather than coming for you. I am learning to respect her intuition where Frey is concerned.' He paused. 'She also believes he might try something tonight.'

'Tonight?'

'It's his best chance of getting close to me, in amid all the chaos. But do not fear. She has men undercover all over my manor, and in the port on the mainland. The *Delirium Trigger* itself is hiding up in the night sky, waiting for a signal if the *Ketty Jay* should arrive.'

Crake felt his stomach sink. First the Shacklemores, and now Trinica Dracken was here? One step ahead of them already? This was getting altogether too dangerous. It was only through

Amalicia's invitations – and because nobody knew Crake and Jez were part of the crew of the *Ketty Jay* – that they'd remained undetected thus far. Crake was beginning to wish he'd never got involved in the first place.

The lavatory door rattled, making him jump. He looked up. There was a pause, then the door rattled again. A moment later, there was a sharp knock on the door.

'Is someone in there?'

It was the butler. Crake was frozen to the spot. He said nothing, in the futile hope that the man outside would go away.

'Hello? Is someone in there?' He sounded angry. There was a knocking again, firmer this time.

The door was locked from the inside. Crake decided that he'd do better to own up, before the butler got really furious.

'I'm in here,' he said. 'Be out in a minute.'

'You'll be out right now, sir!' said the butler. 'I don't know how you got up here, but these are the private rooms of Master Thade.'

'Do you trust her?' said Grephen, from downstairs. His voice was suddenly faint. They'd moved away, walking into another room. Crake strained to hear over the voice of the butler.

'Dracken? As much as I trust any pirate,' Thade replied. 'Besides, we need her. She's our only link to—'

'Sir! I must insist you come out here right now!' the butler cried, knocking hard on the door.

'Give a man a moment to finish his business!' Crake protested, delaying his exit as long as he could. He had the sense that something important was being discussed here, but the words were becoming harder and harder to hear as the speakers moved away.

'. . . we . . . no one else?' Grephen asked. 'I . . . uneasy about . . .'

'. . . Dracken knows the . . . has charts and . . . device of some kind. Only way . . . can find that place. She . . . our . . . has to be escorted in . . . out . . . secret hideout . . .'

'Sir!' bellowed the butler.

'I'm coming!' cried Crake. He flushed the toilet, and was

dismayed when the sound drowned out the last of the conversation from below him. Unable to hold out any longer, he unlocked the door and was immediately seized by the arm. The butler was a short, balding, red-faced fellow, and he was in no mood for Crake's weak excuses. The daemonist was escorted roughly along the corridor and down the stairs, past the startled manservant who was supposed to be guarding them.

'Sir will please stay downstairs from now on, or he shall be thrown from the premises!' the butler snapped, loud enough to draw titters from the guests nearby. Crake blushed, despite himself. He hurried back towards the ballroom as the butler began to vent his anger on the hapless manservant who had let Crake pass minutes before.

Once in the ballroom, he looked for Jez, and found her with Vexford. The older man was towering over her, drunk on sherry and success, bawling about his outrageous exploits during the Second Aerium War. Crake strode up to them and took Jez by the arm.

'Cra—' Jez began, then corrected herself. 'Sweetheart!'

'We're going,' he said, pulling her away.

'Here, now, you boor!' protested Vexford, who was still in mid-story; but Crake ignored him, and Jez was propelled away. Vexford grabbed her wrist to stop her.

'Sir!' she exclaimed, breathlessly.

Vexford leaned closer and murmured huskily in her ear. 'I have a large estate, just outside Banbarr. Anyone in the city will know where it is. If you ever tire of this ruffian, you will be most welcome.' Then she was pulled away again by her impatient companion.

'It's been a great pleasure, sir!' Jez called over her shoulder. 'I hope to meet again!' Then the crowd closed around them, and she turned to Crake with a narrow glare. 'You left me alone with him,' she accused. 'He smells of sour milk and carrots.'

'We'll talk about it later, dear,' said Crake.

'I don't think I want to marry you any more,' she sulked.

Twenty

A Guest On The Path – The Letter
Knife – A Bad End To The Evening

The crowd on the lawns had thinned out considerably – most of them were in the ballroom now – and the chorus of night insects was in full voice. Crake pulled off his earcuff and threw it into a flower bed as they passed. It was useless without its partner, and he wasn't about to retrieve it from Thade's pocket. He'd make more, and better.

'So I take it you found out what you wanted?'

'I found out more than I wanted,' he muttered. 'But right now I'd like to get off this island as quickly as possible.'

Crake looked up into the moonless sky as they walked, fancying he might see a patch of deeper black in the blackness: the *Delirium Trigger*, lurking in wait. Jez, having picked up on his obvious agitation, stayed silent.

They crossed the lawns and came to the old path that led to the manor's landing pad. Here, passenger craft ran a shuttle service to the port of Black Seal Bluff on the mainland. The *Ketty Jay* was hidden in a glade a few kloms out from the port. Shaken by his near-miss with the *Delirium Trigger*, Frey hadn't dared set down in Black Seal Bluff itself. A sensible precaution, as it turned out. Dracken's undercover spies would have spotted the craft immediately.

They'd been fortunate so far. They'd received more than their share of luck. But the circle was drawing tighter now, and the closer they got to the truth behind the destruction of the *Ace of Skulls*, the more it constricted.

The path down to the landing pad was wide and deserted, with a knee-high drystone wall on either side. It wound down the hill, occasionally bulging out into small rest areas with carved wooden benches. Weeping bottlebrush and jacarandas overhung the wall, obscuring sections of the path. Electric lamps, set in recesses, lit their faces from below. Bats feasted on insects in the blood-warm darkness overhead.

Crake was so intent on getting down to the pad and away that he was surprised when Jez suddenly tugged him to a halt.

'Someone's there,' she said. She was staring intently into the foliage, a distant look in her eyes, as if she was seeing right through the leaves and bark to whoever hid beyond.

'What? Where?' He tried to follow her gaze, but he could see no sign of anyone.

'He's right there,' she murmured, still staring. 'On the bench. Waiting for us.'

They stood there a moment, not knowing what to do. Crake couldn't fathom how she could sense this mysterious man, nor how she knew his intention. But he didn't doubt the conviction in her voice. They couldn't go forward without passing him, and they couldn't go back. Crake suddenly wished they'd tried to smuggle in weapons, but it was forbidden for guests to carry arms.

Yet he couldn't just stand here, trapped, a child afraid to move in case he disturbed the spider. That wasn't the way a man ought to act. So he steeled himself, and walked on, Jez following behind.

A dozen paces later the path twisted and widened into a circular rest area, hidden by the trees. There was an ornamental stone pool, with a weak jet of water bubbling from a spike in its centre. Sitting on a bench, contemplating the pool, was Fredger Cordwain. He looked up as Crake and Jez arrived.

'Good night,' said Crake, without breaking stride.

'Good night, Grayther Crake,' Cordwain replied.

Crake froze at the sound of his name. He tensed to run, but Cordwain surged up from the bench, a revolver appearing in his meaty hand. He must have assumed the rule against carrying arms didn't apply to him.

'Let's not make this difficult,' Cordwain said. 'You're worth just the same to me dead or alive.'

'Who's this?' Jez asked Crake. It took a moment before he realised she was still playing in character. 'Sweetheart, what's this about?'

Cordwain walked towards them, his weapon trained on Crake. 'Miss Bethinda Flay,' he said. 'If that is your real name. The Shacklemore Agency have been after your "sweetheart" for several months now. I'm ashamed to say it took me a little time to recognise him from his ferrotype. It's the beard, I think. I don't have a good memory for faces.'

'But he hasn't done anything!' Jez protested. 'What did he do?'

Cordwain stared at her levelly. 'Don't you know? He murdered his niece. An eight-year-old girl.'

Jez looked at Crake, stunned. Crake was slump-shouldered, gazing at the floor.

Cordwain moved around behind Crake, took his wrists and pulled his arms behind his back. Then he shoved the revolver into his belt and drew out a pair of handcuffs.

'Stabbed her seventeen times with a letter knife,' he said conversationally. 'Left her to bleed out on the floor of his own daemonic sanctum. That's what kind of monster he is.'

Crake didn't struggle. He'd gone pale and cold, and he wanted to be sick.

'His own brother hired us to find him,' said Cordwain. 'Isn't that sad? It's terrible when families get to fighting among themselves. You should always be able to trust your family.'

Tears gathered in Crake's eyes as the handcuffs snapped closed. He raised his head and met Jez's gaze. She stared at him hard, shock on her face. Wanting to be reassured. Wanting to know that he hadn't done this thing.

He had nothing to tell her. She could never condemn him more than he already condemned himself.

'If you don't mind, Miss, I'll have to ask you to come along with me, too,' said Cordwain as he adjusted the handcuffs. 'I'm sure you understand. Just until we establish that you've no connection with this—'

Jez lunged for the pistol sticking out of his belt, but Cordwain was ready for her. He grabbed her by the arm and yanked her off balance, shoving Crake down with his other hand. With his hands cuffed behind his back Crake was unable to cushion his fall, and he landed painfully on his shoulder on the stony ground.

Jez slapped and punched at Cordwain, but he was a big man, much stronger and heavier than she was.

'As I thought,' he said, fending her off. 'In on it too, aren't you?'

Jez landed a fist on his jaw, surprising him. But the surprise lasted only a moment. He backhanded her hard across the face: once, twice, three times in succession. Then he flung her away from him. She tripped headlong, flailing as she went, and cracked her forehead against the low stone wall of the pool.

The terrible sound of the impact took all the heat out of the moment. Cordwain and Crake both stared at the small woman in the pretty black dress who now lay motionless on the ground.

She didn't get up.

'What did you do?' Crake cried from where he lay. He struggled to his knees.

Cordwain drew his pistol and pointed it at him. 'You calm down.'

'Help her!'

'I said cool your heels!' he snapped. He moved over towards Jez, crouched down next to her, and picked up a limp hand, pressing two fingers to her wrist. After a moment, he let it drop, pulled her head aside and checked for a pulse at her throat.

Crake knew the result by his expression. He felt a surge of unbelievable, irrational hate. 'You son of a bitch!' he snarled, getting to his feet. Cordwain immediately thrust his weapon towards him.

'You saw what happened!' Cordwain said. 'I didn't mean for that!'

'You killed her! She wasn't anything to do with us!'

Cordwain advanced on him. 'You shut your damn mouth! I told you I could take you in dead or alive and I meant it!'

'Well, you'd better take me dead, you bastard! Because even a Shacklemore doesn't get to kill innocent women! And I'm going to make absolutely sure that everyone knows what you've done.'

'You need to stop your talking, sir, or I will shoot you like a dog!'

But Crake was out of control. The sight of Jez, lying there, had freed something inside him. It unleashed all the rage, the guilt, the horror that he kept penned uneasily within. He saw his niece, still and lifeless, her white nightdress soaked in red, her small body violated by vicious wounds. He saw the bloodied letter knife in his hand.

That was the day he began to run, and he hadn't stopped since.

'Why don't you shoot?' he shouted. 'Why don't you? Save me the show trial! Pull the trigger!'

Cordwain backed off, his gun raised. He was unsure how to deal with the red-faced, spittle-flecked maniac who was stumbling towards him, his hands cuffed behind his back.

'You stay back, sir!'

'End it, you murderer!' he screamed. 'End it! I've had enough!'

And then something moved, quick in the night, and there was a terrible, dull crunch. Cordwain's eyes rolled up into his head and he crumpled, folding onto himself and falling to the ground.

Standing behind him, a rock from the drystone wall in her hand, was Jez.

Crake just stared.

Jez tossed the rock aside and took the keys from the Shacklemore man. She walked over to Crake, turned him around, and undid his handcuffs. By the time they'd fallen free, he'd found words again.

'I thought you were dead.'

'So did he,' she replied.

'But he . . . but you *were* dead.'

'Apparently not. Give me a hand.'

She began to tug Cordwain towards the trees. After a moment,

Crake joined her. As they manhandled him over the drystone wall, his head lolled back, and Crake caught a glimpse of his eyes. They were open, and the whites were dark with blood.

Crake turned away and vomited. Jez waited for him to finish, then said, 'Take his legs.'

He wasn't used to this merciless tone from her. He did as he was told, and together they carried him out of sight of the path and left him there.

They returned to the clearing, where Jez replaced the rock in the wall and threw Cordwain's gun into the undergrowth. She dusted her dress off as best she could.

'Jez, I—' he began.

'I didn't do it for you, I did it for me,' she interrupted. 'I'm not being taken in by any damn Shacklemore. Not when half the world still wants us dead.' There was a weary disgust in her voice. 'Besides, you still haven't told me what you learned in there. The Cap'n will want to hear that, no doubt.'

She wasn't the same Jez who had accompanied him to this party. The change was sudden, and wrenching. Everything that had happened before, every shared joke and kind word, meant nothing in the face of the crime he'd committed. Crake wished there was something to say, some way he could explain, but he knew that she wouldn't listen. Not now.

'It's better that we don't speak about what happened here today,' she said, still brushing herself down. She stopped and gave him a pointed look. 'Ever.'

Crake nodded.

'Right, then,' she said, having arranged herself as best she could. 'Let's get out of here.'

She walked down the path towards the landing pad. Crake cast one last glance into the trees, where Cordwain's body lay, and then followed her.

Twenty-One

Frey Calls A Meeting – Hope – A Captain's
Memories Of Samarla – The Bayonet

'You want to take on the *Delirium Trigger*?' shrieked Harkins. Pinn choked on his food, spraying stew across the table and all over Crake's face. Malvery gleefully pounded Pinn on the back, much harder than was necessary, until his coughing fit subsided.

'Thanks,' he snarled at the grinning doctor.

'Another day, another life saved,' Malvery replied, returning to his position by the stove, where he was working on an artery-clogging dessert made mostly of sugar. Crake dabbed at his beard with a pocket handkerchief.

'So?' prompted Jez. 'How do you plan to do it?'

Frey surveyed his crew, gathered around the table in the *Ketty Jay*'s mess hall, and wondered again if he was doing the right thing. His plan had seemed inspired when he came up with it a few hours ago, but now he was faced with the reality of his situation he was much less certain. It was fine to imagine a crack squad of experts carrying out their assigned missions with clinical precision, but it was hardly a well-oiled machine he was dealing with here.

There was Harkins, reduced to a gibbering wreck by the mere mention of the *Delirium Trigger*. Malvery, lacing the dessert with rum and taking a couple of swigs for himself as he did so. Pinn, too stupid to even swallow his food properly.

Jez and Crake were trustworthy, as far as he could tell, but they'd barely been able to meet each other's eyes throughout the meal. Something had happened between them at the Winter Ball –

perhaps Crake had made an unwelcome move? – and now Jez's loathing for him was obvious, as was his shame.

That left Silo, silently spooning stew into his mouth, unknowable as always. Silo, who had been Frey's constant companion for seven years, about whom he knew nothing. Frey had never asked about his past, because he didn't care. Silo never asked about anything. He was just there. Did he *have* thoughts like normal men did?

He tried to summon up some warm feelings of camaraderie and couldn't.

Oh well, damn it all, let's go for it anyway.

'We all know we can't take on the *Delirium Trigger* in the air,' he said, to an audible sigh of relief from Harkins. 'So what we do is we get her on the *ground*. We lure Dracken into port and when she's down . . .' He slapped the table. 'That's when we do it.'

Pinn raised a hand. When Pinn raised a hand it was only ever for effect. If he had something to say he usually just blurted it out.

'Question,' he said. 'Why?'

'Because she won't be expecting it.'

Pinn lowered his hand halfway, then raised it again as if struck by a new idea.

'Yes?' Frey said wearily.

'Why don't we do something *else* she isn't expecting?'

'I liked the running away plan,' said Harkins. 'I mean, we've been doing pretty good so far with the running away. Maybe we should, you know, keep on doing it. Just an idea, though, I mean, you're the Cap'n. Only seems to me that, well, if it ain't broke it doesn't need fixing. Just my opinion. You're the Cap'n. Sir.'

The crew fell silent. The only sounds were Malvery quietly stirring the pot and a wet chewing noise coming from the corner of the mess, where Slag was tucking in to a fresh rat. He'd dragged it all the way up from the cargo hold in order to join the crew's dinner.

Frey looked at the faces turned towards him and felt something unfamiliar, a strange weight to the moment. He realised with a shock that they were waiting for him to persuade them. They *wanted* to be persuaded. In their eyes, he saw the faintest hint of something he'd never thought to see from them. Something he was only accustomed to seeing in the expressions of beautiful girls just before he left them.

Hope.

Rot and damnation, they're hoping*! They're hoping I can save them. They're hoping I know what I'm doing.*

And Frey was surprised to realise he felt a little bit good about that.

'Listen,' he said. 'Dracken's been catching us up ever since she set out to get us. She was behind us when she got to Quail, she almost had us at the hermitage, and she was even *ahead* of us at the Winter Ball. She knows that we know about Gallian Thade, and she'll assume we'll keep on after him. But what she *doesn't* know is that we know about their secret hideout.'

'We don't even know what this secret hideout *is*,' Jez pointed out.

Pinn looked bewildered. He wasn't sure who knew what any more.

'Crake heard Thade and the Duke talking about Trinica and some secret hideout,' Frey said. 'They mentioned charts and a device of some kind. Seems to me that if we get those charts and that device, then we can find our way there too.'

Pinn raised his hand. 'Question.'

'Yes?'

'Why?'

'Because we need proof. We know Duke Grephen arranged Hengar's murder. We know he's planning a coup. But we don't have any way to prove it. If we can prove it, we can shop those bastards to the Archduke.'

'What good will that do?' Jez asked. 'We still blew up the *Ace of Skulls*.'

'You think they're going to care about the trigger-man if they've got the mastermind?' Frey asked. 'Look, I'm not saying they'll necessarily forgive, but they might forget. If the Archduke gets his hands on *them*, he won't worry about *us*. We're small-time. And without Duke Grephen putting up that huge reward, Dracken's not going to waste her time chasing us either.'

'You think we can actually get ourselves out of this?' Malvery rumbled. He was standing behind Frey, at the stove. He'd stopped stirring and was staring at the pot of dessert.

'Yes!' Frey said, firmly. 'We play this right, we can do it.'

The crew were exchanging glances, as if looking for support from each other. Did their companions feel the same? Were they being foolish, to believe that they could win out against all the odds?

'Whatever's going on at this hideout is something to do with all of this,' Frey said. 'The answers are there, I'm sure of it. There's a way out. But we need to hang on, we need to go a little deeper first. We need to take the risk. Because I'm not spending the rest of my life on the run, and neither are any of you.'

'You said we'll lure Dracken into a port,' said Jez. 'How are we gonna do that?'

'Parley,' he said. 'I'll invite her to talk on neutral turf. Face to face. I'll pretend I want to cut a deal.'

'And you think she'll agree?'

'She'll agree.' Frey was horribly certain of that.

Nobody spoke for a few moments. Slag looked up, puzzled by the pregnant pause in the conversation, then went back to snacking on his rat.

Frey felt the weight of Malvery's hand on his shoulder. 'Tell us the rest of the plan, Cap'n.'

Frey stepped off the iron ladder that ran from the mess up to the main passageway of the *Ketty Jay*. He stopped there for a moment and took a breath. Explaining his plan had been unusually nerve-wracking. For the first time he could remember, he'd actually worried about what his crew thought. There were a few good suggestions, mostly from Jez. Outright shock as he revealed the final part. But they'd liked it. He saw it on their faces.

Well, it was done. Until now he hadn't really been sure they'd go with it. It was frightening to have it all seem so suddenly real.

Because he really, really didn't want a meeting with Trinica Dracken.

Slag scampered up the ladder behind him and thumped down into the passageway, obviously in the mood for some company. He followed Frey into the captain's quarters and waited while Frey shut the door and dug out the small bottle of Shine from the locked drawer in the cabinet. He sat patiently while Frey administered a drop to each eye and lay back on the bed. Then, once he'd determined that Frey was liable to be motionless for a while, he hopped onto the captain's chest, curled up and fell asleep.

Frey drifted on the edge of consciousness, dimly aware of the warm, crushing weight of the cat on his ribs. He was scared of what was to come. He hated being forced into this position. He hated having to be brave. But in the soothing narcotic haze he felt nothing but peace, and gradually he fell asleep.

In seeking to block out one thing he'd rather forget, he ended up dreaming of another.

The north-western coast of Samarla was a beautiful place. The plunging valleys and majestic mountains were kept lush and green by frequent rains off Silver Bay, and the sun shone all year round this close to the equator. It was a land of sweeping vistas, mighty rivers and uncountable trees, all green and gold and red.

It was also swarming with Sammies. Or, to be more accurate, it was swarming with their Dakkadian and Murthian troops. Sammies didn't dirty themselves with hand-to-hand combat. They had two whole races of slaves to do that kind of thing.

Frey looked down from the cockpit of the *Ketty Jay* at the verdant swells beneath him. His navigator, Rabby, was squeezed up close, peering about for landmarks by which to calculate their position. He was a scrawny sort with a chicken neck and a ponytail. Frey didn't much like him, but he didn't have much choice in the matter. The Coalition Navy had commandeered his craft and his services, and since the rest of his crew had deserted rather than fight the Sammies, the Navy had assigned him a new one.

'They're sitting pretty, ain't they? Bloody Sammies,' Rabby

muttered. 'Wish *we* had two sets of bitches to do our fighting for us.'

Frey ignored him. Rabby was always fishing for someone to agree with, constantly probing to find the crew's likes and dislikes so he could marvel at how similar their opinions were.

'I mean, you've got your Murthians, right, to do all your hard labour and stuff. Big strong lot for hauling all those bricks around and working in the factories and what. Good cannon-fodder too, if you don't mind the surly buggers trying to mutiny all the time.'

Frey reached into the footwell of the cockpit and pulled out a near-empty bottle of rum. He took a long swig. Rabby eyed the booze thirstily. Frey pretended not to notice and put it back.

'And then you've got your Dakkadians,' Rabby babbled on, 'who are even worse, 'cause they bloody *like* being slaves! They've, what do you say, *assistimated*.'

'Assimilated,' said Frey, before he could stop himself.

'Assimilated,' Rabby agreed. 'You always know the right word, Cap'n. I bet you read a lot. Do you read a lot? I like to read, too.'

Frey kept his eyes fixed on the landscape. Rabby coughed and went on.

'So these Dakkadians, they're all dealing with the day-to-day stuff, administration or what, and flying the planes and commanding all the dumb grunt Murthians. Then what do the actual Sammies do, eh?' He waited for a response that wasn't going to come. 'Sit around eating grapes and fanning their arses, that's what! Calling the bloody shots and not doing a lick of work. They've got it sweet, they have. Really sweet.'

'Can you just tell me where I'm setting down, and we can get this over with?'

'Right you are, right you are,' Rabby said hastily, scanning the ground. Suddenly he pointed. 'Drop point is a few kloms south of there.'

Frey looked in the direction that he was pointing, and saw a ruined temple complex in the distance. The central ziggurat of red stone had caved in on one side and the surrounding dwellings, once grand, had been flattened into rubble by bombs.

'How *many* kloms?'

'We'll see it,' Rabby assured him.

Frey took another hit from the rum.

'Can I have some of that?' Rabby asked.

'No.'

They came in over the landing zone not long afterwards. The hilltop was bald, and where there used to be fields there were now earthworks, with narrow trenches running behind them. Battered stone buildings clustered at the crest of the hill. It was a tiny village, with simple houses built in the low, flat-topped style common in these parts. The trees and grass glistened and steamed as the morning rain evaporated under the fierce sun.

Nothing moved on the hilltop.

Frey slowed the *Ketty Jay* to a hover. He was surly drunk, and his first reaction was disgust. Couldn't the Coalition even organise someone to meet their own supply craft? Did they *want* to run out of ammo? Did they think he *enjoyed* hauling himself all over enemy territory, risking enemy patrols, just so they could eat?

Martley, the engineer, came bounding up the passageway from the engine room and into the cockpit. 'Are we there?' he asked eagerly. He was a wiry young carrot-top, his cheeks and dungarees permanently smeared in grease as if it was combat camouflage. He had too much energy, that was his problem. He wore Frey out.

Rabby examined the earthworks uncertainly. 'Looks deserted, Cap'n.'

'These *are* the right co-ordinates?'

'Hey!' Rabby sounded offended. 'Have I ever failed to get us to our target?'

'I suppose we usually get there in the end,' Frey conceded.

'Did the Navy tell us anything about this place?' Martley chirped. 'Like maybe why it's so deserted?'

'It's just a drop point,' Frey said impatiently. 'Like all the others.'

Frey hadn't asked. He never asked. Over the past few months Frey simply took whichever jobs paid the most. When the Navy began conscripting cargo haulers into minimum-wage service, the

Merchant Guild responded by demanding danger bonuses. Those employed by the big cargo companies were happy to sit out the war ferrying supplies within the borders of Vardia. Freelancers like Frey saw an opportunity.

By taking the most dangerous missions, Frey had all but paid off the loan on the *Ketty Jay*. They'd had some close scrapes, and the crew complained like buggery and kept applying for transfers, but Frey couldn't have cared less. After seven years, she was almost his. That was all that counted. Once he had her, he'd be free. He could ride out the rest of the war doing shuttle runs between Thesk and Marduk, and he'd never again have to worry about the loan companies freezing his accounts and hunting him down. He'd be out on his own, a master of the skies.

'Let's just load out the cargo and get paid,' he said. 'If there's no one here to collect, that's not our problem.'

'You certain?' said Martley, uncertainly.

'If there's been a screw-up here, it's someone else's fault,' said Frey. He took another swig of rum. 'We're paid to deliver to the co-ordinates they give us. We're not paid to think. They've told us *that* enough times.'

'Bloody Navy,' Rabby muttered.

Frey lowered the *Ketty Jay* down onto a relatively unscarred patch of land next to the village. Impatient and drunk, he dumped the aerium from the tanks too fast and slammed them down hard enough to jar his coccyx and knock Martley to his knees. Martley and Rabby exchanged a worried glance they thought he didn't see.

'Come on,' he said, suppressing a wince as he got out of his seat. 'Quicker we get unloaded, quicker we can go home.'

Kenham and Jodd were down in the cargo hold when they arrived, disentangling the crates from their webbing. They were a pair of ugly bruisers, ex-dock workers drafted in for labour by the Navy. The only people on the crew they respected were each other; everyone else was slightly scared of them.

Jodd was smoking a roll-up. Frey couldn't remember ever seeing him without a cigarette smouldering in his mouth, even when handling crates of live ammunition, as he was now. As captain, he took an executive decision to say nothing. Jodd had never blown them all to pieces before. With a track record like that, it seemed sensible to let it ride.

Frey lowered the cargo ramp and they began hauling the crates out. The sun hammered them as they emerged from the cool shadow of the *Ketty Jay*. The air was moist and smelled of wet clay, and there was a lingering scent of gunpowder.

'Where do you want 'em?' Kenham called to Frey. Frey vaguely waved at a clear spot some way downhill, close to the trenches. He didn't want those boxes of ammo too near the *Ketty Jay* when he took off. Kenham rolled his eyes – *all the way over there?* – but he didn't protest.

Frey leaned against the *Ketty Jay*'s landing strut with the bottle of rum in his hand, and watched the rest of his crew do the work. Since it took two men to a box, a fifth worker would only get in the way, he reasoned. Besides, it was captain's privilege to be lazy. He swigged from the bottle and surveyed the empty site. For the first time he noted that there were some signs of conflict: burn marks on the walls of the red stone houses; sections where the earthworks had been blasted and soil scattered.

Old wounds? This place had probably seen a lot of action. But then, there was that smell of gunpowder. Weapons had been fired, and recently.

He cast a bleary eye over his crew, to be sure they were getting on with their job, and then pushed off from the landing strut and wandered away from the *Ketty Jay*. He headed towards the village.

The houses were poor Samarlan peasant dwellings, bare and abandoned. Wooden chicken runs and pig pens had fallen into ruin. The windows were just square holes in the wall, some of them with their shutters hanging unevenly, drifting back and forth in the faint breeze. As Frey got closer he could see more obvious signs of recent attacks. Some walls were riddled with bullet holes.

His skin began to prickle with sweat. He drained the last of the rum and tossed the bottle aside.

The dwellings were built around a central clearing that once had been grassy but was now churned into rapidly drying mud. Frey peered around the corner of the nearest house. Despite the racket from the forest birds, it was unnervingly quiet.

He looked through the window, into the house. The furniture had long gone, leaving a mean, bare shell, dense with hot shadow. The sun outside was so bright that it was hard to see. It took him a few seconds to spot the man in the corner.

He was slumped, motionless, beneath a window on the other side of the house. Frey could hear flies, and smell blood.

By now his eyes had adjusted to the gloom. Enough to see that the man was dead, shot through the cheek, his jaw hanging askew and pasted onto his face with dried gore. Enough to see that he was wearing a Vardic uniform. Enough to see that he was one of theirs.

He heard a sound: sharp and hard, like someone stepping on a branch. The voices of his crew, suddenly raised in a clamour.

With a cold flood of nausea, he realised what was happening. Panic plunged in on him, and he bolted, running for the only safety he knew. Running for the *Ketty Jay*.

As he rounded the corner of the house, he saw Kenham lying face down next to a sundered crate. Jodd was backing away from the trenches, firing his revolver at the men that were clambering out of them. Rifle-wielding Dakkadians: two dozen or more. Small, blond-haired, faces broad and eyes narrow. They'd hidden when they heard the *Ketty Jay* approaching. Perhaps they'd even had time to throw the bodies of the dead Vards into the trenches. Now they were springing their ambush.

Rabby and Martley were fleeing headlong towards the *Ketty Jay*, as Frey was. There was fear on their faces.

One of the Dakkadians fell back into the trench with a howl as Jodd scored a hit, but their numbers were overwhelming. Three others sighted and shot him dead.

Frey barely registered Jodd's fate. The world was a bouncing, jolting agony of moment after moment, each one bringing him a fraction closer to the gaping mouth of the *Ketty Jay*'s cargo ramp. His only chance was to get inside. His only chance to live.

Dakkadian rifles cracked and snapped. Their targets were

Rabby and Martley. Several of the soldiers had broken into a sprint, chasing after them. A shout went up in their native tongue as someone spotted Frey, racing towards the *Ketty Jay* from the far side. Frey didn't listen. He'd blocked out the rest of the world, tightened himself to a single purpose. Nothing else mattered but getting to that ramp.

Bullets chipped the turf around them. Martley stumbled and rolled hard, clutching his upper leg, screaming. Rabby hesitated, broke stride for the briefest moment, then ran on. The Dakkadians pulled Martley down as he tried to get up, then began stabbing him with the double-bladed bayonets on the end of their rifles. Martley's shrieks turned to gurgles.

The cargo ramp drew closer. Frey felt the sinister brush of air as a bullet barely missed his throat. Rabby was running up the hill, yelling as he came. Two Dakkadians were close behind him.

Frey's foot hit the ramp. He fled up to the top and pulled the lever to raise it. The hydraulic struts hummed into life.

Outside, he heard Rabby's voice. 'Lower the ramp! Cap'n! Lower the bloody ramp!'

But Frey wasn't going to lower the ramp. Rabby was too far away. Rabby wasn't going to make it in time. Rabby wasn't getting anywhere near this aircraft with those soldiers hot on his heels.

'Cap'n!' he screamed. 'Don't you leave me here!'

Frey tapped in the code that would lock the ramp, preventing it from being opened from the keypad on the outside. That done, he drew his revolver and aimed it at the steadily closing gap at the end of the ramp. He backed up until he bumped against one of the supply crates that hadn't yet been unloaded. The rectangle of burning sunlight shining through the gap thinned to a line.

'*Cap'n!*'

The line disappeared as the cargo ramp thumped closed, and Frey was alone in the quiet darkness of the cargo hold, safe in the cold metal womb of the *Ketty Jay*.

The Dakkadians had overrun this position. Navy intelligence had screwed up, and now his crew was dead. Those bastards! Those rotting bastards!

He turned to run, to race up the access stairs, through the passageway, into the cockpit. He was getting out of here.

He ran right into the bayonet of the Dakkadian creeping up behind him.

Pain exploded in his guts, shocking him, driving the breath from his lungs. He gaped at the soldier before him. A boy, no more than sixteen. Blond hair spilling out from beneath his cap. Blue eyes wide. He was trembling, almost as stunned as Frey.

Frey looked down at the twin blades of the Dakkadian bayonet, side by side, sticking out of his abdomen. Blood, black in the darkness, slid thinly along the blades and dripped to the floor.

The boy was scared. Hadn't meant to stab him. When he snuck aboard the *Ketty Jay,* he probably thought only to capture a crewman for his fellows. He hadn't killed anyone before. He had that look.

As if in a trance, Frey raised his revolver and aimed it point-blank at the boy's chest. As if in a trance, the boy let him.

Frey squeezed the trigger. The bayonet was wrenched from his body as the boy fell backwards. The pain sent him to the edge of unconsciousness, but no further.

He staggered through the cargo hold. Up the metal stairs, through the passageway, into the cockpit, leaving smears and dribbles of himself as he went. He slumped into the pilot's seat, barely aware of the sound of gunfire against the hull, and punched in the ignition code – the code that only he knew, that he'd never told anyone and never would. The aerium engines throbbed as the electromagnets pulverised refined aerium into gas, filling the ballast tanks. The soldiers and their guns fell away as the *Ketty Jay* lifted into the sky.

Frey would never make it back to Vardia. He was going to die. He knew that, and accepted it with a strange and awful calm.

But he wasn't dead yet.

He hit the thrusters, and the *Ketty Jay* flew. North, towards the coast, towards the sea.

Twenty-Two

Sharka's Den – Two Captains –
A Strange Delivery – Recriminations

The slums of Rabban were not somewhere a casual traveller would stray. Bomb-lashed and tumbledown, they were a mass of junk-pits and rubble-fields, where naked girders slit the low sunset and the coastal wind smoothed a ceiling of iron-grey cloud over all. In the distance were new spires and domes, some of them still partially scaffolded: evidence of the reconstruction of the city. But here on the edges, there was no such reconstruction, and the population lived like rats on the debris of war.

Sharka's Den had survived two wars and would likely survive two more. Hidden in an underground bunker, accessible only by tortuous, crumbling alleys and an equally tortuous process of recommendation, it was the best place in the city to find a game of Rake. Sharka paid no commission to any Guild, nor any tax to the Coalition. He offered a guarantee of safety and anonymity to his patrons, and promised fairness at his tables. Nobody knew exactly what else Sharka was into, to make the bigwigs so afraid of him; but they knew that if you wanted a straight game for the best stakes, you came to Sharka's Den.

Frey knew this place well. He'd once picked up a Caybery Firecrow in a game here, on the tail end of a ridiculous winning streak that had nothing to do with skill and everything to do with luck. He'd also wiped himself out several times. As he stepped into the den, memories of triumph and despair sidled up to greet him.

Little had changed. There was the expansive floor with its many tables and barely lit bar. There were the seductive serving girls, chosen for their looks but well schooled in their art. Gas lanterns hung from the ceiling, run off a private supply (Sharka refused to go electric; his patrons wouldn't stand for it). The myopic haze of cigarettes and cigars infused the air with a dozen kinds of burning leaf.

Frey felt a twinge of nostalgia. If he didn't count the *Ketty Jay*, Sharka's Den was the closest thing to a home he had.

Sharka came over to greet him as he descended the iron steps to the gaming floor. Whip-lean, his face deeply lined, he was dressed in an eccentric motley of colours, and his eyes were bright and slightly manic. There was never a time when Sharka wasn't on some kind of drug, usually to counteract the one before. He was overly animated, his face stretching and contorting into grins, smiles, exaggerated poses, as if he were mouthing words to some-body deaf.

'Got you a private room in the back,' he said. 'She's in there now.'

'Thanks.'

'You think she was followed?'

'No. I was hiding out there a while. I watched her go in, checked all the alleys nearby. She came alone.'

Sharka grunted and then beamed. 'Hope you know what you're doing.'

'I always know what I'm doing,' Frey lied, slapping Sharka on the shoulder.

Sharka was as much a survivor as his den was. Since the age of fifteen he'd pounded his body with every kind of narcotic Frey had ever heard of, yet somehow he'd made it to fifty-six, and there was no reason to suppose he didn't have thirty more years left. The man's blood must have been toxic by now, but he was tough as a scorpion. You just couldn't kill him.

'Well, I'll leave you to it. You can find your way, eh? Come see me after, I'll make sure you get an escort to wherever you need. Can't have Dracken's men jumping you on the way out.'

Perhaps the stress of what was to come had made him over-emotional, but Frey was deeply touched by that. Sharka was a dangerous man, but he had a heart of gold, and Frey felt suddenly unworthy of his kindness. Even if he didn't exactly trust him, it was nice to know that *someone* didn't want him dead.

'I'm grateful for what you've done, Sharka,' he said. 'I owe you big.'

'Ah, you don't owe me anything,' Sharka said. 'I like you, Frey. You lose more than you win and you tip big when you score. You don't piss anyone off and you don't re-raise when you're holding dirt and then catch a run on your last card. This place is full of cocky kids with money and old hacks playing percentages. Could do with more players like you at my joint.'

Frey smiled at that. He nodded his thanks again and then headed through the tables towards the back rooms. Sharka was a good sort, he told himself. Sharka wouldn't sell him out for the reward on his head. Everyone knew that Sharka's was neutral ground. He'd lose more in custom than he'd gain by the reward if there was the slightest suspicion that he'd turned in a wanted man. Half the people here were wanted by someone.

A serving girl in an appealingly low-cut dress met him at the back rooms and directed him to one of the private gaming areas. Sharka's was all bare brick and brass – not pretty, but Rake players distrusted glitz.

He stepped in to a small, dim room. A lantern hung from the ceiling, throwing light onto the black baize of the Rake table. A pack of cards was spread out in suits across it. A well-stocked drinks cabinet rested against one wall. There were four chairs around the table.

Sitting in one of the chairs, facing the door, was Trinica Dracken.

The sight of her was a jolt. She was lounging in the chair, small and slim, dressed head to toe in black: black boots, black coat, black gloves, black waistcoat. But from the buttoned collar of her black shirt upwards, everything changed. Her skin was powdered ghost-white. Her hair – so blonde it was almost albino – was cut short, sticking up in uneven tufts as if it had been butchered with a knife. Her lips were a red deep enough to be vulgar.

But it was her eyes that shocked him most. Her lashes were almost invisible, but her irises were completely black, dilated to the size of coins. It took him a moment to realise they were contact lenses, and not the product of some daemonic possession. Worn for effect, no doubt, but certainly effective.

'Hello, Frey,' she said. Her voice was lower than he remembered. 'Long time.'

'You look terrible,' he said as he sat.

'So do you,' she replied. 'Life on the run must not agree with you.'

'Actually, I'm getting to enjoy it. Catching my second wind, so to speak.'

She looked around the room. 'A Rake den? You haven't changed.'

'You have.'

'I had to.'

He gestured at the cards on the table between them. 'Want to play?'

'I'm here to parley, Frey, not play your little game.'

Frey sat back in his chair and regarded her. 'Alright, he said. Business it is. You know, there was a time when you liked to sit and talk for hours.'

'That was then,' she said. 'This is now. I'm not the person you remember.'

That was an understatement. The woman before him was one of the most notorious freebooters in Vardia. She'd engineered a mutiny to become captain of the *Delirium Trigger* and her reputation for utter ruthlessness had earned her the respect of the underworld. Rumour held her responsible for acts of bloody piracy and murder, as well as daring treasure snatches and near-impossible feats of navigation. She was feared by some and envied by others, a dread queen of the skies.

Hard to believe he'd almost married her.

Rabban was one of the nine primary cities of Vardia, and like the others it bore the same name as the duchy it dominated. Though it had suffered terribly in the Aerium Wars, it was still large enough to need over a dozen docks for aircraft. These docks were the first thing to be repaired after the bombing stopped six years ago. Some were little more than islands in a sea of shattered stone, but even these were busy with passenger shuttles, cargo haulers and supply vessels. Transport by air had been Vardia's only viable option for over a century and, even in the aftermath of a disaster, there was no way to do without it.

Only a few of the docks, however, were equipped to deal with a craft the size of the *Delirium Trigger*.

She rested inside a vast iron hangar, alongside frigates and freighters: the heavyweights of the skies. A web of platforms, gantries and walkways surrounded it at deck-height, busy with an ant swarm of engineers, dock workers and swabbers. Everything was being checked, everything cleaned, and a complex exchange of services and trade goods was negotiated. A craft like the *Delirium Trigger*, with a crew of fifty, needed a lot of maintenance.

The *Delirium Trigger*'s purser was a Free Dakkadian named Ominda Rilk. He had the fair skin and hair typical of his race, the small frame and narrow shoulders, and the squinting eyes that still elicited much mockery in the Vardic press. Dakkadians were famed and ridiculed for their administrative abilities. Education and numeracy were much prized among their kind: it made them useful to their Samarlan masters. But Dakkadians, unlike Murthians, could own possessions, and they could earn their freedom.

It was unusual to find a Dakkadian in Vardia, where there was still much bad feeling towards them after the Aerium Wars. They were seen as pernickety coin-counters and misers by the more generous souls; the rest thought they were cunning, underhanded, murdering bastards. But still, here was Ominda Rilk. He stood among the crates and palettes waiting to be loaded onto the *Delirium Trigger*, examining everything and making small notes in his logbook now and again. And his squinty eyes were keen enough to spot two men transporting a very heavy-looking crate in a manner that was frankly quite surreptitious.

'Ho there!' he cried. The men stopped, and he walked briskly over to them. They were dock workers, dressed in battered grey overalls. One was large and big-bellied, with a whiskery white moustache; the other was short, stumpy and ugly, with oversized cheeks and a small thatch of black hair perched atop a small head. They were both flushed and sweating.

'What's this?' he asked, motioning at the crate. It was nine feet tall and six wide, and they'd been rolling it along on a wheeled palette towards the loading area, where a crane picked up supplies for transport to the deck of the *Delirium Trigger*.

'Don't know,' said Malvery, with a shrug. 'We just deliver, don't we?'

'Well, who's it from?' snapped Rilk. 'Where are the papers? Come on!'

Malvery drew out a battered, folded-up set of papers. Rilk shook them open and checked the delivery invoice. His eyebrows raised a fraction when he read the name of the sender. *Gallian Thade*.

'We weren't expecting this,' he said, handing back the papers with a scowl.

Malvery gave him a blank look. 'We just deliver,' he said again. 'This box goes on the *Delirium Trigger*.'

Rilk glared at him, and then at Pinn. There was something not right about these two, but he couldn't put his finger on it. Pinn looked back at him, mutely.

'Does he speak?' Rilk demanded, thumbing at Pinn.

'Not much,' Malvery replied. At least, he'd been told to keep his trap shut, for fear he'd say something stupid and ruin their disguise. Malvery hoped he'd implied enough threat to keep the young pilot in line. 'You want us to load this thing on, or what?'

Rilk studied the crate for a moment. Then he snapped his fingers. 'Open it up.'

Malvery groaned. 'Aw, come on, don't be a—'

'Open it *up*!' Rilk said, snapping his fingers again, in a rather annoying fashion that made Malvery want to break them and then stuff his mangled hand down his throat.

The doctor shrugged and looked at Pinn. 'Open it up,' he said.

Pinn produced a crowbar. The crate had been nailed shut, but they forced open a gap in the front side with relative ease, then pulled it the rest of the way with brute strength. It fell forward and clattered to the ground.

Rilk stared at the hulking, armoured shape inside the box. A monstrosity of metal and leather and chain mail, with a humped back and a circular grille set low between the shoulders. It was cold and silent.

'What *is* it?' he asked.

Malvery pondered for a moment, studying Bess. 'I reckon it's one of those pressure-environment-suit-thingies.'

Rilk looked it up and down, a puzzled frown on his face. 'What does it do?'

'Well, you wear it when you want to work on the deck, see. Like, in arctic environments, or when your craft is really, really high in the sky.'

'It's cold as a zombie's tit up there, and the air's too thin to breathe,' Pinn added, unable to resist joining in. Malvery silenced him with a glare.

'I see,' said Rilk, examining Pinn. 'And how is it a dock worker knows a thing like that?'

Pinn looked lost. 'I just do.'

'Lot of pilots come to the dockside bars,' Malvery said with forced offhandedness. 'People talk.'

'Yes they do,' said Rilk. He walked up to Bess, put his face to her face-grille, and peered inside. 'Hello?' he called. The word echoed in the hollow interior.

'He thinks there's somebody in there,' Malvery grinned at Pinn, giving him a nudge. Pinn chuckled on cue. Rilk withdrew, his pale face reddening.

'Box it up and load it on!' he snapped, then made a quick note in his logbook and stalked away.

'Why did you bring me here, Darian?' asked Trinica Dracken.

'Why did you come?' he countered.

She smiled coldly in the light of the lantern overhead. 'Blowing you out of the sky after all this time seemed a little . . . impersonal,' she replied. 'I wanted to see you. I wanted to look you in the eye.'

'I wanted to see you too,' said Frey. He'd scooped up the cards that were laid out on the table.

'You're a liar. I'm the last person you ever wanted to see again.'

Frey looked down at the cards and began to shuffle them restlessly.

'I had people watching you,' said Trinica. 'Did you know that? After you left me.'

He was faintly chilled. 'I didn't know that.'

'The day after our wedding day, I had the Shacklemores looking for you.'

'It wasn't our wedding day,' said Frey, 'because there wasn't a wedding.'

'A thousand people turned up thinking otherwise,' said Trinica. 'Not to mention the bride. In fact, everyone seemed to think they were there for a magnificent wedding right up until the moment the judge called for the groom.' Her expression became comically sorrowful, a sad clown face. 'And there was the poor bride, waiting in front of all those people.' She blew a puff of air into her hand, opening it out as she did so. 'But the groom had gone.'

Frey was rather unnerved by her delivery. He'd expected shrill remonstrations, but she was utterly empty of emotion. She was talking as if it had happened to someone else. And those black, black eyes made her seem strangely fey and alien. A little frightening, even.

'What do you want, Trinica?' The words came out angrier than he intended. 'An apology? It's a little late for that.'

'Oh, that's most certainly true,' she replied.

Frey settled back in his seat. The sight of her stirred up all the old feelings. Bad feelings. He'd loved this woman once, back when she was sweet and pretty and perfect. Loved her in a way he'd never loved anyone since. But then he'd broken her heart. In return, she'd ripped his to pieces. He could never forget what she'd done to him. He could never forgive her.

But an argument would do him no good now. He couldn't take the risk that Trinica would storm out. The object of this meeting was to keep her here as long as possible, to let his men do their job on the *Delirium Trigger*.

He cleared his throat and strove to control the bitterness in his voice. 'So,' he said. 'You set the Shacklemores on me.' He began cutting the cards and reshuffling them absently.

'You were a hard man to find,' she said. 'It took them six months. By then . . . well, you know what had happened by then.'

Frey's throat tightened. Rage or grief, he wasn't sure.

'They came back and said they'd found you. You were doing freelance work somewhere on the other side of Vardia at the time. Using what you'd learned from working as a hauler for my father's company, I suppose. Making your own deals.'

'It was a living,' said Frey neutrally.

She gave him a faint, distracted smile. 'They asked me if I wanted them to bring you back. I didn't. Not then. I asked them instead to let you know – discreetly – how I was doing. I was sure you hadn't troubled to enquire.'

Frey remembered that meeting well. A stranger in a bar, a shared drink. Casually mentioning that he worked for Dracken Industries. Terrible what had happened to the daughter. Just terrible.

But Trinica was wrong. He *had* enquired. By then, he'd already known what she'd done.

Memories overwhelmed him. Searing love and bilious hate. The stranger before him was a mockery of the young woman he'd almost married. He'd kissed those lips, those whore-red lips that now smiled at him cruelly. He'd heard the softest words pass from them to him.

Ten years. He'd thought that everything would be long ago buried by now. He'd been badly mistaken.

'It didn't seem fair, really,' Trinica said, tilting her head like a bird. There was a childish look on her face that said: *Poor Frey. Poor, poor Frey.* 'It didn't seem fair that you should be able to turn your back and walk away like that. That you could leave your bride on her wedding day and never have to think about what you'd done, never take any responsibility.'

'I *wasn't* responsible!'

She leaned forward on the card table, deadly serious, those awful black eyes staring out of her white face. 'Yes,' she said, 'you were.'

Frey dashed the cards across the table, but his fury died as soon as it had come. He sat back in his chair, his arms folded. He wanted to argue but he needed to keep things calm. Keep things together.

Don't let this bitch get to you. Play for time.

'You had the Shacklemores keep track of me after that?' he asked. Trinica nodded. 'Why the interest?'

'I just forgot to call them off.'

'Oh, come on.'

'It's true. At first, I'll admit, I wanted to see what effect my news would have on you. I wanted to see if you suffered. But then . . . well, I left home, and other things got in the way. It was only years later that I realised they'd been keeping the file open on you all that time, drawing a fee every month. My father was paying for them, you see. When you've that much money, it's easy to forget about something like that.'

'You know I joined the Navy, then?' he said.

'I know they *conscripted* you when the Second Aerium War began,' she said. 'And I know you were drinking too much, and you started taking all the most dangerous jobs. I know nobody wanted to fly with you because it was only a matter of time before you self-destructed.'

'You must have enjoyed hearing all about that.'

'I did, yes,' she replied brightly. 'But I didn't find out until after you had disappeared.'

Frey didn't say anything.

'They tell me the position was overrun by Samarlan troops. My guess is, you landed there and they ambushed you. What happened to the rest of the crew?'

'Dead.'

'Naturally.'

'Navy intelligence,' Frey sneered. 'Bunch of incompetent bastards. They sent us out there and the Sammies were waiting.'

Trinica laughed: the sound was sharp and brittle. 'Same old Darian. Picked on by the world. Nothing's ever your fault, is it?'

'How was it *my* fault?' he cried. 'I landed in a war zone because of information *they* gave me.'

Trinica sighed patiently. 'It was a war, Darian. Mistakes happen all the time. You landed in a war zone because you had been flying the most dangerous front-line missions for months. You never used to ask questions; you just took the missions and flew. It was a miracle it didn't happen sooner.'

'It was the best chance I had to pay off the loan on the *Ketty Jay*,' he protested, but it sounded weak even to him. He couldn't forget the desperate tone in Rabby's voice as he closed the cargo ramp. *Don't you leave me here!*

'If you wanted to die, why didn't you just kill yourself?' Trinica asked. 'Why try and take everyone else with you?'

'I never wanted to die!'

Trinica just looked at him. After a moment she shrugged. 'Well, evidently you didn't want it enough, since here you are. Everyone thought you were gone. The Shacklemores closed the file. The loan company wrote off the rest of your repayments on the *Ketty Jay*. And off you went, a corpse to all intents and purposes. Until one day . . . one day I hear your name again, Darian. Seems you're alive, and everyone's looking for you. And I just had to throw my hat in the ring.'

'You just had to, huh?' Frey said scathingly.

Trinica's demeanour went from casual to freezing in an instant. 'That day you disappeared, you cheated me. I thought I'd never get to make you pay. But you're alive, and that's good. That's a wonderful thing.' She smiled, the chill smile of a predator, her black eyes glittering like a snake watching a mouse. 'Because now I'm going to catch you, my wayward love, and I'm going to watch you hang.'

Twenty-Three

Barricades – Bess Awakes – A Lesson
In Cardplay – The Monster Belowdecks – Thieves

The *Ketty Jay* was berthed at a small dock in the outskirts of Rabban, far from the *Delirium Trigger*. The dock was little more than a barely used landing pad set above a maze of shattered and leaning alleyways. Only a few other craft of similar size shared the space. They sat dark and silent, their crews nowhere to be seen. A few dock personnel wandered around, looking for something to do, their presence revealed by a cough or a slow movement in the shadows. All was quiet.

Silo and Jez worked in the white glare of the *Ketty Jay*'s belly lights, rolling barrels from the cargo hold and manhandling them into rows of five. There were several such rows positioned around the *Ketty Jay*. A haphazard kind of arrangement, an observer might think, unless they guessed what the barrels were really for.

They were building barricades.

Harkins was skirting the edge of the landing pad, scampering along in a crouch, a spyglass in his hand. He stayed out of the light of the electric lamp-posts that marked out the landing pad for flying traffic. Every so often he'd stop and scan the surrounding alleyways, then run off in a nervous fashion to another location and do it again. The dock personnel paid him no mind. As long as his captain paid the berthing fee, they were happy to tolerate eccentrics.

The night was still new when Harkins straightened, his whole body frozen in alarm. He adjusted his spyglass, shifted it this way and that, counting frantically under his breath. Then he fled back towards the *Ketty Jay* as if his heels were on fire.

'Here we go,' said Jez, as she saw him coming. Silo grunted, and levered another barrel of sand into place.

'There's *twenty* of 'em!' Harkins reported in a quiet shriek. 'I mean, give or take a couple, but twenty's near enough! What are we supposed to do against twenty? Or even *nearly* twenty. *Ten* would be too many! What's he expect us to do? I don't like this. Not one measly rotting bit!'

Jez studied him, worried. He was even more strung out than usual. The Firecrow and Skylance were not even in the city: they'd been stashed at a rendezvous point far away. Without his craft, he was a snail out of its shell.

'We do what the Cap'n told us to do,' she said calmly.

'But we didn't know there'd be *twenty*! That's almost half the crew!'

'I suppose Dracken doesn't want to leave anything to chance,' said Jez. She exchanged a glance with Silo, who headed up the cargo ramp and into the *Ketty Jay*.

Harkins watched him go, then turned to Jez with a slightly manic sheen in his eyes. 'Here, *that's* an idea! Why don't we just go inside, close up the cargo hold and lock it? They'd never get in then.'

'You don't think they've thought of that? They'll have explosives. Either that, or someone who knows how to crack open and rewire a keypad.' She motioned towards the small rectangle of buttons nested in the nearby landing strut, used to close and open the cargo ramp from the outside.

The belly lights of the *Ketty Jay* went out, plunging them into twilight. The barely adequate glow of the lamp-posts gave a soft, eerie cast to the near-empty dock. Silo emerged carrying an armful of guns and ammo.

Jez gave Harkins a reassuring pat on the arm. He looked ready to bolt. 'Twenty men here means twenty less for the others to deal with,' she said. 'The Cap'n said Dracken would be coming for us. We're ready for it. We just have to hold out, that's all.'

'Oh, just that!' Harkins moaned with hysterical sarcasm. But then Silo grabbed his hand and slapped a pistol into his palm, and the glare the Murthian gave him was enough to shut him up.

Malvery and Pinn rejoined Crake, who was waiting at a safe remove from the *Delirium Trigger* with a worried frown on his brow. Together, they watched Bess being loaded on. The arm of the crane was chained to the four corners of one great palette, on which were secured dozens of crates. It lifted the palette onto the deck of the *Delirium Trigger*. From there, Dracken's crew carried the crates to a winch which lowered them through an opening into the cargo hold. Dockers were not allowed aboard. Dracken was wise to the dangers of infiltration that way.

'I don't like this,' Crake said to himself, for the tenth time.

'She'll be fine,' said Malvery, looking at his pocket watch.

'And if she's not,' said Pinn, 'you can always build a *new* girlfriend.'

Malvery clipped him around the head. Pinn swore loudly.

'She'll be fine,' Malvery said again.

Pinn fidgeted and adjusted his genitals inside his trousers. He was dressed in dock worker's overalls, as were his companions, with his regular clothes beneath them. It would be necessary to change in a hurry later. Until then, exertion and multiple layers had left him sweltering. 'When can we get on with it? My pods are dripping.'

The others ignored him. He smoked a roll-up resentfully as they observed the activity aboard. The palette, once empty, was lifted off the *Delirium Trigger* by the crane and returned to the elevated hangar deck, where more crates were loaded on.

'Right-o,' said Malvery. 'Let's head down there. Crake, keep your mouth shut. Nobody's gonna believe you're a docker with that accent. Pinn . . . just keep your mouth shut.'

Pinn made a face and spat on the ground.

'Now, the Cap'n wants this to go like clockwork,' Malvery said. 'We all know there's bugger all chance of that, so let's just try not to get ourselves killed, and we'll all be having a drink and a laugh about this by dawn.'

They made their way back across the busy dock, weaving between piles of chests and netting and screeching machinery. Huge cogs turned; cage-lifts rattled up and down from the lower hangar decks. Cranes swung overhead, and shouts echoed round the iron girders of the roof, where squadrons of pigeons roosted and shat. A massive freighter was easing in on the far side of the hangar, its aerium tanks keeping it weightless, nudging into place with its gas-jets.

Posing as dock workers, the three imposters were invisible in the chaos. They picked some cargo from a stack of netted crates and barrels that were being loaded onto the *Delirium Trigger*, and made their way towards the huge palette that was chained to the crane arm. The cargo had been piled high on the palette by now. They carried their loads on and went around to the far side of the palette, where they couldn't be seen by the workers on the dock. There, they began unlashing a group of crates, rearranging them to make a space.

Another docker rounded the corner, carrying a heavy-looking chest. Malvery, Pinn and Crake did their best to look focused and industrious. The docker – a grizzled, burly man with salt-and-pepper hair – watched them in puzzlement for a moment, then decided that whatever they were doing wasn't interesting enough to comment on. He put down the chest, secured it with some netting and left.

Once they'd dug out a space, they checked the coast was clear and crammed in. Then they stacked their own crates in front of it, sealing themselves inside.

Their timing was perfect. No sooner had they hushed each other to silence than a steam-whistle blew. They heard the footsteps of dock workers beyond their hiding place, evacuating the palette, and then, with a lurch, it began to lift.

Malvery had to steady the unsecured crates in front of them, for fear of being buried; but the crane moved slowly and the palette was heavy enough to be stable. Though the crates made slight and distressing shifts, nothing moved far enough to fall. Tucked in their little corner, they felt themselves transported across the gap between the hangar deck and the deck of the *Delirium Trigger*.

Crake found himself thinking that this must be how a mouse felt. Hiding in the dark, at the mercy of the world, frightened by every unknown sound. Spit and blood, he hated this. He didn't have it in him to be a stowaway. He was too afraid of getting caught.

But Bess was aboard. He was committed now. He'd committed her.

Why did you do it? Why did you agree to this?

He agreed to it because he was ashamed. Because since their encounter with the man from the Shacklemore Agency, he couldn't look Jez in the eye. Absurdly, he felt he *owed* her something. He felt he owed the crew. He needed to atone, to make amends for being such a despicable, vile monster. To apologise for his presence among them. To make himself worthy.

Anyway, it was too late to turn back now.

'We're nearly there,' Malvery said. 'Do it.'

Crake drew out his small brass whistle. He put it to his lips and blew. It made no sound at all.

'That's it?' asked Pinn, bemused.

'That's it,' said Crake.

'So now what happens?'

'Bess has just woken up to find that she's in a box,' Crake replied. 'I wouldn't want to be in the *Delirium Trigger*'s cargo hold right now.'

By the time the palette bumped down onto the deck, the howling and smashing had begun.

'I suppose you know I'm innocent, don't you?' Frey asked.

Trinica was pouring two glasses of whisky from the drinks cabinet. She looked back at him: a moon-white face partially eclipsed by the black slope of her shoulder.

'You're not *innocent*, Frey. You killed those people. It doesn't matter if you were set up or not.'

'The *Ace of Skulls* was rigged to blow. Those people were going to die anyway, with or without me.'

'*Everyone* is going to die, with or without you. It doesn't mean you're allowed to murder them.'

She was needling him and he knew it. It enraged him. She always had a way of pricking at his conscience, puncturing his excuses. She never let him get away with anything.

'You were in on it, then?' he asked. 'The plot?'

She handed him his whisky and sat down again. The card table lay between them, the cards face down where they'd been thrown by Frey. Skulls, Wings, Dukes and Aces, all hidden in a jumble.

'No. I didn't set you up. I didn't know you were alive until I heard you were wanted.'

'But you know now. You know Duke Grephen is the man behind it all, and that Gallian Thade is in on it too. You know they made me the scapegoat?'

She raised an eyebrow, blonde against white. 'My. You evidently think you've learned a lot. Was that your sucker punch? Should I be awed at how clever you've been?'

'A little awe would be nice, yes.'

She sipped her whisky. 'I assume you're appealing to my better nature? Wondering how I could be part of such a terrible miscarriage of justice? How I could willingly let you take the blame for the death of Hengar when I know it was Grephen's idea?'

'That's about the size of it.'

'Because Grephen is paying me a lot of money. And because, frankly, I'd do it for free. You deserve it.'

'It doesn't concern you to be an accomplice to the murder of the Archduke's son? Don't you think there might be bigger implications involved?'

'Possibly there are,' said Trinica. 'But that's none of your concern, since it'll all be over for you very soon.'

'Come on, Trinica. Hengar's death is only the start. You must know if Duke Grephen is planning something.'

Trinica smiled. 'Must I?'

Frey cursed her silently. She wasn't giving anything away. He wanted to push her for more information, but she wouldn't play the game. Telling her that he knew about Grephen was intended to lead her up the wrong path, but he couldn't reveal that he knew about the coup, or her mysterious hideout. That would tip his hand.

'One question,' he said. 'The ferrotype. The one on the Wanted posters. How did they get that, if you didn't give it to them?'

'Yes, I was surprised, too,' she said. 'We had it taken when we were up in the mountains. Do you remember?'

Frey remembered. He remembered a time of romantic adventure, a couple newly in love. He was a lowly cargo pilot and she was the daughter of his boss, one of the heirs to Dracken Industries. He was poor and she was rich, and she loved him anyway. It was breathless, dangerous, and they were both swept giddily along, careless of consequences, armoured by their own happiness.

'It was my father who gave it to them, I'd imagine,' she said. 'I suppose the Navy had no pictures of you, and they knew you had worked for Dracken Industries before that. They were probably hoping for a staff photograph.'

'He kept *that* one?'

'He kept it because I was in it. I imagine that's how he'd like to remember me.'

The Wanted posters had only shown Frey's face, but in the full picture, Trinica was clinging to his arm, laughing. Laughing at nothing, really. Laughing just to laugh. He remembered the ferrotype perfectly. Her hair blowing, mouth open and teeth white. A rare, perfect capture; a frozen instant of natural, unforced joy. No one would connect that young girl with the woman sitting in front of him.

In that moment, Frey felt the tragedy of that loss. How cruel it was, that things had turned out the way they did.

But Trinica saw the expression on his face, and correctly guessed its cause. She always knew his thoughts, better than anyone.

'Look at yourself, Darian. Cursing the fate that brought you here. One day, you're going to realise that everything that's happened to you has been your own fault.'

'Dogshit,' he spat, sadness turning to venom in an instant. 'I've tried my damnedest. I tried to better myself.'

'And yet here you are, ten years later, barely scraping a living. And I am the captain of a crew of fifty, infamous and rich.'

'I'm not like you, Trinica. I wasn't born with a silver spoon shoved up my arse. I didn't have a good education. Some of us don't get the luck.'

She looked at him for a long moment. Then her black eyes dropped to the face-down cards, scattered on the table.

'I remember when you used to talk about Rake,' she said, idly picking up a card and flipping it over. It was the Lady of Crosses. 'You used to say everyone thought luck was a huge factor. They said it was all about the cards you were dealt. Mostly luck and a bit of skill.' She flipped over another: Ten of Fangs. 'You thought they were idiots. You knew it was mostly skill and a bit of luck.'

The Ace of Skulls came next. Frey hated that card. It ruined any hand in Rake, unless it could be made part of a winning combination, which could hardly ever be done.

'A good player might occasionally lose to a mediocre one, but in the long run, the good players made money while the bad ones went broke,' Trinica continued.

The next card came up: the Duke of Skulls. Any Priest would give her a five-card run to the Ace of Skulls, an unbeatable combination.

She turned the final card: the Seven of Wings. The hand was busted. Her gaze flicked up from the table and met his.

'Over time, luck is hardly a factor at all,' she said.

Belowdecks, the *Delirium Trigger* was in chaos. A slow, steady pounding reverberated through the dim passageways. Metal screeched. Men shouted and ran, some towards the sound and some away from it.

'It's in the cargo hold!'

'*What's* in the cargo hold?'

But nobody could answer that. Those inside the hold had fled in terror when the iron-and-leather monstrosity burst out of its crate and began rampaging through the shadowy aisles. Barrels were flung this way and that. Guns fired, but to no avail. The air had filled with splinters as the intruder smashed through crates of provisions and trade goods. It was dark down there, and the looming thing terrified the crewmen.

Those on the deck above, operating the winch, had peered fearfully through the hatch into the cargo hold at the first signs of a disturbance. The light from the hangar barely penetrated to the floor of the hold. They scrambled back as they caught a glimpse of something huge lunging across their narrow field of view. It was only then that one of them thought to raise the winch.

In the confusion that ensued, nobody noticed three strangers, now dressed in the dirty motley of crewmembers, making their way belowdecks.

Those who had managed to escape from the cargo hold had slammed the bulkhead door behind them and locked it shut, trapping the monster inside. But the monster didn't like being trapped. It was pounding on the inside of the door, hard enough to buckle eight inches of metal. Enraged bellows came from behind.

'Get your fat stenching carcasses over here!' the burly, dirt-streaked bosun yelled. The men he was yelling at had come to investigate the sound, and were now backing away as they saw what was happening. They reluctantly returned at his command. 'Weapons ready, all of you! You *will* defend your craft!'

A rotary cannon on a tripod was being hastily erected in the passageway in front of the door. The bosun knelt down next to the crewman who was assembling the cannon. 'When that thing comes through the door, give it everything you've got!'

Malvery, Crake and Pinn skirted the chaos as best they could, and for a time they were unmolested. The *Delirium Trigger* was only half-crewed, and almost all of them were occupied with the diversion Bess was creating. They did their best to avoid meeting anyone, and when they were seen it was usually at a distance, or by somebody who was already hurrying elsewhere. They managed to penetrate some way into the aircraft before they came up against a crewmember who got a good look at them, and recognised them as imposters.

'Hey!' he said, before Malvery grabbed his head and smashed

his skull against the wall of the passageway. He slumped to the floor, unconscious.

'Not big on talking your way out of things, are you?' Crake observed, as they dragged the unfortunate crewman into a side room.

'My way's quicker,' he said, adjusting his round green glasses. 'No danger of misunderstanding.'

The side room was a galley, empty now, its stoves cold. Crake shut the door while Malvery ran some water into a tin cup. The crewman – a young, slack-jawed deckhand – began to groan and stir. Malvery threw the water in his face. His eyes opened and slowly focused on Pinn, who was standing over him, pointing a pistol at his nose.

Malvery squatted down next to the prisoner and tapped him on the head with the base of the tin cup, making him wince. 'Captain's cabin,' he said. 'Where?'

They left the deckhand bound and gagged in a cupboard of the galley. Pinn was for shooting him, but Crake wouldn't allow it. Pinn's argument that he was 'just a deckhand, no one would miss him' carried little weight.

The captain's cabin was locked, of course, but Crake had come prepared. Given the time and the materials, it was a simple trick for him to produce a daemonic skeleton key. He slipped it into the lock and concentrated, forming a mental chord in the silence of his mind, awakening the daemon thralled to the key. His fingers became numb as it sucked the strength from him. Though small, it was hungry, and beyond the power of any but a trained daemonist to handle.

The daemon extended invisible tendrils of influence, feeling out the lock, caressing the levers and tumblers. Then the key turned sharply, and the door was open.

Malvery patted him on the shoulder. 'Good job, mate,' he grinned. Crake felt oddly warmed by that. Then he heard the distant pounding echoing through the *Delirium Trigger*, and he remembered Bess.

'Let's get this done,' he said, and they went inside.

Dracken's cabin was spotlessly clean, but the combination of brass, iron and dark wood gave it a heavy and oppressive feel. A bookshelf took up one wall, a mix of literature, biography and navigational manuals interspersed with shiny copper ornaments. Some of the titles were in Samarlan script, Crake noticed. He spotted *The Singer and the Songbird* and *On the Domination of Our Sphere*, two great works by the Samarlan masters. He found himself taken by an unexpected admiration for a pirate who would – or even could – read that kind of material.

Pinn and Malvery had gone straight to the desk on the far side of the cabin, which sat next to a sloping window of reinforced windglass. The light from the hangar spilled onto neatly arranged charts and a valuable turtleshell writing set. Crake had a sudden picture of Dracken looking thoughtfully out of that window at a sea of clouds as her craft flew high in the sky.

Pinn pawed through the charts, scattering them about and ruining Crake's moment of reverie. 'Nothing,' he said.

Malvery's eye had fallen on a long, thin chest on a shelf near the desk. It was padlocked. 'Crake!' he said, and the daemonist came over with his skeleton key. The lock was trickier than the one that secured the cabin door, but in the end, it couldn't stand up to the key.

It was full of rolled-up charts. Atop them was what seemed to be a large compass. Malvery passed the compass to Crake, then began scanning through the charts with Pinn. Crake listened to the booming coming from the depths of the *Delirium Trigger* as he studied Malvery's discovery.

Keep pounding, Bess, he thought. *As long as I hear you, I know you're all right.*

The compass was so big that Crake could barely hold it in one hand. It was also, on closer examination, not a compass at all. It had no North-South-West-East markings, and it had four needles instead of one, all of equal length and numbered. Additionally, there were eight tiny sets of digits, set in pairs, with each digit on a rotating cylinder to allow it to count from zero to nine. These set pairs were also numbered one to four, presumably to correspond with the needles. The needles were all pointing in the same direction, no matter which way he turned it, and the numbers were all at zero.

'I think we found 'em!' Malvery said. He scooped up all the charts from the chest and shoved them inside his threadbare jersey, then looked at Crake. 'Is that the device you were after?'

'I believe it is.'

Crake had little doubt that what he held was the mysterious device Thade had mentioned. The strangeness of the compass, and the fact that it had been placed in the same chest as the charts, was enough for him.

'We should—' he began, but then he saw a movement in the doorway, and there was the loud report of a gun.

Malvery had seen it too: one of the crew, a black-haired, scruffy man, drawn by the sound of voices and the sight of the captain's door left open. On seeing the intruders, the crewman hastily pulled his gun and fired. The doctor ducked aside, fast enough so that the bullet only grazed his shoulder.

Another gun fired, an instant after the first. Pinn's. The crewman gaped, and a bright swell of blood soaked out from his chest into his shirt. He staggered back and slid down the wall of the passageway outside, disbelief in his eyes.

'We got what we came for,' said Malvery, his voice flat. 'Time to go.'

The crewman lay in the passageway, gasping for air. Pinn and Malvery passed without looking at him, pausing only to steal his pistol. Crake edged by as if he was contagious, horrified and fascinated. The crewman's eyes followed his, rolling in their sockets with an awful, empty interest.

Crake found himself pinned by that gaze. It was the look of a man unprepared, shocked to find himself at the gates of death so swiftly and unexpectedly. There was bewilderment in that look. The dying man was crushed by the knowledge that, unlike every other desperate moment in his life, there was no second chance, no way that wit or strength could pull him clear. It filled Crake with terror.

Now Crake knew why Malvery and Pinn hadn't looked.

He was trembling as he followed his companions up the corridor. After a moment, he remembered Bess. He put the whistle to his lips, the whistle tuned to a frequency that only she could hear, and he blew. It was a note different from the one he used to wake her up and put her to sleep. This one was a signal.

Time to come back, Bess.

'Any moment now, boys!' the bosun yelled, as the bulkhead door screeched and lurched forward on its hinges. It was possible to see glimpses of movement through the gap at the top of the door, where the eight-inch steel had bent forward under the assault of the creature in the cargo hold. Enough to see that there was something massive behind, something as fearsome as its roaring suggested.

The crew braced themselves, aiming their revolvers and lever-action shotguns. The man operating the tripod-mounted rotary cannon flexed his trigger finger, wiped sweat from his brow and sighted. The door had given up the struggle now. Each blow could be the one that brought them face to face with the thing in the hold.

Doubt was on their faces. All their guns seemed suddenly pitiful. Only discipline kept them in place, crowded in the dim passageway.

The door buckled inwards, its upper hinge coming away completely. One more blow. One more.

But the final blow didn't come. And still it didn't come. And, after a time, it seemed it wasn't going to.

The men let out their pent-up breath, unsure what this new turn of events might mean. Each had been resigned to their fate. Had they been reprieved? They didn't dare to hope.

Some of them began to whisper. What had happened? Why had it stopped? Where had the thing in the hold gone?

From beyond the ruined door, there was only silence.

Twenty-Four

Dynamite – Jez Hears A Call – A Swift
Retreat – The Cards Are On The Table

'To your left! Harkins, to your left!'

Harkins waved his pistol in the vague direction of the enemy and fired three wild shots before cringing back into the cover of the barrels. The shadowy figure he was aiming for ran behind a parked fighter craft and disappeared from sight.

'Nice shooting,' Jez murmured sarcastically under her breath, then resumed scanning the dock for signs of movement. She flinched as three bullets pocked the barrels in front of her, searching her out. But the barrels were full of sand, and they were as good as a wall.

They'd put the *Ketty Jay* down close to a corner of the elevated landing pad, so as to give themselves only two sides to defend when Dracken's men came for them. The barricades gave them good cover, and the largely empty dock meant that Dracken's men had a lot of open space to deal with. But they had twenty men out there, and on Jez's side there were only three. Two, if you didn't count Harkins, and he wasn't really worth counting. She checked her pocket watch and cursed.

They couldn't hold out. Not against these odds.

Silo was crouched behind a barricade to her right, sighting along a rifle. He fired twice at something Jez couldn't see. An answering salvo chipped the wood inches from his face.

There was one unforeseen disadvantage to their choice of position. Being close to the edge of the landing pad meant that they were near the lamp-posts that delineated it for the benefit of aerial traffic. Their attackers, on the other hand, had crossed the pad and were shooting from its centre, where it was darkest. The landing-pad staff – who would use spotlights to pick out places for craft to land – had fled when the battle began, presumably to rouse the militia.

Jez wasn't hopeful. She doubted help would come through these broken alleys soon enough. Besides, being arrested by the militia was as sure a death sentence as Dracken's men were. They'd be recognised as fugitives and hung.

Privately, Jez wondered if she'd survive that.

Don't worry about that now. Deal with the things you can deal with.

'Silo!' she hissed. 'The lights!' She thumbed at the lamp-posts.

Silo got the message. He sat with his back to the barrels and shot out the nearest lamp-post. Jez took out another. In short order, they'd destroyed all the lamp-posts nearby, and the *Ketty Jay* sat in a darkness equal to that of their attackers.

But the distraction had let Dracken's men sneak closer. Even in a quiet dock like this, there were hiding places. The need to fuel and restock aircraft meant there was always some kind of clutter, whether it be an idle tractor for pulling cargo, small corrugated sheds for storage, or a trailer full of empty prothane barrels waiting to be taken away.

There was movement everywhere. A shot could come from any angle. Sooner or later, something was going to get through.

Harkins was whimpering nearby. Silo told him to shut up. She looked at her pocket watch again. Rot and damnation, this was bad. They hadn't expected twenty. Ten they could have held off. Maybe.

Something skittered across the landing pad, a bright fizz in the gloom. It took Jez only a moment to realise what it was. Dynamite.

'Down!' she cried, and then the stick exploded with a concussion hard enough to clap the air against her ears. The barrels murmured and rattled under the assault, but the throw had fallen short. Dracken's men weren't close enough to get it over the barricades. But it wouldn't be long before they were.

She looked back at the *Ketty Jay*, rising above them like a mountain. The cargo ramp was open, beckoning them in. She thought about what Harkins had suggested when he first saw Dracken's men coming. How long could they hold out inside? How much damage would a stick of dynamite do to the *Ketty Jay*?

Of course, Dracken's men might have more dynamite. And a lot of sticks of dynamite could do a lot of damage.

She raised her head and looked out over the barrels, but was driven down again by a salvo of bullets, coming from all sides. Panic fluttered in her belly. They'd keep her pinned, creeping nearer and nearer until they could fling dynamite over the barricade. There were too many to hold back.

And then, almost unnoticed, she felt the change. It was becoming more natural now, a slight push through an invisible membrane: the tiniest resistance, then a parting. Sliding into elsewhere, easy as thought.

The world altered. The dark was still dark, but it didn't obscure her vision any more. She sensed them now: eighteen men, two women. Their thoughts were a hiss, like the rushing of the waves along the coast.

Panic swelled and consumed her. She was out of control. Her senses had sharpened to an impossible degree. She *smelled* them out there. She heard their footsteps. And in the distance, far beyond the range of physical hearing, she heard something else. A cacophony of cries. The engines of a dreadful craft. And its crew, calling her. Calling in one wordless, discordant chorus.

Come with us. Come to the Wrack.

She recoiled from them, trying to focus her thoughts on anything other than the beckoning of that nightmarish crew. But instead of snapping out of that strange state, her mind veered away and fixed on something else. She felt herself sucked in, as she had been in Yortland watching predators stalking snow-hogs. But this time it was no animal she joined with: it was a man.

She felt his tension, the sweat of him, the thrill of the moment. Comfort and satisfaction at being on the winning side. He knew they had the advantage. Don't slip up, though, you old dog. Plenty of graves full of the overconfident (*pleased with that line, use it on the boys)*. Seems like they're keeping their heads down, now. That dynamite scared 'em good.

Need to get closer. Get a good shot on 'em then. Cap'n (*respect awe protectiveness admiration*) would love it if you bagged one for her. Come on. Just over there.

Run for it!

Suddenly Jez was moving, rising, sighting down her rifle. She was in him and she was herself, two places at once. She knew where he was; she saw through his eyes; she felt his legs pumping as they carried him.

Her finger squeezed the trigger, and she shot him through the head at forty metres in the dark.

His thoughts stopped. All sense of him was gone. He was blanked, leaving only a hole. And Jez was thrust back into herself, her senses all her own again, curled in a foetal ball behind her barricade as she tried to understand what had just happened to her.

What am I? What am I becoming?

But she knew what she was becoming. She was becoming one of *them*. One of the nightmare crew. One of the creatures that lived in the wastes behind the impenetrable cloud-wall of the Wrack.

I have to run, she told herself, as a fresh volley of gunfire was unleashed. Bullets ricocheted off the side of the *Ketty Jay*. Another stick of dynamite fell close enough to knock over some of the barrels at the end of a barricade.

'We can't hold out no more!' screeched Harkins.

No, she thought grimly. *We can't.*

The deck of the *Delirium Trigger* was all but deserted. Most of the skeleton crew were in the guts of the aircraft, anxiously listening to the silence coming from the cargo hold. Others had gone to summon the militia. In the face of such alarm, nobody was loading cargo or swabbing the decks. When Malvery, Pinn and Crake emerged from the captain's cabin with their plunder, there were no crew to stop them.

They raced across to the winch, now unmanned. A loaded

palette was dangling over the cavernous hatch that led to the cargo hold. Pinn flustered around the controls for a few moments before finding something that he assumed would lower the winch. As it turned out, he was right. There was a loud screech and the palette began to rattle downwards.

Crake scanned the craft nervously. A crowd of dock workers had gathered around the *Delirium Trigger* on the hangar deck, but nobody dared cross the gangplank. They'd heard men talking about a monster aboard. Now they followed the activity of the newcomers with keen interest, assuming them to be crew.

Crake didn't even see who shot at them. Pinn threw himself back, spitting a foul oath, as the bullet hit the winch next to his head. They scrambled out of the way, searching for their assailant, but there was no sign of one. Crake tripped and sprawled as another rifle shot sounded. Fear flooded him. He couldn't take shelter if he didn't know what direction the attack was coming from.

That didn't bother Malvery overmuch. 'Get to cover!' he yelled, rushing towards an artillery battery, a cluster of massive cannons.

Crake scrambled after him. Another bullet hit. Out of the corner of his eye Crake saw the dock workers shouting in consternation. They were unsure who the villain was here. Some were following Crake's plight, but others were looking at a spot above and behind him.

He looked over his shoulder. There, where the deck of the *Delirium Trigger* rose up towards an electroheliograph mast, he saw movement. A man, crouching, aiming.

Then Crake was behind the cannons, hunkering down next to Pinn and Malvery. 'He's up there!' he panted. 'By the mast!'

Malvery swore under his breath. 'We need to get off this bloody aircraft, sharpish. Before them down below work out what's going on.'

There was a sudden whine of strained metal from the winch. The chain swung sharply one way, then another, pulled from below.

Malvery edged along the barrel of the cannon and peered out

for an instant, then drew back. 'I see the bastard.' He drew a pistol from his belt. It looked tiny in his huge hand. His usual shotgun had been too large to smuggle beneath their clothes.

'Wait,' said Crake. 'Not yet.'

The chain pulled restlessly back and forth. The mechanism shrieked in protest at the weight it was carrying. The weight of the golem, clambering up the length of the chain and out of the cargo hold.

An enormous hand grabbed on to the lip of the hatch. Bess pulled herself up with a low bass groan, hauling her enormous bulk onto the deck.

'Now!' said Crake. Malvery swung out of hiding, aimed his pistol, and fired at the crewman hiding near the mast. The crewman, amazed by the sight of Bess, was taken by surprise. The shot missed by inches, but it startled him enough to send him scrambling out of sight.

The dock workers on the hangar deck were panicking now, beginning to flee as Bess drew herself up to her full height. They'd never seen anything like her, this humpbacked, faceless armoured giant. Those who were nearest fought to get out of the way, pushing aside the men at the back who were crowding closer to see what the fuss was about.

'Bess!' Crake called as they broke from hiding. The golem swung towards him with a welcoming gurgle. He hurried up to her and quickly patted her on the shoulder. The dock workers' fear of Bess grew to encompass Crake and the others now: they were friends with the beast! 'We're getting out of here.'

Malvery sent another blast towards the electroheliograph tower as they ran for the gangplank. There were shouts of alarm from behind them as crewmen were roused by the gunfire. Bullets nipped at their heels. Pinn sent a few back, shooting wild.

Bess thundered down the gangplank and onto the hangar deck, the others close behind. The dock workers melted away from the *Delirium Trigger* like ice before a blowtorch, spreading chaos through the hangar as they fled. All activity came to a halt as crewmen on nearby freighters sensed the disturbance.

Malvery took the lead, heading towards the stairs that would take them to ground level, where they could exit the hangar. But he'd barely started in that direction when whistles sounded from below: the Ducal Militia of Rabban. Beige uniforms began to flood up the stairs that Malvery had been running for.

Too many men. Too many guns. Bess could make it through, but her more fragile, fleshy companions wouldn't.

Malvery came to a halt, pulled out his pocket watch and consulted it. He looked back at the *Delirium Trigger*, where the angry crew was already marshalling for pursuit. The militia had blocked their escape route. There was no way out.

'Alright,' he said. 'Now we've got problems.'

Trinica Dracken looked at her pocket watch, snapped it shut and slipped it back inside the folds of her black coat.

'You need to be somewhere, Trinica?' Frey enquired.

She looked up at him across the card table. She seemed to be weighing a question.

'I think we've beaten around the bush for long enough, Darian. You wanted to parley. Speak your piece.'

Her tone was newly impatient. Frey put two and two together.

'Why the hurry, Trinica? You were happy to make small talk until now. You wouldn't have been trying to buy time, would you? Delaying me here for some reason?'

He caught the flicker of anger in her eyes, and felt a small satisfaction. She'd had the best of this meeting so far: it was good to score a point on her.

'Make your offer,' she said. 'Or this meeting is over.'

Might as well try, thought Frey. 'I want you to give up the chase. Turn your back and leave us alone.'

'What good will that do? You'll still be wanted by the Century Knights.'

'The Century Knights I can handle. They don't know the underworld. I can scatter my crew, duck my head till the worst of it blows over. Maybe I'll get out of Vardia. Sell the *Ketty Jay*, get a real job. But not with you on my heels. Most of them don't even know my face except from some old ferrotype, but you do. I think you'd find me in the end. So I'm asking you to give it up.'

Trinica was waiting for the punchline. 'Grephen is paying me a lot of money to track you down. Certainly more than you've ever seen in your life. What can you possibly offer me that would tempt me to give that up?'

'I'll keep your name out of it if I get caught.'

'You'll *what*?' She was midway between amusement and astonishment.

'You're a traitor. You're a knowing accomplice in the murder of the Archduke's only son. The Coalition Navy never managed to pin anything on you – maybe because the witnesses have an odd habit of dying – but they know what you are and they'll jump at the chance to see you swing from the gallows. You know Grephen is afraid of the Knights getting me before you do. He's afraid I'll make accusations against him.'

'That's the best you've got?' Trinica laughed. 'The accusations of a condemned man, without any proof to back them up?'

'Have you thought what's going to happen if whatever Grephen's planning *doesn't* work?' Frey asked. 'My accusations might not save me, but if Grephen makes a move on the Archduke then he'll prove what I said about him is true. And that will mean everything I said about *you* will be true. Now maybe Grephen will win and everything will be alright for you, but if he loses, you'll have the Navy all over you for the rest of your days. You certainly won't be docking in a place like Rabban anytime soon.'

'Why would you believe he's making a move on the Archduke?'

Frey gave her a look. 'I'm not stupid, Trinica.'

She studied him. Considering. He'd seen that expression a hundred times before at a Rake table, as players stared at their opponents and asked themselves: *do they really have the cards to beat me?*

Then she snorted, disgusted at herself for allowing him to threaten her.

'This is ridiculous, and I don't have time for it any more. It's all

235

over now, besides. I've got you.' She drained her whisky and got to her feet. 'You're done.'

'This is a parley, Trinica. Neutral ground. Sharka guarantees our safety,' he grinned at her. 'Can't get me here,' he added, rather childishly.

'Of course not,' she said. 'But I can get your craft.'

'You don't even know where she is.'

'Certainly I do,' she replied. 'You're berthed in the Southwest Labourer's Quarter. Of course you registered under a false name, but I had every dock master in the city keeping an eye out for a Wickfield Ironclad-class cargo-combat hybrid. There aren't many around with the *Ketty Jay*'s specifications, and I do know that craft quite well. I listened to you talk about her enough.'

Frey was unperturbed. Trinica noted his lack of reaction.

'Obviously, you guessed I'd do something like this,' she said. 'It doesn't matter. How many men do you have, Frey? Five? Six? Can you afford to keep that many?' She looked around the room; he bored her now. 'I sent twenty.'

Twenty, thought Frey, keeping his face carefully neutral, the way he'd learned to at the card table. *Oh, shit.*

'What if I did the same?' he said. 'What if my men are on *your* craft, right now?'

Trinica rolled her eyes. 'Please, Darian. You never could bluff well. You're too much the coward: you always give in first.'

She sighed and looked down at him, as if pitying a dumb animal. 'I know you,' she said. 'You're predictable. That's why I almost caught you at the hermitage. Once Thade told me about you and his daughter I realised that was the first place you'd go. You always did think with the wrong organ.'

Frey didn't reply. She had him there.

'You want to know why I'm a good captain and you're not? Because you don't trust your people. I've earned my men's respect and they've earned mine. But you? You can't keep a crew, Darian. You go through navigators like whores.'

Frey kept his mouth shut. He couldn't argue. There was nothing to say.

236

'And because I know you, I know you'd never trust anyone with your aircraft,' she continued, walking past him towards the door. 'The *Ketty Jay* is your life. You'd rather die than give the ignition codes to someone who might fly off with her. That means your crew are outnumbered, outgunned, and trapped, defending an aircraft that's nothing more than an armoured tomb.' She cocked her head. 'Perhaps you were thinking of some clever flanking manoeuvre. Perhaps you're going to bring in reinforcements behind my men. Whatever you try, it makes no difference. You just don't have the numbers.'

Frey's shoulders slumped. Twenty men. How long could Jez, Silo and Harkins hold out against twenty men? Everything had relied on timing, but it was only now he truly realised how desperate the situation was. The plan had sounded so fine coming out of his mouth. But he was the only one not risking his life here.

Trinica saw how it hit him like a hammer. She touched his shoulder in false sympathy and leaned down to whisper in his ear, her lips brushing his lobe. 'By now they'll be dead, and my men will have filled the *Ketty Jay* with so much dynamite, the explosion will be heard in Yortland.'

She opened the door and looked back at him. 'This will be the second time your crew died because of your hang-ups, Darian. Let's see how far and fast you run without your aircraft.'

Then she was gone, leaving the door open behind her. Frey sat at the table, looking down at the mess of cards before him, feeling pummelled and raw and slashed to ribbons. She'd taken him apart with nothing more than words.

That woman. That bloody woman.

Twenty-Five

*Flight – 'Pick Your
Targets' – No Way Out*

Crake ran hard. His lungs were burning in his chest and his head felt light, but his legs were tireless, filled with strength lent by adrenaline. Bess lumbered ahead, Malvery and Pinn hot on her heels. Bullets scored the air around them.

But they were only delaying the inevitable. There was nowhere left to go.

The hangar deck was crowded with cranes, portable fuel tanks and piled cargo. Massive cogs rose out of the floor, part of a mechanism that clamped aircraft in their berths and prevented heavy freighters from drifting. In the distance, elevated platforms for spotlights and a narrow controller's tower rose almost to the roof of the hangar.

They used these obstacles as cover, darting past and around them, blocking the aim of the *Delirium Trigger*'s crew. Nobody attempted to stop them with Bess leading the way. Dock workers fled for cover, frightened by the wild gunplay of their pursuers.

The mouth of the hangar opened out to the night and the electric lights of the city. But the hangar deck was forty feet up, and there was no way down. The militia had spread out to block all the stairways. They were trapped, but still they ran, eking every last moment out of their liberty and their lives. There was nothing else left to do.

Bess slowed as they passed another pile of cargo waiting to be loaded onto a frigate. She picked up a crate and lobbed it effortlessly towards their pursuers. They scattered and scrambled away as it smashed apart in their midst. Crake and the others raced past her, and she took up position at the rear. A rifle shot bounced off her armoured back, spinning away with a high whine, as she turned to follow them.

Why did I come here? Crake thought. It was the same question he'd been asking himself all night. *Why did I agree to do this? Stupid, stupid, stupid.*

He flayed himself with his own terror as he ran, cursing his idiocy. He could have just refused. He could have stayed out of this and left at any time. But he'd allowed himself to be roped into Frey's plan, driven by self-loathing and his captain's insidious charm. Back in Yortland, he'd been ready to throw it all in and leave Frey to his fate. Yet somehow, he found himself agreeing to join the *Ketty Jay*'s crew.

He'd made an error. He'd momentarily forgotten that time in the dingy back room of a bar, when Lawsen Macarde held a pistol to his head and told Frey to give up the ignition codes to the *Ketty Jay*. He'd forgotten the look on Frey's face, those cold, uncaring eyes, like doll's eyes. He'd allowed himself to believe – *again* – that Frey was his friend.

And because of that, he was going to die.

They dodged around machinery and vaulted over fuel pipes, rushing through the oily metal world of the hangar. Dark iron surrounded them; dim lights glowed; everything was covered with a thin patina of grime. They could expect no quarter here. This wasn't a place for sympathy, but for the unforgiving industry of the new world. Crake had grown up on country estates, surrounded by trees, and had rarely ever seen the factories which had made his family rich. Now a grim fatalism swept over him. It seemed a terrible place to live a life, and a worse one to end it in.

The deck narrowed as they reached the mouth of the hangar, splitting into long walkways that led to spotlight stations and observation platforms. To their left and right, half-submerged below the elevated deck, were freighters and passenger liners, colossal in their shabby majesty. There were people lining the rail, watching their plight with interest, safely remote.

'Up here!' cried Malvery, and they were funnelled onto a gantry that projected out to the mouth of the hangar. It was wide enough for three abreast, but at the end there was nothing but a small observation platform. After that, there was only the fatal plunge to the ground.

It didn't matter. They ran until the gantry ran out, and there they stopped.

The crew of the *Delirium Trigger* slowed, seeing their quarry was trapped. They gathered at the end of the gantry, where there was cover. Between them and the men of the *Ketty Jay* was a long, open stretch. They'd be easy targets there, and they still feared the golem enough to respect its power.

'Now what?' Pinn asked.

'Now we surrender,' said Malvery.

'We *what*?' cried Pinn.

The doctor's grin spread beneath his thick white moustache. Pinn grinned back as he caught on. Crake was appalled to find that he was the only one who seemed nervous at the prospect of imminent death.

'I don't think they're in the mood to take us alive, anyway,' said Malvery. 'Everyone, get behind Bess. She's our cover.'

'Hey, wait a—' Crake began, but they'd already crowded behind the golem, using her bulk as a shield. Bess hunkered down and spread herself out as much as possible. Malvery and Pinn crouched, peering out from either side, their guns ready. Crake, still carrying Dracken's strange compass in his hands, slid in next to them. He listened to the quiet ticks and coos coming from Bess's chest.

'How much ammo do we have?' Malvery asked.

'I got . . . um . . . twelve, thirteen bullets?' Pinn replied.

'I'm on about the same. Crake?'

Crake gave Pinn his revolver and a handful of bullets. 'You take them. I wouldn't hit anything anyway.'

'Right-o,' said the doctor, aiming his gun. 'Pick your targets.'

The men of the *Delirium Trigger* had swelled in number now. Some held back, studying the situation, while others angrily demanded action. One or two even tried to run up the gantry, but were held back by their companions. A chancy, long-range shot spanged off Bess's shoulder.

'Look at 'em,' Pinn crowed. 'Bunch of pussies.'

Directed by the bosun, the crew commandeered crowbars from dock workers and started jimmying nearby bits of machinery. The militia had caught up now – beige uniforms milled in the crowd – but having assessed the situation they seemed happy enough to let the men of the *Delirium Trigger* handle it. Presumably they'd claim the credit afterwards. It was easier than risking any of their own.

'What are they doing out there?' Malvery murmured to himself.

Crake peered out, took one look and went back into hiding. 'They're making a shield.'

He was right. Moments later, ten men started to advance up the gantry, holding before them a large sheet of iron pulled from the side of a crane. They crept forward nervously but with purpose, their guns bristling out around the side of the shield.

'Hmm,' said Malvery.

'What?' said Pinn. 'Soon as they get close enough, we send Crake's girl out to get 'em. She'll squash 'em into paste.'

'Ain't quite that easy,' said the doctor, nodding towards the hangar deck. 'Look.'

Pinn looked. Five men had taken position at the edge of the deck, and were lying on their bellies, aiming long-barrelled rifles at them.

'Sharpshooters,' said Malvery. 'If Bess moves, we lose our cover, and they kill us.' As if to punctuate his statement, a bullet ricocheted off Bess, inches from his face. He drew back a little way.

'Bugger,' said Pinn. 'Why do *we* never come up with plans like that?'

'We did,' said Malvery. 'That's how we ended up here.'

The men of the *Delirium Trigger* crept steadily closer. The narrow angle along the gantry made it impossible to get a good shot at any of them. Malvery tried an experimental salvo with his pistol, but it only rattled their shield. They stopped for a moment, then continued.

Crake was sweating and muttering to himself. *Stupid, stupid, stupid.* He wanted to be sick but there was nothing in his stomach: he'd been too nervous to eat before they set out on this mission.

The shield, having crossed much of the gantry, stopped. The men hunkered down behind it, becoming invisible. There was an agonising sense of calm before the inevitable storm.

'Well,' said Malvery to Pinn. 'I'd say it was nice knowing you, but . . .' He shrugged. 'You know.'

'Likewise, you whiskery old fart,' Pinn smiled, mistaking genuine distaste for comradely affection. Then the men of the *Delirium Trigger* popped up out of hiding with their guns blazing, and all thought was lost in the chaos.

The assault was terrifying. They fired until their guns were empty, then ducked down to reload while the men behind them continued the barrage. Bess groaned and howled as she was peppered with bullets. They smacked into her at close range, blasting holes in the chain mail and leather at her joints, chipping her metal faceplate. She swatted at the air as if plagued by bees, cries of distress coming from deep inside her.

Crake had his hands over his ears, yelling over the tumult, a blunt shout of fear and rage and sorrow. The sound of leaden death was bad enough: the sound of Bess's pain was worse.

Malvery managed to point his pistol around the side of Bess's flank and fire off a shot or two, but it did no good. They crammed in behind the golem as best they could, but bullets were flying everywhere and they dared not break cover. Bess was being driven back by the cumulative impacts of the bullets, which punched at her armour, cutting into the softer parts of her. She stumbled backward, roaring now. The others stumbled back with her. Crake saw a spray of blood torn from Pinn's leg: he went down, his pistols falling from his hands, clutching at his thigh.

And suddenly he knew what was behind a dying man's eyes. He knew what the crewman on the *Delirium Trigger* had known, the one that Pinn had shot. He knew what it felt like to run out of time, leaving a life incomplete, and so much still to do.

There was blinding light, and the bellow of engines. And

machine guns, ear-splitting machine guns smashing through the cool night air of the hangar. The men on the gantry were cut to bloodied shreds, jerking as they were pierced, thrown limply over the railings, plunging to the floor of the hangar.

Crake blinked and stared, stunned by his reprieve. But there was no mistake. Hanging in the air, scuffed and scratched and beautiful, was the *Ketty Jay*. And sitting at the controls was Jez.

Malvery guffawed with laughter, waving one arm above his head. Jez waved back, through the cockpit window. Pinn, rolling on the ground and shrieking, was largely forgotten.

Harkins sat in the autocannon cupola, and he opened up on the hangar deck as Jez rotated the *Ketty Jay* into position. The shots were pitched to scare rather than hit anyone, but they caused sufficient panic to keep the sharpshooters busy. The cargo ramp at the rear of the craft was gaping open, and Silo was standing at the top of it, holding on to a rung, beckoning them.

Jez's control of the craft was clumsy: she backed up too hard, and swung the lip of the cargo ramp into the gantry rail with a crunch. Metal twisted and screeched, but she managed to stabilise the *Ketty Jay* again, and now there was an escape route, a ramp leading into the maw of the cargo hold.

Crake was standing as if in a dream, bewildered by all the noise and motion. Bess scooped him up in both arms as if he was a child, holding him close. Then she thumped forward, leaped onto the ramp, and carried him into the cargo hold.

Behind him there was scrambling, voices, men shouting things he didn't understand. The muffled sound of autocannon fire from above; the whine of prothane thrusters on standby; the blessed safety of walls all around him.

Then the hydraulics kicked in, and the cargo ramp began to close. Malvery was shouting '*Jez! Get us out of here!*' Pinn was wailing. The whole world swung as the craft moved. There was a wrench of metal from outside as the *Ketty Jay* tore off part of the gantry rail.

Acceleration.

★

It took some time before the fog of panic cleared and Crake's senses returned. He realised that Bess had put him down on the floor, and was squatting next to him. He could see the glimmers of light inside her faceplate, like distant stars. Malvery was telling Pinn to shut up.

'I'm bleeding out, Doc! I'm going cold!'

'It's just a flesh wound, you damn pansy. Stop whining.'

'If I don't make it through . . . you have to tell Lisinda . . .'

'Oh, her. Sure. I'll tell your sweetheart you died a hero. Come on, hobble your arse to my surgery, I'll give you a couple of stitches. We'll have you fixed by the time we pick up the Cap'n.'

There was movement, and the umber-skinned, narrow face of the Murthian loomed into Crake's view.

'You alright?' he asked.

Crake swallowed and nodded.

Silo looked up at Bess. 'She's a fine thing,' he said. Then he picked up the compass that was lying next to Crake. The compass he'd taken from Dracken's cabin. Silo weighed it in his hand thoughtfully, then gave Crake a look of approval, stood up and walked away.

Bess was making echoing coos in her chest. Crake sat up and ran his hand along the metal plating of her arm. It was scored with burn marks and dents.

'I'm sorry, Bess,' he murmured. 'I'm so sorry.'

Bess cooed again and nuzzled him, bumping the cold iron of her faceplate against his cheek.

Twenty-Six

A Well-Earned Break – Silo Lends A Hand –
The Captain Is Woken – From Bad To Worse

Frey celebrated his victory in the traditional manner, and was roaring drunk by dawn.

They reclaimed the Firecrow and the Skylance from their hiding place outside Rabban, then flew for three hours, changing course several times until they were thoroughly sure that any attempts at pursuit would be hopeless. After that they began to search for a place to put down. Frey found a hillside clearing amid the vast moon-silvered landscape of the Vardenwood. There they sallied out, built a campfire, and Frey proceeded to get hammered on cheap grog.

It had been a long, long time since he felt this good.

He looked around at the laughing faces of the men who drank with him: Malvery, Pinn, even Harkins, who had loosened up and joined them after a little bullying. Jez was in her quarters, keeping to herself as usual, deciphering the charts they'd stolen from Dracken's cabin. Crake and Silo were nearby, tending to the damage that Bess had suffered. Nobody wanted to sleep. They were all either too fired up or, in Crake's case, too anxious. He was fretting about his precious golem.

But Frey couldn't worry about Crake for the moment. Right now, he was basking in the satisfaction of a job well done. *His* plan had worked. *His* crew had triumphed against all the odds. Despite that cold bitch's condescending words, her cruel pity, he'd screwed her over like a master. He imagined her face when she got back to find her crew in disarray and her precious charts missing. He imagined how she'd smoulder when she heard of the heroic last-minute rescue in the *Ketty Jay*. He imagined her rage when she realised how badly she'd misjudged him.

You thought you knew me, he gloated. *You said I was predictable. Bet you didn't predict* that.

And the best thing was that none of his people had got hurt. Well, except for Crake's little pet and the scratch on Pinn's leg, but that didn't really count. All in all, it was a brilliant operation.

If this was what success tasted like, he wanted more of it.

The bottle of grog came round to him and he swigged from it deeply. Malvery was telling some ribald story about a high-class whore he used to treat back when he was a big-city doctor. Pinn was already in stitches, long before the punchline. Harkins spluttered and grinned, showing his browned teeth. Their faces glowed warmly, flushed in the firelight and the colours of the breaking dawn. Frey felt a surge of alcohol-fuelled affection for them all. He was proud of them. He was proud of himself.

It hadn't been an easy thing, to entrust Jez with the ignition code to the *Ketty Jay*. The code was set during the manufacture of the aircraft, and because it relied on various complex mechanisms it couldn't ever be changed without lengthy and expensive engineering procedures. Jez would forever have the power to activate and fly the *Ketty Jay*. Even now, Frey had to fight the suspicion that Jez might be creeping towards the cockpit, intending to punch in the numbers and run off with his aircraft before anyone could stop her.

It's done now, he thought. *Live with it*.

It had been absolutely necessary for the completion of his plan that someone else fly the *Ketty Jay*. Jez had assured him she could, having grown up flying many types of aircraft. But he'd still found himself unable to give away the code at first. Like marriage, it felt like sacrificing too much of himself to a stranger.

In the end, he'd convinced himself by making an analogy to Rake. He found that most things in life could be related to cards, if only you thought hard enough.

In Rake, it was possible to play *too* carefully. If you waited and waited for the perfect hand, then the obligatory minimum bets each round would gradually whittle you down. You'd run out of time and money waiting for an opportunity that never came. Sooner or later, you had to take a risk.

So he'd bet on Jez, and thankfully he'd won big. She was an odd fish, but he liked her, and he knew she was competent. He even had to admit to a slight sense of relief at the sharing of the secret code, although he wasn't exactly sure why. It felt like he'd let out the pressure a little.

Malvery reached the punchline of his story, and they howled with laughter. Frey hadn't been paying attention, but he laughed anyway, caught up in the swell. He passed on the bottle, and Malvery gulped from it. Later, Frey would think of other things: the task they still had ahead of them, the bitter sting that came from seeing Trinica's face again. But for now, drinking with his men, he was happy, and that was enough.

Crake was anything but happy. Their narrow escape hadn't invigorated him with a sense of triumph, but depressed him instead. He was acutely aware that they'd only made it out because Jez had arrived early. She'd been forced to take off sooner than planned, driven back to the *Ketty Jay* by far superior numbers, and had then headed directly to their pick-up point at the hangar. Once there, she'd spotted the disturbance inside and realised there was trouble. Their estimation of the length of the operation had been off: they'd allowed themselves far too much time.

In the end, they got lucky.

Rather to his surprise, Silo had emerged from the engine room to help him patch up Bess. The Murthian was a silent, solid presence around the *Ketty Jay*, but because he rarely offered an opinion and never socialised, Crake had unconsciously begun to ignore him, as if he was one of the servants back home. He suspected that Silo was simply curious, and saw an opportunity to get a closer look at the golem, to work out what made her tick. Whatever his motives, Crake was glad of the help and the quiet company. Between them, they pulled out bullets, stitched up leather, and soldered her wounds.

Though the damage was all superficial, Crake was wracked with guilt. He'd allowed Bess to be used as an object. What if they had dynamite? What if they had a really big cannon? Could she have stood up to that? For that matter, what would actually happen to her if she was destroyed?

Bess was a shell, inhabited by a presence. That was as much as Crake knew. A vacant suit of armour, a skin surrounding nothing. Where did the presence truly exist? What exactly was in there? Did it occupy the skin of the suit, or was it somewhere inside? Those glittering eyes in the emptiness – did they mean something?

He didn't know. He didn't even truly know how he'd made her. Bess was an accident and a mystery.

'Does it hurt her?' Silo asked suddenly, rubbing his finger across a bullet hole in her knee. His deep, molten voice was heavily inflected. *Doors eet hoort hair?*

'I don't know,' said Crake. 'I think so. In a way.'

The Murthian stared at him, waiting for more.

'She was . . . upset,' he said awkwardly. 'When they were shooting her. So I think she feels it.'

Silo nodded to himself and returned his attention to his work. Bess was sitting quietly, not moving. She was asleep, he guessed. Or at least, he called it sleep. In these periods of catatonia, she was simply *absent*. There were no glittering lights inside. She was an empty suit. Where the presence had gone, or if it had really gone anywhere at all, he couldn't have said.

The silence between them returned, but Crake felt a pressure to say something now that Silo had. It seemed momentous that the Murthian should be out here alongside him, asking him an unprompted question. He began to feel more and more uncomfortable. The rising chorus of birds from the trees all around seemed unnaturally loud.

'The captain seems in good cheer,' he said at length.

Silo only grunted.

'How do you and he know each other?'

Silo stopped and looked up at him. For a few seconds, Silo

regarded him in the pale dawn light, his eyes unreadable. Then he went back to his task.

Crake gave up. Perhaps he'd been wrong. Perhaps Silo really didn't want to talk.

'I escaped from a factory,' Silo told him suddenly. *Arr scorrpt fram a fack-truh.* He kept working as he talked. 'Seven year back. Built aircraft there for the Samarlans. My people are slaves down there. Bet you know that, yuh?'

'Yes,' said Crake. He was shocked to hear such a torrential monologue from Silo.

'The Dakkadians gave up. Stopped fighting long ago, joined their masters. But those of us from Murthia, we never give up. Five hundred year and we never give up.' There was a fierce pride in his voice. 'So when the time comes, some of us, we kill our overseer and we run. They come after us, yuh? So we scatter. Into the hills and the forest. And pretty soon, there's just me. Starved and lost, but I ain't dead and I ain't no slave.

'Then I see a craft coming down. Ain't damaged, but flies like it is. Pilot look like he don't know a thing. Makes a rough landing, and off I go. That's my way out. And when I get there, I find the Cap'n inside. Stabbed in the guts. In a bad way.'

It took Crake a moment to catch on. 'Wait, you mean *our* captain? Frey?'

'Frey and the *Ketty Jay*,' said Silo.

'How did it happen?'

'Didn't ask, and he didn't say,' Silo replied. 'Now, there's plenty food and supplies there on that craft, but I can't fly. I know craft on the inside, but I never flew one. So I take care of the Cap'n. I get him his drugs and bandages and I get him well. And in the meantime, I eat, get strong.' He shrugged. 'When he got better, he said he wasn't never goin' back to the people who sent him there. Said he was goin' to live the life of a freebooter. That was fine by me. He flew us both out, and I been on the *Ketty Jay* ever since.'

'So you saved his life?'

'S'pose. S'pose he saved mine too. Either way, here I am, yuh?

249

We ain't never spoken of it since. I fix his craft, he keeps me in shelter. That's the way it is, and I'm grateful every day I have on board the *Ketty Jay*. Every day, that's one more day I ain't a slave. Lone Murthian wouldn't last long out here in Vardia. Your people ain't exactly fond of us since the Aerium Wars.'

Crake looked over at the fire, where Malvery was holding Frey down and pouring grog into his mouth while the other two cheered. Every time he thought he had Frey figured out, he was bewildered anew.

'You never said.'

'You never asked,' said Silo. 'It's a fool that speaks when there ain't no cause to. Too many loudmouths already on this craft.'

'On that we agree,' said Crake.

Silo got to his feet and stretched. 'Well, I done what I can with your lady Bess,' he said. 'Gonna catch some sleep.'

'Thank you for your help,' said Crake. Silo grunted and began to walk off.

'Hey,' called Crake suddenly, as a new question occurred to him. 'Why do they call you Silo?'

'The name mama gave me is Silopethkai Auramaktama Faillinana,' came the reply. For the first time that Crake could remember, he saw the Murthian smile. 'Think you can remember it?'

'Cap'n.'

Frey was faintly conscious of someone shaking him. He wished with all his heart that they'd go away.

'Cap'n!'

There it was again, dragging him upwards from the treacly, grog-soaked depths of sleep. *Leave me alone!*

'Cap'n!'

Frey groaned as it became clear they weren't going to give up. He was aware of a cool breeze and warm sun on his skin, the smell of grass, and the forbidding portents of a dreadful hangover. He opened his eyes, and flinched as the eager sun speared shafts of light directly into his brain. He blocked the light with his hand and turned his head to look at Jez, who was kneeling next to him.

'What?' he said slowly, making it a threat.

'I've figured out the charts,' she said.

He levered himself upright and groaned again, mashing his face with his palm. His mouth tasted like something had shat in it and subsequently died there. The embers of the fire were still alive, but the sun was high in a blue sky on an unseasonably warm winter's day. Malvery snored like a tractor nearby. Pinn was sucking his thumb, his other hand twitching towards his crotch, around which all his dreams revolved.

'Don't you sleep?' he said.

'Not much,' she admitted. 'Sorry if it's a bad time. You said you wanted to know straight away. You said time is—'

'—of the essence, yes, I remember.' He deeply regretted those words now. 'So you know where Trinica's hideout is?'

'I believe so, Cap'n. The charts weren't easy to work out. It's not just an X-marks-the-spot kind of thing.'

'Uh? A chart's a chart, isn't it?'

'Not really. These are very close detail, marking a route through the mountains. Either we're missing a chart or Trinica already knows the general area where the hideout is. If you don't know where to start, you're just looking at a bunch of mountains.' She gave a quirky smile. 'Lot of mountains in Vardia.'

'But you figured it out?'

'Matched the position of the bigger mountains with my other charts.'

'Good work, Jez.'

'Thank you, Cap'n.'

'Now tell me where we're going.'

'You're not gonna like it.'

'I rarely do.'

'I assume you've heard of Rook's Boneyard?'

'Oh, for shit's sake,' he sighed, and then slumped down onto his back again, his eyes closed. He'd expected bad news, just not quite *that* bad.

Jez patted him on the shoulder. 'I'll be in my quarters when you're ready,' she said. Then he heard her get up and walk back to the *Ketty Jay*.

Everybody who flew over the south end of the Hookhollows knew Rook's Boneyard. They all knew to avoid it if they possibly could. Aircraft that went into that small, restlessly volcanic area were rarely seen again. Those that ventured into the mists spoke of seeing their companions mysteriously explode. Pilots went mad and flew into mountainsides. Survivors talked of ghosts, terrible spirits that clawed at their craft. It was a cursed place, named after the first man to brave it and survive.

Why don't I just lie down and die here? thought Frey. *It'll save time.*

Time. Time was something they didn't have. There was no telling how long it would take Trinica to replenish her crew and familiarise the newcomers with the complexities of the *Delirium Trigger*. A day? A week? Frey had no idea. It really depended on whether there was anyone really vital among the men Jez had machine-gunned on the gantry.

But he knew one thing. As soon as she was up and running, Trinica would be after them with redoubled fury. Without her strange compass and her charts, she wouldn't be able to get to the hideout, but she knew that Frey would be heading that way. She might be able to get word to her allies somehow. He wanted to be in and out before she had a chance to act.

He got to his feet and swayed as his head went light. It took a few moments for everything to stabilise again. He wasn't, he reflected, in good shape for facing certain death anytime soon.

'Alright,' he told himself unconvincingly. 'Let's do this.' And he stumbled off to rouse the crew.

Twenty-Seven

A Perilous Descent – The Puzzle Of
The Compass – Frey Sees Ghosts

The *Ketty Jay* hung in the white wastes of the Hookhollows, a speck against the colossal stone slopes. There were no other craft to be seen or heard. Below them, there was only the bleak emptiness of the mist. It cloaked the lower reaches, shrouding canyons and defiles, hiding the feet of the mountains. Down there, in Rook's Boneyard, the mist never cleared.

High above them were jagged, ice-tipped peaks. Higher still was a forbidding ceiling of drifting ash clouds, passing to the east, shedding a thin curtain of flakes as they went. A poisonous miasma, seeping from volcanic cracks and vents along the southern reaches of the mountain range. It was carried on the prevailing winds to settle onto the Blackendraft, the great ash flats, where it choked all life beneath it.

Frey sat in the pilot's seat, staring down. Wondering whether it was worth it. Wondering whether they should just turn tail and run. Could he really get them out of this mess? This ragged collection of vagrants, pitted against some of the most powerful people in the land? In the end, did they even have a chance? What lay in that secret hideout that was so important it was worth all this?

Their victory against Trinica had buoyed him briefly, but the prospect of flying blind into Rook's Boneyard had reawakened all the old doubts. Crake's words rolled around in his head.

As a group, we're rather easy to identify. Apart, they'll probably never catch us. They'll only get Frey.

Was it fair to risk them all, just to clear his own name? What if he sent them their separate ways, recrewed, and headed for New Vardia? He might make it there, across the seas, through the storms to the other side of the planet. Even in winter. It was possible.

Anything to avoid going down there, into the Boneyard.

Crake and Jez were with him in the cockpit. He needed Jez to navigate and he wanted Crake to help figure out the strange compass-like device, which nobody had been able to make head nor tail of yet. He'd banished the others to the mess to keep them from pestering him. Harkins and Pinn had been forced to leave their craft behind again, since it was too dangerous to travel in convoy, and they were insufferable back-seat pilots.

'It'll be dead reckoning once we're down in the mist, Cap'n,' said Jez. 'So keep your course and speed steady and tell me if you change them.'

'Right,' he said, swallowing against a dry throat. He pulled his coat tighter around himself. He wasn't sure if it was the hangover or the fear, but he couldn't seem to get warm. He twisted round to glance at Crake, who was standing at his shoulder, holding the brass compass in both hands. 'Is it doing anything yet?'

'Doesn't seem to be,' said Crake.

'Did you turn it on?'

Crake gave him a look. 'If you think you know a way to "turn it on" that all of us have missed, do let me know.'

'We don't need your bloody sarcasm right now, Crake,' Jez snapped, with a sharp and unfamiliar tone to her voice. Crake, rather than offering a rejoinder, subsided into bitter silence.

Frey sighed. The tension between these two wasn't helping his nerves. It had been slowly curdling the atmosphere on the *Ketty Jay* ever since they returned from the ball at Scorchwood Heights.

'Where's all this damned mist coming from, anyway?' he griped, to change the subject.

'Hot air from vents to the west blowing over cold meltwater rivers running off the Eastern Plateau,' Jez replied absently.

'Oh.'

The conversation lapsed for a time.

'Cap'n?' Jez queried, when things had become sufficiently uncomfortable. 'Are we going?'

Frey thought about sharing his idea with them. He could offer to cut them loose and go his own way. Wouldn't that be the decent thing? Then nobody had to go down into the Boneyard. Least of all him.

But it all seemed a bit much to try and explain it now. Things had gone too far. He was resigned to it. Easier to go forward than back.

Besides, he thought, in a rare moment of careless bravado, *nothing clears up a hangover like dying.*

He arranged himself in his seat and released aerium gas from the ballast tanks, adding a little weight to the craft. The *Ketty Jay* began to sink into the mist.

The altimeter on the dashboard ticked steadily as they descended. The world dimmed and whitened beyond the windglass of the cockpit. The low hum of the electromagnets in the aerium engines was the only sound in the stillness.

'Come to one thousand and hold steady,' Jez instructed, hunched over her charts at her cramped desk. Her voice sounded hollow in the tomb-like atmosphere.

'Crake?'

'Still nothing.'

They'd puzzled over the compass for most of the day, but nobody had been able to decipher its purpose. The lack of markings to indicate North, South, East or West suggested that it wasn't meant for navigation. The four needles, which seemed capable of swinging independently of one another, made things more confusing. And then there were the numbers. Nobody knew what *they* meant.

They'd established that each pair of number sets corresponded to a different arrow. The pair of number sets marked '1' matched the arrow marked '1'. Each number was set on a rotating cylinder, like the readout of the altimeter, and presumably displayed the numbers zero to nine. The upper set of each pair had two digits, allowing a count from 00 to 99. The lower set had the same, but was preceded by a blank digit. All the numbers except this blank were set at zero.

Frey had the sense that this compass was vital to their survival in Rook's Boneyard. They were in danger until they could work out what it did. But right now it didn't seem to be doing *anything*.

Frey brought the *Ketty Jay* to a hover when his altimeter showed they were a klom above sea level, down among the feet of the mountains. The mist had thickened into a dense fog, and the cockpit had darkened to a chilly twilight. Frey knew better than to use headlamps, which would only dazzle them; but he turned on the *Ketty Jay*'s belly lights, hoping they'd provide some relief against the gloom. They did, but only a little.

'Alright, Cap'n,' said Jez. 'Ahead slow, keep a heading of two-twenty, stay at this altitude.'

'We'll start at ten knots,' he replied.

'Right.' Jez looked at her pocket watch. 'Go.'

Frey eased the *Ketty Jay* forward, angling to the new heading. The sensation of flying blind, even at crawling speed, was terrifying. He suddenly found a new respect for Harkins, who had chased a Swordwing at full throttle through the mist after the destruction of the *Ace of Skulls*. That nervy, hangdog old beanpole was braver than he seemed.

For long minutes, they moved forward. Nobody said anything. Frey could feel a bead of sweat making its way from his hairline, across his temple. Jez called out a change of heading and altitude. Mechanically, he obeyed.

The pace was excruciating. The waiting was killing him. Something was bound to happen. He just wanted it over with.

'I have something!' Crake announced. Frey jumped in his seat at the sudden noise.

'What is it?'

Crake was moving the compass around experimentally. 'One of the needles is moving.'

Frey brought the *Ketty Jay* to a stop and took the compass from Crake. Jez glanced at her pocket watch again, mentally recording how far they had travelled on this new heading.

256

Crake was right. Though the other needles, numbered 2 to 4, were still dormant, the first needle was pointing in the direction that the *Ketty Jay* was heading. As Frey twisted it, the needle kept pointing in the same direction, no matter which way the compass was turned.

The number sets corresponding to the first needle had changed, too. Whereas all the others were still at zero, these had sprung into life. The topmost set read 91. The bottom set, the one preceded by a blank digit, read 30. They were not moving.

'The top one started counting down from ninety-nine,' said Crake. 'The bottom one just clicked to thirty and stayed there.'

'So what does it mean?' Frey asked.

'He doesn't know what it means,' Jez said.

'Do *you*?' Crake snapped.

Jez turned around in her chair, removed her hairband and smoothed her hair back into her customary ponytail again. 'I've some idea. The topmost digits were counting down when we were moving, and now they're not. I'd guess that they show the distance we are from whatever the arrow is pointing at.'

'So what *is* the arrow pointing at?' Crake asked, rather angry that he hadn't worked it out first.

'Something ninety-one metres ahead of us,' Frey replied helpfully. 'So now what? Can we go around it?'

'I'd rather not deviate from the charts if we possibly can,' said Jez. 'They're very precise.'

'Alright,' Frey replied. 'Then we go very, very slowly, and let's see what's up ahead. Crake, read out the numbers.'

He settled back into his seat and pushed the *Ketty Jay* forward at minimum speed. Crake stood behind him, eyes flicking between the compass and the windglass of the cockpit, where there was still nothing but fog to be seen.

'Needle's holding steady. The other set of numbers is still at thirty. The top one is counting down . . . Eighty . . . Seventy . . . Sixty . . . No change anywhere else . . . Fifty . . . Forty . . .'

Frey's mind was crowded with possibilities, tumbling over each other in a panic. What was it that waited there for them? The entrance to the hideout? Or something altogether deadlier?

'Thirty . . . Twenty . . .'

He was so taut that his muscles ached, poised to throw the *Ketty Jay* into full reverse the instant that anything emerged from the murk.

'Ten . . . Five . . . Zero.'

'Zero?' Frey asked.

'Five . . . Ten . . . The needle has changed direction. Now it's pointing behind us. Twenty . . . Twenty-five.'

'Let me have a look,' Frey said, and snatched the compass from Crake. The needle was pointing directly behind them, and the numbers were counting up towards ninety-nine again.

'Um,' he said. Then he handed the compass back to the daemonist. 'Well. That's a puzzle.'

'Perhaps those numbers didn't mean distance after all,' Crake suggested churlishly, for Jez's benefit. Jez didn't reply. He went back to reading them off. 'Ninety . . . Ninety-five . . . Now the numbers have reset to zero, and the first needle has joined the other three.'

'I suppose that means we've gone out of range.' Frey suggested.

'But there wasn't anything *there*!'

'That's fine with me.'

Jez called out a new heading, and Frey took it.

'You might see a—' she began, when Frey yelled in alarm as the flank of a mountain emerged from the fog. He banked away from it and it slipped by to their starboard side.

'—mountain,' Jez continued, 'but there'll be a defile running out of it.'

'I didn't see any defile!' Frey complained, annoyed because he'd suffered a scare.

'Cap'n, I'm navigating blind here. Accuracy is gonna be less than perfect. Pull back closer to the mountain flank.'

Frey reluctantly did so. The mountain loomed into view again. Jez left her station to look through the windglass.

'There it is,' she said.

Frey saw it too: a knife-slash in the mountain, forty metres wide, with uneven walls.

'I don't much like the look of that,' he said.

'Drop to nine hundred, take us in,' Jez told him mercilessly.

Frey eased the *Ketty Jay* around and into the defile. The mountains pressed in hard, narrowing the world on either side. Shadowy walls lay close enough to be seen, even in the mist. Frey unconsciously hunched down in his seat. He concentrated on keeping a steady line.

'More contacts,' said Crake. 'Two of them.'

'Two needles moving?'

'Yes. Both of them pointing directly ahead.'

'Give me the numbers.'

Crake licked dry lips and read them off. 'First needle: distance ninety and descending. The other number reads fifty-seven and holding steady. Second needle: distance . . . ninety also, now. That's descending too. The other number reads minus forty-three. Holding steady.'

'*Minus* forty-three?' Jez asked.

'A little minus sign just appeared where that blank digit was.'

Jez thought for a moment. 'They're giving us relative altitude,' she said. 'The first set of numbers show the distance we are from the object. The second show how far it is above or below us.'

Frey caught on. 'So then the ones ahead of us . . . one is fifty-seven metres above us and the other is forty-three metres below?'

'That's why we didn't see anything the last time,' Jez said. 'We passed by it. It was thirty metres above us.'

Frey felt a mixture of trepidation and relief at that. It was reassuring to believe that they'd figured out the compass and could avoid these unseen things, at least. But somehow, knowing where they were made them seem all the more threatening. It meant they were really *there*. Whatever *they* were.

'Crake, keep reading out the distances,' he said. Crake obliged.

'Twenty . . . ten . . . zero . . . needle's swung the other way . . . ten . . . twenty . . .'

Frey had him continue counting until they were out of range and the compass reset again.

'Okay, Cap'n,' said Jez. 'The bottom's going to drop out of this defile any minute. We come down to seven hundred and take a heading of two-eighty.'

Frey grunted in acknowledgement. There was enough space between the mountain walls for a much bigger craft to pass through, but the constant need to prevent the *Ketty Jay* from drifting was grinding away at his nerve and giving him a headache. He dearly wished he hadn't indulged quite so heavily the night before.

Just as Jez had predicted, the defile ended suddenly. It fed into a much larger chasm, far too vast to see the other end. The fog was thinner here, stained with a sinister red light from below. Red shadows spread into the cockpit.

'Is that lava down there?' Frey asked.

Jez craned over from the navigator's station and looked down. 'That's lava. Drop to seven hundred.'

'Bringing us closer to the lava.'

'I'm just following the charts, Cap'n. You want to find your own way in this mist, be my guest.'

Frey was stung by that, but he kept his mouth shut and began to descend. The fog thinned and the red glow grew in strength until they were bathed in it. The temperature rose in the cockpit, drawing sweat from their brows. They could feel the radiant heat of the lava river flowing beneath them. Pinn came up from the mess to complain that it was getting stuffy down there, but Frey barked at him to get out. For once he did as he was told.

Frey added aerium at seven hundred metres to halt their descent, and pushed onward along the length of the chasm. Visibility was better now. The mist offered hints of their surroundings. It was possible to see the gloomy immensity of the mountains around them, if only as smudged impressions. To descend a few dozen metres more would bring the lava river into detail: the rolling, sludgy torrent of black and red and yellow. The heat down there would be unimaginable.

'Contacts,' said Crake again. 'Ahead and to the left a little. We – oh, wait. There's another. Two of them. Three. Three of them.'

'There's three?'

'Four,' Crake corrected. He showed Frey the compass. The needles were in a fan, all pointing roughly ahead. Frey frowned as he looked at it, and for a moment his vision wavered out of focus. He blinked, and the feeling passed. He swore to himself that he'd never again drink excessively the night before doing anything life-threatening.

'Any of them directly in front of us?'

'One's pretty close. Twenty metres below. Oh!'

'Don't just say "oh!"' Frey snapped. 'Oh, *what*?'

'One of the needles moved . . . now it's changed back . . . now it's gone back again.'

'What you mean, it changed?' Frey demanded. He wiped sweat from his brow. All this tension was making him feel sick.

'It moved! What do you think I mean?' Crake replied in exasperation. 'Can you stop a moment?'

'Well, why's it changing? Is there something there or not?' Frey was getting flustered now. He felt a fluttering sensation of panic come over him.

'There's more than four of those things out there,' said Jez, who had got up from her station and was looking at the compass. 'I'd guess it keeps changing the needles to show us the nearest four.'

'There's one thirty metres ahead!' Crake cried.

'But is it above us or below us?' Frey said.

'Forty metres above.'

'Then *why tell me*?' he shouted.

'*Because you told me to!*' Crake shouted back. 'Will you stop this damn craft?'

But Frey didn't want to. He wanted to get this over with. He wanted to be past these invisible enemies and away from this place. There was a terrible feeling of wrongness stealing over him, a numbness prickling up from his toes. He felt flustered and harassed.

'What the bloody shit is going on, Crake?' he snarled, leaning forward to try and see what, if anything, was above them. 'Some-one talk to me! Where are they?'

'There's one, there's three in front of us, one behind us now . . . umm . . . two above, thirty and twenty metres, there's . . .' Crake swore. 'The numbers keep changing because you're moving! How am I supposed to read them out fast enough?'

'Just tell me if we're going to hit anything, Crake! It's pretty damn simple!'

Jez was staring in bewilderment. 'Will you two calm down? You're acting like a pair of—'

But then Frey recoiled from the window with a yell. 'There's something out there!'

'What was it?' Jez asked.

'We've got one twenty . . . ten metres ahead . . . it's below us though . . .' Crake was saying.

'It looked like . . . I don't know, it looked like it had a *face*,' Frey was babbling. His stomach griped and roiled. He could smell his own sweat, and he felt filthy. He wiped at the back of his hands to try and clean them a little, but all it did was smear more dirt into his skin. 'The ghosts!' he said suddenly. 'It's the ghosts of Rook's Boneyard!'

'There aren't any ghosts, Cap'n,' Jez said, but her face was red in the lava-light and her voice sounded strange and echoey. Her plain features seemed sly. Did she know something he didn't? A blast of maniacal laughter came from the mess, Pinn laughing hysterically at something. It sounded like the cackle of a conspirator.

'Of course there are ghosts!' Frey turned his attention back to the windglass, trying to will the mist aside. 'Everyone says.'

'Two of them are behind us now,' Crake droned in the back-ground. 'One ahead, one passing to the side.'

'*Which* side?'

'Does it matter?'

Something swept past the windglass, a stir in the mist. Frey saw the stretched shape of a human form and distorted, ghastly features. He shied back from the windglass with a gasp.

'What is it?'

'Didn't you see it?'

'I didn't see anything!'

Frey's vision was slipping in and out of focus, and refused to stay steady. He burped in his throat, and tasted acid and rotten eggs.

'Cap'n . . .' said Crake.

'I think something's wrong,' Frey murmured.

'Cap'n . . . the second set of numbers . . .'

'What second set of—'

'The numbers! They're counting up from minus twenty towards zero! It's coming at us from below!'

'Cap'n! You're drifting off altitude! You're diving!' Jez cried.

Frey saw the altimeter sliding down and grabbed the controls, pulling the *Ketty Jay* level.

'It's still coming!' Crake shrieked.

'Move!' Jez cried, and Frey boosted the engines. The *Ketty Jay* surged forward, and a split second later there was a deafening explosion outside, slamming against the hull and throwing Crake and Jez across the cabin. The craft heeled hard, swinging to starboard, and Frey fought with the controls as they were propelled blindly into the red murk. The *Ketty Jay* felt sluggish and wounded. Frey caught a glimpse of the compass on the floor, its needles spinning and switching crazily.

They're all around us!

Crake started shrieking. 'Daemons! There are daemons at the windows!' Frey's vision blurred and stayed blurred. There seemed to be no strength in his limbs.

'Cap'n! Above and to starboard!' Jez shouted.

Frey looked, and saw a round shadow in the mist. Growing, darkening as it approached. A ghost. A great black ghost.

No. A sphere. A metal sphere studded with spikes.

A floating mine.

Jez grabbed the flight stick and wrenched the *Ketty Jay* to port. Frey fell bonelessly out of his seat. Crake screamed.

There was another explosion. Then blackness, and silence.

Twenty-Eight

*Jez Saves The Day – Legends Come To Life – The Dock
Master – Some Tactical Thinking – News From The Market*

Frey came to a kind of bleary awareness some time later, to find himself crumpled on the floor of the *Ketty Jay*'s cockpit. His cheek was pressed to the metal, wet with drool. His head pounded as if his brain was trying to kick its way out of his skull.

He groaned and stirred. Jez was sitting in the pilot's seat. She looked down at him.

'You're back,' she said. 'How do you feel?'

He swore a few times to give her an idea. Crake was collapsed in the opposite corner, contorted uncomfortably beneath the navigator's desk.

Frey tried to remember how he'd got in this state. He was tempted to blame it on alcohol, but he was certain that he hadn't been drinking since last night. The last thing he remembered was flying through the fog and fretting about the numbers on the compass.

'What just happened?' he asked, pulling himself into a sitting position.

Jez had the compass and the charts spread out untidily on the dash. She consulted both before replying. 'You all went crazy. Fumes from the lava river, I suppose. It would explain all the ghosts and hallucinations and paranoia.' She tapped the compass with a fingernail. 'Turns out this thing is to warn us where the magnetic floating mines are. Someone's gone to a great deal of trouble to make sure this secret hideout stays secret.'

Frey fought down a swell of nausea. He felt like he'd been poisoned.

'Apologies for taking the helm without permission, Cap'n,' said Jez, sounding not very apologetic at all. 'Had to avoid that mine, and you were out of action. Close thing. The *Ketty Jay* took a battering. Anyway, we're nearly there now.'

'We are?'

'It's actually pretty easy once you work it out,' she said, although he wasn't sure if she meant following the route to the hideout or flying the *Ketty Jay*.

He got unsteadily to his feet, feeling vaguely usurped. The sight of Jez in the pilot's seat disturbed him. It was an unpleasant vision of the future he feared, in which Jez – now possessing the ignition code – stole away with his beloved craft when his back was turned. She looked so damned *comfortable* there.

Outside, everything was calm and the air had cleared to a faint haze. Though there was still a heavy fog overhead, blocking out the sky, it was possible to see to the rocky floor of the canyon beneath them. A thin river ran along the bottom, hurrying ahead of them, and a light breeze blew against the hull.

Frey rubbed his head. 'So how come it didn't affect you?'

She shrugged. 'Once I saw what was happening, I held my breath. I only took a few lungfuls before we flew out of it.'

Frey narrowed his eyes. The explanation had an over-casual, rehearsed quality to it. As an experienced liar, he knew the signs. So why was his navigator lying to him?

There was a clatter from the passageway behind the cockpit, and Malvery swung round the door. 'Allsoul's balls, what were we drinking?' he complained. 'They're all comatose down there. Even the bloody cat's conked out.'

'You weren't giving the cat rum again, were you?' Frey asked.

'He looked thirsty,' Malvery said, with a sheepish smile.

'Eyes front, everyone,' said Jez. 'I think we're here.'

They crowded around her and stared through the windglass as the *Ketty Jay* droned out of the canyon. And there, down among the fog and the mountains of the Hookhollows, hidden in the dreadful depths of Rook's Boneyard, they found at last what they'd been searching for.

The canyon emptied out into a colossal, gloomy sinkhole, a dozen kloms wide, where the ground dropped seventy metres to a waterlogged marsh. Streams from all over the mountains, unable to find another way out, ended up here, tipping over the edge in thin waterfalls. Mineral slurry and volcanic sludge, washed down from distant vents, stained the surface of the marsh with metallic slicks of orange, green or blue. Ill-looking plants choked the water. The air smelled acidic and faintly eggy.

But here, in this festering place, was a town.

It was built from wood and rusting metal, a ramshackle sprawl that had evolved without thought to plan or purpose. Most of it was set on platforms that rose out of the water, supported by a scaffolding of girders. The rest was built on what little land the marsh had to offer: soggy banks and hummocks. Each part was linked by bridges to its neighbours, and lit by strings of electric lamps that hung haphazardly across the thoroughfares.

The buildings varied wildly in quality. Some wouldn't have looked out of place on a country estate in the tropical south. Others had been thrown together with whatever could be found or brought from the outside. They were made of wood and stone, with slate or corrugated iron roofs. Parts of the settlement were a cluster of shanty-town huts, barely fit for habitation, whereas others were more organised and showed an architect's touch.

Then there were the aircraft. There had to be two hundred or more, crowding around the town. Frigates floated at anchor, secured by strong chains to stop them drifting. Smaller craft ferried their crews to and from the ground. There was one enormous landing pad, occupying the biggest land mass in the marsh, but even that was nowhere near adequate to cope with the number of craft berthed here. Several large landing pads lay on the surface of the marsh. They were temporary-looking things, buoyed up by flaking aerium tanks filled from portable engines to prevent the pads from sinking.

Frey stared at the multitude. He saw freighters, barques,

fighters of all description, double-hulled caravels, ironclads, monitors and corvettes. The air above the town was busy with craft taking off and setting down, a restless to and fro. A Rainbird-class hunter-killer, sleek and vicious, slipped past them to their starboard and headed into the canyon they'd just exited.

'That's a bit more than just a hideout,' Malvery murmured, amazed. 'There's a whole bloody port down here.'

And suddenly Frey knew where he was. Nothing else matched the picture. He'd always believed this place was a myth, a wistful dream for freebooters all over Vardia. But now it was laid out before his eyes; decaying, shabby, but undoubtedly real. The legendary pirate town, hidden from the Coalition Navy and ruled by the famed pirate Orkmund.

Retribution Falls.

Frey could see no indication of where he was supposed to land, no spotlights to guide him in, so he squeezed into a vacant spot on the main pad. When he and his crew opened the cargo ramp to disembark they found someone waiting for them. He was tall and doughy around the belly and face, with one lazy eye and a gormless smile.

'You signed in yet?' he asked Frey.

Frey was momentarily lost for an answer. The man had just watched them set down. He considered asking how he might possibly have got to the dock master's office and back while still in mid-air, but eventually he settled on an easier response.

'No.'

'You should sign in. Orkmund's orders.'

Frey felt a thrill of excitement at the name. That settled it. This was Retribution Falls alright.

'Where's the dock master?'

'You the captain?'

'Yeah.'

'Follow me, I'll take you.'

Frey told the others to wait by the *Ketty Jay*, and then trailed after the man towards the dock master's office. It was a grim, low-ceilinged affair, more like a large shed than an administrative building. Dirty windows were divided into small rectangular panes. The door stuck and had to be wrenched open: the frame had warped in the dank air.

Inside, the gloom was barely leavened by a single oil lantern. The dock master – a thin, old man with a pinched face – was hunched over a desk, writing with a pen. On the other side of the room was a lectern, where a huge book lay open. It was full of names and dates.

Frey waited to be noticed. The man with the lazy eye waited with him. The smell from the swamp lingered in the nostrils, faintly disgusting. Frey suspected that the locals didn't notice it any more.

After a short time, the dock master looked up. 'Well, sign in, then!' he snapped, indicating the book on the lectern. 'Olric, honestly! Why don't you just tell him to sign in?'

Olric looked shamefaced. Frey went over to the book and picked up the pen that lay next to it. He scanned over the entries. Each line bore the name of a captain, the name of an aircraft, and the date and time of arrival and, in some cases, departure. At the bottom of each double page the dock master had signed his name and title in crabbed script.

He flicked back a few pages, idly searching for someone he knew. Maybe Trinica would be in here.

'Busy recently, aren't you?' he commented. 'You usually get this much traffic?'

'Just sign,' the dock master said impatiently, not looking up from his records.

Frey's decision to confine most of the crew to the craft wasn't popular with one man in particular.

'You stinking bastard, Frey!' Pinn cried. 'You didn't even believe Retribution Falls existed until now! I *told* you we should come here when we were back in Yortland, but oh, no! You thought: let's all laugh at Pinn! Well I called it right, and I *deserve* to come.'

'Shut your fat meat-hole, Pinn,' Malvery said. 'Cap'n's given you an order.'

'Oh really? Well he can stuff it up his arse with all the other orders he's given me!'

Frey looked at Silo. 'If he tries to leave, shoot him,' he said, only half-joking.

'Cap'n,' Silo replied, priming his shotgun with a crunch.

Pinn looked around at the rest of the crew, finding no support, and then stamped back into the depths of the craft, muttering mutinously.

'Jez, Malvery, come on,' he said. 'We keep a low profile, have a look around, keep our ears open. And don't anybody call me anything but Cap'n, okay? I don't want to hear my name spoken outside of the *Ketty Jay.*'

'Right-o.'

'Everyone got revolvers? Good. You never know.'

They headed across the landing pad towards the bridge to the town. Frey was rather pleased with himself for standing firm against Pinn's outburst. Pinn was envisioning a night out in this pirate haven, but Frey needed to be able to effect a quick escape if necessary, without the need to go searching under bar tables for his drunken crew. Taking the whole group out would be like trying to herd cats.

He reviewed the tactics behind his choice of landing party. Separating Malvery and Pinn was the key. Pinn wouldn't cause any trouble without the doctor's back-up, and since Malvery was coming along, he didn't care what happened to Pinn. Malvery was useful muscle and had a bluff charm that would play well, but the two of them together in a place like Retribution Falls would result in alcoholic carnage, sure as bird shit on statues.

Jez would also be useful. She was smart, observant, and she had eyes like a hawk. Plus she was the only sensible one among them. He didn't count Crake. Crake dealt with daemons: nobody could say *that* was sensible.

But he had an ulterior motive in bringing Jez. He wanted to keep an eye on her. As grateful as he was that she'd saved their lives, he was suspicious. It puzzled him that the fumes hadn't seemed to affect her, and her explanation was weak. He didn't want to leave her alone on his aircraft. Not now she knew the ignition code. He wasn't so sure he trusted her.

The others wouldn't mind staying on the *Ketty Jay*. Crake, as he was never a freebooter, didn't understand the legend and allure of Retribution Falls. He had no desire to see the place. Harkins didn't like crowds or strangers. He'd rather be secure in his quarters, living in terror of the cat, who would wait for him to fall asleep before trying to suffocate him. And it would be too dangerous to take Silo. A Murthian would attract unwanted and hostile attention in a town like this. Besides, Silo had work to do. He needed to check over the *Ketty Jay* and repair any damage from the mines.

All in all, he had the whole thing figured out.

Not bad, Frey, he thought. *That's the sort of thinking a real captain does. That's how to handle a crew.*

He was in the mood for self-congratulation, despite his near-catastrophic failure to lead them through Rook's Boneyard. The triumph of finding Retribution Falls outweighed all that. This must have been how Cruwen and Skale felt when they discovered New Vardia. He was an explorer now. Whatever happened after this, he had to admit, he felt more . . . well, more like a *man* than he ever had before.

In that moment when he pressed down on his guns and blew the *Ace of Skulls* into a flaming ruin, his life as he knew it had ended. Every day since then had been one clawed back. He'd been forced to fight every step. It was exhausting, and terrifying, and most of the time he hated it. But just sometimes, when he could snatch a rare instant of peace amid the chaos, he felt different. He felt good about himself. And it had been a long, long time since he'd felt like that.

They took the bridge from the landing pad to the nearest platform, and discovered that Retribution Falls was even more unpleasant up close, and a far cry from the legends.

The narrow streets were weathered and worn beyond their years. The marsh air ate through metal, twisted wood, and brought mould to stone. Everything flaked and peeled. Generators buzzed and reeked, providing the power for the lights that hung on wires overhead to stave off the gloom. It was cold, yet their clothes became damp and stuck to them. The smell of the marsh mingled with that of a thousand unwashed bodies.

Retribution Falls was stuffed with every kind of pirate, smuggler, fraudster and criminal that Frey could imagine. Every pub and inn was crammed to capacity. The streets were choked, the whores hollow-eyed and exhausted. Inside, the humidity and the heat of dozens of bodies made things uncomfortable. Drunken men with short tempers fought hard. Guns were drawn, and bodies fell.

There was a wildness here that he found frightening. It was a jostling, stinking pandemonium of rotted teeth and leering faces. Danger surrounded them. He found he actually missed the spectre of the militia. He liked his illegal doings to be conducted within the safety of an orderly civilisation. Total lawlessness meant survival based on strength or cunning, and Frey didn't have too much of either.

They passed raucous bars and stepped over men lying in the thoroughfares, rum-soaked, unconscious and recently robbed. Malvery eyed up the bars as they passed, but without Pinn as his accomplice, he behaved himself and stuck close to his captain. Occasionally he'd shove someone out of their path; his size and fierce glare discouraged arguments.

'Not quite the utopia I'd envisioned, Cap'n,' Jez murmured.

Frey didn't quite understand what she meant by 'utopia' – it sounded like one of Crake's words – but he got the idea.

'All those craft, all these people,' he said. 'Doesn't it seem like there's far more pirates here than this place was built to hold?'

'Certainly does,' she said.

'And what does that say to you?'

'Says they're being gathered here for something.'

'That's what I thought,' he replied.

The market was a little less crowded than the streets and bars, but not by much. It sat on a platform all of its own, linked by bridges to several of its neighbours. Oil lamps hung from the awnings of rickety stalls, adding a smoky tang to the already fouled air. Their flickering light mixed uneasily with the electric bulbs hanging overhead, casting a strange glow on the heaving sea of faces that surged beneath.

Malvery pushed his way through the crowd, with Frey and Jez following in his slipstream. The stalls they passed were guarded by shotgun-wielding heavies. There were all manner of wares for sale: trinkets and knick-knacks, hardware, boots and coats, navigational charts. Dubious fried meats were offered to hungry shoppers, and someone was roasting chestnuts nearby. The noise of yelled conversation was deafening.

'You get the impression that this has all got a little out of control?' Jez screamed in Frey's ear.

Frey didn't hear what she said, so he nodded as if he agreed, and then replied, 'I think whoever's running this show, they've let things get a bit out of control!'

Jez, who also hadn't heard him, said, 'Definitely!'

Frey spotted a stall on the edge of the market platform, where the traffic wasn't quite so oppressive and it was possible to see the darkening marsh in the background. One of several signs that hung from its pole-and-canvas frontage declared:

Breathe the Free Aire! Filters 8 Shillies!

He tapped Malvery on the shoulder and steered him over. The storekeeper saw them coming and perked up. He was a thin, ginger-haired man with an enormous, puckered patch of scar tissue that ran across one side of his face. It looked like he'd been mauled by a bear.

'How did you get that?' Frey asked conversationally, indicating the scar.

'How did I get what?' the storekeeper asked, genuinely puzzled.

Frey thought a moment and then let it drop. 'These filters you're selling. They'd protect us against the bad air in the canyons?'

The storekeeper grinned. 'Guaranteed. Did your old ones let you down?'

'Something like that.'

'That's rough, friend. Well, you can rely on these.' He pulled one out of a crate behind him and put it on. It was a black metal oval with several breathing-slits that fitted over the mouth and nose, secured over the head by a strip of leather. 'Wo wetter n orb wetwibooshun bawls.'

'What?'

The shopkeeper took off the mask. 'I said, no better in all Retribution Falls.'

'Okay. I need seven.'

'Eight,' Jez corrected. When Frey and Malvery both looked at her, she said: 'The cat.'

'Right,' said Frey. 'Eight. Give me a discount.'

'Six bits.'

'Three.'

'Five.'

'Four.'

'Four and eight shillies.'

'Done.'

'You won't regret it,' the storekeeper promised, as he began counting out filters from the crate. 'First time in Retribution Falls?'

'How'd you guess?'

'Lot of newcomers recently. You just got the look.'

'Why so many?'

The storekeeper dumped an armful of filters on the cheap wooden table that passed as a counter. 'Same reason as you, I expect.'

'We're just here for the beer and scenery,' Malvery grinned. The storekeeper laughed at that, revealing a set of teeth better kept hidden.

'You heard about what's going on tomorrow?' the storekeeper asked, as Frey laid down his coins on the counter.

'Like you noticed, we just got here,' Frey replied.

'You know where Orkmund's place is?' He indicated a distant platform. It was too dark to make out anything but a sprinkle of lights. 'Ask anyone, you'll find it. Be there tomorrow at midday.'

'What's happening?'

'Orkmund's got something to say. Reckon it might be time.'

Malvery did a passable job of pretending he knew what the man was talking about. 'You think so?'

'Well, look around,' said the storekeeper. 'Some of these boys are going stir crazy. Can't keep a bunch of pirates cooped up like this. They came to fight, and if they can't fight someone else, they'll fight each other. I reckon he's gonna give the word to start the attack.'

'Let me at 'em,' said Frey. 'Can't wait to show that lot.'

'You know who we're fighting?' the storekeeper gasped, which wrong-footed Frey totally.

'Er . . . what?'

'You know where Orkmund's sending us?'

'Don't *you*?'

'Nobody knows. That's what we're all waiting to find out.'

Frey backpedalled. 'No, I meant, you know . . . the *general* them. Let me at *them*. Whoever *they* are.' He trailed off lamely.

The storekeeper gave him an odd look, then snatched the coins off the counter and called out to a passer-by, trying to lure them over. Dismissed, Frey and the others moved away, distributing the filters between them.

'Orkmund's got himself a pirate fleet,' Jez said. 'That's how Grephen's going to do it. That's how he'll seize power. He's made a deal with the king of the pirates.'

'But there's one last thing I don't understand,' Frey replied. 'How'd Duke Grephen get Orkmund on his side?'

'Paid him, probably,' Malvery opined.

'With what? Grephen doesn't have the money to support an army. Or at least Crake doesn't think so, and he should know.'

'Crake could be wrong,' Jez said. 'Just because he has the accent doesn't mean he has some great insight into the aristocracy. There's a lot you don't know about him.'

Frey frowned. He was getting heartily sick of this tension between Jez and Crake. They'd been barely able to work together when he needed them to navigate through the canyons of Rook's Boneyard. Something needed to be done.

'Back to the *Ketty Jay*,' he said. 'We've learned enough for now. Let's see what Orkmund says tomorrow.'

'We're not going to have a drink?' Malvery asked, horrified. 'I mean, in the interests of gathering information?'

'Not this time. Early start in the morning. I'm not having any trouble tonight.'

He started off back towards the landing pad. Malvery trudged behind. 'I miss the old Cap'n,' he grumbled.

Frey had almost all the information he needed. He was missing only one piece. Someone was backing Duke Grephen, providing the money to build an army of mercenaries big enough to fight the Coalition Navy and take the capital of Vardia. He needed know who. When that last piece fell into place, he'd understand the conspiracy he was tangled up in. Then, he could do something about it.

A serene and peaceful feeling settled on him as they made their way back towards the *Ketty Jay*. Tomorrow would bring an answer. He didn't know how he knew, but he was certain of it.

Tomorrow. That's when we start turning this around.

Twenty-Nine

Intervention – The Confessions Of Grayther Crake –
An Experiment, And The Tragedy That Follows

Crake was shaken out of sleep by Frey's hand on his
shoulder.

'Get up,' Frey said.

'What is it?' he murmured.

'Come on,' insisted the captain. 'I need you in the mess.'

Crake swung his legs off the bunk. He was still fully clothed,
having gone to sleep as soon as Frey left the *Ketty Jay*. He'd hoped
to shake off the headache he'd picked up from breathing the lava
fumes. It hadn't worked.

'What's so urgent, Frey? Stove making spooky noises? Daemonic activity in the stew?'

'There's just something we need to sort out, that's all.'

Something in his tone told Crake that Frey wasn't going to let
this go, so he got to his feet with a sigh and shambled after his
captain, out into the passageway. But instead of going down the
ladder to the mess, Frey walked past it and knocked on the door of
the navigator's quarters. Jez opened up. She glanced from Frey to
Crake, and was immediately suspicious.

'Can you come to the mess?' Frey asked, though it sounded less
a request than an order.

Jez stepped out of her quarters and shut the door behind her.

They climbed down into the mess. Silo was in there, smoking a
roll-up and drinking coffee. He was petting Slag, who was lying
flat on the table. At the sight of Jez, the cat jumped to his feet and
hissed. As soon as the way was clear, he bolted up the ladder and
was gone.

Silo looked up with an expression of mild disinterest.

'How's the *Ketty Jay*?' Frey asked.

'She battered, but she tough. Need a workshop to make her pretty again, but nothing hurt too bad inside. I fixed her best I can.'

'She'll fly?'

'She'll fly fine.'

Frey nodded. 'Can you give us the room?'

Silo spat in his palm and stubbed the roll-up into it. Then he got up and left. Since speaking with Silo, Crake couldn't help seeing the Murthian's relationship with his captain in a new light. They'd been companions so long that they barely noticed one another any more. They wore each other like old clothes.

'Sit down,' Frey said, motioning to the table in the centre of the mess. Jez and Crake sat opposite one another. The captain produced a bottle of rum from inside his coat and put it on the table between them.

'She doesn't drink,' Crake said. He was beginning to get a dreadful idea what this was about.

'Then you drink it,' Frey replied. He straightened, standing over them. 'Something's going on between you two. Has been since you went to Scorchwood Heights. I don't know what it is, and I don't want to know, 'cause it's no business of mine. But I need my crew to act like a crew, and I can't have this damned bickering all the time. The only way we're gonna survive is if we work together. If you can't, next port we reach, one of you is getting off.'

To his surprise, Crake realised that Frey meant it. The captain looked from one of them to the other to ensure the message had sunk in.

'Don't come out of this room till you've settled it,' he said, and then he climbed through the hatch and was gone.

There was a long and grudging silence. Crake's cheeks burned with anger. He felt awkward and foolish, a child who had been told off by his tutor. Jez looked at him coldly.

Damn her. I don't owe her an explanation. She'd never understand.

He hated Frey for meddling in something that didn't concern him. The captain had no idea what he was stirring up. Couldn't they just let it lie? Let her believe what she wanted. Better than having to think about it again. Better than having to face the memories of that night.

'It's true, isn't it?' Jez said.

He met her gaze resentfully.

'What the Shacklemore said,' she prompted. 'You stabbed your niece. Seventeen times with a letter knife.'

He swallowed against a lump in his throat. 'It's true,' he said.

'*Why?*' she whispered. There was something desperate in the way she said it. Some wide-eyed need to understand how he could do something so utterly loathsome.

Crake stared hard at the table, fighting down the shameful heat of gathering tears.

Jez sat back in her chair. 'I can take the half-wits and the incompetents, the alcoholics and the cowards,' she said. 'I can take that we shot down a freighter and killed dozens of people on board. But I can't be on this craft with a man who knifed his eight-year-old niece to death, Crake. I just can't.' She folded her arms and looked away, fighting back tears herself. 'How can you be how you are and be a child-murderer underneath? How can I trust anyone now?'

'I'm not a murderer,' Crake said.

'You killed that girl!'

He couldn't bear the accusations any more. Damn her, damn her, he'd tell her the whole awful tale and let her judge him as she would. It had been seven months pent up inside him, and he'd never spoken of it in all that time. It was the injustice, the right-eous indignation of the falsely accused, which finally opened the gates.

He took a shaky breath and spoke very calmly. 'I stabbed her,' he said. 'Seventeen times with a letter knife. But I didn't murder her.' He felt the muscles of his face pulling towards a sob, and it took him a moment to control himself.

'I didn't murder her, because she's still alive.'

The echo chamber sat in the centre of Crake's sanctum, silent and threatening. It was built like a bathysphere, fashioned from riveted metal and studded with portholes. A small, round door was set into one side. Heavy cables ran from it, snaking across the floor to electrical output points and other destinations. It was half a foot thick and surrounded by a secondary network of defensive measures.

Crake still didn't feel even close to being safe.

He paced beneath the stone arches of the old wine cellar. It was cold with the slow chill of the small hours, and his boot heels clicked as he walked. Electric lamps had been placed around the echo chamber – the only source of light. The pillars threw long, tapering shadows, splaying outward in all directions.

I have it. I have it at last. And yet I daren't turn it on.

It had taken him months to obtain the echo chamber. Months of wheedling and begging and scraping to the hoary old bastard in the big house. Months of pointless tasks and boring assignments. And hadn't that rot-hearted weasel enjoyed every moment of it! Didn't he relish seeing his shiftless second son forced to run around at his beck and call! He'd strung it out and strung it out, savouring the power it gave him. Rogibald Crake, industrial tycoon, was a man who liked to be obeyed.

'You wouldn't have to do any of this if you had a decent job,' he'd say. 'You wouldn't need my money then.'

But he *did* need his father's money. And this was Rogibald's way of punishing him for choosing not to pursue the career picked out for him. Crake had come out of university having been schooled in the arts of politics, and promptly announced that he didn't want to be a politician. Rogibald had never forgiven him for that. He couldn't understand why his son would take an uninspiring position in a law firm, nor why it took over three years for him to 'work out what he wanted to do with his life'.

But what Rogibald didn't know, what *nobody* knew, was that Crake had it worked out long ago. Ever since university. Ever since he discovered daemonism. After that, everything else became petty and insignificant. What did he care about the stuffy and corrupt world of politics, when he could make deals with beings that were not even of this world? *That* was power.

But daemonism was an expensive and time-consuming occupation. Materials were hard to come by. Books were rare and valuable. Everything had to be done in secret. It required hours of study and experimentation every night, and a sanctum took up a great deal of space. He simply couldn't manage the demands of a serious career while pursuing his study of daemonism, and yet he couldn't get the things he needed on the salary of a lawyer's clerk.

So he was forced to rely on his father for patronage. He feigned a passion for invention, and declared that he was studying the sciences and needed equipment to do it. Rogibald thought he was being ridiculous, but he was rather amused by the whole affair. It pleased him to let his son have enough rope to hang himself. No doubt he was waiting for Crake to realise that he was playing a fool's game, and to come crawling back. To have Crake admit that he was a failure, that Rogibald was right all along – that would be the sweetest prize. So he indulged his son's 'hobby' and watched eagerly for his downfall.

Since Crake was unable to afford accommodation grand enough to suit his needs, his father allowed him to live in a house on the family estate which he shared with his elder brother Condred, and Condred's wife and daughter. It was a move calculated to humiliate him. The brothers' disdain for each other was scorching.

Condred was the favoured son, who had followed his father into the family business. He was a straight-laced, strict young man who always acceded to Father's wishes and always took his side. He had nothing but contempt for his younger brother, whom he regarded as a layabout.

'I'll take him under my roof if you ask me to, Father,' he said, in front of Crake. 'If only to show him how a respectable family live. Perhaps I can teach him some responsibility.'

Condred's sanctimonious charity had galled him then, but Crake took some comfort in knowing that Condred regretted the offer now. Condred had envisioned a short stay. Perhaps he thought that Crake would be quickly shamed into moving out and getting a good job. But he'd reckoned without his younger brother's determination to pursue his quest for knowledge. Once Crake saw the empty wine cellar, he wouldn't be moved. He could endure anything, if he could have that. It was the perfect sanctum.

More than three years had passed. Three years in which Crake spent all his free time behind the locked door of the wine cellar, underground. Every night he'd come back from work, share an awkward dinner with his disapproving brother and his snooty, dried-up bitch of a wife, then disappear downstairs. Crake would have happily avoided the dinner, but Condred insisted that he was a guest and should eat with the family. It was the proper thing to do, even if all concerned hated it.

How typical of Condred. Cutting off his nose to spite his face, all in the name of etiquette. Moron.

The only thing that made life in the house bearable, apart from his sanctum, was his niece. She was a delightful thing: bright, intelligent, friendly and somehow unstained by the sour attitude of her parents. She was fascinated by her uncle Grayther's secret experiments, and pestered him daily to show her what new creation he was working on. She was convinced that his sanctum was a wonderland of toys and fascinating machines.

Crake found it a charming idea. He began to buy toys from a local toymaker to give to her, passing them off as his own. Her parents knew what he was doing, and sneered in private, but they didn't say a word about it to their daughter. She idolised their layabout guest, and Crake loved her in return.

Those three years of studying, experimenting, trial and error, had brought him to this point. He'd learned the basics and applied them. He'd summoned daemons and bid them to his will. He'd thralled objects, made simple communications, even healed wounds and sickness through the Art. He corresponded often with more experienced daemonists and was well thought of by them.

All daemonism was dangerous, and Crake had been very cautious all this time. He'd gone step by tiny step, growing in confidence, never overreaching himself. He knew well the kinds of things that happened to daemonists who attempted procedures beyond their experience. But it was possible to be *too* cautious. At some point, it was necessary to take the plunge.

The echo chamber was the next step. Echo theory was cutting-edge daemonic science, requiring complex calculations and nerves of steel. With it, a daemonist could reach into realms never before accessed, to pluck strange new daemons from the aether. The old guard, the ancient, fuddy-duddy daemonists, wouldn't touch it; but Crake couldn't resist. The old ways had been mapped and explored, but this was new ground, and Crake wanted to be one of the first to the frontier.

Tonight, he was attempting a procedure he'd never tried before. He was going to bring life to the lifeless.

Tonight, he was going to create a golem.

He stopped his pacing and returned to the echo chamber, checking the connections for the twentieth time. The echo chamber was linked by soundproofed tubes to a bizarre armoured suit that he'd found in a curio shop. The shopkeeper had no idea what it was. He theorised that it might have been made for working in extreme environments, but Crake privately disagreed. It was crafted to fit a hunchbacked giant, and it wasn't airtight. He guessed it was probably ornamental, or a sculptural showpiece made by some deranged metalworker. At any rate, Crake had to have it. It was so fascinatingly grotesque, and perfect for his purposes.

Now it stood in his sanctum, ready to accept the daemon he intended to draw into it. An empty vessel, waiting to be filled. He studied the armoured suit for a long time, until it began to unnerve him. He couldn't shake the feeling that it was about to move.

Surrounding the echo chamber and the suit was a circle of resonator masts. These electrically powered tuning forks vibrated at different wavelengths, designed to form a cage of frequencies through which a daemon couldn't pass. Crake checked the cables, following them across the floor of the sanctum to the electrical output he'd had wired in to the wall. Once satisfied, he turned them on one by one, adjusting the dials set into their bases. The hairs on his nape began to prickle as the air thickened with frequencies beyond his range of hearing.

'Well,' he said aloud. 'I suppose I'm ready.'

Standing on the opposite side of the echo chamber to the armoured suit was a control console. It was a panel of brass dials, waist-high, set into a frame that allowed it to be moved around on rollers. Next to the controls was a desk, scattered with open books and notepads displaying procedures and mathematical formulae. Crake knew them by heart, but he scanned them again anyway. Putting off the moment when he'd have to begin.

He hadn't been so terrified since the first time he summoned a daemon. His pulse pounded at his throat. The cellar felt freezing cold. He'd prepared, and prepared, and prepared, but no preparation would ever be enough. The cost of getting this wrong could be terrible. Death would be a mercy if an angry daemon got its hands on him.

But he couldn't be cautious for ever. To be a rank-and-file practitioner of daemonism wasn't enough. He wanted the power and renown of the masters.

He went to the console and activated the echo chamber. A bass hum came from the sphere. He left it for a few minutes to warm up, concentrating on his breathing. He had a feeling he might suddenly faint if he didn't keep taking deep breaths.

It's still not too late to back out, Grayther.

But that was just fear talking. He'd made this decision long ago. He steeled his nerve and went back to the console. Steadily, he began to turn the dials.

There was an art to catching a daemon. The trick was to match the vibrations of the equipment to the vibrations of the daemon, bringing the entity into phase with what the uneducated called the 'real' world. With minor daemons – little motes of power and awareness, possessing no more intelligence than a beetle – the procedure was simple enough. It was rather like fishing: you placed a sonic lure and drew them in.

But the greater daemons were another matter entirely. They had to be caught and forced into phase. A greater daemon might have six or seven primary resonances that all needed to be matched before it could be dragged unwillingly before the daemonist. And once there, the daemon needed to be contained. It was a foolish man who tried to deal with an entity like that without taking measures to protect themselves.

Crake wasn't stupid enough to think he could handle a greater daemon yet. He was aiming lower. Something with a dog-like level of intelligence would suit him very nicely. If he could thrall an entity like that into his armoured suit, he'd have a golem dull enough to be biddable. And if it proved troublesome, he had procedures in place to drive it out and back into the aether.

But summoning daemons was dangerous in many ways. A man didn't always know exactly what he was getting. He might fish for a minnow and find a shark on the line.

Crake had made calculations, based on the findings of other echo theorists and his own ideas. He'd identified a range of frequencies where he'd be likely to find what he wanted. Then he commenced the hunt proper.

The echo chamber began to vibrate and whine as he searched along the bandwidth. Daemonism was as much about feel and instinct as science. Crake closed his eyes and concentrated, turning the dials slowly.

There it was. That creeping sensation of being watched. He'd found something. Now he had to catch it before it slipped away.

He set up new resonances, starting high and low and then moving them closer together, feeling out the shape of the entity. He stopped when he felt the resistance of it.

The reaction was more pronounced now: a cold shiver, a slight feeling of vertigo and disorientation. He had to keep his eyes open. When he closed them, he started tipping forward.

He looked at the dials. The thing was huge, spread right across the subsonics.

Let it go, he told himself. *Let it go. It's too big.*

He *had* it now, though. There was no way he could hold on to something like that with his standard equipment. It would simply phase into a different frequency and escape. But with the echo chamber, he could keep it pinned, pounding it with confusing signals that all interfered with one another.

He could *get* this one. Forget the golem, forget everything else. He just wanted to see it. Then he'd send it back. But just to *see* it!

Excited, riding on a fear-driven high, he worked the dials feverishly. He set up more vibrations, seeking the daemon's primary frequencies, narrowing and narrowing the bandwidth until he matched them. The daemon was shifting wavelengths, trying to escape the cage, but he shifted with it, never letting it get away from him. The closer he came, the less space the daemon had to wriggle.

The air was throbbing. The echo chamber pulsed with invisible energies.

Spit and blood, this is working! This is actually working!

Once he had it fixed as best he could, he stepped away from the console and went to peer inside the echo chamber. Through the porthole in the door, he could see that the sphere was empty. But he wasn't disheartened. Inside, perspectives bent out of shape, and the air warped in eye-watering contortions. Something was coming. He could hardly breathe for terror and fascination. Leaning close to the thick glass, he tried to see further inside.

A colossal, mad eye stared back at him.

He yelled, falling away from the porthole, his heart thumping hard enough to hurt. That vast eye had surged out of nowhere, surfacing into his reality, burning itself on to his consciousness. He saw it now, impossibly huge, belonging to something far bigger than the echo chamber could contain.

There was a heavy impact, and the echo chamber rocked to one side. Crake sat where he'd fallen, transfixed. Again, the sound of a giant's fist pounding. The echo chamber dented outwards.

Oh, no. No, no.

He scrambled to his feet and ran for the console. *Get rid of it, get rid of it, any way you can.*

Another impact, sending a shudder through the whole sanctum. The electric lamps flickered. One tipped over, crashing to the ground. Crake lost his footing, stumbled onwards.

And then he heard her scream.

The sound froze him to the bone. It was more dreadful than anything he could imagine; more dreadful than the thing in the echo chamber. His world tipped into the primal, inescapable horror of a nightmare as he looked over at his niece, standing there in her white nightdress. She was just outside the circle of resonator poles, transfixed by the scene before her.

He'd never know how she'd got the key to the wine cellar. Perhaps she'd found an old copy in some dusty, hidden place. Had she been planning this moment ever since? Had she been unable to sleep, so keen was she to see the secret wonderland of toys where her uncle Grayther worked? Had she set her clock to wake her, hoping to sneak down in the dead of night when she thought he wouldn't be there?

He'd never know how or why, but it didn't matter in the end. What mattered was that she was here, and the daemon was uncontainable. The door of the echo chamber flew open, and the last thing he knew before his life changed for ever was a hurricane wind that smelled of sulphur, and a deafening, unearthly howl.

When his senses returned to him, the sanctum was dark and silent. A single electric lamp remained unsmashed. It lay on its side near the echo chamber, underlighting the looming shape of the armoured suit, which was still connected by cables to the dented metal sphere.

Crake was disorientated. It took him several seconds to understand where he was. His mind felt scratched and sore, as if rodents had been scrabbling at it from the inside, wounding his senses with small, dirty claws. The daemon had been in his head, in his thoughts. But what had it done there?

He realised he was standing. He looked down, and saw in his hand a letter knife with the insignia of his university on the hilt. The knife and the hand that held it were slick and dark with blood.

There was a clicking noise from the shadows. Red smears on the stones. He followed them with his eyes, and there he found her.

Her white nightdress was soaked in red. There were slits in her arms and throat, where the knife had plunged. They welled with rich, thick blood, spilling out in pulses. She was gaping like a fish, making clicking noises in her throat. Each breath was a shallow gasp, and her lips and chin were red. Her brown hair was matted into sodden wads.

Her eyes. Pleading. Not understanding. Dazed with incomprehensible agony. She didn't know about death. She'd never thought it could happen. She'd trusted him, with a blind, unthinking love, and he'd turned on her with a blade.

It was the daemon's revenge, for daring to summon it from the aether. It had been cruel enough to leave him his life and wits intact.

Crake hadn't known that pain and despair and horror could reach the heights that they now did. The sheer intensity of it was such that he felt he should die from it. If only the darkness would come back, if only his heart would stop! But there was no mercy for him. Realisation smashed down upon him like a tidal wave, and he staggered and gagged, the knife falling from numb fingers.

She was still alive. Alive, begging him to make the pain stop, like some half-broken animal ruined under the wheels of a motorised carriage. Begging him to make it better somehow.

'*She's a child!*' he screamed at the darkness, as if the daemon was still there to be accused. '*She's just a damned child!*'

But when the echoes had died, there was only the wet clicking from his niece as she tried to draw breath.

What overtook him then was a grief so overwhelming that it drowned his senses. He was seized by an idea, mad and desperate, and he acted on it without thought for consequence. Nothing else was important. Nothing except undoing what had been done, in the only way he could think of.

He scooped her up in his arms. She was so light, so thin and pale, white skin streaked with trails of gore. He carried her to the echo chamber, and gently placed her inside. He pushed the door shut. Despite the abuse it had suffered, the lock engaged and it sealed itself. Then a weakness took him, and he fell to his knees, his forehead pressed against the porthole in the door, sobs wracking his body.

She was lying on her back, her head tilted, looking at him through the glass. Blood bubbled from her lips. Her gaze met his, and it was too terrible to stand. He flung himself away, and went to the control console.

There, he did what had to be done.

Jez had seen men cry before, but never like this. This was heartbreaking. Crake's sobs were deep, wild, dredged up from a depth of pain that Jez couldn't have imagined he held inside him. His story had become almost impossible to understand as he neared the end. He couldn't even form a sentence through the hacking sobs that shook his whole body.

'I didn't know!' he cried, his face blotched and his beard wet with tears. His nose was running, but he didn't trouble to wipe it. He was ugly and shattered before her. It hurt to see him so. 'I didn't know what I was doing! Only it . . . it didn't work like I thought. The tra . . . the tra . . . transfer wasn't perfect. She's *different* now, she's not . . . like she was . . .' He gasped in a breath. 'I just wanted to *save* her.'

But Jez couldn't give him pity or sympathy. She'd hardened herself too much. She saw the tragedy of him now, but if she let herself forgive him, if she gave in even a little, there would be no going back. He could perhaps be excused the crime of stabbing her, if he wasn't in his right mind. But what he'd done next was nothing short of diabolical.

'One thing,' she said. Her voice was so tight that it hardly sounded like her. 'Her name.'

'What?'

'All this time, you never told me your niece's name. You've avoided it.'

Crake stared at her with red eyes. 'You know her name.'

'Say it!' she demanded. Because she needed just this final closure, before she could walk away.

He swallowed and choked down a sob.

'Bessandra,' he said. 'Bessandra was her name. But we all just called her Bess.'

Thirty

Orkmund's Address – A Familiar Object –
Frey Puts It All Together – 'Gotcha!'

By midday, a crowd had gathered outside Orkmund's stronghold.

In a rare moment of architectural forethought, the stronghold had been built in front of a large square which was employed for the purpose of meetings, markets and occasional executions or bouts of trial-by-combat. A wooden stage, now groaning under the weight of spectators, stood in the centre for just this purpose. Another, more temporary one had been erected just outside the stronghold, and was guarded by burly men with cutlasses. This would be Orkmund's podium.

Frey pushed through the press of bodies, with Malvery clearing the way ahead. Pinn and Jez came behind. Pinn had been subdued by his confinement in the *Ketty Jay* the night before, and Frey had extracted promises of good behaviour today. He charged Malvery with enforcing them, knowing how the doctor liked to bully Pinn.

It was fun to torment the young pilot now and then, but Frey knew how much it meant to him to see Retribution Falls before they left. Just so he could say he'd been. Just so he could tell Lisinda of his adventures, on that day when he returned in triumph to sweep her into his arms. Having asserted his authority, Frey was happy to give Pinn a little slack.

The stronghold was constructed in a squared-off horseshoe shape, with two wings projecting forward around a small interior courtyard. It was dull and forbidding, with square windows and iron-banded doors. Its walls were dark stone, streaked with mould.

A place built for someone who had no interest in flair or aesthetics. A fortress.

Surrounding the stronghold was a ramshackle barricade of metal spikes and crossed girders, eight feet high and surmounted by wooden watchtowers. The watchtowers were manned by rifle-wielding pirates, who scanned the crowd below them, no doubt deciding who they'd shoot first if they had the chance. In the middle of the barricade was a crude gate, a thick slab of metal on rollers that could be slid back and forth to grant access to the courtyard.

Frey and the others fought their way to a vantage point as the gate began to open and the crowd erupted in ear-pummelling cheers. The floor shook with the stamping of feet. It occurred to Frey that they were standing on a huge platform that was held up by a scaffolding of girders, and that it might not be built to take this kind of weight. It would be an ignominious end to his adventure, to sink to the bottom of a foetid marsh beneath a hundred tons of unwashed pirate flesh.

It wasn't until Orkmund climbed the steps to his stage that Frey caught sight of him. The pirate captain Orkmund, scourge of the Coalition in the years before the Aerium Wars, who disappeared fifteen years ago and was thought by most to be dead. But he wasn't dead: he was building Retribution Falls. A home for pirates, safe from the Navy. A place where they could conduct their business in peace – with a hefty cut for Orkmund, of course.

Though he must have been in his mid-fifties, Orkmund still cut an impressive figure. He was well over two metres high, bald-headed and thickset, with squashed features that gave him a thuggish look. Tattoos crawled over this throat, scalp and arms. He wore a simple black shirt, tight and unlaced at the throat, to emphasise an upper body and arms that were heavy with muscle. He walked up to the stage with a predator's confidence, surveyed the cheering crowd, and raised his arms for silence. It took some time.

'Some of you know me by sight,' he shouted. His voice, though loud, was still faint and thin by the time it reached Frey's ears, and he had to concentrate to hear. 'Some don't. For them new to Retribution Falls: welcome. I'm Neilin Orkmund.'

The cheer that erupted at that drowned out anything else for a while. When the crowd was relatively quiet again, Orkmund continued.

'I'm proud to see so many men and women here today. Some of the finest pirates in the land. Some of you've known of this place for years. For others, it'd only been legend until recently. But you've come at my call, and I thank you for that. Together, we'll be an unstoppable force. Together, we'll make an army like Vardia's never seen!'

More cheers. Pinn and Malvery cheered along with them, caught up in the moment.

'Now I know some of you are frustrated. Champing at the bit. You wanna get into action, don't you? You wanna break some bones and smash some skulls!'

Another deafening cheer, accompanied by clapping and jostling that threatened to turn into a riot.

Orkmund held up his hands. 'You've enjoyed my hospitality. You've dipped your beaks in the delights of Retribution Falls. And in return, I ask you only one thing: be patient.'

The pirates near to Frey groaned and muttered. Suddenly the fervour had gone out of the crowd.

'I know you're disappointed. No one wants to get out there more than me,' Orkmund hollered. 'But this ain't no small task we're taking on! We ain't here to rob a freighter or steal a few trinkets from some remote outpost. We ain't just a crew of fifty men, or a hundred. We're a crew of thousands! And a crew of thousands takes time to gather and co-ordinate.'

There were reluctant mumbles of concession at this.

'The time's coming very soon. A matter of days,' said Orkmund. 'But I've brought you here today because I've something to show you all.'

As he spoke, a troop of armed pirates sallied out of the stronghold, guarding two dozen men who were carrying a dozen large chests between them. They carried the chests up onto the stage as Orkmund continued.

'I know that there are doubters out there. What are we doing here? Why are we waiting? Who are we attacking, and why's it still a secret?' Orkmund said, prowling back and forth on the stage. 'Well, first ask yourself: why'd you come to Retribution Falls? Why'd you answer my call, when you didn't even know who you was fighting? For some, it was loyalty to me. For some, it was the call to adventure. But for most of you . . . it were this!'

He threw open one of the chests, and a gasp went up from the crowd.

'Loot! Ducats! Money!' Orkmund cried, and the crowd cheered anew, their spirits roused. He went to the next one, and threw that open, revealing that it, too, was full of coins. 'All this, for you! Booty! A share for every man that survives, and a right generous share it is too!' He threw open another one. 'Now ain't this worth fighting for? Ain't this worth waiting a few more days for?'

The pirates howled with glee, shaking their fists in the air, driven rabid by the sight of so much money. If not for the respect they had for Orkmund and the multiple guns trained on them, they might have tried to storm the stage right then.

But while Pinn and Malvery were yelling themselves hoarse, Frey had spotted something. He turned to Jez. 'Can you see the stage?'

She craned to look over the shoulder of the pirate in front. 'Not really.'

'Come here,' he said, and crouched down to offer her a piggy-back.

'No, Cap'n, it's really alright.'

'I need your eyes, Jez. Help me out.'

Since she couldn't think of a good reason to protest, she climbed awkwardly onto his back and he lifted her up.

'You know, my eyesight's not all that great, I mean it's—'

'The last chest on the right,' said Frey. 'Describe it to me.'

Jez looked. 'It's red.'

'Describe it *more*,' he said irritably.

She thought for moment. 'It's very fine,' she said. 'Dark red lacquer. Kind of a branch-and-leaf design on the lid. Silver clasp in the shape of a wolf's head. Oh, wait, he's opening it.'

Orkmund was throwing open each chest, whipping the pirates into a frenzy with the wealth paraded before them. Frey didn't need Jez to tell him that the red-lacquered chest was full to bursting with ducats.

And that was it. The final piece fell into place.

'Everyone!' he said. 'We're leaving.'

Pinn whined in complaint. Malvery raised a threatening hand to cuff him. 'Fine,' Pinn sulked. 'Let's go.'

Frey let Jez down to the floor. 'Seen enough, Cap'n?' she asked.

'Oh yeah,' he said. 'I've seen enough.'

The streets were relatively quiet on their way back. Retribution Falls seemed cold and bleak without the din of drunken revelry. Frey stepped through the sludge of debris and bodily fluids from the night before, setting a quick pace. He was eager to get to the *Ketty Jay*. There was a purpose in his walk.

'What's the story, Cap'n?' Jez asked. 'Are we getting out of here?'

'That's right,' he said. 'There's no reason to stay any more.'

'I can think of lots,' said Pinn. 'Most of them come in pints or bottles, the rest have big wobbling tits. Come on, how about a little shore leave?'

'I'm trying to save us all from the noose, Pinn,' Frey replied. 'Stay chaste for a day. Think of your sweetheart.'

'Thinking of her just makes me want to bang a whore even worse,' Pinn grinned, then held his hands up in submission. 'Okay, okay. Yes, Cap'n. Back to the *Ketty Jay* like a good little pilot. But I still don't get what's going on.'

'Alright, I'll tell you,' said Frey. 'We knew that Duke Grephen was planning a coup against the Archduke. What he didn't have was an army big enough to take on the Navy, or the money to pay for it. Orkmund's providing the army, and now we know who's providing the money.'

'Do we?' Jez asked. 'Who?'

'The Awakeners.'

'What makes you think that?'

'That chest on the podium. I saw them bringing it out of the hermitage where Amalicia was being kept. I didn't know what was in it then, but now we do. Money. And look where it ended up: here in Retribution Falls.'

'The Awakeners are financing the pirates?' Pinn asked. 'Why?'

'Because they want the Archduke out. Him and his wife.'

'What's his wife got to do with it?'

'The Archduchess is the one who's got him talking about all these new laws to limit the power of the Awakeners,' Frey said. He was aware that he was losing Pinn already. 'Look, the Awakeners run themselves like a business. And there's no question they make bucketloads of money from the superstitious. Now if someone as powerful as the Archduke starts saying that the whole idea of the Allsoul is rubbish, people are going to start listening to him. And that means the Awakeners start going the way of all the other religions they crushed a century ago.'

'You're remarkably well informed these days, Cap'n,' Jez commented.

'Been talking to Crake,' he said.

'You know he's not exactly impartial, don't you?' she said. When she spoke of the daemonist, he noted that her tone wasn't as obviously scornful as it had been yesterday.

'So why are the Awakeners funding Duke Grephen?' Pinn piped up.

Frey sighed. This would require careful explanation for Pinn to understand. 'Because Grephen's an Awakener. Just like Gallian Thade. If he becomes the Archduke, then the Awakeners gain power instead of losing it. In fact, they'd become pretty much unstoppable.'

Pinn frowned, pondering that for a moment as they hurried through the narrow, filthy lanes, past peeling walls and rusted steps. 'And the Awakeners hired Dracken to catch us?'

'No!' Frey and Malvery cried in unison. It was Frey who

continued: '*Grephen* hired her to catch us. Because he didn't want us talking to anyone and blowing his plan before he could put it into action.'

Pinn thought some more. Frey had a feeling of dread in his stomach, anticipating the inevitable follow-up question.

'So who hired the Century Knights?'

Malvery covered his face with a hand in despair.

'What?' Pinn protested. 'It's complicated!'

'I swear, mate, you have the brains of half a rock.'

'*Nobody* hired the Century Knights,' Jez said. 'They're loyal to the Archduke. Nothing to do with Grephen. They're after us because they think *we're* the villains here.'

'We did kill the Archduke's son,' Malvery pointed out.

'Accidentally!' Frey said. 'And besides, we were set up. That means it doesn't count.'

Malvery raised an eyebrow. 'I'd like to see you try that line of argument with the Archduke,' he said.

'What Grephen wants,' Frey told Pinn, before he could ask another question, 'is that we get killed, nice and quiet, and he gets to show the bodies to everyone. Hengar's murderers are caught, case closed. That was the idea from the start. We were supposed to die during the ambush.'

'What he *doesn't* want is the Century Knights catching us and giving us a chance to tell our side of the story,' Jez continued. 'He's afraid that we know enough to make them suspicious, and that will blow his big surprise attack.'

'Which is happening in a few days, if you believe that Orkmund feller,' added Malvery.

Pinn gave up trying to figure out who was after who and asked, 'So what do we do?'

'What we do is cut a deal,' said Frey. 'Talk to some people. Set up a safe rendezvous. We'll give them the charts and the compass, let them come see Retribution Falls for themselves. Once they find the army Orkmund's put together, they'll believe us. We'll offer them the big fish, and in return, we demand a pardon.'

Pinn stopped dead. The others walked on a few steps before they noticed.

'You're selling this place out?' he said, appalled.

Frey was confused. 'What do you mean?'

'I mean, you're going to tell the Coalition Navy where Retribution Falls is?'

'You think you could shout it a bit louder, Pinn?' Malvery cried. 'I don't think they heard you in Yortland.'

Pinn looked around furtively, suddenly remembering where he was. Thankfully, the alley they were standing in was deserted, and nobody seemed to have heard. He scuttled up closer to Frey and jabbed him in the chest with a finger.

'This place is a legend! This place was built with the sweat and tears of a generation of pirates. It's been the hope of every freebooter since the Aerium Wars that they could one day find Retribution Falls and live out the rest of their days in pirate wonderland. It's a yoo –, a yoo—'

'Utopia,' Jez said. 'Pinn, it's a dump.'

Pinn was aghast. 'It's Retribution Falls!'

Jez studied her surroundings critically. The sagging roofs, the cracked walls and mildewed corners, the broken bottles and bloodstains. She sniffed, taking in the rank stench of the marsh.

'You know what pirates are really good at, Pinn?' she said. 'Being pirates. And that's all. In fact, if you asked me what would happen if you took a thousand pirates and asked them to build a town, I'd say it would look pretty much like this. This place was better as a legend. The real thing doesn't work.'

'Let me put it this way, Pinn,' said Frey. 'Do you want to get hanged, or don't you?'

Pinn examined the question for a trick. 'No?' he ventured.

'It's either you or this place. Orkmund's working for Duke Grephen, remember? And Grephen wants all of us dead. You too, Pinn.'

Pinn opened his mouth, shut it, opened it again, and then gave up trying to argue. 'Lisinda would never get over it if anything happened to me,' he said.

'Think how proud she'll be when she learns you single-handedly triumphed over an army of pirates,' Malvery beamed.

'I suppose I could dress it up a little,' Pinn mused. 'Alright, spit on this place. Let's get out of here and stab some backs!'

'That's the spirit!' Frey said cheerily.

Back at the *Ketty Jay*, Frey issued instructions for take-off and made sure Slag was trapped in the mess so some unlucky volunteer – Pinn – could force a mouth filter on him during the journey back. Silo was showing Frey some superficial damage to the underwings when Olric, the dock master's assistant, wandered up to them.

'Leaving, are you?'

'Just got an errand to run,' said Frey. 'Orkmund says it'll be a few days yet, so . . .' he shrugged.

'You gotta sign out.'

'I was just about to. Be over there in a minute.'

Olric ambled away again. Frey asked Silo to fetch Crake from inside, and the daemonist came down the cargo ramp shortly after.

'You needed me?'

'You and Jez sort things out last night?' he asked.

Crake didn't meet his eye. 'As best we could.'

Frey wasn't encouraged. 'Can you come with me to the dock master's office? I need to sign out before we fly.'

Crake gave him a puzzled look. 'Two-man job, is it?'

'Actually, yes. I need you to distract the dock master. I mean *really* distract him. You think you can do the thing with the tooth?'

'I can try,' said Crake. 'Did he strike you as particularly smart or quick-witted?'

'Not really.'

'Good. The less intelligent they are, the better the tooth works. It's the smart ones that cause all the problems.'

'Don't they always?' Frey commiserated, as he led the daemonist across the landing pad.

'What are you up to, anyway?' Crake asked.

'Taking out a little insurance,' replied Frey, with a wicked little smile.

The journey out was less traumatic than the journey there. Now they had filters to protect against the strange fumes from the lava river, and they knew the trick of the compass and the mines, things were not so daunting. The only drama came from Pinn, who had a miserable time trying to subdue the cat, until Malvery hit on the idea of getting him drunk first. A quarter-bottle of rum later, and Slag was placid enough to take the mouth filter, after which they headed to Malvery's surgery to apply antiseptic to Pinn's scratched-up arms and hands.

There had been talk of ignoring the charts and flying straight up and out of there, instead of the laborious backtracking through the canyons, but they soon discovered that there was a reason why nobody did that. The area above Retribution Falls was heavily mined, and Jez theorised that these ones could be more magnetic than the ones they'd encountered, meaning that they'd home in on the *Ketty Jay* from a greater distance. Frey decided not to push their luck. They'd follow the charts.

Frey had Jez and Crake up in the cockpit again, one to navigate and one to read from the compass while he flew. The atmosphere between them had changed. Instead of sniping, Jez tried not to talk to Crake at all, beyond what was necessary to co-ordinate their efforts. Crake also seemed very quiet. Something was different between them, for sure, but Frey had the sense that it wasn't entirely resolved yet.

Well, at least there had been progress. They weren't fighting any more. It was a start.

Frey was light-hearted as he piloted them through the fog. He was beginning to feel that things were really pulling together for them now. The changes had been slow and subtle, but ever since they'd left Yortland he'd felt more and more like the captain of a crew, rather than a man lumbered with a chaotic rabble. Instead of letting them do whatever they felt like, he'd begun to give them orders, and he'd been surprised how well they responded once he showed a bit of authority. They might gripe and complain, but they got on with it.

The raid on Quail's place had been a complete success. Jez and Crake's infiltration of the Winter Ball had yielded important information. And the theft of the compass and charts from the *Delirium Trigger* was their crowning glory so far. A month ago, he couldn't have imagined pulling off anything so audacious. In fact, a month ago he couldn't have imagined himself giving anybody orders. He'd have said: *What right do I have to tell someone else what to do?* He didn't think enough of himself to take command of his *own* life, let alone someone else's.

But it wasn't about rights, it was about responsibilities. Whether as passengers or crew, the people on board the *Ketty Jay* endured the same dangers as he did. If he couldn't make them work together, they all suffered. His craft was the most important thing in the world to him, yet he'd never given a damn about its contents until now. It had always been just him and the *Ketty Jay*, the iron mistress to whom he was forever faithful. She gave him his freedom, and he loved her for it.

But a craft was nothing without a crew to run it and pilots to defend it. A craft was made up of people. The *Ketty Jay* was staffed with drunkards and drifters, all of them running from something, whether it be memories or enemies or the drudgery of a land-bound life; but since Yortland, they'd all been running in the same direction. United by that common purpose, they'd begun to turn into something resembling a crew. And Frey had begun to turn into someone resembling a captain.

Damn it, he was getting to *like* these people. And the thought of that frightened him a little. Because if his crew got hanged, it would be on his account. His fault. He'd got them all into this, by taking Quail's too-good-to-be-true offer of fifty thousand ducats. He'd made that desperate gamble, closed his eyes and hoped for a winning card; but he'd drawn the Ace of Skulls instead.

Jez, Crake, Malvery, Silo . . . even Harkins and Pinn. They weren't just badly paid employees any more. Their lives had come to rest on his decisions. He didn't know if he could bear the weight of that. But he did know that he had no choice about it.

'No mines nearby,' Crake reported.

'I think we're through, Cap'n,' Jez said, slumping back in her seat. 'You can start your ascent any time now.'

'Well,' Frey said. 'That was Rook's Boneyard. I hope you all enjoyed your tour.'

They managed weak smiles at that. He cut the thrusters and fed aerium gas into the ballast tanks, allowing the *Ketty Jay* to rise steadily. The fog thinned, and the mountainsides faded from view.

'Never thought I'd miss daylight quite so badly,' Frey said. 'It better be sunny up there.'

There was no danger of sun, this deep in the Hookhollows, with the clouds and drifting ash high in the sky overhead. But the mist oppressed him. He wanted to be able to see again.

The *Ketty Jay* rose out of the white haze, and the sky exploded all around them. The concussion threw the *Ketty Jay* sideways and sent the crew flying from their seats onto the floor. Frey scrambled back into his seat, half-blinded by the flash of light, thinking only of escape.

Get out of here, get out of here, get—

But the blast had spun the *Ketty Jay* around, and now he could see their assailant through the windglass of the cockpit. Her black prow loomed before them, a massive battery of guns trained on his small craft.

The *Delirium Trigger*.

Frey slumped forward onto the dashboard. The first shot had been a warning. Her outflyers had surrounded them, waiting for the slightest hint that they were going to run. But Frey wasn't going to run. It was hopeless. They'd be blown to pieces before he had time to fire up the thrusters.

Not like this. I was so damn close.

The *Delirium Trigger*'s electroheliograph mast was blinking. Jez, who had staggered to her feet and was standing behind the pilot's chair, narrowed her eyes as she watched it.

'What's it say?' Frey asked.

' "Gotcha!" ' Jez replied.

Frey groaned. 'Bollocks.'

Thirty-One

One Is Missing – Frey Is Put To
The Question – Goodnight, Bess

I knew I should have got out when I had the chance, Crake thought, as the men of the *Delirium Trigger* flooded up the *Ketty Jay*'s cargo ramp. Six of them covered the prisoners while the others dispersed through the hold, checking corners, moving with military precision. Wary eyes flickered over Bess, who was standing quietly to one side.

'You tell that thing, if it moves, you all get shot,' snarled one of the gunmen.

'She won't,' said Crake, the words coming out small. 'I put her to sleep.'

He'd been forced to. He couldn't trust that Bess would behave when their lives were under threat.

The gunman jabbed Crake with the muzzle of his revolver. Bess didn't react. 'She'd better not. Or you're first to go.'

The crew of the *Ketty Jay* stood at the top of the ramp, offering no resistance. All except Jez, anyway. Where Jez was, only the captain knew. Crake had seen her speaking urgently with Frey as they were being escorted out of the mountains. Later, after they were instructed to land in the vast wastes of the Blackendraft, she was gone. When Malvery enquired as to her whereabouts, Frey said: 'She's got a plan.'

'Oh,' said Malvery. 'What kind of plan?'

'The kind that won't work.'

Malvery harumphed. 'No harm in trying, I suppose.'

'That's what I thought.'

They were patted down. None of them were carrying weapons,

302

but Crake's heart sank a little further when a crewman pulled his skeleton key from the inside pocket of his greatcoat and held it up in front of his face.

'What's this for?' the crewman demanded.

'My house,' Crake lied. The crewman snorted and tossed it away. It skidded across the floor of the cargo hold and into a dark corner. With it went any hope that Crake had of escaping from the *Delirium Trigger*'s brig and saving their hides.

Once the invaders were satisfied they'd been stripped of anything dangerous, Frey and his crew were herded down the ramp at gunpoint. Crake was sweating and his stomach roiled. The future was closing in on him rapidly, arrowing him towards the gallows. He couldn't see a way out of this one. They were surrounded by overwhelming firepower and completely at Dracken's mercy. There would be no miraculous rescue this time.

Pinn whistled as he walked down the ramp, totally oblivious to the seriousness of their situation. Even now, he believed in his own heroic myth enough to trust that a hair-raising escape was just around the corner. Crake hated him for that happy ignorance.

Outside, the world was as bleak as their prospects. The ash flats to the east of the Hookhollows were desolate and grim, featureless in every direction. Even the nearby mountains were invisible beneath the rim of the great plateau. From horizon to horizon was a dreary grey expanse, a dead land choked beneath the blanket of dust and flakes that drifted from the west. A chill wind stirred powdery rills from the ground and harried them into the distance. The sky overhead was the colour of slate. The disc of the sun was faint enough to stare at without discomfort.

Looming in the sky to their left was the *Delirium Trigger*, its massive keel imposingly close, as if it might plunge down and crush them at any moment. Closer by was the small passenger shuttle used to ferry crew from the craft to the ground and back again. The *Delirium Trigger* was too huge to land anywhere except in specially designed docks.

Their captors halted them at the bottom of the ramp. Standing before them, a short distance away, was a slight figure, dressed

303

head to toe in black. Crake recognised her from Frey's description: the shockingly white skin, the short, albino-blonde hair torn into clumps, that black, fearsome gaze. She regarded them icily as one of her men walked over to her and whispered something in her ear, then she gave him a short command and he hurried back into the bowels of the *Ketty Jay*. After that, she walked up to Frey. Mutual loathing simmered in their eyes.

'The ignition code, please,' she said.

'You know that's not gonna happen,' he said. 'You've got us. What do you want my aircraft for?'

'Sentimental value. The code?'

'She's not worth anything compared to the reward you'll get bringing us in. Leave her here.'

'She's worth everything to you. Besides, the press will want some ferrotypes of the craft that shot down the *Ace of Skulls*. Perhaps I'll present it to the Archduke as a gift. It may encourage him to overlook certain rumours about my activities elsewhere in the future.'

'This is pointless. You won't—'

Dracken pulled a revolver in one quick move and pressed the muzzle against his chest, silencing him. 'It wasn't a request. Give me the code.'

Frey was shaken; Crake could see it. But he bared his teeth into something approximating a grin and said: 'Shoot me if you like. You'll just save the hangman a job.'

Dracken and Frey stared at each other: a test of wills. Dracken's finger twitched on the trigger. She was sorely tempted. Then she took the gun away and stepped back.

'No,' she said. 'You get to live. Duke Grephen will want a signed confession out of you. Besides, there's someone else who may be more willing to talk. I understand there was a woman flying the *Ketty Jay* that night when you stole my charts. I don't see her here. Where is she, Frey? Won't she know the codes?'

Frey didn't reply. Dracken spotted one of her men coming out of the *Ketty Jay* and heading over to her. 'Let's find out,' she said.

She addressed the crewman, a whiskery, heavyset fellow with a steel ear to replace one that had been cut off. 'Anyone else inside?'

'One,' he said. 'In the infirmary. She's dead, though I ain't sure what of.'

Trinica looked at Frey for an instant. 'You're sure she's dead?'

'Yes, Cap'n. She don't have a pulse, and she ain't breathing. I listened at her chest, and her heart ain't beating. I seen a lot of dead men and women, and she's dead.'

'She hit her head,' said Frey. 'When you shelled us.' He indicated Malvery. 'The doc tried to help her, but he couldn't do much. All the damage was inside.'

Malvery caught on, and nodded gravely. 'Terrible thing. Fine young woman,' he murmured.

Crake felt a chill go through him. He was remembering that night on the Feldspar Islands when they'd gone to Gallian Thade's ball at Scorchwood Heights. The night when Jez had *really* fallen and hit her head. Fredger Cordwain, the man from the Shacklemore Agency, had taken her pulse then, too. He'd also been convinced she was dead. At the time, Crake had assumed he was mistaken in the heat of the moment, but now he wondered.

How had she managed to fool them both?

'You want us to get rid of her?' the crewman asked Dracken.

'No,' she said. 'Leave her where she is. We'll need the body to show the Duke. How are they getting on with the golem?'

'Coming out now, Cap'n,' he replied, gesturing at the half-dozen men who were manhandling the inert form of Bess down the ramp.

'What are you doing with her?' Crake blurted in distress, before good sense could intervene.

Dracken's black eyes fixed on to him. Crake had a sudden and dreadful feeling that he'd done something very foolish in drawing her attention. 'That thing is yours, is it?' she asked. 'You're the daemonist?'

Crake swallowed and tasted ash in the back of his throat. Dracken sauntered over towards him, raking her gaze along the line of prisoners as she went.

'Very clever, what you did in Rabban,' she murmured. 'And surprising, too. I'd have expected a daemonist to abandon their golem and make a new one, but you actually *rescued* it from my cargo hold.' She studied him with an intensity that made him squirm. 'That's very interesting.'

Crake kept his mouth shut. He had the impression that anything he said would only damn him further.

'Still, interesting as it is, I'm not stupid enough to fall for the same trick twice,' she said. 'And I'm not having that thing wake up on the journey back. So your golem is staying here.'

Crake felt weakness flood through him. The horror of it almost made him stagger. He looked around wildly, taking in the endless, trackless expanse of grey that surrounded them. There were no signs of life anywhere. No civilisation. Nothing but the tiny smudges of aircraft heading for the coast, hopelessly distant.

To abandon her here would be to lose her for ever.

'I've an idea,' said Dracken, addressing Frey. 'It seems the only other person who knows the ignition code is dead, and I'd rather not kill you until after you've given us a confession. But a daemonist . . . well, he could be problematic. They have all kinds of . . . arts. Probably easier to get rid of him now.'

Crake saw what was coming. She lifted her gun and pointed it at his forehead in what was becoming a depressingly familiar state of affairs.

'Unless you've something to tell me, Frey?' she prompted.

Frey's face had gone stony. Crake had seen that impassive expression before, when Lawsen Macarde put him in a similar situation. Except this time, there was little doubt that Trinica's gun was fully loaded.

A strange calm came over him. *Let it end, then.*

'You have until three,' said Trinica. 'One.'

He was tired. Tired of struggling against the grief and shame. Tired of living under the weight of one arrogant mistake, to think that he might summon one of the monsters of the aether and come away unscathed. Tired of trying to understand that awful twist of fortune that had led his niece to his sanctum on that particular night, instead of any other.

Leave her here, amid the ash and dust. If he didn't wake her up, no one ever would. Let her sleep, and perhaps she'd dream of better things.

'Two.'

He closed his eyes, and to his faint surprise, dislodged a tear. He felt it trickle down the side of his face, over the hump of his cheekbone, to be lost in his beard.

He'd worked so hard to be great. It had ended in ignominy, disgrace and failure. What was a world worth, that treated its inhabitants so?

'Thr—' Trinica began.

'Stop!' Frey snapped.

Crake's eyes stayed closed. Hovering on the razor-blade edge between existence and oblivion, he dared not tip the balance with the slightest movement.

'Seven sixty-seven, double one, double eight,' he heard his captain say.

There was a long pause. His body shook with each thump of his heart. He didn't even hope. He didn't even know if he wanted to be left in the world of the living.

But the choice wasn't his to make. He felt the chill metal of the revolver muzzle leave his forehead. His eyes fluttered open. Dracken had stepped back, and was regarding him like a child who has just spared an insect. Then she turned to Frey and raised an eyebrow. Frey looked away angrily.

Crake felt detached from himself, clothed in a dreamlike numbness. He watched as Dracken's crew carried Bess away from the *Ketty Jay*. Then, with obvious glee, they stood her on her feet. A hunched metal statue, a monument to their victory. He heard Dracken order the man with the steel ear to assign two men to fly the *Ketty Jay* behind them. Frey wouldn't meet anyone's eye: he'd been broken by Dracken, and was burning with a hate and fury such as Crake had never seen him show.

But it all seemed far away and inconsequential. He was still alive, somehow, although he wasn't sure he'd fully returned from the brink yet.

Someone patted his shoulder. Malvery. They were being urged towards the nearby passenger shuttle. From there they'd be taken to the *Delirium Trigger*'s brig. Crake sent a mental message to his feet to get them moving. Dazed, he stumbled along with the group, his boots scuffing up little grey clouds. They were herded up some steps and into the belly of the shuttle, where they sat, surrounded by armed guards.

Crake looked out through the shuttle door at the lonely figure of Bess. The crewmen had deserted her now, and were attending to other tasks. The shuttle was powering up its engines, sending veils of dust to coat her.

Let her sleep, he thought. *Goodnight, Bess.*

Then the door slammed closed, and she was lost from his sight.

Thirty-Two

An Audience With Dracken – Bringing
Up The Past – The Ugly Truth Of It All

'Out, you.'

Frey looked up, and saw a thickset, bald man with a bushy black beard on the other side of the bars. 'You mean me?'

'You're the cap'n, ain't ya?'

He glanced around at his crew, trying to decide whether there was any advantage in protesting. All six of them had been put in the same cell on the *Delirium Trigger*'s brig. There were five cells in all, each capable of holding ten men. The walls were metal, and the lights were weak. The smell of oil was in the air, and the sound of clanking machinery and distant engines echoed in the hollow spaces.

Silo met his eyes with a customarily inscrutable gaze. Malvery just shrugged.

'I'm the captain,' Frey said at length.

'Cap'n Dracken wants to see you,' the bald man informed him.

The gaoler unlocked the door and pushed it open, waving a shotgun to deter any attempts at a breakout. Frey walked through, and the door clanged shut behind him.

'Hey,' said Malvery. 'While you've got her ear, ask if we can get some rum down here, eh?'

Pinn laughed explosively. Crake didn't stir from where he sat in a corner, drowned in his own misery. Harkins had fallen asleep, tired out by being afraid of everything. Silo was silent.

And Jez? What was Jez doing right now? Frey had turned it over and over in his mind, but he still couldn't work out how she could fake her own death convincingly enough to fool Trinica's man. She'd refused to reveal how she was going to do it when she first told him of her plan. She just said: 'Trust me.'

Still, he was beginning to wonder if she actually *had* died.

The bald man took him by the arm and pressed a pistol into his side, then walked him out of the brig and through the passageways of the *Delirium Trigger*. They passed other crewmembers on the way. Some sneered triumphantly at Frey; others gave him looks of abject hatred. Their humiliation at Rabban – not to mention the deaths of a dozen or so crewmen – hadn't been forgotten.

When they reached the door to the captain's cabin, the bald man brought him to a halt. Frey expected him to knock, but he didn't. He appeared to be deliberating some question with himself.

'Are we going in?' Frey prompted.

'Listen,' replied the crewman, turning on Frey with a threatening look in his eyes. 'You be careful what you say in there. The Cap'n . . . she's in one of her moods.'

Frey arched an eyebrow. 'Thanks for the concern,' he said, sarcastically. 'What's she going to do, kill me?'

'It ain't you I'm concerned about,' came the reply, and then he knocked on the door and Trinica called for them to enter.

Trinica's cabin was well ordered and clean, but the dark wood of the bookcases and the brass fittings of the dim electric lamps gave it a close, gloomy feel. Trinica was sitting behind her desk at the far end of the room, on which a large logbook lay open next to a carefully arranged writing set and the brass compass-like device they'd used to navigate the minefields of Retribution Falls. She was looking out of the sloping window. Beyond, night had fallen.

She didn't acknowledge Frey as he was brought in. The bald man stood him in the centre of the room. After a moment, without turning from the window, she said:

'Thank you, Harmund. You can go.'

'Cap'n,' said the big man, and left.

Frey stood uncertainly in the centre of the room for a moment, but still she didn't speak to him. He decided he'd be damned if he'd feel awkward in front of her. He walked over to a reading-chair by one of the bookcases and sat down in it. He could wait as long as she could.

His eyes fell to the compass on the desk. The sight of it inspired a momentary surge of bitterness. That would have been his proof. That device and the charts that came with it would have won him his freedom. He'd been so close.

He fought down the feeling. No doubt Trinica had put it there to inspire just such a reaction. Railing against the injustice of his circumstances would do him no good now. Besides, for the first time he could remember it felt just a little childish.

'You're going to hang, you know,' she said at last. She was still staring out of the window.

'I'm aware of that, Trinica,' Frey replied scornfully.

She glanced at him then. There was reproach in her eyes. Hurt, even. He found himself regretting his tone.

'I thought we should talk,' she said. 'Before it's over.'

Frey was puzzled by her manner. This wasn't the acerbic, commanding woman he'd met back in Sharka's den; nor did he recognise her behaviour from the years he'd loved her. Her voice was soft, the words sighing out without force. She seemed deeply tired, steeped in melancholy.

Still suspicious of a trick, he resolved not to play into her hands. He'd give her no sympathy. He'd be hard and bitter.

'Talk, then,' he said.

There was a pause. She seemed to be seeking a way to begin.

'It's been ten years,' she said. 'A lot's happened in that time. But a lot of things stayed . . . unresolved.'

'What does it matter?' Frey replied. 'The past is the past. It's gone.'

'It's *not* gone,' she said. 'It never goes.' She turned away from the window and faced him across her desk. 'I wish I had your talent, Darian. I wish I could walk away from something or someone, and it would be as if they never existed. To lock a piece of my life away in a trunk, never to be opened.'

'It's a gift,' he replied. He wasn't about to explain himself to her.

311

'Why did you leave me?' she asked.

The question took him by surprise. There was a pleading edge to it. He hadn't expected anything like this when he was led into the room. She was vulnerable, strengthless, unable to defend herself. He found himself becoming disgusted with her. Where was the woman he'd loved, or even the woman he'd hated? This desperation was pitiable.

Why *had* he left her? The memories seemed distant now: it was hard to summon up the feelings he'd felt then. They'd been tinted by ten years of scorn. Yet he did remember some things. Thoughts rather than emotions. The internal dialogues he had with himself during the long hours alone, flying haulage for her father's company.

In the early months, he'd believed they'd be together for ever. He told himself he'd found a woman for the rest of his life. He couldn't conceive of meeting someone more wonderful than she was, and he wasn't tempted to try.

But it was one thing to daydream such notions and quite another to be faced with putting them into practice. When she began to talk of engagement, with a straightforwardness that he'd previously found charming, he began to idolise her a little less. His patience became short. No longer could he endlessly indulge her flights of fancy. His smile became fixed as she played her girlish games with him. Her jokes all seemed to go on too long. He found himself wishing she'd just be sensible.

At nineteen, he was still young. He didn't make the connection between his sudden moodiness and irritability and the impending threat of marriage. He told himself he *wanted* to marry her. It would be stupid not to, after all. Hadn't he decided she was the one for him?

But the more he snapped at her, the more demanding she became. Tired of waiting – or perhaps afraid to wait too long – she asked him to marry her. He agreed, and secretly resented her for a long time afterwards. How could she put him in that position? To choose between marrying her, which he didn't want, or destroying her, which he wanted even less? He had no option but to agree at the time and hope to find a way out of it later.

And yet Trinica seemed blissfully unaware of any of this. Though his bad moods were ever more frequent, they didn't seem to trouble her any more. She was assured that he was hers, and he seethed that she would celebrate her victory so prematurely.

By the time the date of the wedding was announced, Frey's thoughts were mainly of escape. He slept little and badly. Her father's obvious disapproval encouraged him to think that the wedding was a bad idea. A barely educated boy of low means, raised in an orphanage, Frey wasn't a good match for the highly intelligent and beautiful daughter of an eminent aristocrat. Those social barriers, that had seemed laughable in the first flush of love, suddenly rose high in Frey's mind.

He wanted to be a pilot for the Coalition Navy, steering vast frigates to the north to do battle with the Manes, or south to crush the Sammies. He wanted to be among the first to land on New Vardia or Jagos after the Great Storm Belt calmed. He wanted to fly free across the boundless skies.

When he looked at Trinica, and she smiled her perfect smile, he saw the death of his dreams.

That was when she fell pregnant. The wedding was hastily brought forward, and her father's opposition to it transformed into wholehearted support of their enterprise, backed up by veiled threats if Frey should waver. Frey began to suffer panic attacks in the night.

He remembered the sensation of a vice around his ribs, squeezing a little harder with every day that brought him closer to the wedding. He never seemed to have quite enough breath in his body. The laughter of his friends as they congratulated him became a distressing cacophony, like an enraged brace of ducks. He felt harried and harassed wherever he went. The smallest request was enough to send him into a fluster.

He remembered wondering what it would be like to feel like that for ever.

By this point he was absolutely certain he didn't want to marry her. But it didn't mean he didn't want to be with her. Even with all the irritation and buried anger, he still adored this woman. She was his first love, and the one who had teased him from his rather cold, uninspiring childhood into a wild world where emotions could be overpowering and deeply irrational. He just wanted things to go back to the way they were before she began to talk about marriage.

But he was terrified of making the wrong choice. What if she *was* the one for him? Would he be condemning himself to a life of misery? Would he ever meet anyone like her again?

He was paralysed, trapped, dragged reluctantly into the future like a ship's anchor scoring its way along the sea bed. In the end, there was only one way out he could face, and that was not to face it at all. He couldn't make even that decision until the very last minute. He was hoping desperately for some vaguely defined intervention that would spare him from hurting her.

None came, so he ran. He took the *Ketty Jay*, in which was everything he had in the world, and he left her. He left her carrying his child, standing in front of a thousand witnesses, waiting for a groom who would never come.

After that, it only got worse.

'Darian?' Trinica prompted. Frey realised he'd slipped into reverie and fallen silent. 'I asked you a question.'

Frey was taken by a sudden surge of anger. What right did she have to make him explain himself? After what she'd done? His love for her had been the most precious thing in his life, and she'd ruined it with her insecurities, her need to tie him down. She'd made him cowardly. In his heart he knew that, but he could never say it. So instead, he attacked her, sensing her weakness.

'You really think I'm interested in a little catch-up to make you feel better?' he sneered. 'You think I care if you understand what happened or not? Here's a deal: you let me go and I'll have a nice long chat with you about all the terrible things I did and what an awful person I am. But in case it escaped your notice, I'm going to be hanged, and it's you that's taking me to the gallows. So piss on your questions, Trinica. You can go on wondering what went wrong until you rot.'

Trinica's expression was surprised and wounded. She'd not expected such cruelty. Frey found himself thinking that the white-skinned bitch who had taken the place of his beloved might actually cry. He'd expected anger, but instead she looked like a little girl who had been unjustly smacked for something they didn't do. A profound sadness had settled on her.

'How can you hate me like this?' she asked. Her voice was husky and low. 'How can you take the moral high ground, after what you did to me?'

'Broken hearts mend, Trinica,' Frey spat. 'You murdered our child.'

Her eyes narrowed at the blow, but any promise of tears had passed. She turned her face away from him and looked out of the window again. 'You abandoned us,' she replied, grave-cold. 'It's easy to be aggrieved now. But you abandoned us. If our child had lived, you'd never have known it existed.'

'That's a lie. I came back for you, Trinica. For both of you.'

He saw her stiffen, and cursed himself. He shouldn't have admitted that, shouldn't have let the words free from his mouth. It weakened him. He'd waited years to throw his hatred in her face, to confront her with what she'd done, but it had always gone so much better during the rehearsals in his head. He wanted her to wreck herself on his glacial indifference to her suffering. He wanted to exact revenge. But his own rage was foiling him.

She was waiting for him to go on. He had no choice now. The gate had been opened.

'I went from place to place for a month. Thinking things through. A bit of time away from you with all your bloody demands and your damn father.' He cut himself off. Already he sounded surly and immature. He took a breath and continued, trying not to let his anger overwhelm him. 'And I decided I'd made a mistake.' He thought about trying to explain further, but he couldn't. 'So I came back. I went to see a friend in town, to get some advice, I suppose. That was when I heard. How you'd taken all those pills, how you'd tried to kill yourself. And how the baby . . . the baby hadn't . . .'

He put his fist to his mouth, ashamed of the way his throat closed up and his words jammed painfully in the bottleneck. When the moment had passed, he relaxed and sat back in his seat. He'd said enough. There was no satisfaction in this. He couldn't even hurt her without hurting himself.

'I was a stupid girl,' said Trinica quietly. 'Stupid enough to believe the world began and ended with you. I thought I could never be happy again.'

Frey had sat forward in his chair, his elbows on his knees and his fingers tangled in his fringe. His voice was brittle. 'I ran out on you, Trinica. But I never gave up on myself. And I never tried to take our child with me.'

'Oh, you gave up on yourself, Darian,' she replied. 'You were just a little more indirect. You spent three years drinking yourself to death and putting yourself in harm's way. In the end, you took your whole *crew* with you.'

Frey couldn't muster the energy to argue. The weary, conversational tone in which she delivered her accusation robbed him of the will to defend himself. Besides, she was right. Of course she was right.

'We're both cowards,' he murmured. 'We deserved each other.'

'Maybe,' said Trinica. 'Maybe neither of us deserved what we got.'

All the fire had gone out of Frey. A black, sucking tar-pit of misery threatened to engulf him. He'd imagined this confrontation a thousand ways, but they all ended with him demolishing Trinica, forcing her to face the horror of what she'd done to him. Now he realised there was nothing he could say to her that she hadn't already thought of, nothing he could punish her with that she hadn't already used to punish herself more effectively than he ever could.

The truth was, his position was so fragile that it fell apart when exposed to the reality of an opposing view. While he nurtured his grievances privately, he could be appalled at how she'd mistreated him. But it didn't hold up to argument. He couldn't pretend to be the only one wronged. They'd ruined each other.

Damn it, he hadn't wanted to talk. And now here they were, talking. She always had a way of doing that to him.

'How'd you get this way, Trinica?' he said. He raised his head and gestured at her across the gloomy study. 'The hair, the skin . . .' He hesitated. 'You used to be beautiful.'

'I'm done with beautiful,' she replied. There was a long pause, during which neither of them spoke. Then Trinica stirred in her seat and faced him.

'You weren't the only one who turned away from me after I tried to kill myself,' she said. 'My parents were disgraced. Bad enough they had a daughter who was going to give birth outside of marriage; now she'd killed their grandchild. They could barely look at me. My father wanted to send me to a sanatorium.

'In the end, I stole some money and took an aircraft. I didn't know where I was going, but I had to get away. I suppose I thought I could be a pilot.

'I was caught by a pirate two weeks later. They must have seen me in port and followed my craft out. They forced me down and boarded me, then took my craft to add to their little fleet. I thought they'd kill me, but they didn't. They just *kept* me.'

Frey couldn't help a twinge of pain. That dainty, elegant young woman he'd left behind hadn't been equipped to survive in the brutal, ugly world of smugglers and freebooters. She'd been sheltered all her life. He knew what happened to people like that.

'I wasn't much more than an animal to them,' she went on. Her tone was dead, without inflection. 'A pet to use as they pleased. That's what *beautiful* does for you.

'It took me almost two years to work up the courage to put a dagger in the captain's neck. After that, I stopped being a victim. I signed on as a pilot for another crew, learned navigation on the side. I wanted to make myself indispensable. I didn't want to be dependent on anybody again.'

She turned her attention to the window, evading him.

'I'll not bore you with the details, Darian. Let's just say I learned what it takes for a woman to survive among cut-throats.'

The omissions spoke more than any description ever could. Frey didn't need to be told about the rapes and the beatings. Physically weak, she'd have needed to use her sexuality to play men off against each other, to ensnare a strong companion for protection. A rich girl who'd never known hardship, she'd been forced into whoredom to survive.

But all that time, she'd been strengthening herself, becoming the woman he saw before him. She could have gone home at any point, back to the safety of her family. They'd have taken her back, of that he was sure. But she never did. She cut out every soft part of herself, so she could live among the scum.

He didn't pity her. He couldn't. He only mourned the loss of the young woman he'd known ten years ago. This mockery of his lover was his own doing. He had fashioned her, and she damned him by her existence.

'By the time I got to the *Delirium Trigger*, I'd made my way in the underworld. I had a reputation, and they respected me. I knew the crew was troubled and I knew the captain was a syphilitic drunk. It took me a year, building trust, winning them round. I knew he was planning an assault on an outpost near Anduss, I knew it would be a disaster, and I waited. Afterwards, I led the survivors against him. We threw him overboard from two kloms up.'

She gazed across at him. Her black eyes seemed darker in the faint light of the electric lamps.

'And then you turned yourself into a ghoul,' he finished.

'You know how men are,' she said. 'They don't like to mix desire and respect. They see a beautiful woman in command and they belittle her. It makes them feel better about themselves.' She looked away, her face falling into shadow. 'Besides, being pretty never brought me anything but pain.'

'It kept you alive,' he pointed out.

'That wasn't living,' she returned.

He had no answer to that.

'So that's the story,' she said. 'That's what it takes to be a captain. Patience. Ruthlessness. Sacrifice. You're too selfish to make that crew respect you, Darian. You surprised me once, but it won't happen again.'

There was a knock at the door. A spasm of irritation crossed her face. 'I gave orders that I wasn't to be disturbed!' she snapped.

'It's urgent, Cap'n!' came a voice from the other side. 'The *Ketty Jay* has gone!'

'*What?*' she cried, surging to her feet. She tore open the door to the cabin. A crewman was outside, obscured from Frey's view by the door.

'She were following us with her lights on,' came the breathless report. 'All of a sudden, the lights go out. By the time we got a spotlight over there, she were nowhere to be seen. She could've gone anywhere in the dark. She's disappeared, Cap'n. Nobody knows where.'

Trinica's head swivelled and she fixed Frey with a glare of utter malice.

Frey grinned. 'Surprise!'

Thirty-Three

Deliberations – Back In The Blizzard –
The Manes – A Feat Of Navigation

Jez, in the pilot's seat of the *Ketty Jay*, flew on into the night.

The craft was dark, inside and out. The light of the moon edged her face in brittle silver. It fell also onto the two bodies on the cockpit floor, and glittered in their blood. Dracken's men. The iron pipe that had stoved in their heads lay between them.

Jez's jaw was set hard. Navigation charts were spread on the dashboard next to her. She stared through the windglass at the world below, eyes fixed. The *Ketty Jay* slid through the darkness, high above the clouded mountains, a speck in the vast sky.

She could see the lights of other craft, visible at great distance. A flotilla of fighters surrounded a long, rectangular freighter. A prickle of shining dots signified a Navy corvette, cruising the horizon. And in between, there were the invisible vessels, like the *Ketty Jay*, that had reason to stay hidden and wanted to move unobserved. Stealthy shadows in the moonlight. A pilot wouldn't see them unless they were very close, but Jez saw them all.

Even hours later, she was still trembling with the aftershocks of murder. Had there been a gun to hand she might have used it to threaten the men, then tied them up and kept them prisoner. But they had the guns, and she only had a length of pipe. She crept into the cockpit and brained the navigator before he even knew she was there. The pilot turned in his seat in time to receive the second blow across his forehead.

She'd told herself that she was only going to knock them out; but as with Fredger Cordwain, the Shacklemore man, it only took one blow to kill them. She was far stronger than her small frame suggested. Just another aspect of the change, along with her penetrating vision, her ability to heal bullet wounds in hours and the frightening hallucinations.

And the voices. The dissonant voices, the crew of that terrible craft, which loomed out of the endless fog of the Wrack. She could hear them now, their faint cries blowing on the wind that rushed past the hull of the *Ketty Jay*. Calling her. Calling her home.

Why not? Why not just go to them? Turn this crate to the north and get it all over with.

She was tired of this life. The last three years had been spent discarding one crew and joining up with another, never putting down roots. She kept her distance from the men and women she worked with because she knew, sooner or later, they'd find her out. It had been the same with the crew of the *Ketty Jay*. Eventually, she always had to run. Now that moment had come again.

Why stay in a world where you're not wanted?

Every day, it got a little harder to resist the call of the Wrack. Every day eroded her willpower a little more. Was it only stubbornness that made her stay among people who would kill her if they knew what she was? Was it simply fear that prevented her from going to the north, where they lamented her absence, where she'd *belong*? Like the distant howl of a wolf pack, their cries stirred her, and she ached to go to them.

What's stopping you, Jez? What's stopping you?

What, indeed? Where else could she go from here? Did she imagine she could effect some kind of daring rescue in the *Ketty Jay*? No, that would be suicide. She wasn't even very good at flying her. It would take a long time to get used to the many quirks of a craft as patched together as this. And even if she did somehow save Frey and the others, what then? How would she explain how she'd convinced Dracken's crewman that she was dead?

It was just like all the times before, with all the other crews. The small things were adding up: her fantastically sharp eyesight; the way she never seemed to need sleep or food; how animals reacted around her; the uncanny healing after she got shot in Scarwater; the way she'd been unaffected by the fumes in Rook's Boneyard.

And now there was this new ability to convincingly imitate a corpse. The first time, only Crake had seen it, and he hadn't said a word. It could have been passed off as the Shacklemore man's mistake. But twice?

Now the suspicious glances would begin. She'd start to hear that wary, mistrustful tone in their voices. Even on the *Ketty Jay*, where you didn't ask about a person's past, questions would be raised. They could accept a daemonist, but could they accept her? How long before Malvery insisted on giving her a check-up to solve the mystery? How long before they found her out?

The reason Fredger Cordwain thought she had no pulse was because she *had* no pulse.

The reason Dracken's man thought she was dead was because she *was*.

It had happened three years ago.

The first Jez knew of the attack was when she heard the explosion. It was a dull, muffled roar that shook the ground and spilled the soup she was eating, scalding her fingers. A second explosion sent her scurrying to grab her thick fur-and-hide coat. She pulled up the hood, affixed the mask and goggles, and headed out of the warmth of the inn, up the stairs and into the blizzard.

She emerged onto the main thoroughfare of the tiny, remote town in Yortland that had been her home for a month. The dwellings to either side were low domes, built mostly underground, barely visible. The light from the small windows and the smoke from their chimneys pushed through the whirling snow.

There were others already outside: some were Yort locals, others were the Vard scientists who used this town as a base while they worked on the excavation nearby. All eyes were on the bright bloom of fire rising from the far side of the town. From the landing pad.

Her immediate thought was that a terrible accident had occurred, some tragic rupture in the fuel lines. Even before she wondered how many might have died, her stomach sank at the thought of being stranded in this place. The aircraft were their only link to the rest of the world. Here, on the northern tip of Yortland, civilisation was scattered and hard to find. There was no other settlement for a hundred kloms in any direction.

She felt a gloved hand on her upper arm and turned. She knew it was Riss, the expedition's pilot, even though his face was hidden behind a fur-lined hood, mask and goggles. Nobody else touched her arm like that.

'Are you alright?' he shouted over the whistling wind. His voice was muffled.

'Of course I'm alright. The explosion was over there.'

But then someone pointed to a dark shape approaching through the grey chaos in the sky, and the cries of alarm began. Jez felt the strength drain out of her as it took on form, huge and ragged and black. The drone of its engines was drowned out by the piercing, unearthly howling coming from its decks. It was a mass of dirty iron, oil and smoke, all spikes and rivets and shredded black pennants. A dreadnought, come from the Wrack, across the Poleward Sea to the shores of Yortland.

The destruction of the aircraft on the landing pad had been no accident. The attackers wanted to be sure nobody got away.

The Manes were here, searching for fresh victims.

Ropes snaked down as the dreadnought loomed closer, its massive hull swelling as it descended until its keel was only a few metres above the rooftops. By the time the Manes came slipping and sliding to the ground, people were already scattering in terror. They'd all heard the stories. The appearance of the dreadnought, the sheer *force* of its presence, panicked them like goats.

Jez panicked with them, fleeing up the thoroughfare, thinking only of escape. It was Riss who grabbed her arm, more forcefully this time, and tugged her into a doorway. He hurried her down some steps and into a circular underground room full of crates of scientific equipment and boxes of food and clothing. It was cold down here, but not as bad as outside. The sound of their boots echoed from the grey stone walls.

As soon as she was released, she bolted into a corner and huddled there, hugging herself and whimpering. She'd always prided herself on being a level-headed sort, but the sight of the dreadnought was too much for her. The craft exuded terror, an animal sense of wrongness that appealed to the most basic instincts. Whatever the Manes were, her intuition shrieked at their mere presence.

Riss was faring better. He was obviously scared out of his wits, but he was moving with a purpose. He'd grabbed two packs and was shoving dried food and blankets into them.

'We can't stay here,' he said, in response to her unspoken question. 'They'll go through the whole town. It's what they do.'

'We . . . I'm not . . . I'm not going out *there*!' Jez said through juddering lips. She could hear screams and sporadic gunfire from outside.

He pulled the packs tight, hurried over and shoved one towards her. She could see his eyes through the glass of the goggles. He was staring at her hard.

'Listen,' he said. 'When the Manes hit a town, they don't leave people to tell the tale. The ones who aren't taken are killed. You understand? We can't avoid them by hiding down here.'

'Where can we go?'

'The excavation. The ice caves. We can survive there for a night. If we get out of town, we can wait till they're gone.'

Jez calmed a little as his words sank in. Professor Malstrom, their employer, was obsessed with the search for a lost race he'd dubbed the Azryx, whom he believed had once possessed great and mysterious technology. Based on slender evidence and some cryptic writings, he'd divined that they died out suddenly, many thousands of years ago, and their civilisation had been swallowed by the ice. He'd persuaded the university to fund him on various digs over the past year, hoping to uncover relics of that ancient people. So far, he'd not found a thing. But the excavation would provide them with the shelter they needed, and the Manes might not look there.

'Yes!' she said. 'Yes, we can hide out in the caves!'

She clutched at the sanity he offered, soothed by the strength and certainty in his voice. Riss had held a candle for her ever since they'd started working together, as pilot and navigator for Professor Malstrom's expeditionary team. She liked him as a friend, but had never been able to summon up any feelings deeper than that.

He'd always been protective of her. It was a trait she found annoying: she interpreted it as possessiveness. But now she was ashamed to realise she *wanted* a protector. She'd crumbled in the face of the horror bearing down on them, and he hadn't. She clung to him gratefully as he lifted her up and helped her put on her pack.

The thoroughfare was eerily deserted when they emerged. The dreadnought had gone, and the blizzard was closing in, cutting visibility down to fifteen metres. The chill began to seep into them immediately, even through their protective clothing. From somewhere in the skirling mêlée of snowflakes came distant yells and the report of shotguns. Piercing, inhuman howls floated after them.

They stayed close to the buildings. Jez hung on to Riss as he led her towards the edge of town, where a crude trail led up the mountain to the glacier. The excavation site was up there.

They'd not gone far when there was the roar of an engine, and a blaze of light up ahead. Gunfire erupted, startlingly close. Riss pulled Jez into the gap between two domed Yort dwellings, and they hid behind a grit-bin as a snow-tractor came racing up the thoroughfare. The boxy metal vehicles were usually employed to haul supplies and personnel back and forth from the glacier, but someone was trying to escape on one. The Manes had other ideas: there were four of them swarming all over it, trying to drag the doors open or punch their way in through the glass. Jez glimpsed them in the backwash of the headlamps as they passed – ghoulish, feral approximations of men and women – and then the speeding snow-tractor fishtailed on the icy ground. It slewed sideways for an instant before its tracks bit and flung it into the wall of a building.

The Manes abandoned the snow-tractor as several Yorts,

wielding shotguns, came backing up the thoroughfare, firing into the blizzard, where more shadowy figures were darting on the edges of visibility. Manes prowled on all fours along rooftops or slunk close to the ground. They flitted and flickered, moving in fast jerks. They jumped from one spot to another without seeming to pass through the distance between.

Jez cringed as she saw the Manes spread out to encircle their victims. She wanted to run, to break from hiding and flee, but Riss held her tight.

The Yorts wore furs and masks. The Manes wore ragged clothes more suited to a mild spring day in Vardia. The cold, which would kill an unprotected human in minutes, meant nothing to them.

She turned away and burrowed into Riss's arms as the Manes sprang inward as one. She'd closed her eyes to the sight, but she couldn't shut out the screams of men and the exultant howls of the Manes. Mercifully, it was over in seconds.

Once done, there was silence. It was a short while before Riss stirred and looked out. The sounds of conflict still drifted out of the blizzard, but the Manes had moved elsewhere.

'Stay here,' he said. 'I'll be back in a moment.'

Jez obeyed, reluctant to leave the relative safety of the grit-bin. His footsteps crunched across the thoroughfare, fading away. For a time, all she heard were faint gunshots and barked commands, carried on the breeze. Then his footsteps came crunching back. She looked out and saw him carrying a cutlass in one hand. There were several dead men scattered across the thoroughfare, their blood stark against the snow. At least three were missing. Not dead, but taken. Stolen by the Manes to crew their terrible craft.

Riss hunkered down in front of her. 'The man in the snow-tractor is dead,' he said. He held up the cutlass. 'I got this.'

'What about a gun? Don't we need a gun?'

He wiggled his fingers inside his thick glove. Unlike the Yort suits, the scientists' gear was built without much consideration for mobility; warmth was their primary concern. The gloves were too clumsy to fit the forefinger inside a trigger-guard, but without them his skin would freeze to the metal.

They headed away from the thoroughfare, through the gaps between the close-set dwellings. The snow had collected in drifts here, and they forged on with some difficulty, but at least the buildings hid them from view. Jez followed in Riss's wake, allowing him to carve a path for her. Her breath was loud in her ears, trapped inside her mask. Her fur-lined hood obscured her peripheral vision, forcing her to turn to look behind her every few steps. She was afraid something was sneaking up on them, following their trail through the snow.

Something *was* sneaking up on them; but the attack, when it came, was from above.

Jez barely saw it. It was a blur of movement in the confusing whirl of the blizzard. Riss reacted with a cry before he was flung aside to crash into the side of a building. Standing in his place, right in front of her, was a Mane. It was the first and last time she ever got a good look at one, and it rooted her to the spot with fear.

The stories said they'd once been human, and they were recognisably so in form and face. But they'd been changed into something else, something that wore human shape uncomfortably, as a skin to contain whatever hid beneath.

The creature before her was scrawny, wearing a tattered shirt and trousers and no shoes at all. Limp black hair was smeared across a pale, wrinkled brow. Its features were twisted out of true. Lips curled to reveal sharp, crooked teeth. It glared at her with eyes that were the yellow and red of bloody pus. Its fingernails were long, dirty and cracked, and it stood low to the ground in a predator's crouch.

It wasn't what she saw, but what she *sensed* that paralysed her: the intuitive knowledge that she was in the presence of something not of this world, something that broke all laws and ruined all the certainties of a thousand generations of knowledge. Her body felt that, and rebelled.

Then it pounced, and bore her into a snowdrift.

She remembered little of what followed. It didn't seem to make sense when she recalled it later. The Mane had her pinned by the shoulders, and stared into her eyes. Her gaze was locked, as if she were a mouse hypnotised by a snake. She could smell the stench of it, a dead scent like damp leaf mould. Her breathing dropped to a shallow pant.

She felt crushed by the weight of the creature's will, oppressed by the force in its gaze. By the time she realised something was being done to her, it was too late to resist it. She struggled to oppose the invader with her thoughts, but she couldn't concentrate. She was losing herself.

She became aware of a change all around her. The blizzard faded, turning ghostly and powerless. The world was darker and sharper all at once. She could see details where there hadn't been details before: the fine jigsaw of creases in the skin of the Mane's face; the shocking complexity of its feathery irises.

There was a whispering in the air, a constant hiss of half-spoken words. Movement all around her. She recognised the movement of the Manes, prowling around the town. She could *feel* them. She shared their motion. And as she sank deeper and deeper into the trance, she felt the warmth of that connection. A sense of belonging, like nothing she'd experienced before, enfolded her. It was beautiful and toxic and sugary and appalling all at once.

She'd almost surrendered herself to it when she was ripped back into reality.

It took a moment for her senses to cope with the change. She was being pulled to her feet by a faceless man in a hooded fur-and-hide coat. Her initial reaction was to pull away, but he held her firmly and said something to her. When she didn't respond, he said it again, and this time the words got through.

'—re you alright? Jez? *Jez?*'

She nodded quickly, because she wanted him to shut up. He was frightening her with his urgent enquiries. The Mane was thrashing and squealing on the ground. A cutlass was buried in the base of its neck, up to the collarbone, half-severing its head. There was little blood, just a clean wound, exposing bone.

But it still wasn't finished. Moving with jerky, spastic

movements, it got its feet under it and tried to stand. Riss swore and kicked it in the face, knocking it flat. He wrenched the cutlass free and beheaded it with a second stroke.

Riss turned away from the corpse of the Mane and looked up at her. He held out his hand: *come with me.*

Something snapped inside her. The accumulated horror and shock of the attack broke through. She lost her mind and fled.

She ran, through the passageways between the houses, out into the blizzard. The winds pushed and battered her. Snow stuck to her goggles. She could hear Riss calling her name but she ignored him. At some point she realised that she could no longer see any houses, just endless, unmarked snow. She kept running, driven by the terror of what lay behind.

Only when exhaustion drove her to her knees did she stop. She was thoroughly lost, and all traces of her passing were being erased by the fury of the snow. She dared not go back, and she couldn't go forward. The cold, that she'd barely noticed during her flight, had set in deep. She began to shiver violently. A tiredness overtook her, every bit as insidious and unstoppable as the power of the Manes.

She curled up into a foetal position, and there, buried in the snow, she died.

Every day since, Jez had wondered what might have happened if things had gone another way. If Riss hadn't saved her. If she'd succumbed to the Mane.

Would it have been so bad, in the end? In that brief moment, when she touched upon the world of the Manes, she'd felt something wonderful. An integration, a togetherness above and beyond anything her human life had given her.

She'd never borne children, never been in love. She'd always dreamed of having friends she could call soulmates, but somehow it never happened. She just didn't care about them enough, and they didn't care about her in return. She'd always considered herself rather detached, all in all.

So when she felt the call of the Manes, the primal invitation of the wolf-pack lamenting the absence of their kin, she found it harder and harder to think of reasons to resist.

Yes, they killed; but so had she, now. Yes, they were fearsome; but a fearsome exterior was no indication as to what was beneath. You only had to know the secret of Bess to understand that.

Would the process have been half so frightening if she'd been invited instead of press-ganged? Might she have gone willingly, if only to know what lay beyond that impenetrable wall of fog to the north? Were there incredible lands hidden behind the Wrack, glittering ice palaces at the poles, as the more lurid pulp novels suggested? Was it a wild place, like Kurg with its population of subhuman monsters? Or was there a strange and advanced civilisation there, like Peleshar, the distant and hostile land far to the south-west?

Whatever had been done to her by the Mane that day was incomplete, interrupted by a cutlass to the neck. She was neither fully human nor fully Mane, but somewhere in between. And yet the Manes welcomed her still, beckoned her endlessly, while the humans would destroy her if they knew that she walked their lands without a beating heart.

She never found out what happened to Riss. The morning after she died, she woke up and dug her way out of the snow that had entombed her in the night. The sun shone high in a crystal-blue sky, glittering on distant mounds of white: the roofs of the town. She'd run quite a way in her panic, but it had been in entirely the wrong direction if she'd hoped to reach the safety of the ice caves up on the glacier.

The corpses lay beneath the snow now. Whether Riss was among them, or if he'd been taken, the result was the same. He was gone.

Numb, she searched for survivors and found none. She stood in front of the snow-covered wreck of the aircraft she'd navigated for a year, and felt nothing. Then she found a snow-tractor and began to dig it out.

It took her several days to find another settlement, following charts she'd salvaged. Since she felt perfectly healthy she didn't question how she'd survived at first. She assumed her snowy tomb had kept her warm. It was only when she was far out in the wilderness that she noticed her heart had stopped. That was when she began to be afraid.

By the time she reached the settlement, she had a story, and a plan.

Keep moving. Keep your secret. Survive, as much as you can be said to live at all.

But it had been a long and lonely three years since that day.

She passed over the southern part of the Hookhollows, their glowing magma vents making bright scribbles in the dark. The Eastern Plateau rose up before her, and she took the *Ketty Jay* down through the black, filthy clouds. Her engines were robust enough to take a little ash. Once she'd broken through, she brought the *Ketty Jay* to a few dozen metres above ground level, and skimmed over the Blackendraft flats. She glanced at the navigational charts she was following. Charts that had been meticulously kept by Dracken's navigator since they'd commandeered the *Ketty Jay*.

Trust me, she'd said to Frey, when he demanded to know how she was going to fool Dracken's men into thinking she was dead. The kind of trust he'd shown when he gave her the ignition code to his precious aircraft, the one thing he could be said to love. Even though he was afraid she might steal it and fly off for ever, he'd trusted her.

And he trusted her to come back and save him. She wouldn't let him down.

She was under no illusion that she was risking her own life, and she knew that even if she succeeded, she'd probably be despised. They couldn't be her friends. She'd never belong to that crew. If they learned how she was slowly, steadily becoming a Mane, they'd be forced to destroy her. She couldn't blame them for that.

Yet she'd try anyway. Perhaps afterwards she'd go to the north, to the Manes; but first, she'd try.

It made no sense. But sometimes, humans did things that made no sense.

There was one last thing to do before she set off. Though she'd been lying in the infirmary with all the appearance of a corpse, she'd been wide awake. And she'd heard Dracken's men talk. Not *all* the crew of the *Ketty Jay* had been taken on board the *Delirium Trigger*.

She slowed the *Ketty Jay* to a hover and consulted the charts again. She wanted to get this right first time. It was a small challenge to herself. She adjusted the craft's heading, pushed her on half a klom, then stopped again. When she was satisfied, she engaged the belly lights. The ashen, dusty waste below her was flooded in dazzling light. She smiled.

Damn it, Jez. You're good.

There, right where they'd left her, was Bess.

Thirty-Four

Malvery's Story – Something Worse Than
Cramp – Frey Goes To The Gallows

Mortengrace, ancestral home of Duke Grephen of Lapin, stood out white among the trees like an unearthed bone. It was set amid the folds and pleats of heavily forested coastal hills in the western arm of the Vardenwood, overlooking the sparkling blue waters of the Ordic Abyssal to the south. High walls surrounded it, enclosing a landing pad for aircraft, expansive gardens and the grand manse where the Duke and his family resided. Among the half-dozen outbuildings were an engineer's workshop, a barracks for the resident militia and a gaol. The latter was rarely used in these more peaceable times, but it had found employment over the last two days, since Trinica Dracken had delivered six of the most wanted men in Vardia.

Crake sat in his cell, with Malvery and Silo, and he waited. It was all that was left to do now. He waited for the noose.

The cell was small and clean, with stone walls plastered off-white. There were hard benches to sleep on and a barred window, high up, that let in the salty tang of the sea. The temperature was mild on the south coast of Lapin, even in midwinter. A heavy wooden door, banded with iron, prevented their escape. There was a flap at the bottom, through which plates of food were occasionally pushed, and a slot their gaoler used to look in on them.

He was a chatty sort, keen to keep them updated on the details of their imminent demise. Through him, they'd learned that Duke Grephen was at an important conference, and was on his way back just as soon as he could get away and find a judge. 'To execute the sentence nice and legal,' the gaoler grinned, drawing out the word 'execute' just in case they missed how clever he was being by using it. 'But don't you worry. There ain't no hurry, 'cause not a soul knows you're here. Nobody's coming to your rescue.'

There were two guards, in addition to the gaoler, though the prisoners rarely heard them speak. They were there to keep an eye on things. 'Just in case you try any foolery,' the gaoler said, with a pointed look at Crake. They'd evidently been warned that there was a daemonist among the prisoners. Crake's golden tooth would be useless: he couldn't deal with three men. His skeleton key was lying somewhere in the *Ketty Jay*'s cargo hold, equally useless.

No way out.

He'd been swallowed by an immense sense of emptiness. It had come upon him in the moment they'd lifted off from the Blackendraft, to be taken on board the *Delirium Trigger*. The news that the *Ketty Jay* had disappeared did little to alleviate it. Bess was gone.

His thoughts went to the small whistle, hidden in his quarters aboard the *Ketty Jay*. Only that whistle, blown by the daemonist who had thralled it, had the power to wake her from oblivion. He'd never get to blow that whistle now. Perhaps that was best.

He should never have tried to save her. In attempting to atone for one crime, he'd committed one far greater. And now she'd be left, neither dead nor alive, for an eternity.

Did she sleep? Was she aware? Was she trapped in a metal shell in the endless waste of the ash flats, unable to move or scream? How much was left of the beautiful child he'd ruined? It was so hard to tell. She was more like a faithful dog than a little girl now, muddled and jumbled by his clumsy transfer, prone to fits of rage, insecurity and animal violence.

He should have let her die, but he couldn't live with the guilt of it. So he'd made her a monster. And, in doing so, made himself one.

A distant howl made Crake, Silo and Malvery look up as one. The voice was Frey's, coming from the torture room, just beyond the cell he shared with Pinn and Harkins.

'They've started up again,' said Malvery. 'Poor bastard.'

Crake stirred himself. 'Why's he bothering to hold out? What does it matter if he signs a confession or not? We're all going to be just as dead with or without it.'

Malvery grinned beneath his white walrus-like moustache. 'Maybe he just enjoys being an awkward bugger.'

Silo actually smiled at that. Crake didn't take up the humour. He felt Malvery put a huge arm round his shoulder.

'Cheer up, eh? You've had a face like a soggy arse since Dracken caught us.'

Crake gave him an amazed look. 'You know, all my life I've been under the illusion that the fear of death was a common, almost *universal* part of being human. But recently I've come to think I'm the only one on this crew who is actually worried about it in the slightest.'

'Oh, I don't know. I bet the other cell is half-full of Harkins' shit by now, he's so scared,' Malvery said with a wink. 'Then again, he's afraid of just about everything. The only reason he's still a pilot is because he's more afraid of *not* being a pilot than he is of getting shot down.'

'But . . . I mean, don't you have *regrets*? Thwarted hopes? Anything like that?' Crake was exasperated. He'd never been able to understand how the vagabonds of the *Ketty Jay* lived such day-to-day lives, never seeming to care about the future or the past.

'Regrets? Sure. I've got regrets like you wouldn't believe, mate,' said Malvery. 'Told you I was a doc back in Thesk, didn't I? Well, I was good at it, and I got rich. Got a little flush with success, got a little fond of the bottle too.

'One day a messenger from the surgery turned up at my house. There was a friend of mine, been brought in gravely ill. His appendix, was what it was. It was early in the morning, and I hadn't gone to bed from the night before. Been drinking the whole time.'

Crake noted that the light-hearted tone was draining out of Malvery's voice. He realised suddenly that he was in the midst of something serious. But Malvery kept going, forcing himself to sound casual.

'Well, I knew I was drunk but I also knew it was my friend and I believed I was the best damn surgeon for the job, drunk or sober. I'd got so used to being good that I thought I couldn't do no wrong. Wouldn't trust it to anyone else. Some junior doc tried to stop me but I just shrugged him off. Wish he'd tried harder now.'

Malvery stopped suddenly. He heaved a great sigh, as if expelling something from deep in his lungs. When he spoke again it was with a deep resignation in his tone. What had been done had been done, and could never be undone.

'It should have been easy, but I got careless. Slipped with the scalpel, went right through an artery. He bled out right in front of me, on the table, while I was trying to fix him up.'

Even obsessed with his own misery, Crake felt some sympathy for the big man. He knew exactly how he felt. Perhaps that was why they'd instinctively liked each other when they first met. Each sensed in the other a tragic victim of their own arrogance.

Malvery cleared his throat. 'I lost it all after that,' he said. 'Lost my licence. Lost my wife. Spent my money. Didn't care. And I drank. I drank and drank and drank, and the money got less and less, and one day I didn't have nothing left. I think that was about when the Cap'n found me.'

'Frey?'

Malvery pushed back the round, green-lensed spectacles on his broad nose. 'Right. We met in some port, I forget which. He bought me some drinks. Said he could use a doctor. I said I wasn't much of a doctor, and he said that was okay, 'cause he wasn't gonna pay me much anyway.' He guffawed suddenly. 'Ain't that just like him?'

Crake cracked a smile. 'Yes. I suppose it is.'

'I ain't never picked up a scalpel since that day when I killed my friend. I don't think I could. I keep those instruments polished in the infirmary, but I'll never use 'em. I'm good for patching you up and a bit of stitching, but I'd never trust myself to open you up. Not any more. You wanna know the truth, I'm half a doctor. But that's okay. 'Cause I found a home on the *Ketty Jay*, and I've got the Cap'n to thank for it.' He paused as Frey screamed from down the corridor. A spasm of anger crossed his face, but was gone again in an instant. 'He's a good man, whatever faults he's got. Been a good friend to me.'

Crake remembered how Trinica had put a gun to his head, and how Frey had given up the codes to his beloved aircraft rather than see the daemonist shot.

'Yes,' he said. 'To me, too.'

Crake knotted his fingers behind his head and leaned back against the wall of the cell. Silo, Harkins, and now Malvery: Frey certainly had a thing for picking up refugees. Granted, they were all useful to him in some way, but all owed a debt of gratitude and loyalty to their captain that Crake hadn't detected until recently. Perhaps Frey's intentions had been entirely mercenary – it could be that he just liked cheap crew – but at least half his men viewed him as a saviour of sorts. Maybe Frey didn't need them, but they certainly needed him. Without their captain, Silo would end up lynched or sent back to slavery in Samarla, Harkins would be forced to face a life without wings, and Malvery would be a destitute alcoholic once again.

And what of the rest of them? He himself had found a place to hide while he stayed ahead of the Shacklemores. Pinn had found a place that would tolerate him, where he could forever avoid the reality of his sweetheart in his doomed search for riches and fame. And Jez? Well, maybe Jez just wanted to be in a place where nobody asked any questions.

Like it or not, Frey gave them all something they needed. He gave them the *Ketty Jay*.

'We're all running from something,' Crake said wryly. Malvery's words, spoken weeks ago, before they'd shot down the *Ace of Skulls* and all this had begun. Malvery bellowed with laughter, recognising the quote.

Crake looked up at the ceiling of the cell. 'I deserve to be here,' he said.

Malvery shrugged. 'Then so do I.'

337

'Ain't no deserving, or otherwise,' Silo said, his bass voice rolling out from deep in his chest. 'There's what is, and what ain't, and there's what you do about it. Regret's just a way to make you feel okay that you're not makin' amends. A man can waste a life with regrets.'

'Wise words,' said Malvery, tipping the Murthian a salute. 'Wise words.'

Distantly, Frey screamed again.

Frey had been shot twice in his life, beaten up multiple times by members of both sexes, bitten by dogs and impaled through the gut by a Dakkadian bayonet, but until today he'd always been of the opinion that the worst pain in the world was cramp.

There was nothing quite so dreadful to Frey as waking up in the middle of the night with that tell-tale sense of tightness running like a blade down the length of his calf. It usually happened after a night on the rum or when he'd taken too many drops of Shine, but on the cramped bunk in his quarters he often lay awkwardly and cut off the circulation to one leg or the other, even when dead sober.

The worst moments were those few seconds before the agony hit. There was always time enough to try and twist out of it in such a way that the pain wouldn't come. It never worked. The inevitable seizure that followed would leave him whooping breathlessly, writhing around in his bunk and clutching his leg. It invariably ended with him knocking multiple items of luggage from the hammock overhead, which crashed down onto him in a tumble of cases and dirty clothes.

Finally, after the chaos of bewildering, undeserved pain, would come a relief so sweet that it was almost worth going through the preceding trauma to get there. He'd lie half-buried in the luggage, gasping and thanking whoever was listening that he was still alive.

Frey had learned long ago that the violent clenching of the muscles in his lower leg could send him wild with agony. Today, his torturer had introduced him to the joys of electrocution.

Instead of just his leg seizing up, now it happened to his entire body at once.

If he survived this, Frey decided, he'd have to rethink his definition of pain.

Blinding, shocking torment; his back arching involuntarily; muscles tensed so hard they could break bone; teeth gritted and jaw pulled back in a grimace.

And then the pain was gone. The joy was enough to make him want to break down and weep. He slumped forward in the chair as much as his restraints would allow, sweat dripping off his brow, chest heaving.

'Do you *want* to be hurt? Is that it?' the torturer asked.

Frey raised his head with some difficulty. The torturer was looking at him earnestly, wide grey eyes sympathetic and understanding. He was a handsome fellow, square-jawed and neat, wearing a carefully pressed light blue uniform in the ducal colours of Lapin.

'You should have a go at this,' Frey said, forcing out a fierce grin. 'Gives you quite a kick.'

The guard standing by the door – a burly man in an identical uniform to the torturer – smiled at that for a moment, before realising he wasn't supposed to. The torturer tutted and shook his head. He moved over to the machine that stood next to Frey's chair. It was a forbidding metal contraption, the size of a cabinet, with a face of dials and semicircular gauges.

'Obviously it's not kicking hard enough,' the torturer said, turning one of the dials a few notches.

Frey braced himself. It did no good.

The pain seemed like it would never end, until it did. The room swam back into focus. He'd always pictured torture chambers as dank and dungeon-like, but this place was clean and clinical. More like a doctor's surgery than a cell. The electric lights were bright and stark. There were all kinds of instruments in trays and cabinets, next to racks of bottles and drugs. Only the metal door, with a viewing-slot set into it, gave away the true nature of this place.

The confession sat on a small table in front of him. A pen waited next to it. The torturer had obligingly read it out to him yesterday, before they began. It was pretty much as he'd expected: *I, Frey, admit every damn thing. I conspired with my crew to kill the Archduke's son because we're greedy and bad, and then we all laughed about it afterwards. It was all my idea and certainly nobody else's, especially not Duke Grephen's or Gallian Thade's, who are both spotless and loyal subjects of our revered leader, and whose very faeces smell of roses and almond, et cetera, et cetera.*

The torturer picked up the pen and held it out to him. 'End it, Darian. Why struggle? You know there's no way out of here. Why must you make the last few hours of your life so miserable?'

Frey blinked sweat out of his eyes and stared dully at the pen. Why *didn't* he just sign it? It was only a formality. As soon as Grephen arrived with a judge, they'd be tried and hanged anyway, though not necessarily in that order.

But he wouldn't. He wouldn't sign that paper because he didn't want to make it easy on them. Because he'd fight for every moment he had left, eke out every inch of existence there was to be had.

Confessing was giving up. He wasn't resisting in the hope of achieving anything; he was resisting just to resist. It didn't matter how futile it was. He was bitter that he'd got so close, that he'd *almost* managed to get his crew out of the mess he'd got them into. It enraged him.

So he relished the small victories that were left. However she did it, Jez had got away, and taken the *Ketty Jay* with her. The fact that Grephen wasn't hurrying back immediately to dispose of his prisoners suggested that Trinica Dracken had neglected to mention that she'd lost the *Ketty Jay* en route. Unwittingly, Dracken had bought them some time.

He'd embarrassed her twice now. He took solace in that. He hadn't failed to notice that Trinica kept her compass and charts close to her at all times now. She'd been carrying them as they were shuttled from the deck of the *Delirium Trigger* to the landing pad at Mortengrace. She was nervous that they might be stolen again, and didn't want to leave them in her cabin.

Small victories. But victories, nevertheless.

He didn't hold out hope of Jez coming back. Not only would it be stupid, she had no real reason to. They were just a crew, like many she'd taken up with before. Though efficient at her job, she'd always seemed stand-offish, keeping to her cabin most of the time. He didn't imagine she held any particular affection for them, and he had no reason to expect loyalty. After all, she'd barely joined before he turned her into an outlaw.

But the *Ketty Jay* survived, and with a new captain at the helm. That was alright with Frey. If he couldn't have her, he was glad that someone could, and he'd always liked his diminutive navigator. He'd always wonder how Jez did it, though he took consolation in the fact that he wouldn't have to wonder long.

I suppose Slag made it too, he thought. *I wonder how he's going to get on with his new captain.*

'Sign!' the torturer urged, pressing the pen into his hand.

Frey took it. 'Give me the paper,' he said.

The torturer's eyes lit up eagerly. He moved the table closer, so Frey could write on it. The leather cuffs he wore were attached to straps that gave him a few inches of slack. The torturer presumably thought a man couldn't spasm efficiently without a little room to writhe.

'Bit closer. I can't reach,' said Frey. The torturer did as he was asked. 'Can you hold the paper steady? This isn't easy with one hand.'

The torturer smiled encouragingly as he steadied the paper for Frey to sign. He stopped smiling when Frey stabbed the pen into the soft meaty part between his thumb and forefinger.

A third man in uniform burst in through the door, and stood bewildered at the sight that faced him. The torturer was wheeling around the room, shrieking, holding his impaled hand, which still had a pen sticking out of it. The guard by the door was in paroxysms of laughter. Frey had crumpled the confession into a ball and was trying to get it into his mouth to eat it, but couldn't

341

quite reach. He paused guiltily as the newcomer stared at him, then let it drop from his hand.

'*What do you want?*' screamed the torturer, when he got his breath back.

'You can stop now,' said the newcomer.

'But he's not confessed!'

'We'll draft a new one and sign it for him. The Duke is back with a judge. He wants this done.'

'Can't you give me an hour?' the torturer whined, seeing his chance at revenge slipping away.

'I'm to take charge of him immediately,' the newcomer insisted. 'Get him out of that chair. He's coming with me.'

The sky was blue. Clear, cloudless and perfect. Frey squinted up at the sun and felt it warm his face. Amazing, he thought, how the north coast of the continent was gripped in ice and yet it was still pleasant here in the south. Vardia was so vast, its northern edge breached the Arctic Circle while its southern side came close to the equator. He'd always thought of winter as the grimmest season; but like anything, he supposed, it depended on where you were standing.

The spot chosen for his execution was a walled courtyard behind the barracks, where the militia conducted their drills. There was a small raised platform in the centre where a general might stand to oversee proceedings. A wrought iron lamp-post projected from its centre, flying the Duke's flag. Ornamental arms projected out from the lamp-post. They were intended for hanging pennants, but the pennants had been removed and a noose thrown over one of the arms to form a crude gallows. The end of the noose lay loosely around Frey's neck. An executioner – a massive, sweaty ogre with a thin shirt stretched over an enormous gut – waited to pull it taut.

A small crowd was assembled before him. There were two dozen militia, a judge, the Duke, and two witnesses: Gallian Thade and Trinica Dracken. Off to one side was a wagon with bars on its sides. Inside this wheeled cage were the remainder of his crew. They were unusually subdued. The seriousness of their situation had sunk in at last. Even Pinn was getting it now. They were going to watch their captain die. Nobody felt like joking.

He'd always wondered how he'd face death. Not the quick, hectic rush of a gun-battle but the slow, considered, drawn-out finale of an execution. He'd never imagined that he'd feel quite so serene. The wind stirred a lock of hair against his forehead; the sun shone on his cheeks. He felt like smiling.

The Darian Frey they were about to kill wasn't the same Darian Frey they'd set out to frame for their crime. That man had been a failure, a man who lurched from crisis to disaster at the whim of fate. A man who had prided himself on being better than the bottom-feeding scum of the smuggling world, and hadn't desired any more than that.

But he'd surprised them. He'd turned and fought when he should have run. He'd evaded and outwitted them time and again. He'd turned a bunch of dysfunctional layabouts into something approximating a crew. Stories would be told of how they tweaked the nose of the infamous Trinica Dracken in a hangar bay in Rabban. Word would spread. Freebooters all over Vardia would hear of Darian Frey, and his craft, the *Ketty Jay*. He'd come close to unearthing a daring conspiracy against the ruling family of the land, involving a Duke of Vardia, the legendary pirate captain Orkmund, and the mighty Awakener cult.

Only a final twist of ill fortune had stopped him. Trinica had made copies of the charts he stole. Without the compass she couldn't make it through the magnetic mines that guarded Retribution Falls, but she could wait at the point where she knew he'd emerge.

One little slip-up. But he'd led them a merry chase all the same. They might have caught him, but he still felt like he'd won.

He looked at the faces behind the bars: Malvery, Crake, Silo, Harkins . . . even Pinn. He was surprised to find he was sad to be leaving them. He didn't want it all to end now. He'd just begun to enjoy himself.

Frey had stopped listening to the list of crimes and accusations that the judge was reading out. The preliminaries were unimportant. He was thinking only of what was to come. Death was inevitable. He accepted that, and was calm. His hands were tied securely before him, and there were two dozen guards with rifles waiting to fill him with bullets if he should try to escape.

But he still had one trick left to play. The world would remember him, alright. Maybe they'd never know the truth, but they'd know his name.

The judge, an ancient, short-sighted relic who was more than half dust, finished his rambling and looked up, adjusting his spectacles.

'Sentence of death has been passed,' he droned. 'Tradition grants the prisoner the opportunity to make a last request. Does the prisoner have such a request?'

'I do,' said Frey. 'To be honest, I consider it a bit of an insult that the Duke couldn't even provide a decent gallows to hang me by. I request an alternative method of execution.'

Duke Grephen's sallow face coloured angrily. Trinica watched the prisoner curiously with her black eyes.

'I'd like to be beheaded with my own cutlass,' Frey said.

The judge looked at the Duke. Grephen swiped a strand of lank blond hair from his forehead and huffed.

'I can see no objection,' creaked the judge warily, in case the Duke had any objection.

'Fetch his cutlass!' Grephen cried. One of the guards hastened away to obey.

Frey stared at the Duke coolly. Even in his uniform, he looked like a spoiled boy. His deeply set eyes glittered with childish spite. He was a cold and humourless man, Frey surmised that much. He'd murdered dozens on board the *Ace of Skulls*, just to kill the Archduke's son in such a way that it could be pinned on someone else. Frey didn't believe it bothered him one bit. If there was any warmth in him, it was reserved for the Allsoul.

Next to him stood Gallian Thade. Sharp-faced, beak-nosed, with a pointed black beard. He was all angles and edges, where the Duke was soft and pudgy. Thade watched him with an air of

344

smugness. He'd waited a long time to see the man who had deflowered his daughter receive his punishment.

And then there was Trinica. He couldn't tell what she was thinking. Her ghost-white face revealed nothing. Would she be pleased to see him die? Would she finally be able to close the chapter of her life that had begun with him? Or was she even now remembering fonder moments from their past, wondering if she'd done the right thing in bringing him here?

Grephen had destroyed the *Ace of Skulls*; Thade had picked Frey to frame for it; Trinica had caught him.

He had reason to kill them all. But he'd only have time to do one of them. And he'd already chosen his target.

The guard returned from the barracks with his cutlass. Grephen took it and inspected it before passing it to the executioner. The executioner ran his thumb admiringly down the blade, then hissed through his teeth as he slashed the tip open.

'Could you get this thing off me?' Frey asked, jiggling his shoulders to indicate the noose. The executioner thrust the cutlass into his belt and removed the noose with one hand, sucking his bleeding thumb with the other.

'Kneel down, mate,' he said. Frey went to his knees on the wooden platform at the foot of the lamp-post. He shifted his wrists inside their knots of rope and rolled his neck.

He looked over at the cage, where his crew were imprisoned. Once he was dead, they'd follow him. Pinn seemed bewildered. Crake's gaze was heavy with tragedy. Silo was inscrutable, Harkins was cringing in a corner and looking away. Malvery gave him a rueful smile and a thumbs-up. Frey nodded in silent thanks for his support.

'Sentence of execution by beheading,' said the judge, 'to be carried out in the sight of these eminent witnesses.'

The executioner drew the cutlass and took aim, touching the blade to the back of Frey's neck. 'Don't worry, eh?' he said. 'One swipe and it'll be done.'

Frey took a breath. One swipe. He saw the blade descending in his mind's eye. He saw himself dropping one shoulder, rolling,

345

holding up his hands as the daemon-thralled sword slashed neatly through his bonds. He saw the blade jump from the hands of the executioner and into Frey's grasp. He saw the surprise on Grephen's face as Frey flung it from the podium. He saw it slide point first into the Duke's fat heart.

The sword always knew his will. He might go down in a hail of bullets, but the author of his misery would go down with him. And all of Vardia would know how Duke Grephen died at the hands of an insignificant little freebooter, who had outwitted him at the last.

'Kill him,' said Grephen to the executioner.

The executioner raised the cutlass. Frey closed his eyes.

Ready . . .

The blade quivered, and he fancied he heard the harmonic singing of the daemon within.

Ready . . .

And then a loud voice cried: 'STOP!'

Thirty-Five

The Suspicions Of Kedmund Drave – Frey Says His Piece –
The Sticky Matter Of Proof – Death In The Courtyard

T he voice that had halted the execution belonged to Kedmund Drave, the most feared of the Century Knights, who
Frey had last seen lying on a landing pad in Tarlock Cove
after he emptied a shotgun into Drave's chest. His moulded
crimson armour showed no signs of the encounter as he swept
across the courtyard towards Duke Grephen, his thick black cape
swaying around him.

To either side were Samandra Bree and Colden Grudge. Frey
recognised them from their ferrotypes. Samandra was wearing the
outfit she was famous for: battered coat and boots, loose hide
trousers, a tricorn hat perched on her head. Grudge, in contrast,
looked like something half-ape. Shaggy-haired and bristle-faced,
he was a hulking mass of dirty armour barely contained inside the
folds of a hooded cloak. His autocannon clanked against his back.
It was a gun bigger than most men could even carry, let alone fire.

'What exactly is going on here?' Drave demanded, striding up
to the Duke. They could scarcely have been more different: the
soft, spoiled aristocrat in his neatly pressed uniform and the iron-
hard figure of the Knight, his silver-grey hair shorn close to his
scalp and his cheek and neck horribly scarred.

Grephen collected himself, overcame the physical intimidation
and attempted to assert his Ducal authority. 'These men are
pirates,' he said. 'They have been condemned to death. I wasn't
aware there was any law forbidding a Duke to deal with pirates
inside his own duchy. As you can see, I have a judge here to
ensure everything is legal.'

Drave stared at the old judge, who began to look nervous.

'I see,' he said slowly. 'I imagine the trial has been thorough and fair.'

Grephen bristled. 'Remember who you're talking to, sir. You may have the Archduke's authority but even the Archduke knows to respect his Dukes.'

'I'm not in the business of respect,' Drave snarled. He turned to the judge. 'There has been a trial, I assume?'

The judge looked shiftily at Grephen and swallowed. 'I was brought here to oversee the executions. The Duke assured me that their guilt was not in question.'

'You've obtained confessions, then?' Drave asked Grephen.

Frey grinned. There wouldn't have been time to make up and sign another confession after he'd ruined the last one.

'They were caught red-handed in an act of piracy,' Grephen declared, flushing angrily. 'There was no need for a confession, or a trial. I exercised my ducal authority, as is my right. Besides, they admitted it.'

'Did we, bollocks!' Malvery yelled from the cage. 'He's lying!'

'You shut up!' growled Colden Grudge, pointing a meaty finger at the doctor.

'We're innocent!' Pinn cried, joining in happily. For a while his faith in a last-second intervention had wavered; but now here it was, and all was right with the world again.

Drave turned his gaze to Trinica. 'Trinica Dracken. You caught these men?'

'Yes.'

'You know what crimes they are wanted for?'

'I do.'

'And you were hired to catch them by the Duke?'

'I was.'

'Then *he* must know what crimes they are wanted for.'

Trinica looked at Grephen, her black eyes emotionless. 'I'd assume so,' she said.

Drave turned on Grephen. 'Given that, Duke Grephen, why did you see fit to execute these prisoners yourself instead of delivering them to the Archduke for public trial? After all, it wasn't *your* son they killed.'

Grephen had begun to sweat, his limp hair becoming lank. He looked to Gallian Thade, but Thade couldn't help.

'I can answer that,' called Frey. He was still kneeling on the platform, with the executioner standing next to him, Frey's cutlass held loosely in his hand.

'You be quiet, criminal!' Grephen snapped.

Drave's eyes narrowed as he looked for the first time at the man who had almost killed him a few weeks earlier. Frey wondered if the malice in that glare would be the death of him, or if Drave would give him the chance he needed. For a long instant, Drave said nothing; then he held up a hand.

'Let him speak. I'd like to hear what he has to say.'

Frey looked around the courtyard. All eyes were on him now. The guards in their light blue uniforms glanced at each other nervously. Grephen looked nauseous with fear. They'd thought this would be a simple execution: now they realised there was much more to it.

'Can I get to my feet?' Frey asked. 'My knees are getting kind of sore like this.'

Drave motioned for him to get up. The executioner backed away a step. 'Make it quick,' he said. 'And make it good. I will get to the bottom of this, but I'll not lie to you, Darian Frey: I'd like to see you dead as much as anyone.'

Frey got up. He was still possessed of that strange sense of calm that had settled on him with the surety of death. It was as if his body couldn't quite believe there might be a reprieve for him.

'I'll keep it simple, then,' he said. 'Duke Grephen plans to overthrow the Archduke. He's being bankrolled by the Awakeners; they want to see the Archduke deposed because of the political measures he and his wife are introducing to limit their power. They know Grephen is devout, and that he'll act favourably towards them once he seizes power.'

'These are *lies*!' Grephen shouted, but Frey went on anyway.

'The Awakeners don't have an army, and Grephen doesn't

command enough troops to challenge the Coalition Navy, so between them they've raised a force of pirates and freebooters, paid for with Awakener gold. This army is at the hidden port of Retribution Falls, waiting for the signal to move on Thesk and unseat the Archduke. As far as I know, that signal is coming any day now.'

'And what does any of this have to do with the destruction of the *Ace of Skulls* and the death of Hengar?' Drave asked.

'Hengar's death was a preliminary. They wanted to be sure there was nobody left for dissenters to rally round. He was the only surviving member of the Arken family who could inherit the title after the Archduke is gone. His secret affair with a Samarlan gave them an opportunity to get him out of the way and make it look like an accident. And Hengar was the popular one; by killing him and then leaking the information about the affair, they made the Archduke's family look dishonest and immoral. All the better for after the coup, when they could claim it was a revolution to depose a corrupt regime, just like the Dukes when they overthrew the monarchy.'

'This is pure fantasy!' Grephen shrieked. 'I will not stand here and listen to this slander from a pirate and murderer.'

'I can prove it,' said Frey. 'I've been to Retribution Falls, and I've seen the army that's waiting there. I know how to find it.' He stared hard into the eyes of Kedmund Drave. 'I can take you there.'

Drave stared back at him. 'In exchange for a pardon, no doubt.'

'A *pardon*?' cried the Duke, but was ignored.

'For me and my crew,' Frey said. 'The *Ace of Skulls* was rigged with explosives. Any engineer would tell you it's nigh on impossible to blow up a craft that size with the guns I have on my craft. We were set up to take the fall for it, so nobody would suspect that it was part of a bigger plot. They hoped we'd be killed before we ever worked out what was going on, so we wouldn't be able to tell anyone.' He raised his bound hands and pointed across the courtyard. 'The set-up was Gallian Thade's doing. He's in on it too.'

Thade said nothing, but his gaze was murderous.

'You're going to take his word for what kind of guns he has on his craft?' Grephen spluttered.

'I know what kind of guns he has on his craft,' Drave said. 'We have it in our possession.'

Frey's heart leaped. That could mean only one thing: Jez. Somehow, she'd found the Century Knights and told them what was going on. A flicker of real hope ignited in him.

'He's playing for time!' Grephen accused. 'He's leading you on a wild goose chase. You're not really thinking of letting him lead you all over Vardia in search of some mythical pirate port?'

Drave looked at Frey. 'Is that what you're doing? Playing for time?'

'If you'll permit me . . .' said Frey. He reached down into his trousers and began groping around at his crotch. Several guards covered him with guns. Samandra Bree raised an eyebrow.

After a moment, he pulled out a tightly folded piece of paper and proffered it across the podium. Drave looked at it, then nodded at Samandra.

'Me?' she cried in protest. She rolled her eyes. 'Fine!' she groaned.

She took the paper delicately from Frey's hand, touching it as little as possible. 'That's been down there for days, right?'

'Ever since Dracken captured us,' Frey said, with a wink. 'Lucky they didn't search us too closely.'

Samandra wrinkled her pretty nose. 'Ugh.'

She handed the paper to Drave, who unfolded it, apparently unconcerned by the moistness and the smell.

'It's a page from the dock master's book at Retribution Falls. You can see his name and title signed down there in the bottom corner,' Frey told him.

'I see it,' said Drave. He turned the paper over. 'I don't see the *Ketty Jay* on here, though.'

'We weren't calling ourselves the *Ketty Jay* at the time. It would have been a bit stupid with half of Vardia trying to catch or kill us.'

'How convenient!' Grephen crowed.

'I'm not showing it to you to prove *I* was there. The fact that you hold it in your hand is proof enough that I was there,' Frey replied. 'The name you should be looking at is the *Moment of Silence*. If you look up her records you'll find she's a craft registered to the Awakeners. The signature will also match the captain's. She was the craft shuttling Awakener gold to Retribution Falls to finance the army.'

Grephen was becoming short of breath. 'That . . . that piece of paper doesn't prove anything! A forged piece of rubbish!'

There were many tales told about Kedmund Drave. Like all the Century Knights, he had his own kind of legend. One of the less unpleasant stories claimed that he could tell if a man was lying just by looking into his eyes. He looked now: a penetrating gaze, boring into the Duke.

Grephen backed off a step. 'You're going to take the word of a convict over that of a Duke?'

'A Duke who still hasn't told me why he's attempting to execute these prisoners when he *knows* they should have gone to the Archduke for trial.'

'This is ridiculous!' Grephen cried, flailing. 'I'm not answering to you! I don't have to answer to anyone but the Archduke in my own duchy.'

'We act for the Archduke,' said Drave. 'So you answer to me!'

'Come on, Grephen!' Frey jeered. 'Tell him why you want me dead! Tell him about Orkmund and all your pirate friends!'

'And *you*!' Grephen cried, thrusting a shaky finger at him. 'I've had quite enough out of you.' He looked at the executioner, who was still standing on the podium, holding Frey's cutlass. 'Kill him!' Grephen ordered.

Two lever-action shotguns spun out from beneath Samandra Bree's long coat, and fixed on the executioner. 'Raise that sword and you're the first to die,' she said.

The executioner stayed where he was, his gaze flicking between the Duke and the twin barrels aimed at his face. Frey was in no doubt which would prove most persuasive.

The Duke's guards were stirring uneasily now. Their loyalty was to their Duke, and they didn't like to see him bullied. Colden

Grudge, sensing the tension, flung back his cloak to allow himself easy access to the double-bladed hand-axes hanging at his belt.

'Your Grace, I think you had better come with me,' said Drave, 'until we can verify your innocence.'

'You're *arresting* me?' Grephen gasped. He looked left and right, eyes bulging, a cornered animal searching for a way out. The elderly judge had already retreated, distancing himself from the Duke.

'Your Grace!' Thade snapped, seeing the panic on his companion's face. 'Calm yourself!'

'I'm requesting the pleasure of your company on the Archduke's behalf,' Drake insisted steadily. 'You won't be locked up. We just need to be sure you aren't going anywhere. If these allegations are groundless, you've nothing to fear.'

'Nothing to fear?' he screeched. 'I'm a Duke! Spit and blood, I'm a Duke of Vardia! You can't treat me like this in my own house!' He hesitated, gaping, as if shocked by the enormity of what he was about to do. Then he turned to his captain of the guard and shouted: 'Seize them! Arrest those Knights!'

Chaos erupted in the courtyard. The militia surged in on the Knights. Samandra Bree's shotguns bellowed, and two men flew backwards in a cloud of blood. Colden Grudge swung his axes, severing limbs and fingers. Kedmund Drave moved faster than his bulk and armour suggested he could, slipping out of the grasp of two soldiers, coming up with pistols blazing. In seconds, the space in front of Frey's makeshift gallows became a battlefield as the militia tried to overwhelm the Century Knights, and the Knights retaliated with lethal force.

The executioner was standing agape. Frey turned to him, holding out his hands.

'Cut the ropes!' he said. It was addressed to the cutlass rather than the man holding it.

The blade moved of its own accord, slashing through the air and dividing the rope between Frey's wrists. As soon as his hands were free, the cutlass somersaulted from the executioner's hands and into his. An instant later, Frey had the tip at the confused executioner's throat. The man's eyes bulged in incomprehension. Frey delivered a good, solid kick square between the legs. His eyes bulged even further as he sank gently to the ground.

Pinn was cheering from inside the cage. Crake shouted at Frey and pointed. 'Dracken's running!' he cried.

Frey looked. The melee in the courtyard had become fiercer. The Knights were many times outnumbered but they still wouldn't go down. Several bloodied bodies lay on the ground. The militia had given up trying to seize anyone and were just trying to kill them now, but their rifles were unwieldy in such close quarters. Some had reverted to pistols and knives. The Knights slipped between the bullets and blades with practised savagery, and their opponents couldn't lay a hand on them.

Beyond it all, Frey could see Trinica Dracken. She was fleeing towards the door that led into the barracks building, away from the courtyard. Duke Grephen was backing away from the knot of men struggling with the Knights. He looked dazed, startled by the carnage he'd unleashed. Inadvertently, he strayed too close to the cage where the *Ketty Jay*'s crew were imprisoned, and Malvery reached out and grabbed him with his thick arms, hugging him close to the bars.

'I've got this one, Cap'n!' Malvery yelled, as Frey launched off the platform in pursuit of Trinica. He sprinted across the courtyard as she disappeared through the door. From the corner of his eye, he saw Gallian Thade running for the same door. The aristocrat had obviously decided that Trinica had the right idea and had abandoned his Duke in favour of a quick escape.

The two of them raced across the courtyard, and for a moment it looked as if they'd reach their destination at the same time. But then Frey saw Kedmund Drave raise his pistol and fire through the press of bodies that surrounded him. Thade's sprint became a stumble, tripping forward under his own momentum. His face went slack, and he crashed to the ground in a heap of dust, his fine jacket holed and stained with blood.

Frey ran on, fearing a bullet in his own back at any moment, but Drave was too busy saving himself to spare more than a split second to deal with anyone else. Pinn and Malvery cheered him on as he flew through the open doorway, out of the courtyard and into the cool stone corridors of the barracks.

Trinica was just disappearing around a corner, and he gave chase. Her compass and charts were the only bargaining chips he had; if she got away with them, he and his crew would still hang for their part in the crime. As he rounded the corner, he glimpsed her again – her black-clad figure, her roughly cropped white hair. Hearing his footsteps, she looked back at him. Her eyes showed him nothing, not even surprise. She dodged around another corner and was lost from sight.

Frey sprinted, arms pumping, his cutlass cutting the air. The barracks were deserted, and the walls rang with the hollow echoes of his bootsteps. He swung round the corner after Trinica.

She was standing there, a few metres away, her pistol aimed at his chest. Frey felt a moment of dreadful surprise, and then she shot him.

The gunshots were deafening. He didn't even have time to skid to a halt before she pulled the trigger twice in succession, shooting at virtually point-blank range. Frey's momentum was violently checked. He tottered on his heels and fell onto his back.

Trinica had dismissed him before he'd even hit the floor. She holstered her pistol and ran on, not interested in wasting a moment of her escape on sentiment.

Frey heard her footsteps disappear up the corridor. His chest heaved. His brain and body gradually slipped out of a state of shock.

He got up on his elbows. He felt around his chest in disbelief.

There were no holes in his shirt. He was unharmed. He got to his feet, looking around himself as if there might be an answer lying there.

I'm not dead, he thought, dumbly. *Why aren't I dead?*

There was only one thing he could think of. He looked down at his hand, which was still holding the cutlass.

The daemon-thralled blade had deflected the bullets.

'I didn't know it could do that,' he murmured, staring at it in wonder. It wasn't even marked. 'Crake, you're a bloody genius.'

But there was no time for amazement. Matters were too urgent to wallow in good fortune.

The corridor ended in a T-junction, which brought him to a halt. He looked both ways. A door was ajar some way down the left corridor. He crept towards it. As he neared, he heard the sounds of muted rummaging inside, and the click of case-locks. Suddenly, the door flew open and Trinica burst out. His arm snapped up, the edge of the cutlass resting against her throat, and she froze. In one hand was her pistol; in the other was the case he'd seen her carrying when they were shuttled down from the *Delirium Trigger*. The case holding the charts and the compass that would lead him back to Retribution Falls.

'Ah-ah, Trinica,' he said chidingly. 'You're not going anywhere. Drop the gun.'

She stared at him, her eyes black, and said nothing.

'Don't think I'll do it?' he asked. 'Try me. After what you just pulled, I'd be glad to be rid of you.'

Trinica dropped her gun. Frey kicked it away from her. 'Give me the case,' he told her. She did so. She didn't seem surprised that he was still alive, and she didn't ask how.

'They'll kill me, Darian,' she said. 'When Grephen's plan comes to light, they'll hang me as a conspirator.'

'Probably,' said Frey. He was still angry enough not to care. The fact that she'd pulled the trigger on him had wounded him deeply. Somehow, he'd always thought she wouldn't be able to do it. Watching him die was one thing, but this had a whole new level of cold-bloodedness to it. He felt unreasonably betrayed. Their past should have counted for something at that moment. You shouldn't be capable of killing someone you once loved.

Trinica stared at him for a long moment. 'What now? Are you going to take me back to them?'

Frey didn't answer that. He hadn't thought beyond reclaiming the charts. He hadn't considered what he might do with Trinica.

'You know there's no guarantee they'll pardon you, don't you?' she said. 'You know they could just force you to co-operate. They might go back on their word after you've done what you said you would. Because whatever way you cut it, you fired on the *Ace of Skulls*. You were attacking it when it exploded. You think the Archduke is going to want to pardon the man who killed his only son?' The corner of her mouth quirked into a smile. 'You're a traitor and a pirate, just like I am.'

Frey wanted to deny that intimacy. He wanted to tell her that they were not the same. But he knew she was right. She spoke to all his deepest fears. His whole plan relied on making a deal with the authorities, and he knew how authorities could be. There was no fairness or justice in them. They had the power to go back on any deal they made, if it suited them.

'Come with me, Darian,' Trinica said. That shocked him.

'With you?' he sneered, automatically.

'I'll drop you at a safe port. You can make your way from there. We'll be under terms of truce, as one captain to another; I'll see you're not harmed.'

Frey hesitated, the sneer dropping from his face. He believed her. There was honour among pirates of a kind there never had been among the aristocracy. And yet it enraged him how even this slender invitation made his heart jump. Though he'd loathed her all these years, his body seemed never to forget the love they'd once shared. The merest hint of reconciliation, of alliance, ignited a yearning in his guts that disgusted him. He reacted by hardening his resolve.

Damn her. Damn her and her terms of truce.

She was no longer the woman he'd loved. The woman he loved no longer existed. Instead, he was haunted by her ghost.

'Why take the risk, Darian?' she said. 'If you go back there, they'll hang you.'

'If I don't go back, they'll hang my crew for sure.'

'Since when did that matter to you?'

He didn't know the answer to that. It wasn't really important. It had been an accumulation of moments: a clutter of drunken laughter, of triumphant grins, of gunfights and arguments and sarcastic little quips. The feeling had crept up on him stealthily, and by the time he was aware of it, he'd been overtaken.

Maybe he'd decided it when he chose to trust Jez with his ignition code? Or when he'd given it away to Trinica in order to save Crake's life? Maybe it was that he felt the need to repay Jez's loyalty: she'd come back, and he admired her for that.

He didn't know when it had started to matter. He just knew that it did. He wouldn't abandon his crew, no matter what the risks were now.

Trinica saw the decision in his eyes. A faint respect crept into her tone. 'Well,' she said. 'Look at you now.'

But Frey was in no mood to be congratulated. He pressed the tip of his cutlass harder under her chin, tipping her head back. A spot of bright red blood bloomed against her white skin. 'Give me one reason why I shouldn't kill you.'

'There isn't one,' said Trinica. 'This is your chance, Darian. You take me back, I die anyway. So I promise you, I won't go quietly. You'd better kill me now. I'd rather you did it than them.'

Her voice was utterly without fear. It was Frey who was afraid. He had no doubt that she meant what she said. She'd throw herself onto his sword rather than allow herself to be taken prisoner. She didn't just expect death, she welcomed it. At that moment he understood how she'd become one of the most dreaded pirate captains in Vardia. Everything inside her had died with their baby. How could you kill the walking dead?

He looked upon the woman he'd once loved, her chin raised, gazing coolly at him. He knew he'd never be able to do it. Because he owed her. He'd turned her into this creature when he left her so cruelly. Maybe he wasn't entirely responsible for the death of his child, but he bore some of the blame. He'd inspired her to do it. And, bitter as it was, he couldn't lie to himself any more.

Trinica had suffered enough. It was written all over her.

He lowered the cutlass.

'You'll be hunted now,' he said. 'Not a freebooter any more. A straight-out pirate. The Navy will never leave you alone.'

Trinica stepped back, one slender hand going to her throat, covering the cut there. She stared at him with a strange, wounded tenderness.

He couldn't bear it. 'Get out of here,' he told her.

'You're not what I thought you were, Darian,' she said, and there was something soft in her voice, something that reminded him of a voice from long ago that had once melted his heart. He dared not let it do so again.

'Goodbye, Trinica,' he said. And then she turned and ran down the corridor, and he watched her go until she was lost from sight.

By the time Frey returned to the courtyard, the battle had ended. Six of the militia had surrendered. The rest lay in various states of death and dismemberment on the floor, their blood turning the dust into red mulch. Of the Century Knights, Colden Grudge had suffered a superficial wound on his brow. He was covering the Duke and the surviving militia with his autocannon. There had been no opportunity to use it earlier, due to the close-quarters fighting, but he looked eager enough to be given the excuse now.

Kedmund Drave looked up as Frey appeared, alerted by the rousing cheer from the caged wagon where his crew were imprisoned. Frey had stashed the charts and compass he'd taken from Trinica, and his cutlass was jammed through his belt. He walked with a tired step.

'Didn't expect to see you back,' Drave commented.

'Just eager to help out the Coalition,' Frey replied. 'Call me a patriot.'

'Dracken?'

'She got away.'

'You think she might warn the others? Orkmund and his men?'

'I've made sure she can't get to them. But we should move quickly. They won't attack while there's no one to give them a signal, but they'll get wind of what's happened here sooner or later.'

'Tell us where they are. We'll deal with them.'

Frey laughed sardonically. 'No. I'll tell you what'll happen. You assemble a strike force of Navy aircraft. I'll lead them into Retribution Falls. Without me, you won't know where you're going.'

Drave stared at him, searching for signs of deceit. Frey wasn't intimidated. Numbed by his recent torture and the shock of facing his own extinction, he'd become impenetrably calm again.

'I'll need my craft, and my crew,' said Frey. 'And I'll need my navigator back too. How did she find you, by the way?'

Samandra Bree had wandered over by this point. She tilted back her tricorn and smiled disarmingly. 'She told us she'd made the acquaintance of a very important fellow called Air Marshal Barnery Vexford at a party at Scorchwood Heights. Apparently, she had to do some quite appalling things to him to secure an audience with the Archduke's representatives at such short notice. He is quite a filthy old man.' She patted him on the shoulder. 'You do have an admirably loyal crew, Captain.'

Frey could only imagine how loyal Jez had needed to be.

'Once they heard where you were, they sent us,' said Drave. He looked around himself, at the dead lying on the ground. 'By the Duke's reaction, I'd say her story and yours have some truth in them.'

'I want pardons,' said Frey. 'In writing.'

'You'll get them,' said Drave. 'When you've led us to Retribution Falls. Not before.' Frey opened his mouth to protest, but Drave held up one metal-gloved hand. 'Pardons can be revoked. Makes no difference if you have a piece of paper or not. If you're telling the truth, and you do what you say, then you'll get what you want. But you double-cross me, and there'll be no place in the world that's safe for you.'

Frey met his gaze steadily. Threats couldn't faze him now. 'Then I suppose we'll just have to trust each other, won't we? Now get my men out of that cage.'

Thirty-Six

The Return To Rook's Boneyard – Jez Is Brought To The Fold –
The Daemons Between Harkins And Pinn – Frey Takes A Risk

'Turning up ahead, Cap'n. Hold steady till you see it.'

Frey made a murmur of acknowledgement and Jez went back to her charts. The *Ketty Jay* slid on through the mists of Rook's Boneyard.

Behind Frey, Crake consulted Dracken's compass and warned them where the deadly floating mines were hiding in the murk. His voice was muffled by the mask he wore. Frey wore one too.

Jez didn't. She'd given up pretending she needed to.

The cockpit was dim and stuffy, and sounds gave back strange echoes. Dew ran down the windglass, and the soft growl of the *Ketty Jay*'s thrusters filled up the silence. Jez sat in her chair at the navigator's station, plotting their course as efficiently as ever. She absently tapped out a sequence on the electroheliograph with her left hand, warning those who followed of the location of the mines, half her mind still on the calculations.

Frey took off his mask for a moment and yelled, 'How we doing back there, Doc?'

'They're still on our tail!' Malvery bellowed back from the cupola, where he had a view of what was going on behind the *Ketty Jay*. Only he could see the huge shapes in the darkness that drifted after them like malevolent phantoms.

'Bet you never thought you'd see the day when you'd be leading a flotilla of Navy craft,' Jez grinned, looking over at the captain.

'I never did,' he agreed with a wry twitch of the lips, then put his gas filter back on.

There was a dull explosion as a mine was detonated by one of the Navy minesweepers, clearing a path for the fleet behind them. It had been slow progress over many hours, gradually creeping closer and closer to Retribution Falls, removing all threats along the way. Since the other craft didn't have compasses of their own, it was just too risky to try to bring the whole strike force through the mines in single file.

Jez wondered how far the sound carried through the choking mist and deep, sharp canyons. She wondered if they might find the denizens of Retribution Falls waiting for them when they arrived. But despite the danger all around them and the certain knowledge of the conflict to come, she felt content.

The sounds of the *Ketty Jay* soothed her. She'd come to know its tics and groans and they were reassuring. The navigator's seat had found her shape, as if it had somehow moulded itself to her buttocks and back, and its form seemed natural now. The muggy heat of the cockpit had become cosy, a warm sanctuary from the hostile world that waited outside.

It was a strange experience. So much time had passed since the Manes had attacked that small village in Yortland that she'd forgotten what contentment felt like. Three years she'd been wandering, hiding, always afraid of discovery. She'd never put down roots or allowed herself to care for those around her.

But here, at last, she felt like she was home. She'd found her place. She was here to stay.

Her reunion with the crew had been unexpectedly touching. Malvery had almost crushed her ribs with a hug, before planting a big, whiskery kiss on her cheek. Frey was similarly effusive. Pinn slapped her on the arm; Harkins babbled, jubilant. Silo nodded respectfully, which was as close as he ever came to a joyous outburst. Even Crake seemed happy to see her, though there was a wariness in his eyes, as if he expected her to reject his handshake.

'Thank you,' he said, simply.

'I brought Bess,' she said, thumbing behind her at the open maw of the cargo hold. 'She's in there.'

Crake's eyes filled with tears and his face split into an uncontrollable grin that was half a sob; then he hugged her, clutching her tightly to him. She was surprised enough to hug him back. Of all people, Crake had been the one who should have been most enthusiastic in his loathing. He was smart, and knowledge-able in the hidden ways. He'd have guessed her nature by now.

And yet he embraced her, as the others did.

She'd hoped that at best they would let her go on her way. She'd hoped that they'd be grateful enough for their rescue that they'd keep her secret from the Century Knights, no matter how danger-ous they knew her to be. The idea of taking her back was ridicu-lous. They might tolerate an openly practising daemonist on board, but how could you get on with a woman whose heart didn't beat, who didn't need to breathe or sleep or eat? How could you ever trust someone like that? Robbed of the common vulnerabilities of humanity, how could you ever know what they might do next?

She'd accepted that they might turn her in. Gratitude didn't apply to monsters. They might try to destroy her. She'd been ready for that. It was an acceptable risk.

But they greeted her like an old friend.

She hardly dared believe what was happening. Surely they were just relieved at escaping execution, and hadn't had time to think it through? If that was the case, then their suspicions would grow as soon as their happiness faded. She couldn't bear that. She had to know if they accepted her as she was or if they simply hadn't taken in the truth yet.

'I suppose . . .' she said, once Crake had released her. 'I suppose I owe you an explanation.'

'No,' said Pinn, beaming.

Jez frowned at his abruptness, and the twinkle of amusement in his piggy eyes. 'No, I mean, you must be wondering how I did it.'

Silo shrugged.

'Not really,' said Frey.

'Nope,' said Harkins.

'Couldn't give a dog's arse, frankly,' Malvery added.

She looked at the faces of the crew, and she began to under-stand. Perhaps they knew exactly what she was, perhaps

363

not. But it didn't matter, because they didn't care. She was one of them.

'You?' she asked Crake.

'I already know how you did it,' he said. 'No need to tell me.' His smile was warm. Bringing Bess back had indebted him to her for ever. Bringing the *Ketty Jay* back had won the hearts of the rest of them.

Seeing their grinning faces, joined together in a conspiracy of support, she at last let herself believe. The grin spread to her face too.

'Well, then,' she said. 'That's that.'

Harkins flexed his fingers on his flight stick and tried not to throw up in his own lap. His stomach had knotted into a ball and his breath came in shallow pants that offered little relief from the crushing anxiety that pressed in on him. He hunkered down in the cockpit of the Firecrow, eyes darting nervously here and there. He wished the mist would clear. He was also afraid of what he'd see when it did.

Only the metal cocoon of the Firecrow kept him together. The sense of safety it afforded stopped him panicking completely.

It seemed so long ago that they'd left the Firecrow hidden in a remote cave next to Pinn's Skylance. The Cap'n had deemed it too dangerous to travel into Rook's Boneyard in convoy. He'd been right: without masks, the deadly fumes from the lava river would have caused both Harkins and Pinn to crash.

Their fortunes hadn't gone too well since then, though. The Firecrow was Harkins' only security, and without it he was lost. He'd spent most of the subsequent days in blubbering fear; first hiding in the *Ketty Jay* so as not to venture into Retribution Falls, then trembling in Dracken's brig on the *Delirium Trigger*, and later waiting to die in his cell at Mortengrace. Superstitiously, he blamed his bad luck on his separation from the Firecrow. He should never have deserted her. He wouldn't do so again if he could help it.

Vast, angular shapes glided past to port and starboard like

undesea leviathans. Smaller fighters hove between them, their lights bright bruises against the serene fog. Harkins made minute course corrections and fretted about a frigate clipping his wing and sending him spiralling to a fiery death.

The mines petered out after the lava river. Presumably the pirates reasoned that anyone without a compass to detect them would be dead by that point. He'd hoped that leaving the mines behind would ease the tension a little, but he found that it increased it instead. They were on the final leg of the journey. Soon they'd reach the enormous, marshy sinkhole where Retribution Falls lay. Soon the fight would begin.

Survive, said Frey. *That's all you have to do. Don't take any risks. Look out for each other.*

The Cap'n had persuaded Kedmund Drave to let them bring the *Ketty Jay*'s outflyers. They were invaluable pilots, he'd said, and they'd need every craft in the fight. Harkins and Pinn were useless sitting on board the *Ketty Jay*. Since their fighters didn't have Navy markings, they could sow havoc among the pirates, who would be unable to tell them apart from their allies.

Harkins had pointed out that this worked both ways, but Frey had assured him the Navy would know who they were and what they looked like. Harkins wasn't quite so certain. He could just see a Navy frigate firing a shell up his exhaust in the heat of the moment.

The flotilla was packed in tight, a tentative train behind the *Ketty Jay*. Harkins was tucked inside it, with Pinn somewhere nearby. The mist was beginning to thin out noticeably. He could make out the detail on the nearest frigates, their gun turrets and armoured keels.

He fingered his silver earcuff. Having a daemon clipped to his ear only added to his unease, but Crake had offered them and Frey had insisted.

'Anybody out there?' he said. 'This is . . . um . . . this is Harkins. Just wondering if anybody's out there. Say something if you are.'

'Clam it, Harkins,' said Pinn's voice in his ear, making him jump. 'Crake said to use these things only when we had to. They'll drain you if you start gibbering.'

'Oh. I was just testing it, that's all. You think the Cap'n can hear?'

'He's too far ahead. They've got a short range. Now shut up.'

Harkins snapped his mouth closed. His ear was tingling where the cuff touched his skin. He didn't really understand all this daemonism business, but it made him feel a little better to hear a familiar voice.

Ahead, the fleet was beginning to break up and spread out as visibility improved and they dipped below the mist into clear air. Harkins' heart thumped against his thin ribs as craft started to accelerate around him. Beneath them was a river, running along the canyon floor. The last stage of the journey. The moment was imminent. He wanted to curl up and hide.

Then at last the canyon gave out and the river plunged away down the sheer wall of the sinkhole. They'd arrived at Retribution Falls.

It lay as the *Ketty Jay* had left it, a shabby assemblage of scaffolded platforms and ramshackle buildings, steeped in the rancid marsh air. The great sinkhole, many kloms across, was ribboned in slicks of metallic ooze. Where the earth broke through the water, rotting dwellings grew like scabs.

But Harkins wasn't looking at the town. He was looking at the aircraft. Hundreds of aircraft.

The fleet had grown in their absence. The landing pads were choked with fighters and heavy attack craft. Battered frigates floated at anchor; clusters of caravels and corvettes hung pensively over the town; shuttles and small personal craft hummed through the air.

There must have been three hundred, at least. Harkins felt his stomach clench and his gorge rise. He was suddenly glad he hadn't eaten anything that morning.

A swarm of fighters was already scrambling to meet them as Harkins came out of the canyon. They'd been alerted by the sight of the first Navy craft at the head of the convoy. Retribution Falls kept a standing defence force, it seemed, ready to go at a moment's notice. But those few craft aside, the pirate army had been caught completely by surprise.

The guns of the Navy frigates bellowed in a deafening cascade, making Harkins shriek inside his cockpit. Their opening salvo ripped a flaming scar across the sprawling town.

The primary target was the main landing pad, where the greatest number of smaller craft were clustered. It was obliterated in a cataclysm of fire. The other, more temporary landing pads that floated on the marsh were also struck. Those that weren't destroyed outright began to list as their aerium tanks were holed, sending dozens of craft sliding into the sucking bog beneath.

Two of the nearest pirate frigates, anchored close to one another, were smashed with explosive shells. One of them split along its keel in a smoky red bloom, and sank to the ground in two halves. There were enough unpunctured aerium tanks to make the descent slow and terrible, like a ship being pulled to the bottom of the sea.

After the initial assault there was a pause to reload, and the Navy fighters came racing out of the cover of the fleet. Harkins saw the sleek Windblades shoot past him like darts, heading to meet the fighters rising from Retribution Falls. He gritted his teeth. He wanted, more than anything, to stay concealed behind the flanks of the enormous frigates. This wasn't his fight, after all: the pirates weren't his enemies.

But the heavy guns of the pirate craft would start up soon, blasting at the fleet, and a tiny craft like his would be dashed to pieces in the shellfire.

The safest thing to do was attack.

He heard Pinn whoop in his ear, and cursed him for his absurd courage. He could already picture that moron racing ahead of the pack, desperate for the first kill, heedless of the danger. He was the kind that would evade death for ever, simply because he didn't realise it was there. The fearless always survived. It was one of the great unfairnesses of life, in Harkins' opinion.

Well, he was damned if he'd let Pinn mock him for being the

last one into the battle. The thought of that chubby-cheeked face screwed up in laughter made his blood boil. He hit the throttle and plunged out of the flotilla, pursuing the Navy Windblades into the fray.

The pirate fighters were a motley of different models from different workshops, representing the last thirty years of aviation technology. They came on like a cloud of flies, without discipline or any hint of a formation. The Navy fighters were tighter, punching towards them like an arrow. Harkins slipped in near the back.

The Firecrow's engines roared, encompassing him in sound. The craft shook and trembled. Through the windglass bubble on its nose, Harkins could see the vile colours of the marsh blurring beneath him. Two Windblades hung on his wings, their pilots wearing identical Navy-grey helmets, their attention focused on the attack. Harkins swallowed and hunched forward, his finger hovering over the trigger.

The two sides met as the Navy frigates released another salvo, pounding the town of Retribution Falls, pulverising those pirate craft which were too slow to react to the surprise attack. Suddenly the world was full of explosions and machine guns, and Harkins yelled in fear as he opened up on the enemy.

The Windblades spread out, spiralling and rolling as they approached. Harkins jinked left to avoid a lashing of tracer fire, picked his target and sent a long burst back towards them. He aimed where he thought the craft was going, rather than where it was, and his guess was accurate. The pilot flew right through the deadly hail of gunfire. The windglass of the cockpit shattered and the pilot jerked as he was shot through with bullets. The craft tipped into a long, lazy dive towards destruction.

The pirates and Navy fighters broke upon each other like waves onto rocks, spuming in all directions as they scattered. The battle became a mass of individual dogfights.

Harkins threw the Firecrow into a steep climb, raking his guns across the underside of an old Westingley Scout. It corkscrewed out of control and slammed into the tail of another pirate craft as he soared upward. Something thundered past his wing, missing a collision by less than a metre. Dizzy with fear-driven adrenaline, he paid it no mind. He levelled out, letting the G-force off a bit before coming around and on to the tail of a rickety Cloud-skimmer.

Pinn screamed with joy in his ear. Harkins gave a scream of a different kind, and pressed down on his guns.

'Time to go,' said Frey, as the first scattered volleys of return fire from the pirate frigates came smashing into the Navy fleet. He vented aerium and dropped the *Ketty Jay* down beneath the keels of the larger aircraft, then hit the thrusters and sped towards the town.

The pirate frigates had begun to wake up now, shedding their anchor-chains and gliding into action, their gun-crews finally in position. Frey had hung back to hide as best he could among the heavy craft, but like Harkins, he knew it would be suicide to stay once the big guns got going. Besides, he'd done his job. He'd led them here. That was enough to earn his pardon, assuming they intended to give it to him.

Now he had a purpose of his own, and it didn't involve getting tangled up in a squabble between the Navy and Orkmund's pirate gang.

Retribution Falls was a mess. Whole areas were flattened as the dwellings, never built for strength, fell apart from the concussion of a single shell. As he watched, one of the platforms at the far end of the town tipped and fell, its gridwork of scaffolding blasted away on one side. Buildings crumbled into landslides of brick, sweeping people with them as they went. Bodies were mangled and ground to bits as an entire district collapsed into the marsh.

Frey heard Malvery start up on the autocannon, blasting away at a pirate fighter as it screamed overhead. He ignored it, steered away from the main conflict and angled the *Ketty Jay* towards the platform he wanted. The quality of architecture there was the highest in the town, and Frey was pleased to see it had suffered only superficial damage.

That was good, since he planned to land there.

'You sure you want to do this, Cap'n?' Jez asked doubtfully, peering through the windglass. Large sections of Retribution Falls had been wrecked. Plumes of smoke billowed from their ruins. 'There's no telling how long it'll be before someone shells the shit out of that platform, too.'

Frey was anything but sure. 'They're concentrating fire on the pirate frigates now,' he said, mostly to convince himself. 'The town itself isn't a threat.' Malvery cheered in triumph from the cupola. Frey assumed he'd made a hit.

'Your call, Cap'n,' she said. 'But we can get out of this now if we want to.'

'I hear you, Jez,' he said. But he was committed in his heart now. He couldn't turn back.

At least this time he'd consulted his crew. He'd outlined his plan and asked them if they wanted to be part of it. Nobody was being forced; nobody was being duped. He wasn't going to order anyone into this.

Some were reluctant. Some thought it would be better to cut their losses. They weren't keen on the risk. But in the end, all of them agreed. Because they trusted him. Because he was their captain.

Frey took the *Ketty Jay* closer to the platform. Jez leaned over his shoulder and pointed. 'There's the square.'

'Malvery!' he yelled. 'Get out of the cupola and get ready!'

Jez picked up her rifle from beneath the navigator's station as Frey brought the *Ketty Jay* down in the square. Those few people who were nearby went running as she came in to land, hard and heavy because Frey was too nervous to be careful. She bumped down with a jolt that made Jez stagger.

Frey sat there for a moment. Overhead, shells exploded and pirate fighters weaved through the sky. He should just take off again. He didn't have to do this. Maybe this was just history repeating, another all-or-nothing hand of Rake that might win him everything or lose it all, when he should have just laid down his cards and walked away with what he had.

You've got a craft, a crew, and the whole world to explore. Nobody's your master. Now that's not so bad, is it? If you're lucky, the Coalition will pardon you when all this is done. Drave may be a mean bastard but he doesn't seem like a liar. You'll be free.

Whether Drave would honour his word or not was a moot point. He wasn't sticking around to see. As soon as he'd done what he came here to do, he planned to run. The Navy would be tied up here for a while. Let them pardon him in his absence.

But first, there was the small matter of fifty thousand ducats. Fifty thousand ducats that had been promised him by the brass-eyed whispermonger Quail. Fifty thousand ducats that he felt he'd damn well earned by now.

This was their chance to be rich. To leave the rogue's life behind and allow themselves a bit of comfort. Equal shares for them all, because everyone had done their part.

He looked out of the cockpit at the barricade surrounding Orkmund's stronghold. The square they'd landed in lay right in front of it. A few days ago, they'd stood here to hear the great pirate speak. Somewhere inside that building was a red chest with a silver wolf clasp that he'd first seen being loaded onto the *Moment of Silence* when he visited Amalicia Thade at the Awakener hermitage.

The thought of Amalicia surprised him. From the moment he left the hermitage, he'd completely forgotten about her. To suddenly encounter her in his memory was a jolt, like rediscovering a discarded trinket that he thought was lost for ever.

'Are we going?' Jez asked.

'We're going,' said Frey. He got out of his chair and ran down the corridor to the steps that led to the cargo hold, where the rest of the crew were assembled, armed to the teeth.

In the few moments before the cargo ramp opened, he belatedly remembered that Gallian Thade had been killed at Mortengrace. That meant Amalicia was free from the hermitage where she'd been imprisoned. Free, and unbearably rich.

Damn it, I should have just married her when I had the chance, he thought.

Then he remembered that Trinica Dracken had also been the daughter of an enormously rich businessman, and he'd been only moments from making himself a part of that inheritance. He swore under his breath.

Damn it, I should have married her, *too!*

By the time they went rushing down the cargo ramp and out into Retribution Falls, Frey was quite eager to shoot someone.

Thirty-Seven

*Treasure Hunt – Harkins Gets
Into Trouble – Orkmund Again*

Pirates and whores ran in panic across the square, heads covered against the thundering concussions and the threat of falling rubble. Their aircraft had been destroyed on the landing pad, cutting off any hope of escape. Now they were helpless witnesses as the Navy pummelled the pirate frigates overhead and fighters wheeled and spat bullets. They fled for what shelter they could and hoped that fate would be merciful.

Frey led his crew down the cargo ramp, cutlass swinging against his leg, pistols raised. The stink of the marsh hit them as they came out into the open air and took up positions around the *Ketty Jay*. He'd been expecting some resistance from the locals, but he found himself pleasantly disappointed. The freebooters who were passing through the square couldn't have cared less why they were landing their craft here. As long as they weren't wearing Navy colours, they could do what they liked. The sight of Bess coming down the ramp deterred any thought of further enquiry.

Frey glanced at the Navy fleet, visible in the distance, a few kloms away. They were spreading out defensively as the pirate craft increased their assault. Half the pirate army's larger craft were destroyed, but the others were giving as good as they got. Frey saw a Navy frigate slip into a groaning descent, its flanks aflame.

As far as he was concerned, both sides could blow themselves to pieces. He had little love for either. As long as some Navy craft survived to tell the tale and exonerate him, that was fine.

'Alright, let's go!' he cried. Silo closed up the cargo ramp and they hurried towards their target with the Murthian covering their backs.

There was a barricade surrounding Orkmund's squat, grey stronghold. The watchtowers surmounting the mass of crossed girders and spikes were empty, but the gate was still closed. It was an enormous slab of metal on rollers, heavy enough to need three men to move it and presumably secured on the other side.

'Bess! Open that gate!' Frey called.

The golem stamped past him. She dug her massive fingers into the metal and wrenched. The gate shrieked in protest as a bolt on the inside resisted, but Bess's strength was inexorable, and it slowly gave way.

Frey could see one or two men who had stopped at the edge of the square and were staring. Clearly, they were puzzled to see several men who looked like pirates breaking in to the pirate captain's stronghold. Malvery raised his shotgun and sighted at one of them; Silo took aim at the other.

'Keep moving, lads. This doesn't concern you.'

They decided that it didn't concern them after all. There was a loud snap of metal and the gate rolled out of the way with a screech.

'Nice work, Bess,' said Frey. Crake patted her on the arm as they sallied inside.

Orkmund's stronghold wasn't large – certainly not the size of somewhere like Mortengrace – but it was secure. The grey, mould-streaked walls were thick, and the windows were small and deeply set. Too small to climb through.

Once inside the barricade they were faced with a squat, three-storey building with two projecting wings on either side, making a three-sided square. The entrance was set between the wings, at the far end of the square.

Frey led them to the nearest wall, at the tip of one of the wings. He pressed himself against it and looked around the corner. He was sweating with the tension. At any moment he expected to be shot at by an unseen foe or obliterated by a shell from above. But the stronghold was quiet, and the sounds of destruction had retreated temporarily into the distance.

'I don't see anyone, Cap'n,' Malvery said at his shoulder.

Frey didn't like the idea of rushing up to the entrance. There were too many windows facing inward on either side. Anyone up there with a gun could pick off attackers with ease.

'We'll make our own way in,' he said. He turned to Bess. Her eyes glimmered behind her face-grille. 'Can you get through this wall?'

Bess could.

There was a pirate standing in the doorway of the room on the other side. The sight of the hulking figure crashing through the wall in a cloud of dust and rubble scared him witless. As with anything that scared him, his first reaction was to shoot it. Bess pushed her way through the debris as bullets ricocheted from her armoured torso. She tore a chunk of stone from the wall and flung it at her attacker. It hit him in the forehead hard enough to take his head off. The remains of the pirate staggered a few steps before tipping over.

'Damn good shot!' Malvery exclaimed, climbing through the hole in the wall.

Frey climbed in after him. 'Our treasure's in this building somewhere,' he said. 'Let's get looking.'

Pinn yowled and whooped like an over-excited monkey as he dodged between swaying trails of tracer fire. The Skylance screamed happily along with him, obedient to his every command, banking and rolling through the chaos of a packed sky. Pinn was flying the fight of his life and the Skylance was in the best shape she'd ever been, with her tanks full of the finest prothane and aerium, courtesy of the Coalition Navy. Together, nothing could touch them.

It was almost too easy. The pirates never saw him coming. Their eyes were all on the Navy Windblades; they considered Pinn's Skylance as one of their own. The last thing they expected was a fellow pirate to turn against them. Those few seconds of confusion were usually all it took.

He glanced down at the ferrotype of Lisinda that swung on a chain from his dash, and grinned fiercely. 'You should see me now!' he cried. 'Sweetness, you should see me now!'

This was what his world might have been like, day after day, if only those Sammies hadn't pulled out of the Second Aerium War just as he was about to join in. This was living.

His machine guns rattled as he drew a line of puncture-marks across the flank of a pirate corvette. He darted away before anyone could see who had done it. The corvette – a medium-sized attack craft with two sets of wings and a fearsome battery of guns – was too busy dealing with Windblades to pay him any mind.

'*Pinn!*' Harkins squealed in his ear, at a pitch high enough to make him wince. 'Pinn, where are you? There's three of them on me!'

Pinn scanned the melee frantically, but he could find no sign of Harkins amid the swooping tangle of fighters that surrounded him. Belatedly he remembered that Frey had instructed them to look out for each other. The object was survival, not kill-count.

'I can't see you!'

'Pinn! Bloody help me!' Harkins yelled.

'I can't help you if I can't see you!' Pinn yelled back. Then, in a rare and remarkable moment, he had an idea. 'Climb up! Climb out of the pack! I'll find you up there!'

He pulled the Skylance into a steep climb, making his way free of the main mass of combat. The higher they got, the fewer aircraft would be in their way to complicate things.

'Pinn! They're right on my tail!'

'I'm coming, you noisy chickenshit! Hold on!'

He spotted the approach of tracers from his port side and rolled the Skylance a moment before a blast of machine-gun fire ripped past the belly of the craft. A quick glance told him that it had come from a Windblade.

'I'm on your side!' he yelled. He could feel a strange tiredness settling into his bones, and remembered the daemonic earpiece.

376

Every whoop and comment he made was sucking a little more energy out of him, and now he'd begun to notice it. He nearly cursed, but at the last moment remembered to keep his mouth shut.

The Windblade had realised its mistake, and was peeling away to search for fresh targets. Pinn craned around in his seat to look for Harkins, and spotted him a klom away, shooting skyward at an angle close to vertical. Three aircraft chased him, sending weaving lines of tracer fire ahead of them.

Pinn hit the throttle and the Skylance responded. He streaked across the dull sky, the battle beneath him and the mists above, his eyes fixed on the steadily ascending quartet of aircraft. Harkins was jinking and twisting as best he could, but the sheer volume of gunfire made it unlikely he could evade them long enough to make it to cover.

Pinn found himself in the grip of an unfamiliar sensation. He was worried. As much as he scorned Harkins, he didn't want to be without him. Harkins was just about the only person on the crew he could push around.

You better not get shot down, you stuttering old lunatic.

Smoke began to pour from the Firecrow's wing.

'I'm hit! I'm hit!' Harkins screeched.

Pinn thumbed his trigger and his machine guns clattered, tearing through the foremost of Harkins' pursuers. The aircraft exploded in mid-air, sending chunks of itself flying away. The others were too close to avoid the debris: a slab of wing, spinning end over end, whipped through the air and into the cockpit of another pirate, smashing him out of the sky. The third aircraft went into evasive manoeuvres immediately, searching for the author of the surprise attack, and then decided that the chase wasn't worth it and plunged back down towards the main mass of the fighting.

Pinn whooped and slapped the side of the cockpit, then scooped up the ferrotype of Lisinda and gave her a kiss. 'Harkins!' he called. 'How bad is it?'

Harkins levelled out and then banked experimentally. He looked wobbly, but the smoke had stopped.

'I . . . er . . . I lost one of my thrusters . . . had to shut it down. Not good, really, then.'

Pinn looked regretfully at the combat going on below them. 'We're done here. You're not gonna last another skirmish. Let's go help out the Cap'n.' He matched Harkins' turn and fell into position behind him.

'Hey, Pinn? Hey?'

'What?'

There was a pause. 'Um . . . thanks.'

Pinn smiled to himself. 'Didn't I tell you to clam it?' he said.

'Where's the treasure kept?' Malvery demanded. The pirate's reply was incoherent, mouthed as it was around the barrel of a shotgun.

'Take the gun out?' Crake suggested.

Malvery withdrew the shotgun a little way. The pirate – still shocked at being collared by the bulky doctor – bent over and gagged. By the time he'd recovered, there was sullen defiance in his glare.

'The treasure. Where?' Malvery demanded again.

The pirate suggested some anatomically improbable places where Malvery could shove his mother. Malvery broke his nose with the butt of the shotgun, then looked around at his companions and shrugged. 'That's me out of ideas,' he said.

Silo and Jez were covering either end of the corridor. The stronghold was mostly deserted – the pirates had evidently fled – but Frey was taking no chances. The pounding of the guns outside seemed worryingly close now, echoing through the empty spaces, bouncing off the unadorned walls. Dust shook from the ceiling, bringing new cracks.

'We haven't got time for this,' he muttered. He seized the pirate, who was holding his bloodied nose, and pointed at Crake.

'This is my friend Grayther Crake. He's got quite a remarkable smile. Why don't you show him, Crake?'

Crake grinned. The pirate stared at him for a moment. His gore-streaked hands came away from his face, the pain of his nose forgotten, and he craned forward in admiration.

'Here,' he said. 'That's a nice tooth.'

Half a minute later, they were on their way, newly furnished with directions. Malvery had insisted on clubbing the pirate once more for that crack about his mother, but afterwards they let him go, minus his pistols and several molars.

They hurried through the corridors, keyed up to face resistance at any moment, but they found few people to stand against them. One man ignored them completely, presumably running for the exit. Another took a pot-shot at Bess and was gunned down for his trouble.

A particularly heavy concussion shook the building and sent plate-sized flakes of plaster raining from the ceiling. Frey stumbled to his knees, and Silo caught his arm as he fell. As he was helped to his feet, he met the Murthian's eyes. Both of them were thinking the same thing. They should get out of here now, while they still had the *Ketty Jay* and their lives.

Just this last thing, Frey told himself, shakily. *Our luck'll hold.*

Silo saw the resolve in Frey's gaze and gave him the tiniest of nods, then reached out one long-fingered hand and squeezed his shoulder in reassurance.

Frey found himself suddenly grateful for the constant presence of the engineer in his life. Though Frey rarely even noticed him, he was always there, a silent strength, working invisibly behind the scenes to keep the *Ketty Jay* running. Frey realised how important Silo had been to him all these years, a friend who asked for nothing but who would offer unquestioning support whenever it was needed. Silo had saved his life after the ambush in Sammie territory, and been with him through all the bitterness that followed. Frey had never wanted a confidante; he wanted someone who he felt would never betray him, no matter what. That was Silo.

Driven by an absurd and overwhelming urge, he hugged his engineer. Silo stiffened in surprise.

379

'Rot and damnation, Cap'n, this isn't exactly the time!' Malvery cried.

Frey withdrew, his face colouring. 'Right,' he said. 'You're right.'

A few more turns brought them to the vault. It was exactly where the pirate had told them it would be. Unfortunately, it was where most of his friends were, too.

The vault door was standing open as they arrived, and a dozen pirates were busy carrying out chests full of treasure. Orkmund himself was there too, directing his men. He was more physically imposing in person than he'd been from a distance: muscular and tattooed, with a bald head and a boxer's face.

Frey had wanted to get the drop on them, but with Bess in tow it was impossible. By the time they'd rounded the corner, the men were alerted. Only the puzzling nature of the metallic clanks and leathery creaks had stopped them pulling out their guns. But now the golem stepped into sight, with Frey and his crew behind her. Some of the men went white and backed away, dropping their end of the chests. Others let their burden fall and drew guns. But Frey's crew had their guns out already, and at the first sign of violence they started shooting.

The first volley cut down half of Orkmund's men, most of them with their revolvers still half out of their holsters. The crew of the *Ketty Jay* ducked around the corner as the answering fire came, but it was mostly directed at Bess, who went stamping up the corridor, roaring as she did so. Those who hadn't been killed in the initial volley stumbled backwards in the face of the metal giant, tripping over the chests, and scrambled to their feet to flee. Frey could hear Orkmund shouting something incoherent at them, urging them to stand and fight; but then there was a terrific explosion from above, and the calamitous sound of falling stone.

Dust billowed out of the corridor and engulfed his crew where they hid. Frey coughed into his fist and looked around the corner. It took some seconds for the dust to clear, but when it did he saw Bess standing there, dirty but unharmed. A section of the ceiling had caved in, burying all but one of the chests. Of Orkmund and his men, there was nothing to be seen. They'd either fled or been buried. Frey didn't care which.

What he did care about was the red-lacquered chest that lay near Bess's feet. A chest with a beautiful branch-and-leaf intaglio on the lid and a clasp in the shape of a silver wolf's head. He ran to it and tugged at the lid. Locked. Stepping back, he blasted the clasp away with his revolver.

There would be no mistakes. He had to be sure.

The others had gathered around him as he knelt down and threw open the chest. Inside was a golden mass of ducats. Thousands upon thousands of coins. Even in the dust-hazed air, it seemed to him that they glimmered.

Bess leaned in over his shoulder to look. She cooed as she saw the wealth within.

Frey could hardly breathe. He had it at last. *They* had it at last. After all the years of scrabbling in the dirt, they were rich.

He stepped back, and looked at the joyous faces of his crew, transfixed by the sight of more money than they'd ever dreamed of.

'Bess, pick that up,' he said. 'We're getting out of here.'

Thirty-Eight

Shells – The Duel –
Malvery's Hour – Out Of The Mist

Frey didn't hear the explosion.

It took some seconds for his stunned senses to recover, but even then, all he could remember was the sensation of being squashed from above by an enormous force, like an insect trodden on by an invisible boot. After that, there was the taste of grit in his mouth, the stinging in his eyes, and the high-pitched whine in his ears, like the squeal of a turbine.

He looked around. Everything was muffled and clouded. The air was grey with pulverised stone. He was on his hands and knees. Ahead of him, what had once been a corridor was now a wall of broken stone.

A shell, he thought, numbly. Orkmund's stronghold must have taken a direct hit.

Suddenly he was being pulled to his feet. He looked up dazedly to see Silo holding his arm. The Murthian was saying something, but he couldn't hear. Silo stood him up and spoke with exaggerated volume and clarity, but to Frey it still sounded like it came from a great distance through the cottony pressure in his ears.

'Cap'n? You hear me?'

'A little bit,' he replied. His voice sounded strange in his own head.

'You hurt?'

Frey checked he had all his arms and legs. 'Don't think so.'

There was a faint yell. Silo looked towards the rubble that had filled the corridor. Frey followed his gaze.

'Hey!' It was Malvery. Had it not been, Frey probably wouldn't have heard him, but the doctor's bellow could wake the dead.

'Doc!' Frey cried. 'You okay?'

'Cap'n! We're fine over here. Cuts and bruises. Silo with you?'

'He's okay.'

'Okay!'

The conversation faltered. The dust was settling, and now Frey could see the section of ceiling and wall which had collapsed into the corridor. Frey and Silo had been lagging behind, guarding the rear of the retreating group. Frey stared at the tons of rubble in front of him, and thought how lucky they were that nobody had been beneath it.

'Wait there!' cried Malvery. Frey glimpsed him momentarily through a gap in the rubble. 'We're going to get Bess to dig through to you!'

Silo grabbed Frey's shoulder and shook his head. He pointed up at the ceiling. 'Ain't a good plan, Cap'n.'

Frey caught on. 'Silo says no!' he cried. 'The roof could come down on you.'

Malvery considered that for a moment. 'I expect that'd hurt quite a bit,' he said.

'Go on to the *Ketty Jay*. We'll find another way round.'

'You sure?'

'You've got the treasure with you?'

'Safe and sound.'

'Get it on board. We'll get there as fast as we can.'

'Right-o.'

'And Malvery? If they start shelling us again, you tell Jez to get her airborne and get you out of there.'

'Without you, Cap'n?'

'Yeah.'

'I'd rather choke on my own shit,' Malvery replied cheerily. 'See you on board.'

Frey shook his head to clear it of the ringing. It was about as effective as he'd expected. At least his hearing was getting less muffled with time.

He picked up his revolver from the ground where it had fallen, and thumbed in the direction they'd come. 'That way, I suppose.'

They hurried back down the corridor and through a doorway, into a crude kitchen. They could see an exterior window, but even though it had been smashed by the explosion it was too small to get through. Frey led the way into a simple eating-hall with benches and a fireplace. He stayed close to the exterior wall, hoping for a door, but room after room confounded him. Eventually, they came out into another corridor, like the one they had left.

'Damn it, how hard can it be to get out of a building?' he complained, and that was when they ran into Orkmund.

He must have heard them an instant before they came around the corner, and that small warning meant he was faster than they were. He was emerging from a doorway as they came into sight, carrying a small jewellery box in his arms. Frey and Silo skidded to a halt as Orkmund dropped the box and pulled a revolver. By the time their own guns were halfway raised, Orkmund already had his levelled.

'Drop 'em!' he cried, and they froze.

Frey thought desperately, but he couldn't force an idea through the fog in his head. This wasn't a war: there was no question of taking prisoners. If they dropped their guns, he'd shoot them. If they drew, he'd shoot them.

'Drop 'em!' Orkmund shouted again, allowing no time for deliberation.

Frey looked at Silo. Silo looked back at him. And in that moment, Frey realised what the Murthian was thinking.

He could only shoot *one* of them. And Silo had decided it was going to be him.

'Don't—' Frey began, but it was too late. Silo moved, raising his revolver to fire. Orkmund reacted, shifting his aim to Silo. Frey followed Silo's lead, an instant behind him: but Orkmund had already committed to his target.

Three shots fired, almost simultaneously. Orkmund fired first, and his bullet took Silo in the chest. Silo's own shot went wild.

Frey's, hastily aimed, clipped the side of Orkmund's revolver and sent it spinning away with a spark and a metallic whine.

Silo fell to the ground. Orkmund hesitated, surprised to find that his gun was no longer in his hand. Frey aimed square at his head and pulled the trigger.

The hammer fell on an empty chamber. He was out of bullets.

Orkmund lunged at him, drawing a cutlass from his belt. Frey threw his revolver down as his own cutlass leaped from its scabbard, flying into his hand, the blade moving of its own accord. The two cutlasses met hard with a ringing chime. Orkmund swung again, pressing the attack, slicing at his ribs and then his thigh. The daemon-thralled blade parried both, blurringly fast, moving with a speed far beyond anything Frey would have been capable of alone. Orkmund was an expert swordsman; Frey had an expert sword.

There was no time to think of Silo. The necessity of survival wouldn't permit it. All he saw was Orkmund's blunt face, twisted in fury, the blades darting between them. He backed away under a flurry of blows, knocking away the pirate's strikes. The cutlass in his hand was doing its work with little help from him, but it could barely manage to keep up with Orkmund's attacks. There was a sharp bite of pain in his shoulder as Orkmund nicked him; a moment later, it was followed by one on his forearm.

The pain set loose the rage. In the corner of his eye, he could see Silo lying motionless on the ground. Possessed by a sudden recklessness, he pushed forward, switching from defence to attack. His cutlass sensed the change, moving with renewed vigour. It felt eager in his grip. Adding his strength to the blade's forced Orkmund to retreat. Suddenly Frey was the one hacking and thrusting while his opponent blocked and parried.

Then, an all-consuming roar, bone-shakingly low. The corridor shook as a tremor ran through it from a nearby shell. Orkmund stumbled back, Frey overreached and lost his balance; but it was Frey who went tumbling to the floor and Orkmund that kept his feet. Frey rolled onto his back, parried aside a downward thrust aimed at his heart, and kicked the pirate's legs away. Orkmund went down, and suddenly they were on equal terms again. They rolled apart and sprang to their feet, panting, facing each other.

There was surprise and a little amazement in Orkmund's eyes. 'You can *fight*!' he exclaimed.

'Yeah,' said Frey, hatefully. 'I can fight.'

He lunged forward again. He was taken by a loathing for this man, a need to eradicate him from existence. The very sight of him was unbearable: the broken planes of his nose, the pattern of tattoos over his neck, skull and arms. This man had pulled the trigger that sent the bullet into Silo's chest. Maybe the quiet Murthian was already dead. Maybe he was even now gasping his last. The one thing worse than the fact that Orkmund had shot him was the fact that he was now preventing Frey from doing anything about it. Every minute was a minute his friend could be bleeding out. Every minute could be the one that ended him.

Silo had taken a bullet for him. He was damned if he'd have that man's death on his conscience for the rest of his life.

Had it not been for the cutlass Crake had given him, the wildness of his attack would have seen him dead at the hands of a swordsman like Orkmund. But with the blade guiding itself, and his murderous strength behind it, he became formidable. Orkmund parried and blocked, but Frey's blows were so vicious that he could barely hold on to his weapon. Steel rang again and again, punctuating the distant explosions.

Then Frey's hands were wrenched back, and his cutlass withdrew of its own volition, in preparation for a mighty strike. Frey panicked, struggling against the wishes of his own blade: he'd been left wide open. Orkmund, seeing the advantage, thrust inside Frey's guard to skewer him. But then Frey's cutlass twisted impossibly, almost breaking his wrist as it did so, and Frey felt the blade cut through meat and bone.

Orkmund's cutlass clattered noisily to the floor. The pirate captain staggered back a step, dazed, gazing at the severed stump of his forearm. Blood fountained with the pulse of his heart. White-faced, he stared at Frey in disbelief.

Frey gritted his teeth and ran him through.

The square in front of Orkmund's stronghold had become a battleground. Shells pounded the grey sky and gunfire cracked and snapped all around. A lumbering pirate frigate was cruising slowly overhead, terrifyingly low and close, its cannons bellowing as it fired at distant Navy frigates. The return barrage exploded deafeningly above the square. Stray artillery ploughed into the town itself, demolishing whatever it hit. A row of buildings along one side of the square had dissolved into rubble and slumped inward after one such misplaced shell.

In the centre of the square sat the *Ketty Jay*. Its cargo ramp was open and guarded by Bess. Its crew had taken cover inside the mouth of the hold or behind the hydraulic struts, firing on anyone who came close. Pinn and Harkins hovered in support, laying down machine-gun fire from their fighter craft, staying just high enough to avoid potshots from below.

An increasingly desperate group of pirates were shooting from the cover of the rubble. The square was scattered with the bodies of those who had already tried to rush the craft, seeing the *Ketty Jay* as their only hope of escaping the cataclysm around them.

Frey hurried through the gates of Orkmund's stronghold with Silo on his back, heedless of the gunfire criss-crossing the air. The ground shook beneath his feet; there was a vast groan of metal from deep below. It felt like the platform they were on might collapse at any moment. He ran low and hunched over in an attempt to keep the Murthian from sliding off. Jez called out at the sight of him and the crew redoubled their fire, keeping the pirates' heads down as their captain came closer.

Frey was exhausted, running on adrenaline alone. The constant noise of the explosions, the effort of carrying almost ninety kilos of dead weight on his back, and the emotional shock of the past few minutes had put him into a shallow trance. He hardly noticed when a shell obliterated one of the buildings nearby, spraying him with stone chips and pushing him sideways with the force. He staggered, corrected himself, and ran doggedly onward.

Bullets whined past. He didn't know if they were meant for him. All he wanted was to get to the *Ketty Jay*.

He stumbled onto the ramp and was met by helping hands from Malvery and Jez, propelling him up into the dim safety of the hold. Bess stepped back onto the ramp, surveying the square threateningly, and Crake pulled the lever to raise it. The pirates screamed with frustration as they saw their chance of escape narrowing, but none of them dared to take on the golem.

All Frey wanted to do was lie down and sleep, but he didn't have that luxury. He hardened his resolve. This wasn't over yet.

He let Malvery take Silo from his back. Warm blood had soaked into his coat where the Murthian lay against him. They laid him on the floor of the hold while the doctor looked at his wound. Malvery's face was pale and fearful.

'Fix him,' Frey told Malvery.

'He's losing too much blood,' Malvery said.

'Fix him, damn you!' Frey snarled. Then he headed for the stairs that led out of the hold. He went up to the passageway that ran along the spine of the *Ketty Jay*, then through the doorway into the cockpit, where he flung himself into the pilot's seat and punched in the ignition code. Jez was moments behind him, dropping into her spot at the navigator's station as Frey flooded the aerium tanks to maximum.

Another explosion rocked the *Ketty Jay* as she began to lift her weight off her landing struts. Frey flinched and ducked as a bullet hit the windglass panel in front of his face, leaving a small circular shatter-mark. The pirate frigate loomed above them and to starboard, shells bursting in the air all around it in a pummelling cascade of light and sound. Its keel suddenly came open, unbuttoned in a sequence of detonations that raced along its flank from stern to bow. Frey willed his craft to lift as the frigate tipped sideways towards them with a moan like the death-cry of some enormous metal beast.

'Come on, come on!' he murmured under his breath, as the *Ketty Jay* hauled her bulk into the air and began to ascend. Jez was staring in horror at the black, flaming mass of the frigate as it grew in their vision, threatening to crush them on its way down. The *Skylance* and *Firecrow* shot past him on either side and streaked away; they couldn't help him now, and they had their own safety to consider. Screams from the square could be faintly heard over the concussion of artillery and the sound of the *Ketty Jay*'s engines. The men and women of Retribution Falls had seen their fate descending on them.

The *Ketty Jay* had barely cleared the tops of the nearest buildings before Frey kicked the throttle to maximum and the prothane thrusters opened up with a roar. He was thrown back in his seat as they accelerated, their landing struts scraping the roof of an inn, tearing off slates as they powered out of the shadow of the frigate. Frey gritted his teeth as the colossal craft bore down on them from above.

The deck of the frigate plummeted past their stern with a bellow of displaced air, raging with smoke and flame, and collapsed into the square with the force of a landslide. The *Ketty Jay* carried Frey and his crew away as Orkmund's stronghold was obliterated, and the great scaffolded platform cracked in half.

For once, Frey was glad that he couldn't see behind his craft. The appalling destruction in their wake was left to his imagination. A stab of grief surprised him – not for the dead, but for Silo, whom he'd dumped into Malvery's care as if he was luggage. He forced himself to be cold. He had a responsibility to the others. Time to wallow in remorse after he'd got them safe.

He vented aerium to curb the *Ketty Jay*'s excessive lift and took her around the rim of the sinkhole, skirting the Navy fleet and avoiding the worst of the fighting. Pinn and Harkins fell into position behind him. To starboard, he had a view of the whole battle. Retribution Falls was a ruin, a half-submerged junkyard. The stern ends of broken pirate craft jutted out of the brackish, rancid water, leaking flaming slicks of fuel. Smoke choked the scene. From within came rapid flashes of guns and the sound of explosions.

The Navy had blocked off one route into Retribution Falls, but there were evidently other ways out, and the pirates took them. The defence of the town had been abandoned and the pirates were retreating, melting into the mist overhead, vanishing into gullies and canyons. The Navy had taken losses, but the surprise attack had kept them light.

Frey flew the *Ketty Jay* behind the Navy fleet, who were still looking in towards the town and not out towards the rim. If anyone noticed the three insignificant aircraft sneaking past, then perhaps they recognised them for who they were and held their fire. In any case, the *Ketty Jay* passed unmolested into the canyon that led out of the sinkhole and away from the battle. The rocky slopes of the Hookhollows closed around them, blocking out the sight of Retribution Falls. Soon they'd left the pirate town behind, and all was quiet again.

Malvery and Crake carried Silo into the tiny infirmary and laid him on the surgical table. The Murthian was unconscious, his breathing shallow and rapid. His eyes moved restlessly behind their lids. The air smelled of oil and blood, and the floor moved with the tilting of the *Ketty Jay* as she flew.

Crake's hands were covered in gore. He felt somehow that he should have been sickened by that, but he was too intent on the moment to allow himself weakness. He remembered the Silo that had helped him patch up Bess after the gunfight at Rabban, the one who had talked and joked with him on that grassy hillside. They were no longer strangers to each other. Crake would do whatever he had to.

Malvery ripped open Silo's shirt, exposing the wound. A ragged hole had been punched through one slab-like pectoral. Rich blood welled out of it in awful quantity. He swore under his breath.

'He's bleeding inside,' said Malvery. 'I can't do anything.'

'You've got to!' Crake protested. 'Open him up. Stop the bleeding!'

'I can't,' Malvery said. He adjusted his round green glasses and tugged anxiously at the end of his white moustache. 'I just can't.'

He opened a drawer and pulled out a bottle of medicinal alcohol. He'd unstoppered it and brought it to his lips before

Crake snatched it from him and slammed it angrily down on the operating table.

'You're the only one who can do this, Malvery!' he snapped. 'Forget what happened to your friend. You're a surgeon! Do your damn job!'

'I'm not a surgeon any more,' Malvery replied, staring at the man on the operating table in front of him. Blood pumped up from the bullet wound and spilled down Silo's chest in grotesque washes of red. Crake clapped his hands ineffectually over the wound, then began looking around for something better to staunch the flow.

He understood Malvery's pain, but he'd no time for sympathy while Silo lay dying. If only Crake had been a better daemonist, he might have used the Art to heal the Murthian. But he didn't have the equipment, so he couldn't do anything. Silo's only chance was Malvery, and the doctor was paralysed.

'Spit and blood, you're just going to stand by and watch?' Crake cried.

'What do you want from me?' Malvery bellowed. 'A miracle? He's dying! I can't stop that!'

'You can try!' Crake shouted back with equal ferocity. Malvery was shocked at the force in Crake's usually quiet tone. 'This isn't like the last time. He's going to die anyway. Nobody will blame you if you fail, I'll make sure of that. But I wouldn't want to be in your shoes when the captain finds out you didn't even *try*.'

Just then, the *Ketty Jay* yawed to port, making him stumble; he had to put out a hand on the operating table to steady himself. The bottle of alcohol tipped from the table, but Crake caught it before it fell. Malvery's eyes went to it.

'Give me the bottle,' he said.

Crake just glared at him.

'I'll need a swig to steady my hand!' Malvery insisted.

'Your hand's plenty steady, Doc. Do it. Earn your place.'

'*Me?*' Malvery roared. 'You've been barely four months aboard, you arrogant shit!'

'Yes. And I saved you all at Tarlock Cove. Bess saved you from

Kedmund Drave. I uncovered Grephen's plans at Scorchwood Heights, and we'd never have taken the charts from Dracken without Bess. We've done our part. Pinn and Harkins fly, Jez navigates, Silo keeps the craft running. What do *you* do that one of us couldn't? Fire a shotgun? Work the autocannon occasionally? You're a surgeon who doesn't operate, Malvery! You're dead weight!'

Malvery's face twisted in anger. He lunged across the table to grab him, but Crake was too fast, and pulled himself out of the way.

'Then prove me wrong!' he cried. 'Cut him open! Stop the bleeding and save his life!'

Malvery's huge fists bunched and unbunched. His face was red with rage. For a moment, Crake though he really would attack; but then he turned away, and stamped over to the wooden cabinet that was fixed to the wall. He pulled it open and drew out a scalpel. The surgical instruments were the only clean things in the grimy room. Malvery came back to the table and stared at Crake.

'I'll cut him, damn it,' he snarled. 'And you're staying to help.'

Crake rolled up his sleeves. 'Tell me what to do.'

Frey sat in the pilot's seat, staring out at the fog. His air filter still hung round his neck, though more than an hour had passed since they crossed the lava river and its noxious fumes. Jez read out directions and co-ordinates from the navigator's station behind him, and he followed them automatically. Once in a while she consulted the compass and warned of some distant mine that the Navy minesweepers had failed to catch, but it was always too far away to be a threat.

Frey barely paid attention to the job at hand. This was the fourth time he'd flown along this route, and it had lost its fear for him now. He trusted Jez. Harkins and Pinn were following his lights through the murk. As for the Navy, they could find their own way out.

He was thinking of Silo. The black spectre of loss hovered over him. It wasn't only the thought that Silo himself might die – Frey had already been surprised by the depth of feeling he had for the taciturn foreigner – but the idea that one of his crew would be lost. With each new peril they survived, he'd thought of them more and more as one indivisible whole. Whereas he'd often dreamed in the past of ditching his crew and flying off alone, now he couldn't stand the thought of it. They'd become a miniature society, the denizens of the *Ketty Jay*, and they needed one another to survive. Somehow they'd achieved a balance that satisfied them all, and when they were in balance they'd been able to achieve extraordinary things. Frey feared losing any of them now, in case that balance would be upset. He feared a return to the way things were.

All this time he'd armoured himself against loss by refusing to care for anyone. Now, somehow, he'd been blindsided. He tried to be angry for allowing himself to become so vulnerable, but he couldn't muster the feeling. It had all been part of a greater change, one that had seen him gain a level of self-respect he'd never had before the destruction of the *Ace of Skulls*. He wouldn't trade the days between that moment and this. Not for anything.

But now Silo lay on the edge of death, left in the hands of an alcoholic doctor and an untrained assistant. Silo, who had taken a bullet so Frey wouldn't have to. Frey didn't want to live with that responsibility.

What's taking them so long? Aren't they done yet?

As if in response, he heard the infirmary door slide open. He hunched his shoulders as if expecting a blow. Footsteps came up the passageway, boots rapping on metal. They were too light to be Malvery, so it had to be Crake. Frey turned in his seat to be sure, and saw the daemonist arrive in the doorway. His hands were gloved with blood, and he was still wearing his filter mask. He pointed to it and said something quizzical which nobody understood.

'You can take it off now,' Jez said, guessing his meaning.

Crake pulled off the mask and took a few deep breaths. 'That's better,' he said. 'Those things are so stuffy.'

'Mmm,' said Jez in mild agreement.

'Everything alright?' Crake enquired.

'Will you bloody well tell me what's going on back there?!' Frey exploded, unable to bear the tension any more.

'Oh, yes,' said Crake. He grinned. 'The doc stopped the bleeding and got the bullet out. He says the patient is going to be alright.'

Jez gasped and gave a little clap, a surprisingly girlish reaction from someone Frey had come to think of as rather unfeminine. Frey slumped back into his seat with a sigh, and a huge sense of relaxation spread through his body. Exhaustion and relief piled in together. At last, it was over. A broad smile spread across his face. Crake laughed and slapped him on the shoulder, leaving a grotesque handprint there.

'Good work, boys,' Frey said. 'Bloody good work.'

'Well, I've got to go and help Malvery finish up,' said Crake. 'Just thought I'd let you know.' He disappeared down the passageway again and into the infirmary.

'We're here, Cap'n,' said Jez. 'All stop. You can start ascending now.'

Frey brought the *Ketty Jay* to a halt and set her rising through the fog. The haze gradually thinned and the darkness brightened by degrees. The flanks of the mountains became discernible again as forbidding slabs of shadow.

Frey looked up. A smile was still on his lips. Up there was light and freedom. Up there was the prospect of a new life, a luxurious life, one financed with the chest full of Awakener gold they'd stolen from Orkmund. Up there was a second chance for all of them.

'Never seen you smiling like that, Cap'n,' Jez said.

'It's just, for once, I really feel that everything's going to be okay.'

Then they broke free of the mist, and a shattering explosion hammered the *Ketty Jay*, filling the cockpit with dazzling light, shaking them about like rag dolls.

When no further explosion came, Frey blinked away the shock and pulled himself back into his seat.

A swarm of Norbury Equalisers surrounded them. Looming ahead of them, with all of its considerable arsenal trained on the *Ketty Jay*, was the *Delirium Trigger*.

Frey blew out his cheeks and huffed a sigh of resignation. 'Bollocks!'

Thirty-Nine

'This Is Where Mercy Gets You' –
Dracken's Choice – Conclusions

A cold wind chased puffs of grey ash across the Blackendraft plains. Frey's coat flapped restlessly. Bleak horizons encircled them. Overhead, the sky was the colour of an anvil. The *Delirium Trigger* hung at anchor a short distance away, its hard, cruel lines stark against the emptiness.

The crew of the *Ketty Jay* stood in a row at the bottom of the cargo ramp. Pinn and Harkins had grounded their craft and been rounded up. Silo, Bess and Slag were missing. Silo was still in the infirmary. Crake had put Bess to sleep to prevent her going berserk and getting them all killed. Slag had vanished into the vents and airways, on some mysterious errand of his own. Nothing would ever separate him from his aircraft.

Facing them was Trinica Dracken and a dozen men from the *Delirium Trigger*. The men covered Frey and his crew with their pistols while Trinica looked down into the red-lacquered chest that sat at her feet. She stared at the wealth within for a long time, but her ghost-white face and unnatural black eyes revealed nothing of what she was thinking. Finally, she looked up.

'You did well, Darian,' she said. 'Kind of you to carry this all the way from Orkmund's stronghold, just for me.'

Pinn muttered something unsavoury under his breath. Malvery clipped him round the ear.

'I should have killed you when I had the chance,' said Frey. There was no rancour in it; it was simply an observation. 'I suppose this is where mercy gets you.'

Trinica gave him a dry smile. 'Consider this the price of a lesson well learned.'

Frey and Trinica gazed at each other across the dusty gap that separated them. The huge silence of the Blackendraft filled the moment.

He couldn't feel hate for her. He couldn't manage to feel much more than a distant disappointment. This felt right, somehow. It had been greed that made him jump at Quail's too-good-to-be-true offer. And while he didn't blame himself for the many deaths aboard the *Ace of Skulls* – they were doomed with or without him – he'd played a part in it. He might have saved the Archduke and done a great service to his country, but he did it by initiating a massacre at Retribution Falls. It didn't seem fair that he should profit from his own stupidity, at the expense of all those lives.

Maybe he owed the world something. For the crew he'd taken into Samarla and left to die. For every Trinica Dracken and Amalicia Thade whom he'd discarded and forgotten as soon as they showed signs of wanting more than he was prepared to give.

For his baby, that died for its parents' cowardice.

He'd condemned them all when he agreed to take on the *Ace of Skulls*. But since then, he'd clawed back all he'd lost, and more besides. He'd forged a crew, and he'd reclaimed himself. Perhaps that was all that was needed, in the end.

'What happens now, Trinica?' he asked her.

'I expect Grephen will hang,' she said. 'The Awakeners . . . well, they're too powerful to be brought down, even by this. But I think the Archduke will redouble his efforts to cripple them from now on.'

'I mean, what happens to us?'

Trinica gave him a bewildered look. 'How would I know? I expect you'll get your pardons, even if you're not there to collect them.'

'You're letting us go?'

'Of course I am,' she said. 'Everyone who put a bounty on your head has either withdrawn it or is in no position to pay any more. Why would I want you?'

His crew visibly relaxed. Frey brushed away a lock of hair that was blowing across his forehead.

'And you?' he asked.

'I'll be heading off somewhere,' she replied, nonchalant. 'I suppose I'll have to keep out of the Navy's way from now on, but I'll survive.'

She motioned to her bosun, who filled a leather bag with coins from the chest. He tied it with a thin piece of rope and gave it to her. It was almost too big to hold in one hand. She weighed it thoughtfully, then hefted it towards Frey, who barely caught it.

'Finder's fee,' she said. 'That, and you can keep your craft.'

'That's uncommonly merciful of you, Trinica.'

She smiled, and this time it wasn't the chilly, guarded smile he'd come to know. It was the smile of the old Trinica, from a time before her world had become full of horrors, and it flooded him with a bittersweet warmth.

'I'm feeling sentimental,' she said. 'Goodbye, Captain.'

She turned her back on them then, and walked towards the shuttle that sat a short way distant. Her men closed the chest and gathered it up. Frey and his crew watched as they disappeared inside the craft, and it lifted off from the ground, taking them back to the *Delirium Trigger*.

'Well,' said Malvery, squinting against the dust as he watched them dwindle into the distance. 'That's just about our luck.'

'Cheer up!' said Frey. 'We've got three aircraft, enough ducats to keep us in the sky for a year, and the world at our feet. I'd say we're the luckiest crew in Vardia right now.'

'I'd feel a damn sight luckier if that witch hadn't buggered off with our loot,' Malvery griped.

Frey slapped him on the shoulder. 'Look on the bright side. She might have killed us.'

'There is that,' Malvery conceded.

'Is . . . um . . . I was wondering, is anyone else hungry?' Harkins enquired.

'We should probably take Silo to a hospital,' Jez suggested. 'Get him a good bed and some nurses.'

Frey looked at Malvery. 'How long before Silo's capable of getting back to work? In your expert opinion?'

'Three weeks, I'd say,' Malvery said. 'Maybe four.'

Frey scratched the back of his neck. 'Well, what with all we've been through we probably deserve a little port time.'

Pinn's eyes lit up at the prospect of booze and whores. Frey held up the bag of coins. 'Drinks are on me tonight!'

There was a cheer from the men.

'Jez!' he barked.

'Cap'n!'

'Find us a nice, out-of-the-way port with a good hospital, lively nightlife and a place where a man can find a game of Rake.'

'Skinner's Gorge?'

'Skinner's Gorge sounds good to me.'

There was another cheer, and they slapped each other's backs and shook hands in wild and vague congratulations. The chest full of ducats was forgotten already. They had all they needed. They were glad just to be alive.

Frey couldn't keep down a grin. As he looked at the laughing faces of his crew, he was consumed by a surge of affection for these people, these men and women who shared his aircraft and his life. They were happy, and free, and the endless sky awaited them.

It was enough.

How to Play Rake

HISTORY

Rake is a variant of poker, in which the player must make the best
five-card hand to win. The game has existed for centuries, since
before the fall of the monarchy: the first recorded mention was as
far back as 87/29 (UY3069). For most of that time it was confined
to the peasantry, and was viewed as a rather vulgar pastime by the
rich. It was popularised in Vardia during the First Aerium War,
when the mingling of conscripted troops allowed the game to
spread. Soon, even the aristocrats who commanded them had
caught on, and Rake passed from the taverns and dens into the
drawing-rooms of the wealthy. Since then it has become the most
popular card game in Vardia.

THE DECK

Rake is played with a standard 52-card Vardic deck, comprising 13
cards of each of the four suits: Skulls, Wings, Fangs and Crosses.
Each suit comprises (in order of value) the numbers 2–10, followed
by the face cards: Priest, Lady, Duke, Ace. The Ace, the highest
card, also functions as the number 1 for the purpose of runs.

SCORING

The object of a hand of Rake is to achieve to best possible combination of five cards. These combinations are scored below, in order of
rank. Two pair beats three-of-a-kind, Suits Full beats a run, etc.

High Card

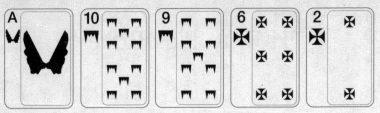

In this case, with no combination possible, only the highest card in the hand is counted. Therefore, a player whose highest card is an Ace beats one whose highest card is only a Priest.

Pair

Two cards of the same value. In the above example, the player has two tens. A higher pair, such as Ladies, will beat him. The remaining cards are disregarded, unless two players have identical pairs, in which case the one with the highest value remaining card wins.

Two Pair

Two pairs of the same value. If two players should have two pair, then the player with the highest pair wins. If both players have the same high pair, the player with the next highest pair wins. In the unlikely event that both have the same two pairs, the remaining card comes into play: again, the player with the highest card wins.

400

Three-of-a-kind

Three cards of the same value. If two or more players have three-of-a-kind, the highest triplet wins. The above hand would be referred to as Three Dukes.

Run

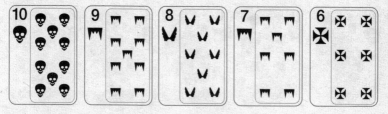

Five cards of sequential value, but different suits. An Ace in this case can count as either a one or an Ace. If two or more players have a Run, the one incorporating the highest card wins.

Suits Full

Five cards of the same suit. They are referred to as Wings Full, Crosses Full and so on. As in a Run, in the case of two players holding Suits Full, the one whose hand incorporates the highest card wins. If it is the same, they go to the next highest, etc, until the hand is resolved.

Full Pack

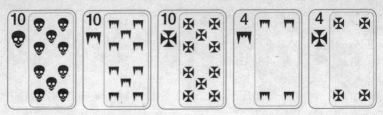

A Full Pack is three-of-a-kind of one value and a pair of another. In the case of two players holding it, the higher value three-of-a-kind wins.

Quads

Four cards of the same value. The last card is disregarded. The above hand would be referred to as Four Ladies, or Quad Ladies.

Rake

Five cards of the same suit in sequential order. This is the highest scoring hand in Rake. If two people should have it, the one incorporating the highest card wins.

The Ace of Skulls

The Ace of Skulls is the most dangerous card in the game of Rake, both for the player who holds it and their opponents. A player who holds the Ace of Skulls must incorporate that card into a scoring hand of three-of-a-kind or higher, or they will automatically lose the hand. The Ace of Skulls must be part of the scoring combination (eg, one of the three cards that forms the three-of-a-kind) – it cannot be a redundant card in the hand, or the player loses. Similarly, if the player cannot manage better than High Card, Pair, or Two Pair – whether the Ace of Skulls is involved or not – the player loses. However, should the player manage to incorporate the Ace of Skulls into a scoring hand of three-of-a-kind or higher, they automatically win the hand, regardless of what their opponents are holding.

PROGRESSION OF PLAY

Rake is played with 2–8 players, though 6 at a table is considered optimum.

The Ante

Players make a minimum bet before the hand commences, the value of which is agreed and determined beforehand. This goes into the pot – the money available to be won – and will be taken by the victor of the hand.

The Deal

Each player is dealt three cards, face down. The player does not show these cards to anyone, but may look at them.

First round of betting

The players bet based on the cards in their hand. A player's bet must be matched or raised by the players to their left, or they may fold, forfeit their ante and take no further part in the hand. Betting continues until all bets are even, at which point the money goes into the pot. There is no limit or restrictions to the betting in Rake. Players can choose to bet nothing, as long as nobody around the table raises them.

The Middle Cards

Now the Middle Cards are dealt. For each player at the table, one card is dealt face up, and one face down. So if there are six players, six cards are dealt face up and six face down, along the middle of the table. These are cards available to be picked up by all the players.

First Pick-up

Each player now takes one of the Middle Cards, hoping to improve their hand. The player to the left of the dealer picks up first, followed by the player to their left, until all players have picked one up. Players may take a face-up card or a face-down card. Face-up cards have the obvious advantage that the player knows their value, but they also give away information about the player's hand to their opponents. They may also be useless to some players, who would rather take an unknown card in the hope of picking one up that helps their hand. Experienced Rake players may use their choice of cards in the pick-up to bluff and deceive their opponents, by misrepresenting the cards they hold.

Second round of betting

Another round of betting, identical to the first.

Second Pick-up

Now the remaining cards are picked up, in the same order as before: left of the dealer, and clockwise after that. In Rake, the dealer is at a considerable disadvantage, being the last person to pick up a card. However, they are also the last one to bet, and have the advantage of studying their opponents' bets before deciding their own.

Third round of betting

A final round of betting.

The Reveal

If there are still two or more players contesting the hand – those who have not dropped out during one of the rounds of betting – they now reveal their cards. The winner takes all the money in the pot. The position of dealer moves one place to the left, and the sequence of play begins again.

The following text originally appeared in blog format in the months preceding the release of *Retribution Falls*.

The Logbook of the *Ketty Jay*

Being an account of the misdeeds and adventures concerning the aforesaid craft and its crew, by its captain, Darian Frey.

Flaxday Middleweek, Fieldfire, 147/32

Midsummer. It's bloody hot. The days are far too long, the *Ketty Jay* is like an oven, and I think the cat has melted. Pinn has been pining all day for his sweetheart and I can only ignore him for so long before I have to shoot him. I don't even have any Shine to take the edge off, since I found out yesterday that my dealer has disappeared under mysterious circumstances. The folks in the tavern gave me a bunch of different stories as to why, but they all agreed that he isn't likely to emerge again, unless it's in bite-size pieces. So for lack of any other damn thing to do, I hereby make my first entry into the Captain's log. I, Darian Frey, proud owner and captain of the *Ketty Jay*, do put pen to paper. Only took me fourteen years to get round to it.

We're low on aerium. Again. The stuff I bought last month was depleted; it's not giving out the lift that it should. It's already been through two or three engines before it got to mine. No way to prove it, of course, except that I know my craft and she's flying like a leprous cow at the moment. Some days I get sick of this cut-price, breadline shit. We nearly blew up last winter 'cause some bastard sold Silo a faulty prothane injector. Just once it'd be nice to buy something with a guarantee, something *proper*, from a Guild-approved shop. Just once it'd be nice not to have to haggle and threaten and promise just to get what I need.

We've put down in Craven's Nook for a few days so we can see what's what. We don't have the money for straight-up aerium but

I know a guy who owes me a favour. Maybe he can put me on to something. Either that or we whore out Pinn and Harkins for some dodgy small-scale courier work. Their aircraft are still running fine, since their fighters hardly use any aerium at all and they're still on the old supply. Harkins is still fretting, of course, but when isn't he?

Either way, we'd better hope that any job we get is local. We're on our last half-canister of aerium, and I don't want to leave us dry. No aerium, no take-off. And you never know when you're gonna have to run.

Millersday Middleweek, Fieldfire, 147/32

Seems I overestimated my old friend's gratitude. Turns out Edley Gotch doesn't think he owes me a favour after all. In fact, he's actually pretty mad at me. Apparently the information I gave him last time we met – information given freely and out of the goodness of my heart, I might add – wasn't quite as accurate as I'd thought. I'd neglected to inform him about the armed guards swarming all over the warehouse he wanted to rob. Not my fault; I told him everything I knew. Can't help it if he wants to base his shabby little criminal empire on semi-reliable hearsay, can I?

Anyway, he wasn't best pleased about having to replace two of his men and one of his ears (the latter with a pretty fetching tin substitute). I suspect if the Doc hadn't been with me, I'd be missing a few exterior organs myself right now. But people don't like to mess with Malvery. Something in his manner, I suppose. You just can't be sure about a man who laughs that loud and that often. He sort of makes you feel like he knows something you don't.

A swift bit of smoothing-over later, and we had ourselves a deal, though not as favourable as I'd like, given the circumstances. He has four canisters for me – and believe me I'm gonna *test* them this time – but first he needs some help with a little problem he's got. Edley Gotch has some competition in town, and he's looking to drive the new gang out. Needs a few extra guns. That's where we come in.

Between you and me, Log, I don't like gunfights. They carry a high risk of making me dead. So I told him half up front, and he laughed, and then Malvery laughed and Gotch went a bit pale and offered one up front and three after. We shook on that.

The crew were suitably unenthusiastic, except for Pinn, who's too dumb to be scared of getting shot. The situation's not ideal, I'll admit, but we need the aerium or we're not flying anywhere. And I'm damned if I'll rot in Craven's Nook too much longer. This place stinks in the heat. I want to get up north where the temperature is suitable for humans.

The crew like to bitch, but they'll warm to the plan once they're drunk. I know I will.

Kilnday Middleweek, Fieldfire 147/32

The great outdoors. I'm on a hillside west of Aulenfay with Lake Elmen glittering in that yellowy-setty-sun kind of glow. There's all these bright isnects around and Malv is starting up a fire even though we don't need one cause it's really nice out. Bit cooked from being out in the sun and probably shouldn't have started drinking *quite* so early but hey. New destnation tomorrow. Where, you ask, little Captain's Log?

Wouldn't you like to know?

Right, well you can probably tell that I'm not dead since I'm wirting this. In fact it all went pretty swimmingly, truth to tell. Everybody still here, no need to go trawling for replacements. I hate taking on new crew, I worked bloody hard to get those ones. It's not easy finding men who'll work for what I pay 'em, hahaha.

So here's what happened. Yesterday we met Gotch and his thugs in the port like we agreed, and they brought a canister of aerium and even rolled it on board for us which was pretty nice. Then they all piled into some junker and we were supposed to follow them in the *Ketty Jay*, Pinn and Harkins flying cover in the Skylance and the Firecrow. Plan was that we set down someway from the bad lot's hideout – which was out of town a way – and then we plough in there guns blazing and hpefully catch em on the hop. So there's twenty of us, or therabouts, me and the crew included. Not Silo though, they got all funny about having a Murthian with em. Silo couldn't care less so he stayed in the engine room which is practically where he lives anyway.

We set down, we creep up to the hideout, so far so good. Then we get there and alarm bells start ringing, cause there's something like thirty buildings there, I mean it's a whole little town. I say why don't we just fly in and machine gun the shit out of it but Gotch doesn't like that, he says they might get away. But I saw it on his face that he knew he'd screwed up but he couldn't go back without looking like a coward. Bad information, tut tut. You'd think he'd learn.

Well, someone sees us then cause to be honest we werne't hiding very well. Someone's clanging a bell, people start coming out, and already I can see there's loads of them and half of them are still probably inside. Doesn't stop Gotch. He's all flush with the element of surprise. He jumps to his feet. 'Get em boys!' I jump up and go 'Come on, men!' or something, then all his men go charging down the hill and all my crew run the other way cause we're not stupid. We could still hear em shooting in the distance by the time we made it back to the craft and got out of there. Dunno what happened to Gotch but I reckon he'll need more than a tin ear this time.

I have a keen sense of things sometimes. Instinct, if you like. I'm good at picking sides. And one look at that lot flooding out of those buildings told me I was on the wrong one. There's gonna be a changing of the guard in Craven's Nook, if it hasn't happened already. Gotch is out. Someone I dont know is in.

Still, I reckoned that coming away with single canister of aerium wasn't exactly fair. I mean, thanks to Gotch we could've all been killed. So we flew back to his little hideout, since just about all his men were off fighting or dead, and we robbed the rest of the arium and a bunch more besides. There were couple of guards, but we had more 'n a couple of shotguns. Anyway, they were nice enough about it once I said they could have what we didn't take.

After that I reckoned it wasn't smart to be around Craven's Nook for a while so we headed off and fetched up here. Breeze off the lake is nice. Might go to Aulenfay later, find a game of Rake. Oh, wait, I can't, I forgot. We made a plan, that's right. I'm tapping my nose with my free hand but I suppose you can't tell cause you're a book.

Okay, enough. Tonight we're having a celebration. Me, Malvery, Pinn, Harkins, Keddle. Maybe Silo will come out, not that he'll actually say anything. Even Slag might come and watch, but he won't come past the cargo ramp. He's never been off that craft, not since he was a teeny kitten. He can beat the crap out of rats the size of your arm but he's scared blind of the sky.

Fourteen years? Damn, shouldn't he be dead soon? That's one old cat.

Queensday Middleweek, Fieldfire 147/32

It appears the cautiously optimistic tone of my last entry was misplaced. We had a fine old night on the grog by the lakeside. Silo came out and sat with us. He drinks hard as Malvery but he doesn't get any more conversational. Doesn't seem to affect him at all, in fact. Anyway, weather was scorching the next morning, everyone staggering about squinting, all of that. I had a feeling like a vicious dwarf kicking me steadily in the brain, but there's a kind of triumph to it. This feeling like you've survived. You know you're alive, even if you don't much want to be.

That was when we found out the *Ketty Jay* was broken.

Silo reckoned it was something to do with the heat. Something wasn't venting out properly, I don't much care, but whatever it was, something melted the something something all over the something and the upshot was we needed some new connectors that Silo didn't have. I raged a bit about carrying spares before he pointed out that we were using the spares and he'd asked me three times in the last three ports to buy some more. Can't say I remember but Silo doesn't lie so I suppose he's right.

Pinn volunteered to fly over to Aulenfay in the Skylance and pick up the bits. That kid's dumb as a raisin loaf but Harkins wouldn't go – he doesn't much like crowds and he started up with a panic attack the moment I suggested it. So I said fine, Pinn could go, and gave him a bit of money.

Three days later, we're getting pretty bored by this lake, I can tell you. Pinn better be dead, because if he's not and he's stupid enough to come back without the best damn excuse in Vardia, Malvery is going to rip a new arse in his face.

Scaleday Thirdweek, Fieldfire, 147/32

Well, he came back, and quite a tale of heroism and gallantry he brought with him. The story of a plucky young pilot, eager to please his captain by returning with the necessary parts to get the *Ketty Jay* airborne again. A worthy quest tragically interrupted by some ruffians who mugged him and left him for dead in an alley. Robbed of all but a few shillies, unwilling to return and face the shame of failure, he gambled his last coins and won. Riding his luck, he won again. What followed was a frankly amazing display of skill that ended in our hero making all his money back, enough to buy the necessary components for his captain and save the day. On the way he won the affection of an improbably busty beauty who indulged his every sordid whim (said whims were described in gloating detail later to his crewmates).

Malvery listened to Pinn's entire story with admirable patience and then punched him.

What actually happened was this: Pinn arrived in Aulenfay with some money in his pocket. Within a few hours he'd spent a sizable fraction of that money on booze and whores. The next morning he presumably did some maths and realised he couldn't afford the stuff he'd been sent for. I don't know how he made up the difference and I don't want to know – he probably just stole it –

but at least he got the right parts, which is no small feat for someone who is regularly outsmarted by his own shoes.

It's exhausting listening to Pinn sometimes. Having spent the previous half hour describing all the things he'd done to his imaginary goddess – actually a ropey old slut with gout – he went into a lament for the sweetheart he left back home, declared that he hated himself for giving in to his manly urges, and then tried to drink himself into a stupor. Malvery snatched the bottle and downed it in front of him just to spite the kid.

Pinn moaning pathetically as I write this. Silo fixing the engine. I can't be bothered any more . . .

Flaxday Thirdweek, Fieldfire, 147/32

Yesterday was a very strange day.

We've picked up two new passengers. One is a daemonist, of all things. The other . . . well, I don't know *what* the other one is. I wonder if I should have allowed them on board, but they seem pretty quiet so far. Still, they paid passage for a year. A *year*. What was I thinking?

Oh yes. I was thinking that I'm now the proud owner of the finest damn cutlass in Vardia.

We finally made it to the cheerily named Cloud Cradle Heights after our extended layover by Lake Elden, only to find that I'd missed my contact by a day and he'd buggered off elsewhere without leaving word. So that was my infallible money-making scheme shot to shit. I won't bore you with the details, Log. Suffice to say it was brilliant and we'll leave it at that.

So while we're kicking around aimlessly in the dock wondering what to do next, this milky-looking fellow named Grayther Crake comes up to me. I make him as a down-on-his-luck aristocrat: he's shabby and smells like he hasn't bathed for a while, but he's still got the accent and a poncey way of putting things. He says he wants to get out of Cloud Cradle Heights, right now. That's no surprise – Cloud Cradle Heights isn't as pretty as it sounds, and he wouldn't be the first man on the run I've helped out, for the right price. The surprise is, he says he wants to book passage on the *Ketty Jay* for a year.

I ask him why. He says he wants to keep on the move. Do we keep on the move? I tell him we've been kicked out of half the ports in Vardia so we don't have much choice. I ask him what he's running from. He says part of the deal is that I don't ask.

Fine with me. Allsoul knows we've got enough secrets on this craft, and we don't ask questions about the past. So I ask him what he's paying with.

'This,' he says, and he holds out a cutlass. 'It's the only thing I have left.'

Now this is one lovely cutlass. I've never been much of a swordsman, and I don't know blades, but this is a work of art. Still, it's probably not worth a year of this bloke's company, so I kind of curl my lip.

'That?' I say.

Then he tells me that this isn't just an ordinary cutlass. He puts it in my hand and tells me to pick the best swordfighter from my crew. Nobody's any good with swords, so I pick Pinn because he's the one I'd most like to stab right now. Crake gives him an iron bar – no swords handy – and tells him to try and hit me.

Pinn obligingly does so. The cutlass sort of *leaps* into the parry, carrying my hand with it. Pinn tries again – I parry again. It's not even me that's doing it, it's the blade. I swear it's possessed. After a couple more times, I sort of accidentally-on-purpose jab Pinn in the arm with it. It's a beautiful thrust, just goes in far enough to hurt like hell but not enough to cause any damage. Don't want to give him an excuse not to fly – if he wasn't such a good pilot, he'd be totally useless.

Of course Pinn wails like he's being murdered and Malvery drags him off to the infirmary to put some antiseptic on the cut. I make some practice swipes with the cutlass. By now I've worked out that Crake is either a daemonist or he stole this from someone who was. Turns out it's the first one.

'That sword in return for our passage,' he says. 'One year. We go where you go. We won't be any trouble.'

I'm so full of visions of swashbuckling my way into the boudoirs of various ladies that I almost miss the plural. '*Our* passage?'

Well, I couldn't really say no. I really wanted that cutlass. I thought I might sell it, but I'd only waste the money. I reckon I'll keep hold of this. It's nice to have something that's not broken, dirty, patched-together or similar. Just one fine thing.

Harkins and Keddle were uneasy about having a daemonist on board. Harkins doesn't like strangers and Keddle is just a moaning so-and-so. I think he's secretly an Awakener or something – there's just a shiftiness about him that gets my back up. Thing is, the luck I have with navigators, I'm not about to go looking for a new one. Keddle might be mediocre at his job, but at least he's stuck with us so far.

Hand is cramping now. I'll tell you about Bess later. That's its (her?) name. Bess.

I really think I'm gonna live to regret letting those two on board.

Kilnday Thirdweek, Fieldfire, 147/32

Quiet few days. We're flush with aerium so we sold off a bit to some desperate merchant for a good profit. Since then we've been slopping around a pretty little nook known as Ock's Fallow. Small port off the trade lanes. The folks round here are pretty respectable. Naturally, they don't like us, but I can just about bear the way they scoff into their wine glasses when we walk in. It's worth it to see them trying to shift Malvery later when he's beached and snoring on the bar.

It's nice to drop out of the race for a while, put your feet up. I reckon those days by the lake last week don't really count, 'cause we were all mad at Pinn. Not good for the blood. We're mostly over that now, although Malvery is still bullying him with a shade more enthusiasm than usual.

Not that everything's sweet, of course – it never is. Keddle is still bitching about the daemonist. He reckons we shouldn't have taken him on. They hang daemonists, so you can bet they have a dim view of those that help them out. I think he's worrying over nothing, though. It's not like he looks different from any other aristocrat. Honestly, you wouldn't know he was a daemonist at all if it weren't for the eight-foot metal golem in the hold.

Oh, yes. The golem. That's Bess. She came on board loaded in a crate. Couldn't believe my eyes when we crowbarred it open. Why our guest saw fit to call it female is beyond me – that's a woman even Pinn would balk at, and he's rutted a hound or two in his time. I don't know what lives inside that armour and I don't care to know. But those little glittery eyes behind her face-grille give me the chills.

They're an odd pair, Crake and Bess. I gave Crake the passenger's quarters, since he paid – Harkins is doubling up with Pinn – and I've barely seen him leave them. The only time is when he goes down to the hold to check on Bess. He talks to her like she's a pet or something. It's weird, but I don't see any harm in it.

Keddle's complaints gave me something to think about, but I reckon for now the benefits outweigh the risks. For one thing, I got me a damn fine cutlass out of it. Plus, as long as we keep that golem inside and out of sight, then the *Ketty Jay* has just picked up one bastard of a watchdog. Crake is just as concerned as I am about being discreet – he only told me he was a daemonist 'cause it would be pretty difficult to explain Bess and the cutlass otherwise – so I've no worries on that score. And having a daemonist around might come in handy. I should ask him what he can actually *do* one of these days. Beyond conjuring up massive hulking armoured bodyguards, that is.

He's running from someone, there's no doubt of that, and part of the deal was that I couldn't ask him who. Still, he only paid for his passage, not my protection. If this someone catches up to us, I'm not standing in their way. And if it's the law, I can always plead ignorance. Us dumb freebooters wouldn't know a daemonist if he bit us on the nose. The golem? We thought it was just a wondrous machine. Simple folk, we.

I'll keep my eye on the situation. He's paid in advance, so kicking him off isn't a problem. If he gets to be trouble, he and his tin missy are out the cargo door.

Just to be sure, though, I'd better find out what they actually *do* to people caught aiding daemonists . . .

Dyersday Thirdweek, Fieldfire, 147/32

Awakeners came to town today. Shame. I kinda liked this place.

Ock's Fallow doesn't have a shrine or temple or whatever they call those places where they live, so we reckoned they were all busy in the big cities where the money is. Turns out they move in squads, heading from town to town, setting up for a few days at a time then packing up for the next destination. Me and Malvery went into the square this morning hunting coffee, and there they were, tents all up and ready. Spooky how they just appeared like that.

We stayed and watched for a while. All these prim and proper folks milling around the tents, going in to see the Awakeners, asking for this and that. I confess I don't get it and I've never really wanted to. All I know is they reckon they can tell your future, and if you pay them enough, they reckon they can change it. Sounds like a scam to me, but if it is, it's the best one I ever saw. Half the country believes in this Allsoul junk.

It's something to do with the last King, the crazy one that all the Dukes ganged up on when they formed the Coalition. After they slung him into one of his palaces and imprisoned him there he got to all kinds of raving, and they wrote it all down in some book, and then reasoned that since they couldn't understand him and he was obviously important then he must be a prophet. It's the old trick educated folk pull over and over: if you don't understand it, it's 'cause you're not smart enough, not that it's incomprehensible dogshit.

Crake was nervy when we told him about the Awakeners. I wonder if it's the Awakeners that are after him? He is a daemonist, after all, and nobody would be hanging daemonists at all if the Awakeners weren't stirring them up all the time. Still, I didn't get that impression. I don't think he's scared of them; I think he hates

417

them. And he's been making noises about moving on for a couple of days.

It's probably time to go, anyway. Malvery, Pinn and high-end booze are a dangerous combination. They get excitable, and that usually ends up involving the militia. Always better to leave before someone kicks you out.

So, I suppose we're going. No idea where to yet, but I reckon we'll know when we get there.

Scaleday Firstweek, Swallow's Reap, 147/32

Got a hot tip last night. Man I met at a card table gave me the news about a freighter, loaded up and ripe for the picking. Piracy's not gone well for me in the past, but still . . .

It went like this. I was on fire, taking down everyone at the table. Cash betting, all of that. This guy's good but he's desperate. Turns out after I beat him that some of his stake had been in the form of an IOU he couldn't pay. Things like that make me angry. I'm not an unreasonable man, but people who bet money they don't have just burn me up. So I pulled my gun on him and things got a bit strained. He was trying to talk his way out of it for a while, but a quick pistol-whipping took care of all that. Never let it be said that I lack finesse.

Finally he started blubbing. Turns out he used to work as assistant navigator on this freighter route before they fired him. He knows the times and the places where it's most exposed. The cargo is junk, but once a month they carry a heap of ducats, part of some accounting process they have. He offered up the information in return for me not clubbing him any more.

Fair enough, I said, since I wasn't getting any money out of him anyway.

I told the boys at dinner in the mess. Harkins went grey and looked rather unsteady. Pinn whooped and started dancing about until Malvery clipped him round the head with a spoon. Keddle grumbled. Silo didn't say anything, but he hardly ever does. The passenger just looked miserable. Morose so-and-so. This cloud of gloom follows him around everywhere. I wish I'd noticed it before I took him on.

Anyway, that's about as close to a vote of confidence as I ever get, so it looks like some light, refreshing piracy might be on the cards. Our window isn't for a little while though, so tonight, the only thing on the cards is cards. I'm going back to win me some more ducats. Feel like I've got a roll coming.

Note to self: Silo is complaining about spares again. Seems that no matter how many times I stock up on parts, there are never any spares. I should do something about it.

Flaxday Firstweek, Swallow's Reap, 147/32

Woke up this morning in a bin. Not one of my better starts. Since I was upside down it took me a while to get out of it, after which I stumbled around trying to work out where in buggery I was. I was covered in all kinds of vile crap, and I had one of those hangovers where I could feel my eyes throb every time my heart beat. I would have been sick, but I think I left it all behind in that bin.

I was feeling so bad I didn't realise I'd been beaten up and robbed for quite some time.

Somehow I found a street I recognised and got back to the *Ketty Jay* without being stopped by the militia. Barely a flicker of surprise from anybody. The passenger made an inquiry about my well-being, but I just snarled at him. The cat obviously likes my new scent: he started following me as soon as I set foot on the craft and he hasn't left me alone all day. I went to my quarters and did my best to sleep, but the hangover and three tonnes of cat on my chest didn't make it easy.

Took me a long time to work out what happened, but from the bits and pieces I remember, I'm pretty sure someone spiked me. Second day I went back to the den they were playing Rake, and that's my game. I was flying. Came away considerably richer, and with the promise of a game the next day. So I went back for that one, and after that . . .

Well, I remember I was doing well. I remember I kept taking

risks and coming up good. I remember beating Wings Full with a Run to the Ace of Skulls. Poor bugger I was playing with almost broke down in tears.

After that, it gets hazy. Someone sat down to play. Grinning at me, front teeth missing. He stank like sweat. Bought me a drink. The owner. Feller named Feckley, as I recall. It was him that did me. Guess he didn't like my run of luck.

Well, at least they were decent enough not to kill me. They didn't know who I was. Probably thought I was just someone passing through, possibly a professional cheat. Not that they'll find me grateful. I think I'd rather they *had* killed me right now.

But they didn't. So as soon as I start feeling a little less bloody awful, I'm going back there. For once, I won that money honestly, and I'm damned if I'm not getting it back with interest.

Kingsday Firstweek, Swallow's Reap, 147/32

Feel rather heroic today, actually. There's nothing to make a man feel like a man like setting right some wrongs.

Now I'm not going say I haven't pulled off a few injustices in my time, but Feckley's little trick was just low. I beat those guys fair and square at Rake, and he spiked and robbed me. It's not often I beat anyone fair and square at anything, so when I do I'm kind of precious about it.

Once I'd got out of bed and had my bowels back under control (an unpleasant-yet-strangely-satisfying side-effect of the spike) I gathered up the boys and we went down to Feckley's den. Harkins I left to guard the *Ketty Jay*. He's a fine pilot but his bravery ends at the limits of his cockpit. He's not cut out for the physical stuff. Confrontations turn him into a gibbering wreck. He's likely to accidentally shoot someone out of nervousness. Quite possibly one of us.

I took Silo along this time. He doesn't often get off the *Ketty Jay* on account of his being a Murthian and liable to get lynched when he's on his own. It's been a good few years now, but nobody's forgotten the war. Suppose the wounds run pretty deep. Me, I'm not fussed about Sammies or Dakkadians or Murthians or whoever – live and let live, that's what I think – but my guts still twinge when I think about that time in Samarla. The end to my illustrious career hauling cargo for the Coalition Navy. Still got the scars on my belly.

Silo and Malvery are the muscle, so I let them go in first. Pinn next, cause he's eager. I follow him in – can't go last, that'd just look weird – and behind me comes Keddle. I'm thinking I should start getting the passenger involved in this kind of thing, maybe. An extra pair of hands never hurts. And that golem would be pretty damn useful, if slightly unsubtle. Seeing Bess walk through town would raise a few eyebrows, though, and I like to keep my profile a little lower than that.

We boot our way into the den, bristling with guns. Feckley's got some muscle, too, but they're slow to their weapons. 'Don't you even think it,' I warn 'em, but there's always one. He thinks he's being ever-so-sneaky as he moves his hand towards his holster. Malvery spots him and shoots him with that big lever-action shotgun of his. Takes his head off above the jaw. Nobody messes with us after that.

Card dens have a lot of money lying around, and this one was no exception. There was much more than was taken from me, anyway. I figure I deserve it. Just to be nice, though, I let the players keep the money in their pockets and what they have on the table in front of them. I'd be a bit of hypocrite if I didn't. It's not their fault that Feckley's a cheating pusbag.

He glares at me all balefully as we empty out his den. I can tell he's wishing he killed me when he had the chance. I know he's thinking up some kind of revenge if he ever lays eyes on me again, so I get my retaliation in first and shoot him in the foot. That'll teach him for glaring.

After that we reckoned it was best to get out of town, so we did, and then followed the obligatory grog-soaked celebrations of a job well done. It's not often we have a genuine reason to celebrate – we usually just make one up. So this time was a bit special. Put me back to bed for a day, but it was worth it.

Where next, Log?

Killing time till our date with the freighter. Crew are restless, as ever. The passenger is showing signs of thawing out. Malvery's decided to start dragging him to the bar with us whenever he can. The Doc doesn't talk like it, but he used to live the high life once upon a time. He doesn't have a problem with Crake's accent like Pinn does. Me, I'm easy. He seems like an alright feller once you unjam that cane from his arse.

The golem is well-behaved, at least, although I do sometimes hear her charging around in the hold. I think Crake's playing ball with her. She doesn't seem violent, but I wouldn't want to get in her way while she's barrelling around. It's all a bit weird, but every time I think of kicking them off, I take out my cutlass and swoosh it around and everything's better. Pity I wasn't carrying it when I got spiked; I think I could have carved up the room blind drunk with this little wonder in my hands. It just seems to know what I want it to do.

I asked Crake if he could make any more stuff like that. He said no and went a bit funny. Mumbling about equipment this and sanctums that, but I could tell what was really bothering him. He's frightened of the idea. Seems a shame to know how to craft miracles and then not do it, but it's not my business, I suppose. Pity. I was going to ask him for a pistol that never missed, or something. Still, I'll set Malvery to pestering him, see what comes of it.

Not long till the freighter. Half the crew think the information's probably bad. The other half agree with the first half. But we've got sod all else to do, so we might as well check it out.

Scaleday Thirdweek, Swallow's Reap, 147/32

You'll forgive me, Log, if I haven't written in you for a while. I do have a good excuse, though. My right hand has been out of operation for some time. As to how it actually happened . . . well . . . your guess is as good as mine.

We picked up the freighter. I mean, we actually did. That poor guy I beat the information out of was dead on. It came cruising over the Splinters with two piddling little Caybury Interceptors as escort. They crossed at night, following a course between the mountaintops, trying not to be noticed. Probably it's worked up till now. But we knew their route, it was a clear night and we had the moon.

Pinn came screaming out of the mountain pass and blew one of the outflyers out of the sky before they even knew what had happened. Harkins was a bit slower than Pinn – he always is, but that's still quick in most people's book. Quick enough to empty his machine-guns into the other outflyer's flank, anyway.

The freighter had some guns on it, cannons big enough to do the *Ketty Jay* some damage. But they were occupied with the smaller craft and they didn't see us coming up on their blind side. The bigger the craft, the easier it is to sneak up on. I raked my guns across its underside, right where the aerium tanks were. Perfect shooting, even if I do say so myself. Holed the tanks and the craft started venting aerium, faster than they could pump it back in.

The art of it is to make them leak enough but not too much. You don't want to rip the tanks apart or they'll dump all the ultralight gas and drop out of the sky. But a steady leak is like a slow puncture. They start losing altitude, and the pilot has to make a choice: set down while he still can, or crash his craft hard. Most of them choose the first option. Ours did, anyway.

Once it was down, we boarded them. They were pretty cooperative, all in all. They opened the door rather than make us blast it open with dynamite. Then we were all in there with our guns, the whole crowd control routine, everybody down, show us the stuff, etc.But there was no stuff. See, the guy I met knew the route alright. But that shit-wit, accidentally or on purpose, had me intercept them on the *return* route. *After* they'd delivered the money. We'd boarded an empty cargo craft.

The mood soured after that.

The boys were giving me dangerous looks on the way back. I

really think that we got close to mutiny that night. I don't mind admitting I was worried, but then I hit on an idea. I told 'em that I'd take 'em all out on the town, and I was paying for everything. So we did. At first they were still grumbling, the ungrateful bastards, and things were nasty for a while. But then Pinn and Malvery started singing, and everyone joined in, even Crake. Soon we were all best friends, at least temporarily. Soon after, we'd forgotten who we were.

At some point in the night, long after I'd lost the capability to make sound decisions, something happened to my hand. I think I got it jammed in a door, or some fat sod stamped on it, or something. Either way, it hurt like a bitch and went sort of purply blue. Taken a week or so for the swelling to go down, but I'm pleased to report that the incident with the freighter has been all but forgotten, and all is normal again. As normal as it gets, anyway.

Dyersday Firstweek, Howl's Batten, 147/32

Things have calmed a bit lately, and I for one am happy for some peace. Seems like everyone's forgotten about the freighter debacle, anyway. I should steer clear of piracy for the time being, I reckon. Sometimes a man has to accept there are things he's not good at.

What I *am* good at is ripping off low-level criminals and getting away with it. See, it works like a cycle. You get a small port, middle of nowhere, and sooner or later the bad men move in. They swagger about a bit, running the place down, and eventually they get shot by even badder men or the Coalition Navy go in there and sort 'em out. Either way, they've got short lifespans. They're replaced, and it all begins again.

Way I figure it, as long as I don't revisit any town where I've stolen from the local crime-boss for a few years, chances are he'll be gone by the time I go back. Clean sheet for me. Then I rip off the next feller. The trick is to spot the ones that have got too big for their boots, the ones who are gonna get 'emselves killed soon.

Once or twice I met fellers who were just dangerous enough to make it into the big leagues. Those, I left well alone.

You might call it a bit risky, making enemies like that, but it's only because my memory is so bloody patchy that I keep on stumbling across folks that want to settle a score. I should keep a list, or something.

This one was a straight theft. I persuaded this feller to let me haul a load of rare glassware for him. Top quality stuff, which he'd no doubt robbed off someone else. We were all smiles as we loaded it on, and then we buggered off out of there, never to be seen again. Made a tidy profit selling it on the other side of Vardia. Would've made a tidier one if I hadn't smashed half of it with a slightly clumsy landing. I didn't think we came down *that* hard, though I suppose it did make Malvery fall down the stairs into the cargo hold. I blame my mysteriously damaged hand.

The passenger's settled in well enough. He's a bit plummy but otherwise a good sort. No idea what his deal is, and more than once I've caught him glancing over his shoulder in public places, like he thinks he's being followed. Still no sign of whoever it is, though. Malvery seems to like him. Keddle likes him as much as he ever likes anyone, the moaning little bastard. The only one Crake can't get on with is Pinn. Not that that's a bad thing. Anyone who *doesn't* think Pinn is an idiot is an idiot themselves. I've met smarter furniture.

Bess gave us all a shock last night. Someone tried to get into the *Ketty Jay*. Most of us were out, and I suppose Silo and Harkins were asleep. Harkins says he got woken by this roaring noise in the hold that scared him silly. Silo went down – Harkins wouldn't, obviously – and found Bess trying to put some poor bloke's limbs and head back on, like he was a doll she was playing with. At least Silo was considerate enough to clean it all up before I got back (I wasn't back till this afternoon, by the way – entertaining a lady, if you know what I mean).

Better make sure Crake has that thing on a lead, in case she thinks about doing the same thing to us. Crake assures me she won't, but nobody's convinced.

Note to self again: Silo is still after a bunch of spares for the engines. I swear I bought some in the last port but they aren't there now. I don't know if the cat's eating them or something, but we only ever seem to have just enough to keep the *Ketty Jay* halfway running. Can't think where they're going but it's getting on my nerves.

Queensday Firstweek, Howl's Batten, 147/32

Got round to picking up my mail today, and there was something interesting inside. I've got mail drops all over Vardia. People I trust, as much as I trust anyone. They hold the letters for me. I stay on the move a lot, and this is the only way I stay in touch. Normal people use the post office for the same thing, but I trust the post office even less than the barmen and low-lives I pay to be my points of contact. Some of the parcels I get are questionable, to say the least. Wouldn't like to turn up asking for it and find myself staring down the business end of a Navy revolver.

What I got this time was a message from a guy called Xandian Quail. He's a whispermonger that lives over in Marklin's Reach. He says he has a proposition for me. Me in particular. A proposition that might make me very rich. And that's all the detail he gave, other than I have to be there by the end of the month. That's two weeks away. Twenty days. Can't hardly stand the suspense, to tell you the truth, Log.

Of course, you can no doubt tell by my jaunty pen-strokes that I'm kidding. This whole thing is suspicious as Pinn's imaginary girlfriend. I've sold a few titbits to Quail in the past and he always pays fair, but he's a big-money information peddler. Never been able to afford to buy anything from him.

So why me? What do *I* have to do with anything?

The sensible part of me is telling me to ignore it. Anything too good to be true usually is. Thing is, my sensible side doesn't have the stamina that my stupid side does. It'll be tired in a few days. I might as well give up now and say I'll be going. Just to talk. I can't think of any reason why Quail would want to kill me, but he could well be working for someone that does.

Still, though. What it'd be to be rich, eh?

I also got a message from an old acquaintance, some horrible bastard called Lawsen Macarde. He's the dominant smuggler in Scarwater these days. One of the fellers I pegged to make it to the top, so I never screwed him too badly on a deal. He's in the market for some aerium, if I can get my hands on any. I could do with some myself; we're getting a bit low. I'll maybe head over to Scarwater sometime soon, see what I can do.

Desperately trying to think of anything I've done to wrong Quail. Can't.

What's it all about?

Daggersday Secondweek, Howl's Batten, 147/32

So here's the plan. We need aerium, badly. The last lot we got hold of has pretty much run dry. Lawsen Macarde wants aerium too, but he doesn't want to pay full price for it. I don't even have enough to buy it for cheap, and if I could find some I'd keep it for myself.

There is, however, a way around this.

I'm not too proud to go trawling round junkyards for aerium. See, abandoned aircraft are not that uncommon, and plenty get shot down. Scavengers just strip what they want and leave the rest, but the higher-ups don't like to leave wrecks rusting all over the place. So sooner or later the big haulers turn up and take them off to the junkyards. Thing is, what a lot of people don't realise is that good aerium can be run through the engines four or five time before all the gas is released. Sure, by the last couple of times your craft flies like a whale and you're liable to drop out of the sky in a storm, but many's the time I've ended up flying on recycled aerium, and I'm not dead yet.

If it's good enough for me, it's good enough for Macarde. So we've been haunting the junkyards, siphoning tanks, and we've got twelve canisters all sealed up and ready to deliver. We're going to flog them to Macarde and use the money to buy three or four canisters of the real stuff from a legit supplier. The supplier will charge and arm and a leg, of course, but I'll pay this time. If you cut corners, you might get some seedy bastard delivering you a load of useless aerium, after all.

All this will mean two things. One, we'd better make ourselves scarce before Macarde finds out what we've done. Two, we're never coming back to Scarwater. I'm fine with both. Macarde's probably not that desperate for aerium that he'll immediately fuel up with the stuff we give him, and Scarwater's a dump anyway.

One more enemy to add to the list. It gets difficult to remember them all, sometimes.

Kilnday Thirdweek, Howl's Batten, 147/32

Son of a bitch. Son. Of. A. Bitch.

Keddle. That rot-damned moaning sack of crap. All he ever did was complain and grumble, in between the odd bit of semi-competent navigation. He wasn't the best, by any chalk, but he did his job. I thought that finally, after all these years, I'd found a navigator I could stick with. One that was sensible enough not to get shot, strong enough so that he wouldn't die of some unknown illness, unambitious enough not to betray me, unromantic enough not to desert for the love of some random whore. By the warty bowels of the Allsoul, I've had shitty luck with navigators. But Keddle . . . damn it, I really thought he was going to be a stayer.

Turns out he isn't. Turns out Silo was getting suspicious about all those engine parts going missing. So when we set down in Jander's Maw, a half-day from Scarwater and our meeting with Macarde, Silo decided to hide out in the engine room and see what happened. Saw Keddle rifling through the spares. Followed him all the way down to the workshops in the town, where he saw Keddle selling them off to a craftbuilder. After that he came back to get me.

Keddle screeched to the high skies when we turned up at the tavern where he was drinking. Course, he said he was innocent, but if Silo says otherwise then there's no question. We dragged him back to the *Ketty Jay*. Me and Malvery were pretty angry, to tell you the truth. We probably didn't conduct ourselves too glamourously as we were kicking the stuffing out of him. I came close to shooting the bastard, but in the end Silo stopped me. Sure, it wasn't a lot of money, but he was stealing! From me! I mean, damn it, there are limits!

Well, I had to get him out of my sight, so I put my boot in his arse and shoved him off the cargo ramp, hands tied behind his back. He went down pretty hard on his face, but he can count himself lucky I didn't put a bullet in his back.

After that, we took right off. Couldn't stay there a moment more. Figured we might as well go overnight to Scarwater. It was close enough that I could find it myself.

It's almost dawn now. We've put down in Scarwater, waiting for the place to wake up. Later today I'll go see about ripping off Macarde. Later today I'll get looking for a new navigator. After that, I'm gonna get roaring drunk and get into some kind of fight. It just feels like one of those days.

Why me, Log?

Why me?

Transcriber's note:

At the time of writing, this was the final entry in the Logbook Of The Ketty Jay. Darian Frey was never known for his diligence, and he apparently forgot about updating the logbook after this date. Considering what happened afterwards, however, he can, perhaps, be excused. The affair which followed has been luridly recounted by various pulp biographers, but I direct your attention to the only official and unbiased account of the tale, written by this humble scribe: Retribution Falls, *available now in bookshops all over Vardia.*

Turn the page for a sneak preview of the
sequel to *Retribution Falls*

THE
BLACK LUNG
CAPTAIN

Available now

One

An Escape – 'Orphans Don't Fight Back' –
Pinn Flounders – Destination: Up

Darian Frey was a man who understood the value of a tactical retreat. It was a gambler's instinct, a keen appreciation of the odds that told him when to take a risk and when to bail out. There was no shame in running like your heels were on fire when the situation called for it. In Frey's opinion, the only difference between a hero and a coward was the ability to do basic maths.

Malvery was to his left, huffing and puffing through the undergrowth. Alcoholic, overweight and out of shape. Pinn, who was no fitter but a good deal dimmer, ran alongside. Behind them was an outraged horde armed with rifles, pistols and clubs, baying for their blood.

The maths on this one was easy.

A volley of gunfire cut through the forest. Bullets clipped leaves, chipped trees and whined away into the night. Frey swore and ducked his head. He hunched his shoulders, trying to make himself small. More bullets followed, smacking into earth and stone and wood all around them.

Pinn whooped. 'Stupid yokels! Can't shoot worth

a damn!' His stumpy legs pumped beneath him like an enthusiastic terrier's.

Frey didn't share Pinn's excitement. He was sick with a grey fear, waiting for the moment when one of those bullets found flesh, the hard punch of lead in his back. If he was especially unlucky, he might get blinded by a tree branch or break his leg first. Running through a forest in the dark was no-one's idea of fun.

He clutched his prize to his chest: a small wooden lockbox, jingling with ducats. Not enough to be worth dying for. Not even worth a medium-sized flesh wound. But he wasn't giving it up now. It was a matter of principle.

'Told you robbing an orphanage was a bad idea,' said Malvery.

'No, it was *Crake* who told me that,' Frey said through gritted teeth. 'That's why he wouldn't come. *You* thought it was a *good* idea. In fact, your exact words were: "Orphans don't fight back." '

'Well, they don't,' said the doctor defensively. 'It's the rest of the village you've got to watch out for.'

Frey's reply was cut off as the ground disappeared from under his feet. Suddenly they were tumbling and sliding in a tangle, slithering through cold mud. Frey flailed for purchase as the forest rolled and spun before his eyes. The three of them crashed through a fringe of bracken and bushes and ended up in a heap on the other side.

Frey extricated himself gingerly from his companions, wincing as a multitude of bumps and scratches announced themselves. The lockbox had bruised his ribs in the fall, but he'd kept hold of it somehow. He looked back at the moonlit slope. It was shallower and smaller than it had seemed while they were falling down it.

Malvery got up and made a half-hearted attempt at wiping the mud off his pullover. He adjusted his round, green-lensed glasses, which had miraculously stayed on his nose.

'Anyway, I've reconsidered my position,' he said, continuing his train of thought as if there had been no interruption. 'I've come to believe that stealing from a bunch of defenceless orphans could be seen as a bit of a low point in our careers.'

Frey tugged at Pinn, who lay groaning on the ground. He'd been on the bottom of the heap, and his chubby face was plastered in muck. '*I'm* an orphan!' Frey protested as he struggled with Pinn's weight. 'Who were they collecting for, if not for me?'

Malvery smoothed his bushy white moustache and followed Frey's gaze up the slope. The forest was brightening with torchlight as the infuriated mob approached. 'You should tell them that,' he said. 'Might sweeten their disposition a little.'

'Pinn, will you *get up*?' Frey cried, dragging the pilot to his feet.

Even with the moon overhead, it was hard to see obstacles while they were running. They fended off branches that poked and lashed at their faces. They slipped and cursed and cracked their elbows against tree trunks. It had rained recently, and the ground alternately sucked at their boots or slid treacherously beneath them.

The villagers reached the top of the slope and sent a hopeful barrage of gunfire into the trees. Frey felt something slap against his long coat, near his legs. He gathered up the flapping tail, and saw a bullet hole there.

Too close.

'Give up the money and we'll let you go!' one of the villagers shouted.

Frey didn't waste his breath on a reply. He wasn't coming out of this without something to show for it. He needed that money. Probably a lot more than any bloody orphans did. He had a crew to look after. Seven mouths to feed, if you counted the cat. And that wasn't even including Bess, who didn't have a mouth. Still, she probably needed oiling or something, and oil didn't come for free.

Anyway, *he* was an orphan. So that made it okay.

'Everything looks different in the dark,' Malvery said. 'You sure this is the way we came?'

Frey skidded to a halt at the edge of a cliff, holding his arms out to warn the others. A river glittered ten metres below, sparkling in the moonlight.

'Er . . . We might have taken a wrong turn or two,' he ventured.

The precipice ran for some distance to his left and right. Before them was a steely landscape of treetops, rucked with hills and valleys, stretching to the horizon: the vast expanse of the Vardenwood. In the distance stood the Splinters, one of Vardia's two great mountain ranges, that marched all the way north to the Yortland coast, thousands of kloms distant.

Frey suddenly realised that he had no idea where, in all that woodland, he'd hidden his aircraft and the rest of his crew.

Malvery looked down at the river. 'I don't remember this being here,' he said.

'I'm pretty sure the *Ketty Jay* is over the other side,' said Frey doubtfully.

'Are you really, Cap'n? Or is that a guess?'

'I've just got a feeling about it.'

Behind them, the cries of the mob were getting louder. They could see the bobbing lights of torches approaching through the forest.

'Any ideas?' Malvery prompted.

'Jump?' suggested Frey. 'There's no way they'd be stupid enough to follow us.'

'Yeah, we'd certainly out-stupid them with that plan.' Malvery rolled up his sleeves. 'Fine. Let's do it.'

Pinn was leaning on his knees, breathing hard. 'Oh, no. Not me. Can't swim.'

'You'd rather stay here?'

'I can't *swim*!' Pinn protested.

Frey didn't have time to argue. His eyes met the doctor's. 'Do the honours, please.'

Malvery put his boot to the seat of Pinn's trousers and shoved. Pinn stumbled forward to the edge of the cliff. He teetered on his toes, wheeled his arms in a futile attempt to keep his balance, and then disappeared with a howl.

'Now you'd better go rescue him,' Frey said.

Malvery grinned. 'Bombs away, eh?' He put his glasses in his coat pocket, ran past Frey and jumped off the cliff. Frey followed him, feet first, clutching the box of coins. He was half way down before he thought to wonder if the river was deep enough, or if there were rocks under the surface.

Hitting the water was a freezing black shock, knocking the wind out of him. Icy spring melt from the Splinters. The sounds of the forest disappeared in a bubbling rush that filled his nose and ears. His plunge took him to the river bed, but the water cushioned him enough to give him a gentle landing. He launched himself upward, shifting the lockbox to one arm and swimming with the other. Only seconds had passed, but his chest was already beginning to hurt. He panicked and struggled for breath, clawing at the twinkles of moonlight above him. Finally, just when it seemed there was no air left inside him, he broke the surface.

Sound returned, unmuffled now, the hissing and splashing of the river. He sucked in air and cast about for signs of his companions. With the water lapping round his face he couldn't find them, so he struck out for the bank. The river wasn't fast, but he could still feel the current pulling him. He vaguely hoped Pinn was alright. He'd hate to lose a good pilot.

He hauled himself out, dragging the lockbox with him, which had inconveniently filled with water and was now twice as heavy as before. Jumping in the river had seemed a good idea at the time, but now he was sodden and cold as well as being dog-tired. He was beginning to think that getting lynched would be preferable to all this exertion.

Once he got to his feet, he spotted his companions. Malvery was swimming towards the bank with one hand, in great bearlike strokes. He was towing Pinn, fingers cupped around his chin. Pinn had gone limp, giving himself over to Malvery's strength.

Frey squelched along the bank to where the current had carried them, and helped them both out. Pinn fell to his hands and knees, retching up river water.

'You rot-damned pair of bastards!' he snarled, between heaves.

'Oh, come on, Pinn,' Frey said. 'I've seen you take down four aircraft without breaking a sweat. You're scared of a little water?'

'I can't *shoot* water!' Pinn protested. He burped noisily and another flood spilled over his lips.

'There they are!' someone yelled from the clifftop. Bullets pocked the bank and threw up little fins of spray from the river.

'Move it!' Frey scrambled away towards the trees. 'It'll take them ages to find a way round.'

He'd barely finished his sentence before the villagers began to fling themselves off the cliff. 'We just want our money back!' an unseen voice called. 'It's for the orphaaaaans!' The final word lengthened and trailed off as the speaker pitched over the edge and plummeted into the water.

'*I'm an orphan!*' Frey screamed, infuriated by

their persistence. He'd done enough to deserve his escape. Why couldn't they just let him go?

His words fell on deaf ears. Angry faces broke the surface of the river and came swimming towards them.

'Don't those fellers give up?' Malvery complained, and they ran.

It was more luck than design that brought them to a familiar trail, which led them back to the *Ketty Jay*. The villagers had stopped shooting – their guns were soaked – but they showed no signs of abandoning the pursuit. In fact, they were gaining. A lifetime of unhealthy habits and too little exercise had not equipped anyone on Frey's side for a lengthy foot chase. Their waterlogged clothes weighed them down and chafed with every step. By the time they made it to the clearing where their companions waited, Malvery looked like he was about to burst a lung.

The *Ketty Jay* loomed before them, dwarfing the two single-seater fighter craft parked nearby. Frey had long ceased to see her with a judgemental eye. He would never have called her beautiful, but she wasn't ugly to him either. After fifteen years she was so familiar that he no longer noticed her squat, hunched body, her stub tail or her ungainly bulk. He knew her too well for appearances to matter. That wasn't something Frey could often say.

Harkins, Jez and Crake stood before her, shotguns and pistols in their hands.

'Get to stations!' Frey panted as he burst into the clearing. 'Harkins! Pinn! Up in the sky, right now.'

Harkins jumped as if stung and fled towards one of the fighter craft, a Firecrow with wide, back-swept wings and a bubble of windglass on its snout. Pinn lurched off towards the other: a Skylance, a sleek racing machine, built for speed.

'We heard gunfire,' said Jez, as Malvery and Frey approached, soaking and bedraggled. She eyed the doctor, who was unsuccessfully trying to catch his breath. 'Has he been shot or something?'

Malvery's retort was little more than an irate wheeze. He staggered off towards the cargo ramp on the *Ketty Jay*'s far side.

'Robbing the children didn't go to plan, then?' Crake asked the captain, one eyebrow raised.

Frey shoved the lockbox full of coins into Crake's hands. 'It went well enough. Where's Silo and Bess?'

Crake regarded the leaking lockbox disapprovingly. 'Silo's in the engine room, trying to fix the problems we had on the way over here. Bess is asleep in the hold. Should I wake her?'

'No. Get on board. We're going. Last one in, shut the cargo ramp.'

He spared a moment to check on his outflyers before boarding the *Ketty Jay*. The Firecrow and the Skylance were rising vertically from the clearing as their aerium tanks flooded with ultralight gas. Satisfied they were on their way, he ran up the ramp.

Malvery was beached and gasping just inside the

hold, surrounded by a large puddle. Frey paid him no attention. Nor did he spare a glance for the hulking metal form of Bess, standing dormant and dark by the stairs. She'd long ceased making him uneasy.

He sprinted up the steps to the main passageway. It was cramped and dimly lit, the cockpit at one end and the engine room at the other, with doors to the crew's quarters and Malvery's tiny infirmary in between. Hydraulics whirred as the cargo ramp closed, sealing the aircraft.

He pushed into the engine room, a small space cluttered by black iron gantries, allowing access to all parts of the complex assembly overhead. It was warm and smelled of machinery. Frey cast around for signs of his engineer, but the only crew member in sight was Slag the cat, a scraggy clump of black fur, watching him from an air vent.

'Silo! Where are you?'

'Up here, Cap'n,' came the reply, although Frey still couldn't see him. He guessed his engineer was working around the other side of the assembly. The *Ketty Jay*, like most aircraft, had two separate sets of engines: aerium for lift and prothane for thrust. Both were tangled together in this room in a confusing jumble of pipes, tanks and malevolent-looking guages.

'Are we ready to go?' Frey asked, addressing the room in general.

'Wouldn't advise it, Cap'n.'

'Can she *fly*?' he persisted. 'It's a bit urgent, Silo.'

A short pause. 'Yuh,' he said at last. 'Gonna fly like a slug though.'

'That'll do,' said Frey, and pelted out of the engine room, his feet squishing in his boots.

Jez was already at the navigator's station when Frey bundled into the cockpit and threw himself into his seat.

'Destination?' she asked.

'Up,' he replied, and boosted the aerium engines to maximum. The *Ketty Jay* groaned and shrieked as her tanks filled. Frey leaned forward and peered through the windglass of the cockpit. The first of the villagers had reached the clearing now, but they were too late. The *Ketty Jay* was dragging herself off the ground and into the air.

Some of them aimed rifles and tried to fire, but their weapons were too wet to work. One of them made a suicidal dive for the *Ketty Jay*'s landing struts as they retracted. Luckily for him, he fell short. The villagers raged and yelled and threw what stones they could find, but the *Ketty Jay* kept on rising.

Frey felt secure enough to make an obscene gesture at his pursuers. 'Thought you had me, didn't you? Well, let's see you yokels fly!' He slumped back in his seat as they cleared the tree-tops. Deep relief sank into his bones.

Jez got up from the navigator's station and stood next to him, staring into the night sky with sudden and worrying intensity. Frey followed her gaze.

There were several small, dark shapes in the distance, coming closer.

'Tell me those aren't what I think they are,' he said.

'Yeah,' said Jez. 'It's the villagers. They've got planes.'